Walls of Leonyla

Stinos

MEGAN WHALEN TURNER

RETURN

OF THE

THIEF

A QUEEN'S THIEF NOVEL

GREENWILLOW BOOKS
An Imprint of HarperCollins*Publishers*

Return of the Thief
Text copyright © 2020 by Megan Whalen Turner
Illustrations copyright © 2020 by Paul O. Zelinsky

The text of this book is set in 12-point ITC Galliard.
Book design by Paul Zakris

Library of Congress Control Number: 2020943465

ISBN 978-0-06-287447-4 (hardcover)

First Edition

20 21 22 23 24 25 PC/LSCH 10 9 8 7 6 5 4 3 2 1

GREENWILLOW BOOKS
An Imprint of HarperCollins Publishers

To Sounis

Table of Contents

EXORDIUM

Unlike others who claim to be well-informed, I am an eye-witness to the events I describe, and I write this history so that future scholars will not have to rely, as do so many staring into the past in my day, on secondhand memories passed down over the years, their details worn away by time and retelling. I will include in my account what I did not see and hear myself only if I learned of the events as they occurred and from those who were present. If my readers trust me, then they may trust my sources. If I cannot record exactly what words were spoken at every moment, I can say with confidence what those words might have been, and in some cases what they must have been, as I saw what resulted from them being spoken, and can we not derive the words when we know the consequences of their utterance?

I am only a man and I know, and my readers must also

know, that there will be errors in my account. I call on Moira to guide my pen in this endeavor and accept the sovereignty of no other. No matter how many times I have come to my study to find words have been inked over or mocking comments added to my manuscript, I have simply recopied those passages. Where the comments have been enlightening, I have incorporated the information into my work and where other uninvited readers have left their questions, I have sought to answer them. No man's reticence can obscure Moira's history, nor should it obscure mine. As I hope to make my chronicle of the high king live and breathe, I will dispense with the language of scholarship and to you who read this account, I say that on my honor it is as true and faithful a narrative as it is in my means to provide.

THE
BOOK
OF
PHERIS

VOLUME I

CHAPTER ONE

Though I was born to the house of Susa, I am Erondites. My mother, the only daughter of the Baron Erondites, was disowned when she married herself to a younger son of the Susa family. My father was an uncomplicated, easygoing man, and I have never known what drew the two of them together, as my mother was ambitious enough for two, and far more conniving. Resenting her restriction to family life on a Susa country estate, she entertained a steady stream of visitors from the capital who brought her all the news of the court, of the queen, and of her father's many machinations. She was far more his child than either of her surviving brothers, and she hated him for casting her out.

When it became clear that I had been born with the infirmity that ran in my family, she declined the conventional response, and not because of any maternal feelings. Knowing it would anger her father, she arranged for a wet nurse and recorded my birth in the capital. She held my naming ceremony in the great temple, with free wine and food for all who attended, and only after that turned me over to the nurse of her own childhood, never to show any interest in me again.

I grew up in an outbuilding on the grounds of the Villa Suterpe, my nurse, Melisande, keeping me alive through my infancy and continuing to care for me as I grew older. She was nurse to my brother, Juridius, as well, though once he was old enough, he was moved to the main house. I never was, and if Melisande had had her way, I would have stayed forever in the two small rooms of our little home, as I was blamed every time the milk soured or someone fell ill. "Out of sight, out of mind, little one," she cautioned me.

Despite the dangers, and her warnings, I was drawn to the main house like a moth to flame. Attention for an ugly child such as I was never positive, but I had my repertoire of seemingly accidental defenses. To my nurse's distress, I enjoyed tipping plates of food or wine into my tormentors' laps or wiping the spit from my mouth on their sleeves and watching with an assumed air of bewilderment as their audience laughed at them instead of me. I came to understand something my nurse never did: the less people want to see you, the easier it becomes to be invisible in plain sight.

My story begins in late summer. The days were still hot, but the grain was ripe, and the end of the year was on the horizon. It was late in the afternoon, the dry air like powder on the skin, and I was behind the stables watching a swarm of bees settle into a hollow tree. They had abandoned the clay pipes stacked for them in the kitchen garden, and the beekeeper had not yet tracked them down. Fascinated by an orderliness I glimpsed in their movements, I sometimes watched the bees for hours, though the longer I was still, the more painful it was when I tried to move again.

Just as my father returning from the hunt would linger at the threshold, handing off his horse, his weapons, his prizes to this servant or that servant before taking the wine from his cupbearer, so would a bee pause at the entrance to the hive to bow and spin in circles, to greet the doorkeeper bees and be greeted in turn. If the hunt had been successful, my father would pour out a libation in thanks; if a bee returned with pockets stuffed full of pollen, the doorkeeper bees escorted the successful hunter inside while other bees flew off, retracing her flight. All had a role to play.

The blue had washed out of the sky except where the sun was just settling on the hills to the west, and a house cat had joined me to begin his evening hunt in the litter under the trees. The birds overhead were making a racket as they found their roosts for the night, and I didn't hear my nurse at first. Her voice was just loud enough to carry into the bushes, where she knew I liked to hide.

"Quickly, come quickly, boy," she called, though she knew how difficult it is for me to get to my feet when I've been still for a long time.

The cat was crouched for a pounce. I had no desire to interrupt his pursuit of dinner, but Melisande called again, so I worked myself up from the ground—carefully enough that the hunter, focused on its mouse, took no notice of my going. The slope behind the stables was steep and I had to move in small steps, placing my bad leg with strict attention to avoid tumbling downhill. My nurse, once she caught sight of me through the brush, urged me with anxious waves of her hand to hurry. Obedient to her, if to no other, I did try, but she was bobbing her head in distress by the time I reached her. She had a bag, which she pushed into my good hand.

"You take this," she said. "You go to the shrine of Agalia, you know the one I mean, where the roof has come down. You stay there until I come for you, do you understand?"

I nodded but waited for more, watching her face. "Erondites is here," she said, and I froze as still as the mouse behind me hiding in deadly peril from the cat. Erondites. My grandfather who hated me. She had no time to say more, and I wondered later: if I hadn't sought an explanation, if I'd gone as soon as I'd been told, slipping away into the bushes, would I have made it to the old shrine in the hills—a half day's walk away for anyone else, an entire day for me or my old nurse? And if I had made it there, what might have been different then?

One of the housemen rounded the corner of the stable, moving fast, followed by another. Melisande said to me, "Go, go," but of course I could not. The first houseman snatched the bag and threw it on the ground, then picked me up, grabbing me around the chest and swinging me. I cried out in pain and Melisande sank her hands into my shirt, twisting the fabric as if, feeble as she was, she could pull me out of the houseman's arms.

"No," she said, her voice breaking, "no, he cannot have my little Pheris."

As I watched in horror, the houseman struck her with his fist, knocking her to the ground. I bit him hard on the ball of his shoulder, making him shout and then swear, but he did not drop me as I expected. He only changed his grip, easily shifting my weight and sending fire through my leg again. He locked an arm around my neck.

"Your time is up, little monster," he said as he tightened his hold.

I'd never been treated so by a servant. Certainly by my family members, but the servants only spat when they saw me, or made a hex sign. Any physical harm they did was indirect: something placed for me to trip over, something unpleasant left on the paths for me to find. If they'd laid a hand on me, Melisande would have had them chopped and boiled and fed to the pigs. But Melisande was still on the ground, sobbing into her hands as my vision grew dark and the blood roared in my ears.

The next thing I knew, I was falling. My head hit the stone floor of the living room at the center of the main house, and I sprawled bonelessly until the darkness began to clear. When I could, I rolled into a crouch so that if I was kicked, as I sometimes was, I had a chance of taking the blow on my good leg. I'd spent a long winter in bed after my father had kicked the bad one.

My mother reclined on a couch, apparently at ease, the beads woven into the thin braids near her face hanging quite still. I'd often longed to set those braids in motion, to hear the clink of the brightly colored glass beads, but knew that any attempt to draw near to her would end with a slap. The man beside her was bald and running to fat the way powerfully built men often do as they age. He clutched a wine cup in his fist and stared at me in disgust—my grandfather, who'd never spoken to my mother since her marriage, who was much reviled in the villa, who'd wanted me dead since the day I was born. I knew what he saw.

Not taking my eyes off him, I tipped my head to one side to let the drool from my mouth spin in a thin line to the floor. Erondites curled his lip and looked away. My mother, fiddling with the beads she wouldn't let me touch, snorted in amusement.

"Meet your heir, Father," she said. "Juridius tells me I should have named him Pheris Monstrous instead of Mostrus."

"You shouldn't have named him at all. You should have had him got rid of." It was no longer considered civilized to leave babies like me out on a hillside for a fox to take, though it still happened. More often, they were quietly drowned by a midwife, or left unfed, uncared for, until they faded away.

"And where would you be now if I had?" my mother asked.

Erondites didn't like that.

"He does not speak?"

"No," said my mother.

"Play chess?" he asked acidly.

"Melisande knows better. She keeps him out of sight."

To my surprise, he laughed in what seemed genuine amusement. "He'll do very well."

"Be sure you remember our bargain," my mother warned.

Erondites shrugged. "You have my word. When your firstborn has served his purpose, Juridius will be my heir."

My brother was younger than I by less than a year, taller and healthy and a credit to his house.

"Juridius will suit you, Father. He knows what he owes his family."

"Better than you," said Erondites.

"I know what a woman owes her family. Have I not provided my husband with sons?" Her smile was ugly.

"But now you are restored, daughter, to the family of Erondites."

"Juridius is my family, and my loyalty will be to him and my other children. If you mean to use my little monster and then reinstate Sejanus as your heir when you have secured his freedom, beware. Sejanus is no match for me."

"Rest easy," said her father while looking at me with both ownership and contempt. "From this, we will proceed to rebuild the House of Erondites."

CHAPTER TWO

In a small audience room made smaller by the granite pillars holding up its high ceiling, with walls paneled in red agate veined in black, the king of Attolia waited. The candles in every sconce couldn't lighten the room—or the king's temper. He was awaiting the arrival of the new heir to the estate of Erondites, as stipulated, a child young enough to be raised in the palace away from the malignant tendencies of his family. The baron had proposed his oldest grandchild, the king had approved, and the boy had been delivered, but Hilarion, who'd met his coach in the stable yard, had sent a warning that all was not as expected.

The doors to the audience room opened with a crash, and everyone recoiled except the king. He leaned forward, elbows on knees, heels hooked on the rung of his massive chair, as the attendants dragged me in, the expressions on their faces warning everyone of the smell before it hit.

"His 'coach' was a wagon with a box in the back," Hilarion announced, coming in behind us. "Locked from the outside."

They'd put me into the box with a bucket and a bottle of water. The bucket upended at every bump, and the jug of water, still half full, had cracked on the second day.

"Is this Erondites's grandson Juridius?" asked the king, as if he doubted it.

"No," said Hilarion grimly. "Juridius is the second child of the baron's daughter, Marina. This is her first."

"Ah," said the king.

"His birth was recorded in the temple," Hilarion admitted defensively. "There's been no sign of him since. Everyone assumed he'd died." He didn't need to say why.

But being invisible is not the same as being dead, and it was obvious that a grave mistake had been made. Feet shuffled and heads bowed as those who might be held responsible ducked the king's gaze. The men holding my arms released me and I sank into my crouch, wrapping my arms around my knees, staring malevolently at the king as he stared back. As angry as I was helpless, I squeezed the spit from my mouth, drooling onto the floor in front of me, but unlike my grandfather, the king didn't look away. Eventually I did.

Knowing that every eye was on me, and there was no escape but the one in my head, I dipped my finger into the small puddle in front of me and made a triangle of three carefully placed wet spots. There was a communal exhalation of disgust, and the weight of stares lightened. I added a third row to my triangle with three spots, then another with five.

"Why didn't they expose him?" I heard someone ask.

"Put him back in his box," someone else advised the king.

"Return him to Erondites."

And Erondites, having had his joke, would kill me and make Juridius his heir. Helpless to alter my fate, I concentrated on the ever-widening triangle. The first wet spot was drying out, so I worked up a little more spit. Eyeing the king, I let it run out of my mouth.

"Your Majesty, get rid of him!" I heard someone protest, but the king watched me seriously as I dipped a finger into my self-made ink and re-created my first point.

"No," he said, coming to a decision. "Get him clean. Find him a bed in my apartments. He will fit in very well with my attendants."

I lifted my head, thinking I had misheard. If I was surprised, the attendants were horrified—obviously, unmistakably horrified—yet not one of them dared protest. That was the first I knew of the king.

They took me through the palace, past the stares of strangers, to a large room filled with scattered furnishings that I later learned was both guard room and waiting room of the king's apartments. They stripped off my clothes and left me to stand shivering and naked as servants brought in a circular tub and pitchers of water to pour into it. My silent angry tears had become shaking breathless sobs by the time it was full, and Hilarion sighed heavily as he crouched in front of me and pointed to the tub.

I shook my head. My leg hurt too much to take my weight. I was considering whether I might steady myself with one hand on the edge of the tub when Hilarion ran out of patience and shoved me in. The attendants jumped back, all cursing together as water splashed everywhere. I dragged myself upright, gasping in pain.

"He hoots like a drunken owl," said the narrow-faced one with long fair hair, the one I later learned was Xikander. Scooping the water with my good hand, I flung it in his direction.

He raised a hand and called me a cursed monster. He didn't want to get close enough to hit me, though.

One of the servants came forward, with toweling to soak up the water. "You wash him," said Hilarion, but the servant made a sign to avert the evil eye and backed away.

"Gods damn it," snapped Hilarion, and I snatched up the soap left by the tub, hastily dragging it across my body, preferring to wash myself than to risk being drowned. By accident or on purpose.

By the time I'd soaped and scrubbed myself, Hilarion had realized that I couldn't get out of the tub on my own. He lifted me with one hand while one of the other attendants rinsed away the soap, soaking Hilarion in the process.

"Take him to the bed," he directed, shaking off some of the water.

They wrapped me in sheeting, and one of them carried me down narrow hallways to drop me on a mattress laid out on the floor. I struggled free of the constricting fabric, only to find myself surrounded by headless people. Hearing the thin, whistling sound of my terror, the man standing nearby laughed. I do not remember now who it was, nor do I want to. I do remember Philologos, though, for his kindness.

"He's frightened," Philo said from the doorway.

"You stay with him, if you want," said the other attendant, brushing past.

Philo crouched down to reassure me. "They are just dummies," he said, "made of stuffing. They hold the king's coats." Encouraged, I looked more closely and saw that he was right. The dim figures only appeared to be shifting in the flickering lamplight from the hallway. I had not been cast into an underworld dungeon with headless monsters. I was in a closet.

"He has a lot of coats," said Philologos soberly. Then he smiled and I managed to take a breath, in and out, with only a tiny leftover hiccup in the middle. Tentatively, I plucked at the sheeting to make it more like bedclothes and less like a shroud.

"Lie down," Philologos suggested.

I put my head on the pillow. He straightened the sheeting and laid a blanket over me before he left. I curled around the pain in my hip and my leg. Too tired to force my limbs to be still, I lay with the muscles in my leg jumping and cramping until I fell into a restless, twitching sleep.

"Send him back," said the queen. "Erondites has had his joke at your expense."

Eugenides went on pacing.

"Then what?" he asked. "I have already agreed that his eldest grandson could be reinstated as his heir. I can send this child back to Suterpe—I can't force Erondites to send Juridius to the palace in his place."

"Keep the boy or send him back, Juridius will be raised by his grandfather," said the queen. "And when the baron is satisfied that Juridius is loyal only to the Erondites, he will eliminate this pretend heir he has foisted on you."

"Unless he thinks I will someday free Sejanus. Then he will cut both of them out of the inheritance."

"I do not think Marina would be pleased by that," said Attolia.

I woke in the dark with my throat on fire. Even the meager light from the lamp in the hall was gone. I longed for my nurse. Melisande would have known what was wrong: too much banging in that box on wheels, too many days without real rest, too much shouting, too much of everything. She would have stroked my head and fetched me cool water to drink, but I was alone and the palace silent all around me. Weeping into my hands, I eventually fell asleep again, to be surrounded in my dreams by looming headless figures.

Nudged by a foot, I woke again, this time in the diffuse light from the closet's small opening to an airshaft. The owner of the foot leaned over me briefly and then backed away, leaving me alone again in my misery. I was often ill, and used to it, but I'd never been without Melisande to comfort me. I was very afraid I would die and was in no way relieved by the appearance of a thin, balding man in the doorway.

"Has anybody brought him a drink?" the man asked angrily. "Has anyone done anything for him at all?"

"Well, we didn't put a pillow over his face," said someone out in the passage.

"Get some water," snapped the man as he bent down beside me. He took away the covers, even as I clutched at them. Having worked for years at the charity hospital, he was used to ungrateful patients. "If you bite, I will put a stick between your teeth," he warned, but he needn't have worried. I hardly had the strength to bite by then. He poked me in the stomach and counted my ribs, listened to my breathing, and looked in my ears as well as down my throat. He was very thorough, and when he was done, he tucked the covers back around me.

"You'll be fine in a day or two," he said, with a reassuring gentleness. "I will give you very nasty-tasting medicine to be sure of it," he added, taking the cup that had been brought to him and mixing into it a vile liquid that was everything he had promised.

"Miras's golden balls," said Dionis behind him. "He can't even drink."

Petrus—because this was indeed the royal physician—sighed. "Not everything that is easy for you is easy for the rest of us. Why don't you go away, Dionis?"

"The king wants to know if he'll live."

"It's a diseased throat. If he throws off the fever, he will be well in a few days."

Dionis left, and Petrus leaned over me again with the cup. "I know it tastes bad, and I know it's hard to swallow," he said. "But drink it up. You're better off sleeping through today's festivities anyway."

The next time I woke, it was night again. The dark figure crouched over me seemed an apparition from my fevered dreams.

"Shh," said a heavily accented voice. "Sit up now and have a drink."

Melisande, I thought. Even far away, she knew what I needed. Imagining her melting honeycombs in the fire, calling on Ula, goddess of the hearth and healing, to aid me, I struggled to sit up, took the cup pushed into my hand, and sipped cool water, scented with lemon, sure that this strange messenger had been sent in answer to my nurse's prayers.

"Better than that oily piss Petrus makes you drink," he said, his words rough and rolling like bobbins. I wondered that Ula's messengers were so vulgar.

Heaven-sent or not, the water was delicious, and I drained the cup to the last drop before holding it out for an unseen hand to take away. I lay down, and the same hand rested on my forehead for a moment like a blessing before he was gone.

Petrus came to check on me every day as my sore throat and fever waxed and waned. With his high forehead and his chin beard, he looked like a satyr missing his horns, but he was far kinder than his appearance suggested. The man with the strange accent came as well, but only in the night. He was not one of Ula's messengers, as I'd first thought, and might have been a servant or one of the attendants. He never said.

When Petrus finally reported that I was well enough to be up, Philologos brought loose-fitting underclothes and a robe, and when I was dressed he led me to the king's waiting room. He instructed me to sit on the bench that ran around its walls and then went to take his part in the morning ritual of dressing the king. Used to the elegance of the Villa Suterpe, I was unimpressed by the king's apartments. The attendants' sleeping quarters were a tight warren of narrow passages and curtained doorways, while the guard room and the waiting room were one and the same, separated from the king's bedchamber by a single door. The waiting room's furniture was mismatched, its hearth was small, and its paneled walls mostly plain. The only interesting things to look at were the decorative medallions hung where the panels joined. They held meticulously carved hunting scenes of men and dogs and horses. I did not think it an odd choice at the time.

The door to the king's bedchamber was arched like the entry to a skep. I was strongly reminded of bees as the attendants went in and out, conferring in low voices as they brought items of clothing or returned them to their closets. Some of the items went by more than once. I saw a gold sash twice and a blue one four times. Eventually the back-and-forth slowed down and the king strolled through the room without stopping, not even pausing to glance in my direction. Those who would attend him that day followed after, the double doors to the passageway closed behind them, and everyone left in the room stared at me.

"He's to have clothes for tomorrow," said Hilarion heavily.

I had been sent to the palace in time to be an eyesore

at the wedding of Sounis and Eddis. Instead I had been ill and slept through it. Having recovered, I was expected to attend the elaborate ceremony during which Attolia and Eddis and Sounis would swear loyalty to Eugenides as the high king over all the rulers of the Little Peninsula. I might have been left in my closet for the day, but the king had decreed otherwise.

Just then, a tall, elegant man swept into the waiting room, Ion, second only to Hilarion in authority over the attendants. With his dark curls held back in his fist, he was obviously in search of a hair tie. "Lamion, have you stolen my velvet . . . Oh, the little monster is better," he said in surprise. "Does it speak? Do you speak?" he asked me directly, and I stared back at him.

Hilarion shook his head. "Erondites's men say he doesn't."

"So, it's a quiet monster. We should count our blessings. Gods willing it will not snore like Dionis." He bent to stare into my face. "Do you understand me, do you understand what I am saying?" he said, and I looked down.

"The king wants him outfitted as an attendant," a stocky man grumbled. That was Dionis.

"Fetch the tailor, then," Ion said with a shrug.

"Why don't you do it?" But Dionis was speaking to Ion's disappearing back. He'd seen his velvet hair tie on Lamion and gone to find himself another.

The tailor must have been in the palace, as he arrived

very quickly with a stool he wanted me to stand on. Even he could see that if I do not keep my feet well spread I will fall over, so huffing and puffing with irritation, he put his stool aside and crouched down to take my measurements. While he measured, the attendants watched and talked. Ion returned and I listened carefully, learning their names as I heard them.

"Hard to believe that a man would send out in public a grandson like that," said one. Sotis.

"Seems like he's the butt of his own joke if that's the kind of heir he has." Dionis.

"He is a step up from Sejanus." Sotis again, and everyone laughed.

Sejanus was my uncle, every bit as beautiful as Ion and highly esteemed in the palace, or so I'd previously believed. My mother's brother, he had always been received at the Villa Suterpe with open arms, as he was an excellent hunting companion to my father and brought delightful tidbits of gossip from the capital. The servants fawned on him, and even I looked forward to his visits. He'd once slipped me a cake without alerting anyone else to my presence underneath a table. That was more kindness than I'd had from any other member of my family.

"He's Susa's grandson, too. Susa can't be happy to have him paraded about." That was Xikander.

"The king is going to send him back, isn't he?" asked

Xikos, Xikander's brother. There was a communal sort of shrug. Clearly none of them knew what the king would do.

Snarling in exasperation, the tailor seized me by the arm and shook me violently. I bared my teeth at him, and he smacked me.

"None of that," said Hilarion.

"He won't stand still!" said the tailor.

"He's still enough, get on with it." Sullenly, the tailor hunched back down. I moved again, easing the weight off my bad leg, daring the tailor to object.

"Does anyone know what his name is? The king said to find out."

"If he's the firstborn of Susa's family, he should have been Juridius."

"I heard from Xippias that his mother gave him Erondites's name for spite," said Dionis.

"Pheris," Ion said, and I turned obediently to look at him, knowing it would annoy the tailor again.

"Are you Pheris?" Ion asked, and I nodded.

"Pheris Mostrus Erondites?" asked Ion, and I nodded again, hesitantly, unaccustomed to the new house name.

Sotis laughed. "Pheris *Monstrous* Erondites." He thought he was clever.

"Quiet, Sotis," said Ion.

Hilarion was also amused, but it wasn't me he was laughing at. "That's what they call his grandfather, you know."

"So?" asked Sotis.

I was equally surprised.

"So, so, so," confirmed Ion. "Not to his face, of course."

I could understand that.

"He is Pheris, then," said Xikos.

"Unless he nods at everything," said the sleek, black-haired Medander. He leaned toward me. "Are you horse? Are you dog?" he asked. "Are you filth?"

"He's Pheris," said Hilarion. "Stop teasing him."

"What do you think, Pheris?" Medander asked, modulating his tone. He was always reluctant to take orders from Hilarion but wouldn't defy him directly. "Do you want to go home to Grandfather?" My whole body shuddered at the thought, and they all laughed.

When the tailor was finished, they gave me some watered wine and honey cakes and sent me back to bed. Out of sight of the attendants and the guards, I explored the labyrinth of the king's apartments, finding storage and bedchambers and the necessaries. Back in my closet, I sat on my pallet of blankets, sipping from my cup. The sound of my nurse's wails as they had carried me away from the villa still rang in my ears. Out of sight, out of mind, she'd taught me. That was the way to stay safe. As I considered what I had seen and heard, I saw no chance of staying out of sight and no safety at all in my future. To be honest, I saw no future.

✦ ✦ ✦

The results of the tailor's hard work arrived that evening. Not even my brother Juridius, apple of my mother's eye, had clothes like the ones Xikos casually tossed at my head.

"Put those on," he said, "and then get out of the way. We need to dress the king for dinner."

I sorted through the collection in my lap and found a fine white undershirt, plain, stitched at the seams with stitches so small I could hardly see them, a sleeveless velvet vest in Attolian blue embroidered in gold, and a pair of trousers, loose in the leg, with a tight cuff at the bottom. I was relieved to see that they buttoned at the top, which meant I wouldn't have to ask anyone to tie the strings on my pants. The vest was double-breasted in the Eddisian style. When the frogs were secured, the embroidery across the front resolved into a gryphon on one side facing a lion on the other, with lilies in between. I remember this as the first time I'd seen the unified crest of the Little Peninsula. There were slippers in the same sky blue as the vest. They'd measured me for boots, but those would have to be specially made to accommodate my foot, and that would take more time.

Once I was dressed, I retreated to a corner, watching Dionis, the gray-haired attendant, stripping coats from the dummies and collecting pants and sashes from the racks that ran along the walls. His hands appeared to be as full when he returned and began to replace the coats on their holders. Ion came to help.

Dionis looked put out, Ion only amused. As they finished their work and left, I heard muffled voices from the waiting room and then the sound of hurrying feet. I dove under the racked clothes, but not fast enough to evade Sotis. Grabbing me by my good foot, he pulled me out.

"The king says you dine with us, and when the king commands, we obey. That means little monsters, too." By the scruff of my neck, Sotis pushed me out of the attendants' quarters to where the king was waiting. As he looked me over, I had my first chance to study Eugenides closely.

He was missing a hand.

I had not seen this before. I was raised by my nurse in an outbuilding—all I knew of this king was that he was an Eddisian who'd married our queen after some sort of trickery. I thought it unlikely he'd been born unnatural, much more likely he'd lost the hand in battle or perhaps in some prosaic way. One of the masons at the villa had had most of his lower arm cut off after his hand was crushed by a falling stone. I'd heard his fingers turned black.

Philologos must have noticed the direction of my gaze. When the king finished his inspection and turned away, Philologos leaned close to say in a whisper, "The queen cut it off."

I think he meant merely to inform me and would have

added more explanation, but Xikos added also in a whisper, a spite-filled one, "Don't annoy the queen."

Philologos glared at him and then shook his head at me, as if I should pay Xikos no attention. But all the while, Xikos, eyebrows high, was nodding his head up and down.

Philologos hissed, "Stop it."

"Don't annoy the king, either," said Sotis, leaning in.

"Don't annoy any of us," said Hilarion, flipping my ear painfully and pointing to the empty doorway. I hastened through it.

We proceeded to the megaron, the only space in Attolia's palace large enough to hold the combined courts of Sounis, Attolia, and Eddis. Attolia joined us on the way, her guards and her attendants mirroring the king's own. Furtively, I watched her, catching glimpses of her face as she turned to speak to the king. Sotis, I judged an unreliable informant, but Philologos had seemed quite sincere. I could see that the queen, for all her beauty, commanded respect. Everyone watched her just as they watched the king, ready to respond in an instant to their least direction.

The first time I saw Attolia's megaron, I could not imagine even a temple could be bigger or more astonishing. The rows of marble columns held the ceiling impossibly high. The gold leaf on the beams glittered in the light of candles in chandeliers that were great wheels of iron illuminating the room below. The famous blue-and-gold mosaic floors were almost invisible under the tables and benches needed to seat so many people.

At the high table, Eddis and Sounis waited to greet the king and queen of Attolia with an exchange of kisses. When they sat, everyone else moved in concert to their own places. Philologos pointed and I went where I was told, scrambling awkwardly over the bench seat as the servants began bringing in trays of food; boys with ewers and amphorae moving from person to person, filling cups and brightly colored glasses.

At the Villa Suterpe, Melisande and I had eaten on the couches that were our beds at night, from bowls made of plain fired clay. While I was staring at the wealth of sparkling, shining ceramic and glass—running a finger across the raised pattern on my plate—others were casting their glances at me and then at the king. Elbows were dug into rib cages and jokes were made. The king was pointedly speaking with the queen of Eddis to his left, ignoring it all.

"Gods damn it," said Hilarion beside me, too late.

Sometime after that, the king said over his shoulder, "Sotis, where is my little Erondites?"

Sotis leaned in to speak quietly. "Under the table, Your Majesty. It appears he is not used to sitting for his dinner."

I glared at his shoes. I was not allowed to sit at the table with my family. All my familiarity with tables such as these came from slipping under the cloths before the servants came to set them and creeping away when I was sure the diners had gone.

"Hilarion thought it best not to make a scene," explained Sotis.

The king agreed. "People love a dancing bear," he murmured. "No one wants to be one."

Under the head table, with people seated on only one side and a cloth that dropped almost to the floor on the other, I felt safe for the moment. I was hungry, but used to that. While everyone above me dined, I took my time admiring the embroidery on the queen's dress. As the queen was very still, I could look my fill. Her skirts were covered in a pattern of interlacing branches, each leaf and blossom perfect in every detail. There was even a tiny nest at the hem, with two even smaller golden eggs nestled inside. I wondered who else but me would ever see them.

Unlike the queen, the king twitched his feet in boredom or irritation and I moved past him warily, in spite of what Sotis had said about avoiding a scene. I'd been dragged out from under tables before. I did notice that the cuffs of the king's trousers matched the embroidery on the queen's dress. A pair of thrushes perched side by side on an embroidered branch, just visible above his boots.

Beyond the king was the queen of Eddis. Her dress was less interesting, plain fabric and no embroidery. Beside her, also in plain clothes, was another man, not the king of Sounis, as he was sitting on the far side of Attolia. Hearing the man speak and Eddis answering, I recognized the rolling sounds in their words.

"Cleon has called for a trial," said the rumbling voice.

"He's not the king of Eddis," said the queen, her voice sharp, though still quiet enough that no one but me, crouched by her feet, was likely to hear.

I stayed to listen, but nothing more interesting was said.

The dinner went on for what seemed like hours. The music was dull. There were speeches and no dancing afterward and worse, no storyteller. I grew more and more uncomfortable on the cold stone floor, until at last there was a scraping of benches and chairs as those seated at the high table stood to leave. By that time my hip and leg had grown so stiff, I had to press the flesh of my thigh, willing the knee to straighten. Painfully, I flattened myself to see from under the cloth. As the kings and queens moved to the door, drawing eyes away from the table, I crawled out and got to my feet with the help of a chair. Seeing platters still filled with food, I snatched half a game bird. Keeping it close to my leg, hoping no grease would drip on my fine new clothes, I limped awkwardly toward the other attendants, waving my arm for balance.

Hilarion drew back Xikander, who must have just been on his way to fetch me. I reached the door in time to follow the last of the attendants through it, gritting my teeth until the stiffness in my leg eased.

Back in my closet, I sat on my pallet, gnawing the meat off the game bird and turning over in my mind what I'd seen of the king and his potentially even more terrifying wife. When I'd licked the bones clean, I threw them out the ventilation window into the airshaft.

CHAPTER THREE

*I*n the morning, before the sun was in the sky, Xikander woke me and told me to dress. Reaching for my clothes, I saw by the light of the lamp outside my door the damage from the previous night's meal. The juices of the game bird had indeed dribbled down the leg of my trousers. There was no help for it, as I had no way to clean them off, not even a washbasin and water, so I scrambled into them as quickly as I could.

In the king's waiting room, all the attendants were gathered, as well as people I would come to recognize as important members of the Attolian court. This was an historic occasion. Everyone present had a role, held clothing or jewel boxes or a tiny amphora. Even I was given an earring to keep in my good hand. Philologos pushed me into place in line beside him, and Ion checked that all was in order. When he saw the stains on my trousers, he briefly closed his eyes.

Recognizing that there was nothing to be done, he nodded at Hilarion, who rapped on the door of the bedchamber. When there was no response, he opened the door and stepped through.

Filing in after Hilarion, we found the king lying on his back in his bed surrounded by the cloth of gold drapery, as perfect as any honeybee in a hive, with his arm over his face. He refused to get up.

"Your Majesty." Hilarion was close to begging. "Everyone is waiting."

"Tell them I died."

"Your Majesty?"

"Died, Hilarion. In the night. Peacefully."

"Why would I do that?"

"Because then you could all go away and leave me alone."

Holding a vest in his hands and trying hard not to crumple the velvet, Hilarion looked at the other attendants for support. Lamion slowly lifted his shoulders all the way to his ears. Philologos hesitantly cleared his throat.

He said, "Your Majesty, if you were dead, we couldn't just leave you alone."

There was silence from the bed.

"The body would have to be washed," said Ion, with an air of the most delicate pragmatism. "And we'd have to dress it for a funeral. An elaborate funeral."

"We'd have to call the doctor," Hilarion warned.

"Doctors," corrected Ion.

With a mumbled curse, the king levered himself slowly up. "That was a cheap shot, Ion," he said bitterly, as everyone else in the room sighed with relief.

The king's hook had a series of straps that ran over his shoulders and was the first thing he was helped to put on. He stood to have his pants pulled up, sat again while his attendants placed his feet in boots, lifted his arms while an undershirt was slipped over his head. It was clear that he did not relish the attention. He already looked tired.

Sotis and Ion did his hair, clipping it and combing it and adding a little oil, then carefully dusting it with powdered gold.

"Robe," said Ion sharply, and Lamion went to fetch it.

Sighing, the king got back to his feet.

They slipped jewels on his fingers and chains around his neck. Ion plucked the single red ruby out of my hand, rubbed it on his coat, and hung it in the king's ear. Then Lamion brought in the robe, sky-blue velvet embroidered with gold thread and trimmed in spotted ermine, with the lilies of Attolia on the back in a deeper blue and white. I watched in awe as it was draped around the king's shoulders. He saw me staring and smiled for the first time.

"You've impressed the imbecile, Your Majesty." Medander

said it as if it were a joke, but there was an edge I didn't miss. It was not just me that Medander was mocking.

"I am so glad someone is pleased," murmured the king.

Hilarion looked daggers at Medander, but he shrugged them off.

It was going to be a very long day.

We first went to the queen's apartments, which were lavish in direct contrast to the king's. Arriving in her reception room, the king blamed the attendants for his lateness. They seemed neither resentful nor amused at this lie, just unsettled, eyeing him as if he might erupt like the Sacred Mountain or, worse, return to his bed. Sagging as he settled into his chair, he might have been thinking of just that.

"Sounis's barons have urged him to repudiate his promise to you," said Attolia.

"He won't," said Eugenides, closing his eyes. "Eddis's barons have been putting the idea in their heads."

"Your cousin looked as if he meant to kill you last night at dinner."

"Cephus has always hated me."

"That wasn't the cousin I meant."

"They have all remembered how much they hate me. I was a hero very briefly when I was stealing your throne and am back to being a villain now that I am stealing Eddis's."

"You are stealing nothing. Eddis is their sovereign, and it is Eddis who has chosen this course!"

"You are expecting a sensitivity to nuance, my queen, that you will not find in Eddisians."

Attolia subsided. "They are demanding a rewording of Eddis's oath. They want something less stringent. 'Advise' rather than 'rule.'"

"I'm sure they do. But that's not the oath Eddis agreed to take, and it's not the one she will swear today." The gold powder from his hair had smeared across the back of the chair. One of the attendants, the old woman Phresine, rolled her eyes at the mess, but the king didn't see.

"Sounis has had to browbeat his barons into supporting him," he was saying wearily. "Eddis has far more authority. She doesn't waste her time the way we do keeping your horrible council of barons appeased."

"No ruler's power is ever absolute," the queen warned.

"If the Eddisians want to dethrone Helen, they know it will be over my father's dead body. Over the dead bodies of my brothers. Possibly over the dead bodies of my sisters—and believe me, no one wants to cross them. If my father says his niece is queen, then she is queen, and if Helen says she will be loyal, she will be loyal. If the Eddisians hate it, they'll be too preoccupied being angry at me to gloat over your barons or Sounis's once I am high king."

"Is that why you continue to be so provoking?"

He opened his eyes to slits. "I have no idea what you mean, my queen," he said.

Attolia raised an eyebrow, too much a queen to say anything else.

The king's procession began at the front of the palace, winding around it to the gates where the Sacred Way left the city and climbed to the temple heights above it, and what I remember most clearly now was the unforgiving, uneven paving stones. All my attention was concentrated on picking my way across them in fear of what might happen if I moved too slowly.

I had never seen a public ceremony. Melisande and I had performed hearth rites together, but since I was not welcome when the family gathered, I had very little knowledge of more formal rituals. I'd visited the small shrines in the valley around our villa but had not been in a real temple since my naming ceremony.

I wouldn't be in one that day, either. After recovering from the climb, I peered through the crowd of people around me, first in curiosity and then in disappointment. The new temple of the goddess Hephestia was nothing but an open foundation, a windswept plaza surrounded by ramshackle workshops made of sticks and clay. There was a single small building, no bigger than the shed I'd shared with Melisande: Hephestia's Treasury. Now its walls are faced with white marble and its dome leafed with gold. It is enclosed within the temple and sits just behind the great statue of Hephestia. Work on that statue had not even begun, and the treasury was an unassuming little building of undressed stone.

I was no more impressed by the ceremony, which was just a lot of talking. One voice did stand out, with a resonance that made my heart thrum in my chest, but when cautious maneuvering brought the speaker into view, the Oracle, high priestess of Hephestia, turned out to be a stout, middle-aged woman with her hair in tight braids like my mother's, no more extraordinary to look at than her temple.

In the old days, a young bull would have been sacrificed and then roasted to be eaten that evening. By the time I realized the high priestess was only going to tap the bull with her thyrsus before it was led away to join the temple's herd, I'd lost interest in the whole process. My back and leg ached. I longed to sit down but didn't dare.

The procession down the Sacred Way moved more slowly than it had going up, luckily for me. The king stopped at each altar we passed to leave an offering for old and new gods alike. Twice he prostrated himself to pray. At a very minor goddess's altar, to everyone's confusion, he closed his eyes and lay still for some time before he got up and continued. When we'd passed through the town gates, the king stopped even more often, humbly bowing his head while coins and flower petals and sweets were thrown for the children. Shaking with exhaustion, sick from the noise and the shouting, I was relieved to reach the palace. I didn't realize the day had only just begun. In the ceremonial courtyard, the king climbed up onto a high platform, where he sat on a figured gold chair to accept as every single person of any importance at all offered him loyalty and gifts in honor of the occasion.

Attolia went first, standing proudly before her people as she promised to be ruled by the will of the gods and the high king. After her oath, she climbed the steps to sit in a no less ornate silver chair on his left. Eddis's oath was just as the king had said it would be, and then she climbed to sit on his right. Sounis followed, placing his hand on the king's foot and looking up to him with an easy smile before swearing his loyalty and obedience—his informality an exception to the crushing etiquette of the hours that followed.

One by one, the Attolian barons approached the king, swore their loyalty, and then offered their gifts, either directly to the king or to one of the attendants standing below the dais. When my grandfather who was Erondites stepped forward, I shrank back behind Ion and didn't see him offer up the ornate hunting bow he'd brought, though I heard the king thank him and saw my grandfather's smirk as he withdrew. Next, a baron carefully placed a golden pomegranate into the king's outstretched palm. The king passed it to Ion without a second glance and the baron hesitantly cleared his throat.

"It opens, Your Majesty," he said.

"Does it?" said the king, sounding bored. Perhaps he thought this was another gift useful only to a man with two hands.

"If I may?" the baron asked, reaching up to retrieve it. Holding the pomegranate in just one hand, he released the hidden catch, and the upper half of the gold fruit lifted. The king leaned forward, and then, as if regretting his show of interest, slowly sat back again.

Hastily, the baron explained, "It can be filled with powder, and the powder then shaken from the openings in the calyx of the fruit, Your Majesty. Or it can hold scent and serve as a pomander, as Your Majesty prefers."

Solid gold, it was a valuable offering to the king; the baron was probably trying very hard to recover from some past offense. I often saw the pomegranate in use over the years, but I do not remember whose gift it was—there were so many trying to improve their relations with the king at that time.

I was surprised to see one baron step forward to make his vow with his daughter beside him. She gave the king a very winning smile as she delivered her family's gift, and I looked to the queen to see her reaction. Her face remained unreadable.

"Heiro," said the king. "These are your earrings."

"I noticed that you admired them, Your Majesty."

"No one has ever given me earrings," said the king, sounding delighted. In the past, he'd stolen them, but those earrings, and whatever the Thief of Eddis stole, could only be used in the service of his god or surrendered on his altar. Heiro's earrings, he would be able to keep. "I will treasure these," he said, and seemed genuinely pleased, rewarding her with a smile as winning as her own. A hundred men who'd offered him far more expensive gifts ground their teeth in frustration, and Heiro's father sighed with visible relief.

That was the king's last smile. After that, he appeared to be almost as miserable as I was, and I was thoroughly miserable. Unable to stand for another minute, I first crouched, and then sat, ignoring Lamion, who hissed at me, and Hilarion, who surreptitiously poked me with his foot. In my head, I could hear Melisande begging me to get up, and all I could do was assure her that at least I was out of sight behind the other attendants. I'd heard Sotis the night before—no one wanted a scene. When the last baron passed by, I looked up in relief, only to see that a line still stretched around the courtyard and that the mayors of various towns as well as the heads of the larger guilds must have their turns. I dropped my gaze back to the striations in the paving stones underneath me and tried to pass the time imagining they were waves with ships sailing on cool marble seas.

Foreign heads of state had sent their own gifts to mark the investiture of the high king. Lengths of linen and dyed wool from the Braelings, a silver dish in the shape of a fish from the Pents, and a beautifully decorated sword from the Gants—another item that was unlikely to be useful, as it would not be weighted for a left-handed man. I think this was a matter overlooked by the Gants and not a deliberate offense.

The Mede ambassador, Melheret, gave the king a scroll. "I was so hoping for a statue," the king commented ungraciously as he received it. Most of those who heard him looked uncomfortable. The ambassador smiled condescendingly and said, "This is a story of my people, Your Majesty, the Epic of Omarak, who overreached and was struck down for it. I thought you might find it instructive."

"Ambassador, I will certainly give it the attention it deserves," the king promised.

Finally the ceremony was over. The king rose with a display of stately dignity and descended from the dais. As he left the courtyard and moved toward the royal wing of the palace, protocol winnowed away one by one those who followed him. We had not yet left the public areas, and there were still bystanders as well as his guards and attendants when he paused in a hallway to complain to Attolia about her gift.

"You gave me a horse," he said, his voice breathy and aggrieved. Indeed she had, a splendid white warhorse whose hooves had drummed against the paving stones as it was paraded through the ceremonial court. "Eddis gave me scrolls from her library," said the king. "Sophos gave me a book of poems." Presents he evidently preferred.

If offended, Attolia sounded neither angry nor sympathetic. "With a scroll and a book, you will look like a scholar," she said. "On that horse, you will look like a king."

"I might have to be a king. I don't have to look like one."

"You said you meant to be a figurehead," Attolia reminded him. "'A king in appearance only,' you said."

Stymied, the king changed ground. "I don't need a warhorse, because I fight on foot."

Attolia didn't respond.

"Gen," said the queen of Eddis, uncomfortable in the expanding silence.

"I picked out the horse," stuck in Sounis hastily, and the king turned to him, swaying a little, as if with surprise.

"You, Sophos? I thought you were my friend."

"I am," the king of Sounis assured him. "He has all the fighting spirit of an apricot. His trainers had given up and sold him for farm work."

"Honestly?"

"Like riding a slowly moving sofa." Sounis swore, "On my honor."

For a moment, it seemed we might proceed, but the king didn't move and the guards aborted their steps, half taken.

The king repeated himself. "I fight on foot," he said, this time probing deliberately for a response.

Attolia didn't give him one, only waited in perfect serenity as he reflected over the day's events.

"My queen," he said at last, "you crafted those oaths very carefully, didn't you?"

Indeed, Attolia had defined the terms of her loyalty, as well as those of Eddis and Sounis, with precision.

"I swore my obedience to you and to your future children, not to your wife," Eddis confirmed.

"And I the same," said the king of Sounis, sounding very serious, when he'd been so boyish a moment before.

"You are the linchpin of this treaty, Gen," said Eddis. "You cannot be risked in battle."

The king's face suddenly lost all its color. He was so pale the scar on his face stood out darker than the skin around it. Eddis crossed her arms and even Sounis braced himself. Attolia narrowed her eyes, as if daring the king to do his worst, but he just drew a long, shaking breath and exhaled it as slowly.

"We will talk about this later," he said. "For now, I shall retire to my room and read . . ." He paused to swallow. "About poor Omarak . . . for my edification."

He didn't make it to his room. He had stopped because he needed to rest and then, taken by surprise, he'd lost his carefully maintained equilibrium. After no more than a few steps he stopped again, his guards circling back like flocking birds, their dress capes swinging. When the king pointed to a door nearby, no one knew why. They all stared. It was just a door to one of many small reception rooms off this hallway. Then the king was stumbling toward it, and his guards were leaping ahead of him to get it open and check the room before he entered.

Two startled men who probably expected their conversation to be undisturbed were summarily ejected as the rest of the royal entourage surged in after the king. Swept along like a small rock in a flood, I went with them. I heard the queen say quite bitterly, "You fool," and heard the king breathily concede. I could see nothing but the backside of the man ahead of me. I did not see her turn and stalk away from him, only heard the people around me catch their breath. In the shocked silence, there was a soft patter of objects hitting the floor as she lifted a bowl from a side table and ruthlessly emptied it.

"My king." Evidently, she offered it to him just in time.

"Unkingly," he said when he was done being sick, still bent over, his hand on his thigh. The queen pulled the bowl away and passed it to her attendant, who received it without any change in expression and immediately passed it on.

Without any warning, the king's knees buckled. The

queen tried to catch him, but he slid through her arms, too heavy to hold. Unwilling to let him go, she dropped as well, velvet and silk robes billowing all around as they sank to the ground together.

"Poison," someone whispered, and I heard the dreadful word repeating through the room.

"But he hasn't eaten anything!" a horrified Philologos protested.

"He ate no breakfast," Hilarion confirmed. "He didn't touch his dinner last night."

"He hasn't drunk anything today, either," said Sotis.

"Nothing?" said the queen.

"Nothing," they assured her.

"*Nothing?*"

Assurances died on their lips.

The king wasn't poisoned; he was ill and none of them had noticed. She lifted a shaking hand to his forehead to feel the heat burning through his skin. I'm surprised his attendants had the courage to stay still in the face of her rage. I was moving already.

"He was sick in the night," confessed Verimius. He must have seen the evidence.

"Your Majesty, I am sorry. I assumed it was just the nightm—" Hilarion said, before he checked his runaway tongue.

The queen bent down over the king. "Why didn't you say something?" she asked.

The king, eyes still closed, waved his hand at the scene all around him. "I can't imagine," he said.

"We cannot lose you," said the queen fiercely.

"So, so, so," whispered the king, deeply weary. "I just heard."

In the doorway, a large man in the green sash of a healer was forcing his way through the crowd.

"Galen," said the king with a sigh. "Can you tell him I died?"

"He is my patient," Petrus insisted, following along in the other healer's wake.

Galen ignored him. "Has anyone else been taken ill?" he asked, and every head swung as they sought and could not find me because I had long since squeezed myself underneath one of the couches along the wall. Only the king, almost flat on the floor, could have seen me, and I prayed to Agalia that he would not. He opened his eyes and deliberately winked at me before closing them again.

Galen asked, "Has Erondites's grandson been near the king?"

"No," they said.

Yes.

"Has he touched him?"

"No!" they said.

Yes.

✦ ✦ ✦

More afraid of the queen's growing impatience than jealous of each other, Petrus and Galen finally agreed that the king had not been poisoned, that he had a stomach ailment and should be carried back to his room to be bled and then dosed with lemon and salt.

"The king shall return to his chamber," Eugenides allowed in a thin voice. "On his feet, and he will not be bled. And he will have hot lemon and no salt."

Galen and Petrus reluctantly accepted the amendments, their acquiescence only provisional, as they helped the king to his feet so that his return to his apartments under his own power might mitigate the rumors already flying around the palace that he had fallen down dead.

When the room was empty, I struggled out from my hiding place, the exit from under the low couch far more difficult than the entrance had been. I limped around the room, stretching my sore body and collecting the oranges scattered on the floor. Then I pushed the couch a little away from the wall and settled in behind it. My hands shook, making it difficult to peel the fruit, and I wondered if it was going to hurt very much to die. I knew Melisande would be grieved, but not surprised, at the news that I was dead. Would my grandfather be blamed for introducing a diseased grandson into the king's household? I hoped so.

I laid out the sections of an orange on the floor as I freed them. There were eleven, a frustrating number. Oranges mostly have ten. I peeled another, hoping not to get another eleven, and got a nine, which was a pleasant surprise. The curved sections of an orange make a good spiral, and with twenty sections, I could make three complete rotations with no section left over. Once I'd laid out the pattern, I ate every part of it, savoring each bite as if it were my last.

When I had eaten all the oranges and no one had come for me, I moved to sit on the couch instead of behind it. The room was meant for private meetings and was not large. One side table held a vase full of flowers. The other had held the fruit I'd just eaten. There was a mosaic on the floor with the storm god in the center medallion, surrounded by his children. Alyta, goddess of the gentle rain, had a gold garland. Her sisters and brothers, less welcome in their attention, had silver ones.

In addition to the doorway the king had stumbled through, there were windows and a doorway to the courtyard outside. I went to look at it. There was nothing interesting to see, only empty pavement and the rectangular reservoir in the center to collect water. The reservoir was empty, probably cracked, as it had recently rained.

When the latch on the door behind me lifted, there was no time to get back to my couch to hide. I slid around the doorpost into the courtyard, where there was not even a flowerpot to conceal me. On hands and knees, I scuttled across the pavement and dropped into the empty reservoir,

rolling myself up against the side and hoping that anyone checking the courtyard from the doorway might
overlook me.

I heard someone say, "Sir, the juice is still wet. He can't
be far."

"He isn't," said Teleus, captain of the guard.

I opened my eyes to see him staring down at me.

With his hand wrapped around my upper arm, Teleus
marched me through the waiting room and directly to the
bedside where the king lay propped up on pillows, sweaty
and pale. Medander saw me first and lunged forward, fist
raised.

"Stop," whispered the king.

"He is pest-ridden, Your Majesty. He needs to be got
rid of."

"Petrus said he had an infection in his throat. Galen and
Petrus agree my disease is in my stomach. It's the only thing
they agree on. It could not be Pheris who made me ill. He's
never even been close."

He lied. I knew by then who had come with the lemon
water in the night, even if he sounded very different by day.

"Go get your bedding and bring it here," he said to me,
and over the protests from the attendants, I did as I was told.

They were still arguing when I returned with my rolled-up
blankets. The king pointed to a corner, and I retreated there

to make a nest and climb into it. None of the attendants disagreed with Medander's recommendation. They wanted me gone, but the king wouldn't listen.

"He is Erondites's grandson and heir," said the king, "and I have conceived a great desire to see him live to adulthood. Now all of you go away."

"I will stay with the king," said Petrus officiously. Galen opened his mouth, and I could tell he meant to say that *he* would stay with the king. Petrus had been kind to me and I hoped the king would choose him, but he refused them both. "All of you go," he said. "Don't make me say it again."

"May I stay, Your Majesty?" asked Ion, sounding deferential. I noticed the contemptuous glance Xikos and Xikander sent his way when the king said yes.

Ion sat in a chair as the room fell quiet. "Would you like me to read something, Your Majesty? Or I could get my instrument."

The king shook his head. "Send for some food."

"Of course." Ion leapt back up. "Some broth, Petrus said, or some fruit."

"Some lamb in plum sauce," said the king. "They were making it for tonight."

"Your Majesty, no."

"Lamb," he whispered. "Plum sauce," almost mouthing the words.

When the food came, he appeared to have changed his mind. Waving away the platter Ion carried, he said, "Give it to the little Erondites."

I sat in my nest of blankets and ate everything, even the meat, which had been cut up into very small pieces and was easy enough to chew. By the time I was done, the king was asleep and my own eyes were closing. I pushed the tray away and fell asleep, not waking until there was a quiet knock at the door in the morning.

"Your Majesty," said Hilarion, stepping into the room, "your cousin who is Eddis wishes to speak to you." Eddis was already in the doorway behind him, coming in whether she was welcome or not. Ion, who'd spent the night in the chair, rose to his feet, blinking the sleep out of his eyes. Eddis smiled at him, and he ducked his head and withdrew to the door before he remembered me.

"The little m—Erondites, shall I take him out?"

Eddis looked at me very seriously. When she smiled, I found myself smiling back.

"I think we can rely on his discretion," said Eddis, and Ion bowed and left.

When the door closed behind him, the king said to Eddis, "You are leaving?"

"Sounis and I will return to Eddis as quickly as we can, to reduce my worries about someone dying in the near future."

"I doubt very much that I am going to die."

"You aren't the one I'm worried about."

"That bad?"

"Cleon has called for a trial."

"Oh, Cleon," said Gen. "Stupid as ever."

"He insists you cannot be allowed to rule over me without the approval of the Great Goddess." Eddis dropped into the seat Ion had vacated and slouched down with her legs crossed at the ankle, much as the king habitually did.

"Does he expect me to rise from my deathbed to fight with him?" the king asked.

"I thought you said you weren't dying."

"I've reconsidered."

"He says that the illness is a sign that you do not have Hephestia's favor."

The king growled and I hunched deeper into the corner, pulling my blankets around me.

"Alternatively," said Eddis, "he says you are malingering. You don't dare to stand trial."

"I am not, Eddis," said the king flatly.

"Nonetheless."

"No. Not nonetheless. You are Eddis. Go smack him."

Eddis shook her head. "Smacking people will not persuade them. I must go home and explain myself and see if they will ever forgive me for what I've done."

"Nonsense," said the king. "Eddis would not forsake you

if you'd sold them all for cannon fodder. It's me they hate. Is your Mede ambassador going to remain with you?"

"I suppose he is," said Eddis, not sounding very happy about it.

"I wish he and Melheret would both go," grumbled the king.

"So does Sophos. Melheret is, this very minute, lecturing him again about shooting his ambassador."

"I hope Sophos is being equally rude in return."

"No, and you know that Sophos is truly sorry to have shot that idiot Akretenesh. He is still worried the gods will take him to task." After a pause, she said abruptly, "You are sick, aren't you, Gen?"

I could not see the king lying among his covers, but I heard him sigh. "Yes."

"Why?"

"People do get sick, you know."

"But I thought you were getting better."

"I do not know why I am a magnet for every contagion. I think—"

Eddis leaned forward.

He lowered his voice to a whisper. "I think the life of kings is not the rosy experience the epics make it out to be."

Eddis's tense shoulders dropped in exasperation. "Idiot," she said fondly, and went away.

✦ ✦ ✦

Hilarion, Lamion, Xikos, and Medander returned to wash the king and change his shirt. Galen came to examine him and found Petrus already in the waiting room ready to rush to the king's bedside.

The king sent both of them away.

Next, the Mede ambassador arrived, having finished lecturing the king of Sounis. He insisted that there must be recompense for the assault on Sounis's ambassador and that it would damage trade with the empire if there was not some immediate remedy.

"I so admire your diplomatic skills, Melheret," said the king. "Ten thousand Mede soldiers landed in Sounis and you are pretending to be outraged because Sophos winged his ambassador. I have an idea. I won't say anything about the invasion of a country under my protection and you won't ever raise the issue of that idiot Sophos shot again. And you can stop making idle threats, because I know you are going to agree."

"And how do you know that, Your Majesty?" said Melheret down his nose in his best affectation of curious condescension.

"Because you don't like your 'brother ambassador' and you're secretly *delighted* Akretenesh got what was coming to him."

Melheret opened his mouth and then closed it again.

"Let us not behave like children, Melheret. You and your

ambassador in Eddis will remain because it suits the empire to have you here spying on us. The emperor browbeat us into the exchange of ambassadors, not the other way around. While you may keep up this pretense in public—that we are civilized nations at peace with one another—we both know that your emperor means to crush the Little Peninsula under his sandal as he advances on the Continent."

There was a long pause before the ambassador responded.

"I am sure that if the king of Attolia were to refrain from behaving like a child, it would be appreciated by all," he said.

The king seemed genuinely amused. "You really should have given me the statue."

"The king is tired," said Melheret, standing to end the interview, though that should have been the king's prerogative.

When he was gone, the king put his arm across his face and mumbled into his sleeve, "The king is tired of the whole Mede empire. That's what the king is tired of."

CHAPTER FOUR

*T*he next morning, the king informed his attendants that he would be getting up, and in spite of the protests I could already see were formulaic and half-hearted, a very abbreviated form of his morning rituals followed.

"Pheris," he called when he was dressed, and the attendants, reminded of my existence, swiveled their heads, wondering where I'd got to. The king knew, waving me out from my hiding place me as I hesitantly peered around the corner of his desk.

"You are coming with me," he said. "I don't want anyone pitching you out a window while I'm not looking."

In the afternoon, the king went to lie down, not in his own apartments, but in the queen's. Attolia had moved into these rooms when she'd seized the throne. Eugenides, once he was king, might have displaced her, or might have taken the apartments directly adjacent, which had traditionally belonged to the queen. He had done neither, choosing instead to inhabit a smaller apartment, usually occupied by minor or more distant relatives of the king. It had previously belonged to Attolia's older brother and had been empty since his death.

The queen's apartments had a guard room to pass through before one reached the spacious waiting room set aside for visitors. There were separate sleeping spaces for each of the attendants, and closets and antechambers, audience and dressing rooms. There were two rooms for the attendants to wait in. The queen's women had precedence in her apartments, so they gathered in the room nearer the royal bedchamber, decorated with scenes of war and statecraft. The king's attendants kicked their heels in rooms farther away, paneled with images of pastoral beauty and domestic tranquility.

"Medander," said Hilarion, with a look at me and then a firm shake of his head. Medander settled back into his chair, whatever he'd been planning in regard to me reconsidered. I held very still until the other attendants turned their attention to the card game that Ion and Sotis were playing. Sotis was arguing that Ion had broken some trivial rule, and when no one was looking in my direction, I slipped off my chair and sank down behind it.

"So, Ion," I heard Xikos say, "if the king dies after all your efforts to curry his favor, how will that work out for you?"

Ion ignored him.

"Even if he lives, you'll never get into his good graces."

"He could have chosen new companions and he hasn't," Philologos pointed out.

"He's not going to send *you* away, Philo. You are his darling."

Ion said very firmly, "This is not the place, Xikos."

"Yes, leave it, Xikos," said Sotis. "I'm ahead and I want to finish this round."

Just then one of the queen's oldest attendants, Imenia, came in, interrupting the game again to announce that the king had awakened. Hilarion stood to go to him and waved at Philologos to attend as well.

Imenia shook her head. "He asked for the little Erondites."

Startled, they all turned to find me sitting back on the chair as if I'd never left it.

"Oh, Philo, you have been replaced after all," said Medander as I dutifully followed after Hilarion.

Medander was talking nonsense, of course. Philo was always a favorite of the king and, no matter how much they teased him, a favorite of the other attendants as well. I was merely a pawn and in the game of kings, even pawns are counted with care. I was kept under a watchful eye almost every waking moment for the next few weeks as the king made clear his unequivocal wish for my continued well-being.

As they grew resigned to my presence, the other attendants tried to set me tasks.

"Pheris," Cleon would say, "bring me that wine." Or Lamion might tell me, "Hang up this coat."

Melisande had taught me well. I kept my eyes down and my face blank as an empty plate. I stared off to one side as if I hadn't heard them, or studied the wine bottle for a leisurely count of ten before slowly delivering it. I would take whatever clothes they handed me with a puzzled look and subsequently drop them on the floor.

"We could leave it there," said Sotis, looking at a shirt sure to be wrinkled when the king next called for it. Lamion just sighed and bent to retrieve it.

It took very little time for them to give up on me. I could not be sent to fetch a lamp, could not be asked to bring a pillow. Sooner than even I expected, I was ignored, which is not to say that I was free from all abuse, any more than I had been at home. Xikos was a man who resented his betters and mistreated his inferiors. He thought I was a suitable target to exercise his resentment on, but he was mistaken. Those same means I used in my defense at the Villa Suterpe were useful to me at the palace: the sticky fingers wiped on his sleeve, the accidental spills, and the many small mishaps in his day for which I could not possibly be blamed. Xikos soon learned to despise me, as I despised him.

I sat through the business of the court until my leg grew so stiff that walking was an agony. I walked until I was so tired that I fell asleep when we stopped, nodding off beside the king's chair. Used to the meager diet afforded to an aging nurse and an unwanted child, I ate rich food for the first time, too much of it, and made myself sick. Hiding it better than the king, I threw up into the necessaries in the middle of the night. What I could not hide was myself. I was pointed at, laughed at, seen in a way I never had been before. I was overwhelmed, and in spite of all my efforts, my eyes were often leaking my woes to the world. Whenever we returned to the king's apartments and he released me to the quiet of my closet, I went sobbing with relief, longing to be with my nurse in our own little outbuilding on the farm, longing for a sense of safety I would never know again.

Slowly I came to tolerate the ceaseless activity of my new home. The weight of watching eyes faded, and the people of the court began to ignore me, just as the attendants had. They talked over my head about affairs of state, and about the state of very private affairs, as I sat on the floor, arranging and rearranging the small items I collected in my pockets. Moving the coins and buttons and pebbles, I paid close, if invisible, attention to everything I heard. Studying the king, I saw how he, too, hid himself in plain sight, how his outward flamboyance helped him keep his secrets, how much he also disliked the noise and the lack of privacy.

Whenever there was an opening in his schedule, he visited the queen's garden, the section of the palace grounds reserved for the royal family. He said the birdsong was restorative, but I knew it was the solitude he savored. Once the guards had confirmed that the garden was free of intruders, he would leave both guards and attendants behind and disappear down the graveled paths. The guards remained at attention at the top of the stairs leading from the terrace down into the garden, watching for any glimpse of the king, ready to rush to him at a moment's notice. The attendants sat around the table where the king and queen frequently breakfasted during fine weather. Neither the guards nor the attendants would leave their places unless the king failed to return in time for his next appointment. When that happened, the attendants would have to wander through the shrubbery calling for him. It offended their dignity and they hated it.

Each time we sat waiting, I felt the pull of the garden. It called to me with the acrid scent of the cemphora bushes released in the sun's warmth, the sound of water pattering in fountains out of sight, the birds chittering in the trees, the wasps that came to collect any crumbs left from the royal breakfast, and the bees that buzzed in the potted plants before heading off in the direction of the kitchen gardens.

With the invisibility I'd felt at the Villa Suterpe settling around me, I inched farther and farther away from the other attendants. One day I crouched down near the guards to lay out my patterns, and on the next visit to the garden, I chose a step halfway down the stairs. Then I moved to the very bottom of them. Finally, holding my breath, I stepped as quietly as I could across the gravel and slipped between the cemphora bushes on the other side. I waited there for an outcry. When there was none, I took a deep breath and moved farther into the garden, sticking to the spaces between the hedges instead of traveling the noisy gravel paths. I didn't go far, meaning to return before any of the attendants noticed I was gone, but I lay down in the soft dirt and inhaled the smell of bark and leaf and flower, feeling as if I was breathing freely for the first time since I'd come to the palace. Then I fell asleep.

When I woke, I was in a panic, with no idea how much time had passed. Afraid the king had already returned to the terrace and my escape had been discovered, I hurried back to the stairs. Stepping in haste between the cemphora bushes, I tripped over the stones edging the path at the base of the terrace stairs and landed face-first in the gravel. The guards looked down at the sound, then turned away, entirely uninterested. As my heart slowed its racing, I limped up the steps, brushing the sharp little rocks off my stinging palms, and settled near the other attendants. Their conversation continued uninterrupted. The king returned a few minutes later, and we went on to his next appointment.

After that, if the king went into the garden, I followed soon after. I did not dare go as far as the kitchen gardens to watch the bees, but thoroughly explored the secret spaces between the hedges and behind the planted beds that only the gardeners knew.

I was lying on my stomach, with my chin propped on my good hand, watching a determined ant arrive home from a long journey between the bushes when I heard "Your Majesty? Your Majesty?" float through the air, and realized my time had run out. I sighed in frustration.

"Duty calls, Pheris," said the king, behind me.

Taken completely by surprise, I dragged myself around to look for him.

"Or at least, Sotis does," he added.

He was sitting not far away, with his back against the trunk of a tree and his legs splayed in front of him. He'd been watching me through the leaves. He continued to watch as I struggled to my feet; then he got up, almost as slowly. We dusted off our clothes.

"Now I know why we are both such a mess after these visits," he said. He still had dirt down one leg of his trousers, and I squatted beside him to wipe it off. He thanked me very seriously and led the way, moving no faster than I did, out to where his attendants were impatiently waiting.

That evening, he informed Hilarion that he wanted me to see a tutor. Hilarion laughed.

"Find one of the indentured who'd like a break from the taxes," said the king.

"Your Majesty is joking?"

He wasn't joking. I began weekly visits to meet a tutor in the palace library. Medander or Xikos or Philologos would escort me until I decided that the chance to move through the palace alone was worth the risk of revealing that I could find my own way. I had no such internal debate about revealing myself to the tutor. Melisande had taught me too well.

Every week my tutor showed me my letters and every week I pretended not to recognize them. I have deliberately omitted his name here. It was not his fault that I was a poor pupil, nor his fault that I was soon as sick of him as he was of me.

To my continuing surprise, I had not died. That did not mean I expected to live. I was not meant to be my grandfather's heir, and I did not delude myself that I was beyond his reach. I might dream of being sent home to the Villa Suterpe—to the familiar outbuildings, the wooded hill behind the stable, the pond at the edge of the kitchen garden—but it was only ever a dream. I did not expect to ever learn what had become of the bees that swarmed the day I was taken away, or whether the red mare had borne twin foals. My brother Juridius was the one meant to inherit. My grandfather intended to kill me himself, or have me killed. That is how one disposes of an unwanted heir.

When the king informed his attendants that he meant to visit the temple heights and address the Great Goddess, they said they would arrange for horses.

"I'll walk," he said.

"Your Majesty—"

"I remind you, Ion, that I am in the pink of health."

This was not true. He'd been feverish a few days earlier and was pretending it hadn't happened.

Ion did not argue, only pointed out how impressed the citizens would be to see their king ride past.

I thought he might be teasing the king about his birthday gift from the queen. Checking the expression on the king's face, I was certain of it. Step by step, the wiser of the king's attendants rehabilitated themselves, Ion, Hilarion, and Cleon risking the occasional needling humor that amused him, while Philologos, deeply ashamed at having followed Sejanus's lead instead of his own conscience, deliberately set aside his self-doubt and took on more responsibility. Lamion, Dionis, Verimius, Sotis—more followers than leaders—did as they were told and took their futures as they came. Medander and the two brothers, Xikos and Xikander, had burned their bridges, or so they must have thought.

While they, too, did as they were told, it was always with a hint of derision or contempt. The very same words that were companionable from the lips of Ion or Hilarion were insulting from the three of them.

The court seemed to have accepted the explanation that the king had kept his wayward attendants in deference to their powerful families. I think the king was more forgiving than they realized. There was always a deep conflict in his nature between his ruthlessness and his compassion. Neither characteristic was ever dominant for long.

"You are no doubt right, Ion," the king said. "Were I going to inspect the construction of the temple, I might even agree. As I approach the Great Goddess in search of wisdom, I'll walk the Sacred Way, as a humble petitioner should."

"A humble petitioner, Your Majesty?"

"One can imitate a humble man without being one, Ion. You should try it sometime." Bowing deeply to hide a smile, Ion went to make the arrangements.

At home, the stable hands had always driven me away from the horses, swearing they would go lame if I touched them. I had snuck back whenever I could, wondering what it would be like to sit on their backs. Secretly, I agreed with Ion that it would be more impressive for the king to ride.

Early the next morning, the king, with all of his attendants, crossed the plaza toward the Sacred Way. It was a long journey around the palace and then back and forth up the hill to where the temples overlooked the city, a sign of the Attolians' wealth and power as much as their piety. I was tired when we reached the heights, though not nearly so much as I had been the first time I'd made the climb.

The workers had been given the day off and the area around the temple was deserted, the double wooden doors to the treasury closed and unwelcoming. When the king nodded, Lamion and Xikos pulled on the doors' bronze rings, putting their backs into it, slowly swinging them open to let the sun pierce the darkness within, revealing an acolyte standing with her hands raised as if to welcome the light.

The king rolled his eyes.

"No knock, Your Majesty?" asked the acolyte. Her voice was ordinary, if condescending, without the oracular tones of Hephestia's high priestess.

"Insellia," the king said, addressing her by name. "I'm sure the Great Goddess needs no knock to be aware that I have come again to petition at her altar."

Insellia frowned and put out her hand. "I will take your petition to the Oracle, and she—"

"Thank you," said the king, ignoring the hand. "But I would be loath to disturb her. I will carry the petition myself."

"Very well." The acolyte turned her rejected gesture into an invitation, though a reluctant one. If any man could approach the gods, what need would there be for priests and priestesses? She eyed the crowd of guards and attendants behind the king.

"I would not see the sacred space before the altar over-crowded," said the king politely.

"A single companion, then."

To everyone's surprise and the acolyte's outrage, the king pulled me forward. "You said one. He is hardly even half of one." The king steered me around her and into the dark entryway of the treasury.

The inside of the treasury of the Great Goddess is no mystery, though it is a place few have seen. Once the king and I had circumnavigated Insellia's obstruction, we moved to the left through a heavy black curtain. When it fell closed behind us, we were in pitch darkness. The king knew his way and guided me to the right, into more curtains, soft and heavy, and this time with no obvious opening between them. In rising fear, I batted my hands in front of me.

"Shhh," said the king, bending close to my ear. "There is no opening, and if you step on the bottom of the curtain, you are fighting against yourself. Slide a foot forward, yes, like that, now again." Step by step, we pushed on, the king's hand firm at my back. The soft heavy curtain slid up past my face, and I found myself in the central room of the treasury, lit by the smoke-filled rays of light that came through the lenses set all around the base of the dome in its ceiling. Four pillars supported the dome, and between them was the altar of the Great Goddess.

Her statue sits facing away from the doorway where Insellia had awaited us, looking in the opposite direction from the enormous statue that now occupies the center of the completed temple. The larger statue of the Great Goddess lifts her staff. The smaller avatar of Hephestia keeps her staff against her shoulder and raises the orb of Earth to the heavens instead. Around her feet, the smoke from smoldering coleus leaves, constantly renewed, pours over the lips of their braziers.

As the king began to walk around the pillars to the altar in front of the Great Goddess, I followed until yanked back by the collar by the acolyte, who'd followed us through the curtains. At my squawk, the king turned to frown at us both. Then he waved me to a bench along the wall. The acolyte sat beside me. She nodded with approval as the king placed a small bag on the altar, with the deliberate clink of coins.

"I am Eugenides, by the will of the Great Goddess high king over Attolia and Sounis and Eddis, and I have come to ask . . . if war comes to my people, should I not lead them in battle?" He dropped to his knees and from his knees to his stomach and laid himself out very gracefully on the stones before the altar. The smoke from the braziers drifted over him in irregular billows, as if moved by a breeze I could not feel. The king breathed deeply and did not cough.

After a while, I assumed he had fallen asleep. Increasingly bored, I examined everything I could see in the dim light. There were shelves on all the walls, some of them already bearing treasures dedicated to the goddess. There were pitchers for pouring out libations, some gold and some silver, one shaped like the head of a lioness. There was a matching set of gold cups, figured with bulls and flowers. My bottom hurt. I shifted uncomfortably and the acolyte frowned.

I studied the Great Goddess, shining in the darkness. The treasury was new, but her statue was much older; the wood from which she was carved showed through the gold leaf. The pillars supporting the dome were tree trunks, smoothed of their bark and inverted, so they were wider at the top than at the ground. They too were older than the treasury, had once held up some other dome in some other temple of Hephestia.

The sunlight shifted while I sat, illuminating the orb of the Earth from a slightly different angle. It had phases, then, like the moon, and could have been read like a sundial if I had been sufficiently familiar with its aspect. Distracting myself from the growing ache in my hip, I figured how one might estimate the time. My feet did not touch the ground. It was an increasingly painful way for me to sit, and every time I moved, the acolyte's frown deepened.

I had long since begun to regret being chosen, wishing Xikos in my place, when between one heartbeat and the next, Moira appeared. She stepped into view from behind a pillar too narrow to have concealed her, and I sat straight up in surprise. The acolyte hissed, and I turned to her in disbelief. Did goddesses appear every day?

Goddess of scribes and messenger of Hephestia, Moira was robed all in white, except for a shawl over her shoulder, which was a thousand different colors. Her coiled hair was held in place with silver wire. Her feather pen was tucked into her belt. She smiled at me, and I was stunned like a rabbit hit with a stone.

The reader may believe a goddess came bearing a message for the king or believe it was only the effect of the smoke from the braziers. The acolyte can offer no corroboration. From the slightly bored expression on her face, I gathered that she saw only the king lying on the floor, not Moira bending over him, the pattern on her shawl changing in the dim and uneven light.

"Eugenides," said Moira, and I heard for the first time what the Oracle's voice only echoed. "Tell me again why you pester the Great Goddess?"

"I ask humbly for instruction," he replied, without lifting his head, speaking in the accent I hadn't heard since I'd been ill, without the diplomatic overlay of Attolian vowels.

"You ask to have all things made plain to you. How is that humble?"

"Asking for guidance is not humble?"

"Asking may be. Expecting an answer is not."

"I no more than hope, goddess."

Moira sighed, shaking her head. "Lies, lies, Eugenides." She crouched beside him and pushed his hair to one side, tucking it behind his ear so that she might whisper softly into it. "Here is your answer then, humblest of mortals. You will fall, as your kind always fall, when your god lets you go." She patted him on the shoulder. "Now you know what many men do not."

She straightened, and stepping behind the pillar, did not reappear on the far side.

It was a little longer before the king pushed himself to his feet. As he rose, so did the acolyte beside me. Relieved, I slid myself from the bench and held on to it while I eased my leg.

"Have you received your answer, Your Majesty?" the acolyte asked dryly.

"Indeed, I have," said the king, in a speculative kind of voice. I turned to see him watching me. I think I had that air of a stunned rabbit still.

"You are one surprise after another, Pheris," he murmured, patting me on the back before leading the way out of the dark treasury.

✦ ✦ ✦

"You have had your answer," said Attolia.

"Indeed," said the king, evidently pleased with it.

"Not the answer to the question you asked, though."

He shrugged, dismissing her concern. "Moira said I will die of a fall, not by the sword. Galen and Petrus can stop wrangling over my health."

"Men fall in battle."

That stopped the king.

"They fall ill," added Attolia, spearing an entirely harmless pastry and transferring it to her plate. They were dining together in a private room after the king's morning training with his guard. "Eddis cannot force her barons to bow to me, nor can Sounis," said the queen. "I cannot force mine to bow to them. Not even to stop the Mede will they unite, except through you. The Eddisians accept you as high king over your cousin who is Eddis—"

"Except all the ones who don't," muttered the king.

"Because you are *Eddisian*. The barons of Sounis may not like to see their king bow to you, but they know that otherwise they would be ruled by the Mede. My barons do not like a foreign king, but they comfort themselves with the fact that the king of Attolia is Annux."

The king tipped his fork back and forth, watching the light reflecting on the tablecloth. He knew this. He knew all of this. There was no reason to say it except to force him to admit that it was true.

"To send people to their deaths and not risk my own is contemptible," he said.

"Is it?" Attolia said, her words leached of any emotion.

The king had the grace to look embarrassed, and the queen, having made her point, moved on. "A letter has come from Eddis. She reports that someone named Therespides is a cause for concern. He stirs up trouble, suggesting you have no right to be ruler over Eddis."

"He's right. That's why Helen rules over Eddis."

"She suspects he is being paid for his efforts. Who is he?"

"He used to be on your payroll, or rather, the payroll of your former master of spies. Relius used to give him money in exchange for information," said the king.

"Eddis has no evidence of clandestine meetings, and the Mede ambassador is only one possible source of the money," said Attolia, delicately chewing her lip.

"She should send that ambassador back to the Medes," said the king.

"And admit she is no longer sovereign and no longer in need of her own ambassador?" Attolia countered.

The king conceded, waving his hand. "You're right. Sounis can shoot him instead." The queen was not amused.

"Did your cousin Cleon truly break your fingers?" she asked abruptly.

Startled, the king said, "Cleon broke one of them, mostly

by accident. My exceptionally more vicious cousin Lader broke two more. Why do you ask?"

"Cleon offers the most amenable ear to Therespides. Eddis says she would like to have him out of her court."

"She should exile him, then."

"My suggestion as well, but she feels she cannot without causing more difficulties. You and I agreed you would have new attendants once the scandal over Sejanus died down."

"We agreed I might have attendants who didn't hate me, or at least ones who weren't standing around watching while someone tried to kill me."

"Eddis asks, if you have gotten over your unfortunate history with him, whether Cleon might be one of them."

With only an appearance of consideration, Eugenides said, "Cleon Omeranicus is already my attendant. Wouldn't it cause confusion having two Cleons?"

The queen deferred with an almost invisible shrug. It would hardly serve to pick one's government servants by the convenience of their names, but she knew an excuse when she heard one and didn't press further.

"Maybe Lader?" she suggested.

The king's laugh was light, but bitter. "Only if he comes back from the dead."

Most of my days were spent in the waiting room. It was not a requirement; officially I was free to come and go just like any of the other attendants. Unlike them, I was afraid to venture too far from the king's protecting presence. I walked alone to the library to meet my tutor through well-traveled passage-ways and did not give in to the temptation to explore beyond them. Instead I tucked myself into a corner of the waiting room where the light from the window above obscured my presence. Safe enough there, I could think my own thoughts or listen to the talk around me.

Much of the conversation was boring. Philologos pined for a young woman named Terse, without any sympathy from me. Verimius pursued the poet Lavia, who wrote terrible poetry about Celia, one of the queen's attendants. Cleon was in love with a girl whose father was a devoted member of the queen's party at court, which was awkward, as Cleon's family was deeply in debt to my grandfather who was Susa.

"At least you're not an Erondites," Verimius consoled him, with a sidelong glance at me.

Indeed, one of the satellite members of the house of Erondites had been found very bruised at the bottom of a staircase. He insisted that he'd tripped.

Some things I saw I did not yet understand: why a guard stared at Layteres, the second son of Baron Xortix, and why Layteres pretended so poorly not to notice. The other guards in Aristogiton's squad watched them both with expressions I couldn't read. Medander's purpose as he surreptitiously carved the edge on a die was more clear. He saw my eyes on him and put the die in his pocket, scowling.

Verimius and Medander talked openly about their dislike of the king, oblivious not only to my attentive ears but also to the reaction of the guards standing duty at the doors and the squad leader sitting on the bench nearby.

"He knows nothing of how to rule," Verimius sulked.

"He did not agree to let you have the disputed land?"

"He said it is the queen's decision."

"Pathetic," said Medander. "He is supposed to be king. It is the queen who rules while he keeps low company. Promoting filthy okloi."

"Well, Costis was a patronoi."

"Two olive trees and a goat don't make an estate. He should have been hanged. His friends, too."

One of the guards standing by the door was Clopius, a good friend to one of the men in Aristogiton's squad, the men Costis had risked his life to shelter from the queen's rage. I remember this moment particularly because Clopius died trying to protect the king after the ambush at the roadside tomb.

Xikos was less direct.

"So, Hilarion, are you for the king now?" he asked in his needling way.

"And if I am?" Hilarion responded.

"Well, it hardly matters, does it? The king is not for us, is he? None of our bootlicking will make him treat us as real companions." He'd used "our," but he meant "your." He just didn't have the nerve to insult Hilarion outright.

"I wouldn't think your bootlicking would make anyone treat you as a real companion, Xikos," said Hilarion, laughing at him. "I am for the king because I am for the king. That is all."

"Oh, surely there is some self-service there? Convince him of your loyalty and improve your fortune?"

"And do you think my fortunes are in doubt, Xikos?"

It was Xikos who needed to have his fortunes repaired. It had been a godsend to his family to have him made an attendant of the new king, and he'd squandered the opportunity. Rather than blame himself, Xikos pretended it was the king who was at fault.

On the rare occasions the king and queen were in the king's bedchamber together, the waiting room also held the queen's attendants, but it was mostly filled with men. Hilarion was married, his wife sometimes joined him in the evenings, but she always left before the heavy drinking began. Dionis, Lamion, and Verimius were married, but their wives lived in the country. That left them free to participate in all the flirtations of the court, which Lamion did to a lesser extent and Verimius to a greater.

One person who was always welcome in the waiting room was the ambassador of the Braelings, Yorn Fordad. He often joined the attendants at the card table and could count on being waved into the bedchamber for a private audience if he caught the eye of the king. Fordad was a solid man with a kind face and a deep, friendly laugh. Unlike so many Braelings, he was not blond, but his skin was just as fair as his countrymen's, and when he was too long in the sun, it burned a bright pink. He kept his chin bare, but when he was playing cards, he liked to stroke his luxurious mustache.

His fellow ambassador, Besin Quedue, who represented the Pents, no one liked. He'd only recently been sent to serve in the Attolian court, having gotten into some sort of trouble at home. Before his arrival, the small state of Attolia hadn't warranted an official ambassador from the mighty Pents; they had relied instead on Fordad as an extraordinary ambassador to protect their interests. Fordad bore Quedue's company patiently and did his best to guide him, but the Pent ignored his advice.

In everyone's hearing, Quedue had assured Fordad that he didn't expect to be stuck in a backwater like Attolia for long. "Father says there will be a spot for me in the subordinary council in a year or two. All I need do is amuse myself in the meantime. The queen is lovely, hmmm?"

"She has a husband," the Braeling cautioned him.

"He is an infant. It is a marriage of convenience."

"Mmm," said Fordad.

"I've heard he pretends not to recognize the Mede ambassador. He won't play games like that with me!" said the Pent.

The Braeling rolled his eyes to the heavens—we all saw it. We also saw that when the door to the king's bedchamber opened and people rose to their feet, the Pent ambassador bowed as low as anyone else.

Later Verimius remarked to Cleon, "Please gods, no one tell that Pent what happened to Nahuseresh. Talking right in front of us as if we were furniture. If he's going to be rude, you'd think he would do it in his own language."

More perceptive, Cleon asked, "If we couldn't understand him, how would we know we were being insulted?"

As the days grew warmer and the rains tapered off, my grandfather began to worry that it would not be as easy as he'd anticipated to get rid of me once his little joke had played out. He knew he would need to remove me from the king's proximity, and he started laying his groundwork. As if to underscore the precariousness of all things in life, Baron Hippias, the secretary of the archives, went to bed and was found dead in the morning.

CHAPTER FIVE

Spring was well begun when Eddis and Sounis returned to Attolia for the Festival of Moira. Cenna of Eddis was competing that year for the Golden Pen, and they came to see the plays performed. Though they were greeted with open arms by the Attolians, their retinues seemed stiff, and some of the Eddisians appeared outright sullen. Lamion commented on it and Ion said they always looked like that.

The city was full for the presentation of new plays and the selection of the best of them for Moira's prize. The Invaders may have built Attolia's amphitheater, across the river from the city, but it was the plays written in Moira's honor that filled it every day in fine weather. It was the first time I'd seen a play, and I still remember every word of all three presented that year, though the first two were nothing out of the ordinary. No one, of course, has forgotten the third play, Cenna's "Royal Favor."

When the narrator first strode out on the stage to introduce his play, the people who came to the theater to chatter with one another and enjoy the sunshine hardly paid attention.

Sing, Goddess! Of the lazy king! Emipopolitus, who connived
  his way to the throne
by marrying the king's daughter Bythesea! Oh, foolish
  princess,
swayed by a pretty face!

Tell us, Moira! Of our indolent king, stuffing himself at the
  banquet table,
shirking responsibilities and shouting of enemies
only he can see!

"Beware! Beware!" The king endlessly warns of war, sending his
  dinner guests to hiding
so that he can go place to place, drinking up the wine
left in their cups!

Oh, Emipopolitus, it is you who must beware as your enemies
  unite against you!
Oh, sorry king, who sees his doom upon him!
How shall he save himself?

Watch now and see
how cunning a man can be,
how hard a lazy man will work
when he serves himself.

As the actors filed onto the stage behind the narrator, the audience gasped. If Emipopolitus's showy costume had left any doubt who was the target of this satire, the oversized hook the actor wore made it unmistakable. By the time the narrator finished the prologue and waited for royal permission to proceed, the whole theater was dead silent.

Many corrupt businessmen or conniving courtiers have seen a thinly veiled version of themselves vilified in Moira's plays, or painfully ridiculed as a lesson to others, but mocking the powerful is not without risk. Only success protects a writer from retribution. The king, with no real choice, gave his permission for the play to go on, but settling back into his seat, he murmured to the queen, "Swayed by a pretty face."

Cenna was engaged in a dangerous business indeed.

Fortunately for Cenna, we laughed until our sides ached as Emipopolitus ran around the stage creating more and more complicated plans that succeeded only by accident in confounding every attempt to unseat him. I was delighted at the end of the play, when all of the lazy king's enemies, including the narrator himself, climbed into a boat to be carried off to exile, convinced they were on their way to colonize the moon. The actor playing Emipopolitus waved them goodbye. When the boat had been lifted into a flyway above the stage, he turned to the audience.

> *Chorus and all are flown away, and though*
>> *I could close the play myself*
> *Give all its elements in capsule form for latecomers*
>> *and the inattentive*
> *I beg you to excuse me, as I must retire*
> *to drink the wine they left behind.*

He waved his hook and wobbled off the stage as the audience roared, and the amphitheater filled with claps and whistles and cheers. The king said very mildly, considering how he'd been abused, "I feel I am missing something in the references to wine."

"I have increased the royal requisitions of it, as well as the other crops we are stockpiling," Attolia said grimly.

"I don't see why that's my fault," said the king. "Why isn't *Queen Emipopolita* the main character of this play?"

Because not even an Eddisian would have dared. It was astonishing that Cenna had gone as far as she had. No

Attolian would have had the nerve to create the character of the Princess Bythesea.

At the banquet in the palace that evening, there was talk of nothing but Cenna's play. Most people had the sense to keep their conversations very quiet, one eye on the high table as they spoke. Only the Pent was sufficiently rude or stupid to laugh out loud.

The Mede ambassador had tried to engage the ambassadors of the Epidi Islands and Kimmer on the subject. Diplomatically, the Epidian claimed not to have seen it. The ambassador of Kimmer said the same, going on at some length about his health and the inadvisability of spending all day in the heat. It might have been diplomacy or truth. "Large crowds inevitably breed disease," he told Melheret. "I never see plays."

"Pity," said the Mede. "It was most amusing." Turning to Quedue, he finally got the response he had been fishing for.

"Quite riotously funny!" the Pent shouted, loud enough to draw everyone's attention. He quoted the silliest bits of the play while looking straight at the king as Melheret smiled and the king smiled, the smiles more and more ferocious, and only the Pent failing to notice.

There was no way to deny Cenna the Golden Pen. She had given a voice to all those who resented the high taxes and the requisitions levied to support the war effort, who thought the Medes, twice driven off the Little Peninsula, were no longer a threat. To deny her play the prize might enflame them further.

When she came forward to take the pen, Cenna turned out to be a surprisingly small woman with a head full of curly hair and a cheerful smile. She didn't look like a troublemaker.

"I have exiled people for less than a play like that, Cenna," said the king sourly.

"But it was funny, Gen, wasn't it?"

"Time will tell," said the king. And indeed, it is a play still performed in the capital every year or two, to the delight of its audiences.

"Moira's priestesses will be more careful how they select the judges for their contest in the future," said Attolia, sitting at her dressing table. She had sent away Phresine, who usually undid the pins from her hair, and made no move to remove them herself. Her hands remained folded in her lap.

"We have more important things to worry us," Eugenides pointed out. "The Namreen are still on the hunt. Costis may still be alive."

Attolia nodded absently.

"Irene?" Eugenides prompted.

"It's nothing," she said. "Sophos asked my advice about a prisoner he is holding."

"Ion Nomenus," Eugenides guessed. "Is he still in that pig shed?"

"He was moved down to a cell in Hanaktos."

"I suppose Sophos wants to release him."

"Of course he does," snapped Attolia. "Sophos would let a viper nest in his shoe if it said pleasssssse."

Eugenides laughed, but she was too angry to join him. She said, "Nomenus betrayed him. Sophos should have killed him on the spot and he didn't have the stomach for it."

"He didn't," Eugenides agreed.

"He let a traitor play on his weakness, and the result of his mercy is that he is asked for even more mercy." She finally began to work at the pins in her complicated braids, pulling them too hard, catching a few hairs with each pin and pulling anyway. "Nomenus has petitioned to be pardoned."

"Many of Sophos's barons did worse and suffered not at all." Eugenides crossed the room to stand behind her.

Meeting his gaze in the mirror, Attolia glared. "We are kings and queens, not all-powerful gods. We cannot reward the good men and punish the bad ones just as we would prefer. He should leave Nomenus to rot and I told him so," she said, daring her king to disapprove.

Eugenides wisely let a moment pass, and when he spoke it was not to argue over the just deserts of a traitor. "You're angry at Sophos for asking you to make that decision so he wouldn't have to."

"I do what I must because I am queen of Attolia. I am not here to cut Sophos's food for him." She yanked on a pin.

He stilled her hand with his own. Startled, she regretted her choice of metaphor, but he lifted her hand away gently and began to free the pins himself.

"Give our friend more credit than that," he asked of her. "He came to you because you have greater experience. You gave him your counsel. The decision is his, and Sophos of all people would never try to evade that responsibility."

As the pins painlessly slipped free, Attolia said, more sympathetically, "I told him he should save a better man. Nomenus is a liar who will only lie to him again."

She was eyeing him once more in her mirror.

"Whereas I am filled with truth as a hive is with honey," he said, his voice sticky-sweet.

"Oh, what a lie that was," she said, her expression finally softening.

By this time, I was ranging farther from the king's side. If people still saw me and warded off ill luck with a flick of their fingers, they did no more than that, and I was careful never to venture where the king's favor might not protect me. The day after Cenna's play, as I returned from another pointless visit to my tutor, I was surprised to see Juridius. I thought he might be an apparition until he threw an arm over my shoulder.

"Hello, brother. My grandfather who is Susa invited me to the festival." So he, too, had seen the plays. I wondered what he had made of them, but he had not sought me out to talk about Moira's competition. I should have guessed it by the way he said "my grandfather who is Susa," as if Susa was not my grandfather as well.

We stood for some time, arm in arm, in a brotherly fashion, while people passed by, and he told me the news of home, none of it what I wanted to hear. Having talked quite loudly about the family and our mother's prestigious visitors, and her reconciliation with her father, he said more quietly, "My grandfather who is Erondites misses having an informant among the king's attendants, Pheris."

I tried to pull away and he tightened his grip.

My mother's charming brother Sejanus had used his position as attendant to torment the king and further an assassination attempt. My uncle's crimes were the very reason I'd been sent to the palace as a pretend heir.

"Erondites wants to know when they will move grain to the stockpiles at Perma," Juridius whispered in my ear. "I told him I could find out from you."

I yanked my head back to look him in the eye, thinking it a cruel joke, not believing my brother would betray me so, and to my grandfather, of all people. Juridius made a pretense of reassuring me. "Melisande is an old woman, scared of shadows," he said. "You have nothing to fear from Erondites."

Having revealed that I was no fool, he still thought he could treat me like one. I tapped a finger to his temple. He was empty-headed if he thought I didn't know that my grandfather wanted me dead.

Slapping my hand away, his smiles all gone, Juridius said, "You are his heir, Pheris, heir to the house of Erondites. You must do what is best for the family."

I shook my head. My treacherous brother shook his, mocking me.

"Tell me, Pheris," he said, "do your new friends know that you are not the idiot you pretend to be? Does the king?" He tightened his arms further, making it hard for me to breathe.

Melisande knew how dangerous it was to be me. It was her hope that people might take pity on a poor witless boy, where they would fear and despise a clever one. She had taught me to play the fool and led my family to believe I was one. In Attolia's palace, they'd taken my idiocy for granted. If they found out that I had understood all the secrets I'd overheard, that I knew the significance of the things I had seen, they would murder me.

My weak, traitorous body shuddered, and Juridius laughed.

"So," he pressed again. "When are they moving the grain wagons to Perma?"

I shook my head again.

"Pheris." He lingered over my name. "Do you want them to know about Emtis?"

If not for the wall, I might have fallen. Emtis was the illegitimate son of one of my father's cousins, a servant, but with a few tenuous privileges of family. He had come to the villa when I had recently lost Juridius's companionship.

Juridius, less than a year younger than I was, had grown from an infant into a sturdy boy with no need of a nurse. My father had sent for him to join the rest of the family in the villa, to learn to ride and hunt and sit at the table as the heir to our father, a son to be proud of. Forlorn, I had tried to approach him in the house, to invite him back to our former games. At first Juridius had been puzzled by the way I was treated, then uncertain, and then, when it was clear to him that he could not be my companion and also the proud son of my father, he'd joined the others in chasing me off.

People are frequently cruel in just such an artless, unreflective way. Juridius was only doing what everyone expected of him. Not Emtis. He burned to pass along the humiliation he felt to someone else. Melisande could threaten the other servants, but she couldn't protect me from him. She could only beg me to stay inside our home, the only place I was safe, and I had refused. I would not give up my freedom, so Emtis had followed me from the house to the stables, to the kitchen garden and anywhere I tried to hide from him. He was a grown man and I was a child, and eventually, driven to my wits' end, I did something terrible. I became the monster people had called me all my life. Emtis lived, but he would never hurt me again.

Juridius was the only person who had suspected the truth of what happened, and he'd used it to rid himself of my company. He'd said, "I hate it when you try to sit next to me in the hall, and I am sick of seeing you looking at me from the doorway with your weepy eyes. I am the heir of my father. I am the son who should be oldest." He warned me to stay away from him or he would tell everyone what had caused our cousin's accident.

He never had, though. He'd kept my secret and I'd thought he always would, that somewhere still inside him was the brother I'd played with on Melisande's hearth, my beloved companion.

"Don't look at me like that," he said, standing in the passage outside the palace library. "You're the one who is the monster," he reminded me. "You're the one who refuses to help his own brother." He drove his elbow harder and harder into my chest. Afraid for myself, thinking of nothing else, I finally gave in. And when Juridius was gone, I staggered back to the king, telling myself over and over that nothing had changed. I had never been meant to live long.

The king was not an early riser. After a week of nightly banquets, he was moving particularly slowly the next day. He had promised to meet Sounis to spar, but he yawned and stretched and took so long to get up that in the end, he threw on his own clothes and raced out the door, moving too fast for me to follow. Wary of running into Juridius on my own, I went with Lamion and Sotis to prepare the breakfast room near the guest apartments.

Eddis and Attolia were already seated and waiting when Sounis arrived from the morning exercise, freshly washed, his hair still wet.

"Gen is still going at it," he said. "Whereas I am an idle layabout who refuses to be bullied into sparring all morning." He dropped onto a chair and flinched as it creaked under his weight. Sotis brought him coffee and he took a cup from the tray without bothering to pinch the tiny delicate handle between his fingers, then blew on it before downing the contents in a single swallow.

Just then we heard the king. He was making his way along the terrace below the window, singing loudly. I saw Eddis wince, and not at his sour notes. He had to have known we would hear him and that we would recognize the song.

Without a word, Sounis pulled himself back out of his chair. He reached for the pitcher of water on Sotis's tray and, looking to Attolia, he waggled it suggestively. After a moment's uncharacteristic hesitation, she gave a tight nod just as the king reached the chorus.

Keeping his own dear love in mind
he said, you are more beautiful,
but she is more k—

Sparkling in the morning light, the water arced out the window, the king's outraged shout proof that Sounis's aim had been true. The room filled with laughter as Sounis turned to replace the pitcher. When he turned back, probably intending to shout something rude out the window, he did not expect to be face-to-face with his target.

The king's attendants had watched, open-mouthed, as he'd thrown his practice sword aside, rushed directly at the wall, and gone straight up it—as if the power that pulls all things toward the Earth had tipped on its side just for him. He toed the rough stones with his soft boots and made it all the way to the windowsill, where he'd had just enough time to snatch at Sounis's sleeve before he began to drop. While Sounis squawked like a surprised rooster, Eugenides shifted to get a better grip. Sounis tried to shake him off and was pulled halfway out the window. The expressions on the faces of the men below were changing from shock to horror. If Sounis got free, the king would fall. If Eugenides pulled him any farther, they both would.

Attolia and Eddis tried to draw Sounis back, but Eugenides had planted his feet flat and was pulling with everything he had. Everyone was shouting or laughing, even Attolia.

Sounis's face was growing redder by the moment. Because it was three on one, or more likely because he outweighed the king, Sounis was slowly hauling himself back inside, and bringing Eugenides with him. They had their arms locked around each other's necks, Eugenides still not giving up, when Attolia said, very quietly, "Gen, enough."

They both froze, though neither let go. In the sudden silence, Sounis's breath was whistling in his throat.

"You've made your little monster cry," said Attolia, and ludicrously, the king of Attolia and the king of Sounis, still without releasing each other, twisted to look at me where I stood with tears running down my face.

Sounis said in a kind, if strangled, voice, "He doesn't mean it."

I hadn't realized I was crying and, realizing it, found I couldn't stop. The king untangled himself from Sounis and came to drop on one knee beside me.

"It's just a game," he reassured me. "No one is angry."

But I only cried harder, until the sobs shook my whole body and I struggled to breathe.

"Chloe," said Attolia, restored to her usual formality, "take him and a few of the sweets up to the apartments. He needs a rest."

Chloe was something of a dogsbody among the queen's attendants, tasked with the less pleasant errands. She had offended the queen, I believe, and been sent home for a while. I'd heard her complain about it, and I'd heard the older attendants trying to make her see that the queen offered her a way to prove herself, that a diligent performance of the unwelcome tasks was the path back into the queen's good graces. I thought Chloe dim-witted, though, and I doubted that she would ever learn.

She kept her expression pleasant until we'd left the room and the queen of Attolia was out of sight.

"Ugh," she said, pulling her hand out of mine. She wiped her hand on her skirts. She wasn't unkind, so she didn't hit me, merely suggested I pull myself together.

"Here," she said, handing me a sticky ball of honey and sesame seeds. "You'll be too busy sucking it out of your teeth to cry." Which was not untrue.

Very soon I was back in the quiet of the king's apartments, my ragged breathing evening out. I thought Chloe would leave me there, but she had taken her instructions to heart and followed me every step of the way, past the guards at the door and through the attendants' waiting room to the warren of rooms behind it. When I lay down, she put the handful of sweets beside my head, then flicked a bedsheet over me. She crouched there a moment, looking down at me.

"I have little brothers, though none as ugly as you," she said, "and they only cry when they are ashamed of themselves. I wonder: what are you ashamed of, little monster?" She searched my face as I stared back at her. Then she stood, brushed her skirts straight, and went away, not as dim-witted as I'd thought.

I cried off and on for the rest of the day. When it was time to dress the king for dinner, I pretended to be asleep and the attendants stepped around my bedding without speaking to me.

Cenna rode back to the mountains with Moira's Golden Pen. Eddis and Sounis sailed away to his capital city. I hid from the king.

If I was anywhere nearby, he could always find me, so I took to slipping off to the closets to hide behind the clothes. When he sent the attendants to hunt for me, they returned both resentful and empty-handed. The king, in turn, began to call me to his side just as I took my first step away, as if this was a game we were playing, as if he were winning. I could not look him in the eye without thinking of how I had betrayed him, while he thought I was trying to avoid the tedium of his meetings.

"If I have to sit through another interminable session with the western barons about road taxes, then you will, too," he insisted.

The only way I could escape from him was to follow the queen when she and the king went their separate ways. The king was careful to call no one to account in front of Her

Majesty and I knew he would not risk drawing her attention to my disobedience. That's why I was present when matters came to a head with the Pent ambassador. Attolia was not scheduled to meet with Quedue. She was to meet with her architects that afternoon, to discuss the new aqueduct. I had trailed behind as she had left the royal apartment, purely to avoid remaining in it with the king. I was unexpectedly entertained.

The little town of Attolia first took root on the heights above the mouth of the Tustis River. The Tustis was brackish near the coast, and the town drew its water from the clean and clear Chelian Spring uphill from it. After the Invaders came, the city grew larger and more powerful. It was rebuilt closer to the shore, and it needed more water, so the first aqueduct was built to bring it from the upper part of the Tustis River, where it was fresher. As the city continued to grow, the second aqueduct was built during the Trading Empire and the third finished after the traders were gone.

By the time the first aqueduct was destroyed in an earthquake, the city's growth had slowed. Although an ambitious project to build a much longer system had begun, the work on it had stopped and started over the years. Attolia was determined not only to see the aqueduct finished, but to erect a beautiful public fountain at its terminus, where the water would be delivered to her people. The engineers reviewed the history and explained their plans. They talked of drop and flow rate, and the precision of measurements and construction required to bring water hundreds of miles without ever allowing it to overflow its course, and I listened, rapt.

The council room was one of the largest in the old part of the palace, one level below the royal apartments, with a table in the center big enough to seat all the architects, the engineers, and the advisors associated with such a monumental project. There were doors at either end and a wall of windows overlooking the city. Opposite the windows was a row of alcoves, each with its own potted lemon tree. I was behind one of them. The queen did not look upon me with the same indulgence as the king, and it was always better to be out of her line of sight.

The lemon trees are long gone now, replaced with pedestals holding the busts of famous admirals. The beautiful landscapes that used to cover the walls have been painted over with pictures of the naval battle at Hemsha—a shame, as the work was not well done and war should not be made beautiful to look at.

Once the talk of the aqueduct moved from engineering to money, how much might be raised and from whom, I dozed off, waking only when chairs scraped across the floor as people rose from the table and bowed to the queen. I stretched and rubbed my leg while waiting for everyone to leave. They were very likely to forget me, and then I would be free to go to the garden. To my disappointment, Phresine said, "Your Majesty, the Pent ambassador requests a private audience."

I made a face. Sitting on the stone floor had left me cold and stiff. I did not want to listen to the Pent, who might drone on until dinnertime.

Complaints had been made to the queen and to the king about Quedue, about bills he'd run up with the palace tradesmen, the unwanted attention he paid to the women of the court, his insults to minor patronoi and his rudeness to the servants. The kitchens hated him, as he complained about the food and demanded dishes be made to order at all hours. No one, not even his fellow ambassadors, liked him, but there was little that could be done. He was the ambassador of one of the most important countries on the Continent. Only the Braelings were more powerful.

Quedue's request for an audience was out of the ordinary, and almost any other ambassador would have been turned away. Fordad, the Brael ambassador, would have been welcome, but Fordad would never have asked. He was meticulous in adhering to the rules of protocol—unlike the Pent, who'd made it clear he felt those rules were for lesser men from less powerful countries.

The queen allowed the ambassador to be admitted, so I shifted, trying to find a more comfortable position, and watched balefully as the Pent minced into the room tick-tacking on his high-heeled shoes. Lamion said he wore them in order to seem taller than the king.

"My dear Irene," said Quedue, waving at the attendants and the guards. "This is hardly private." The queen had not given him permission to use her name, nor to sit, which he did. "I had hoped to meet you without your shepherdesses, who guard so assiduously their one precious sheep."

"Do queens have privacy where you come from, ambassador? We do not have it here, I assure you." Attolia rose and moved away from him. The council room had been a dining room once, back when guests reclined as they ate. That had not been the style at court for years, but the couches from those days still lined the walls and the queen stopped next to one. Chloe leapt forward to plump the pillows and Attolia settled onto her left side, her elbow on a curving rest and her hand under her chin, her expression remote. Chloe adjusted Attolia's dress, smoothing the fabric and tucking it around her legs before stepping back, the picture of deference.

Quedue immediately left his chair and crossed the room as well. Attolia had deliberately left no room for him on the couch, so he dropped and sat cross-legged on the floor in front of the queen. Phresine's eyes widened. The queen's expression remained unchanged.

"You can depend upon me," the Pent said. I didn't know what he meant.

Attolia also seemed puzzled. "For what, ambassador? Is

there a new matter we need to discuss?"

"Yes," said Quedue in a low voice. "A vitally important matter. We have a saying in my country, that a beautiful woman deserves love."

Phresine's expression was almost worth the ache in my hip.

"Ugly women do not?" asked the queen, as if genuinely curious.

This was not what the Pent had expected, and after a brief hesitation, he ignored her. "My king has often said it is wrong for a beautiful woman to enter a marriage of convenience." He lingered over the words, and the queen appeared to consider them carefully.

"But he married your queen to preserve peace on the border with Gant, did he not? Surely he would not imply that she is not . . . ?"

The Pent said hastily, "Oh, my king never ceases to praise the beauty of his queen."

"Really?" said Attolia. "I thought he called her a cow. From a land of cows."

The conversation, which Quedue had obviously practiced in advance, was going further and further astray. "Is cow . . . not a compliment here in Attolia?"

Someone snorted, but Attolia only said very seriously, "Cow-eyed is, ambassador. It has something to do with the eyelashes and the demurely lowered gaze."

"Well then, let me call you cow-eyed, dear queen, for your lashes are lovely and no one can rival you for low—I mean, no one can rival your demure nature." He took the queen by the hand, trying to regain the initiative. "I think what my king meant was that true love should not be constrained, and a certain flexibility is important in a political marriage." He was stroking his thumb across her knuckles.

Her reply was cold. "On the contrary, Ambassador. Your king may not expect his wife to be faithful. He may call his queen a cow, and I wish her joy of him. In Attolia, the most important thing in a marriage is—"

She was pulling hard enough that he was probably hurting her hand. She stopped and stared him down. Reluctantly, he released her.

"—respect," she finished.

"Nonsense," said the Pent. He paused to glare at the attendants all around them before he leaned in to whisper, "You are hemmed about with his spies, but I can silence them. I know what you would say, if you felt free to speak."

Phresine stepped forward to end this fiasco. Too late. The ambassador had raised himself up on his knees, seized the queen's face in both hands, and pressed his lips against hers.

The king, assuming the meeting with the engineers was dragging on, had, like the Pent, waived formalities.

Descending the flight of stairs from the royal apartments, he'd walked down the hallway trailing his attendants behind him, to arrive in the open doorway precisely as a whole roomful of people stood by watching the queen of Attolia in the Pent ambassador's arms.

No one paints moments like these on walls.

Seeing him pale, I understood why even Eddis had braced herself after the oath-taking ceremony when the king was told he could not fight in his own battles. That had been illness. This was rage.

The ambassador, sensing his dangerous exposure, swiveled his head. Seeing the king, he waffled over how alarmed he should be. Attolia pushed him away. She pointed to the second set of doors on the far side of the room.

"Run," she said.

After another moment of hesitation, the ambassador jumped to his feet but failed to take her advice, only circling to the far side of the council table before he paused to look back. The king hadn't moved, except to lift his hand to his heart, like a man slowly realizing the fatal nature of a wound. He even looked down, as if expecting to see a blade protruding from his chest.

When he lifted his head and fixed his eyes on the Pent and the ambassador saw the knife that appeared in the king's hand, he began to flee in earnest, his hard-soled shoes rattling as he raced away. The king went after him, leapt to the top of the table in a single jump, and landed at a run on the other side. The ambassador was going so fast as he left the room that he bounced off the opposite wall of the passage outside.

The queen shouted at the guards to shut the doors. The king, without time to countermand the order, swerved to one side, reversed the knife in his hand, and hurled it through the diminishing space between them. There was a ring of metal on stone outside and a wail from the ambassador, then a slam that reverberated through the room and probably the entire palace. Slowing to a stop, the king stood with his shoulders hanging.

Then he spun in a slow circle, looking at the guards, his attendants, the queen's attendants. Frozen in place, they might have been devotional statues at an altar.

"Get out," he ordered.

No one protested, but no one moved, either.

"OUT!" he shouted. The guards who'd just closed the doors began furiously pulling them open again. Floor to ceiling and solid bronze, they weighed as much as ten men and it was no easy task.

Once they were open, the queen's attendants began to file out. Phresine hesitated. Attolia waved her hand, ever so slightly, and Phresine went too. At the other doorway, Hilarion stood aside to let Xikander pass him. Then he, too, hesitated. The guards behind him were moving more cautiously than the men who'd probably saved the Pent ambassador's life, and the doors behind him were not yet closed.

"Out, Hilarion," said the king, his voice lower but no less intense.

Hilarion bowed and stepped back, disappearing from sight, leaving the king, the queen, and me, behind the lemon tree, too frightened to breathe.

The king swung to face the queen, looked down again at his hand held to his chest.

"It hurts," he said. His voice breaking.

"Serves you right," said the queen, every word as cold as ice.

"Serves me right?" said the king. Incredulous as well as angry, he said, "Serves me right?"

"You dare," said Attolia, rising to her feet like a thundercloud. "You dare impugn *me*."

"He was kissing you!"

"*He was insulting me!*"

"You told them to shut the doors!" the king shouted.

They stood facing each other.

"Why? Why?" wailed the king, until Attolia gritted her teeth and gave the answer that should have been obvious.

"If I cannot kill the Pent ambassador, then neither will you."

The fire in the king flickered. His eyes fell away from her

face. There was another long silence until, in a milder voice, he inquired, "Can we not kill him?"

"Do not pretend with me when you know the answer." The queen sat, recovering her poise. "Though he will be on the next ship headed west, if I have to send him home in a rowboat."

The king sighed heavily. He continued to look all around the room, as if for a previously unseen exit, and then said quietly, "I'm sorry."

The queen nodded. She held out her hand, and he crossed the space between them and fell to his knees. He put his head down on her lap.

Voice muffled, he said, "It still hurts," as if the pain should have lessened now that the cause of it was gone.

She stroked his hair. "Serves you right," she said again, but gently.

I exhaled in relief. The king lifted his head. My mouth went dry as he fixed his eyes on the potted lemon I was hiding behind.

The king pushed back on his heels. He'd reached me in the space of a few heartbeats and had me out by the collar and stumbling toward the door in a few more. The metal cuff on his hook made a sharp tap, no more, on the solid bronze doors. After a long moment of hesitation, one began to swing open. The king stopped it with his foot, shoved me through the narrow opening, then used his weight to close it again.

I fell as he let me go and scuttled away, afraid to leave a foot to be caught by the weight that was swinging on hinges toward me. From the floor, I looked up at a circle of faces. They were asking if the queen was dead, had the king stabbed her, had she stabbed him?

"He can't speak," Hilarion reminded everyone as he pulled me to my feet.

"He can nod!" shouted someone at the back of the crowd. The hallway was filling up, as everyone within earshot had come to gawk. "Can't you ask the little monster to nod?"

"Pheris," Hilarion said, hands on his knees beside me. "Did the king . . . hurt . . . the queen?"

I shook my head.

"Do you think he—" He was searching my face as he spoke, and he stopped himself before the question was complete. Straightening up, he said very loudly, "This is futile. He is an idiot and can't tell us anything."

He'd seen how frightened I was, my fear a reflection of the realization reverberating through me. I was no ambassador with diplomatic protection. No one was going to intervene to save me. When the king learned who had betrayed him— and my grandfather who was Erondites would be sure he knew—I would not be sent home, I would have not even a day to spend again with Melisande. My earnest, self-loathing shame at my own actions had been nothing but a means to hide the truth from myself. It was not Erondites who was going to kill me. It was the king.

Too afraid of the possible answer, Hilarion dropped his question. He did not want to know if the king had murdered the queen, or if she was going to murder him. He didn't want to be the one who had to decide what to do next. When Phresine, with several of the queen's other attendants, circumnavigated the council room and arrived to speak to him, his relief was palpable. She was old enough to be his mother, and Hilarion bent head and body to listen to her.

Phresine told him she had sent one of the queen's attendants to each of the royal apartments and divided the rest between the two entries to the council room, to wait on whoever emerged. Grateful for her example, Hilarion did the same. After that, he dismissed everyone he had the authority to send away and persuaded most of the rest to go by asking them if they were sure they wanted to be the first person the king or queen saw when the doors finally opened. The crowd retreated to await developments out of sight. Hilarion sent Xikos and Sotis to fetch furniture from the nearby rooms, and we all sat down.

Hours passed. The dinner hour was over, the skies dark, the moon shining, and nothing had been heard from the king or the queen. Finally, after conferring again with Phresine,

Hilarion directed the guards to open the doors. At first little could be seen in the council room; the soft light of the moon coming in through the windows made impenetrable shadows elsewhere. Someone yawned from the far side of the room, where two couches had been pushed together and cushions piled high.

"What is the time, Hilarion?" the king asked sleepily.

"Nearly midnight, Your Majesty."

"Is there a problem," asked the queen, also waking, "that you disturb us?"

Hilarion had no answer ready. It was Chloe who piped up. "You said to bring you the map of the new course for the aqueduct . . . when you'd finished with the Pent ambassador."

From the shadows, the queen laughed. "Tomorrow will be soon enough," she said.

Softly the doors were closed. In the morning, the king was in his bed and the queen in hers when their attendants went to wake them.

CHAPTER SIX

The Pent ambassador was still demanding an apology as he was hustled onto a ship and dispatched home. His attachés, left behind, continued to insist on one. Between the outrageous behavior of the Pent and that of the king, the court was divided. Ion and Hilarion, usually in fast agreement, were opposed on this issue. Ion, who was meticulous about protocol, defended the king and delighted in every joke at the Pent's expense. Hilarion disapproved. He felt the king's misbehavior overshadowed that of the ambassador and had allowed Quedue to avoid the condemnation he deserved. Verimius said the king had embarrassed the Attolians. Xikos despised the king, but despised the Pent even more, and voiced to Xikander a savage wish that the king had succeeded in killing the ambassador. "If only we could have been rid of them both," he grumbled.

There were rumors about a meeting of the Greater Patronoi, the heads of the great families, or even an assembly of all the barons, to censure the king. On their own, the Greater Patronoi could overrule certain royal decrees, and the assembly of barons, when unified, was powerful enough to dictate to the throne. Attolia, for all her strength, had always been careful to maintain allies in both assemblies.

"They can't unite themselves long enough to agree on what wine to have with dinner," said the king. "It will be forgotten in a day."

Indeed, when Susa made it clear he would not support a motion against the king, the murmuring died down. The Brael ambassador, who was again the extraordinary ambassador for the Pents, brought the subject up in court with obvious reluctance. "In these tempestuous times, Your Majesty, I would like to hear from you that we are safe here in your home, that our diplomatic immunity is inviolable."

The king pretended to take offense. He assured the Braeling in a high-handed manner that he wasn't going to start firing at ambassadors the way Sounis had, lingering for so long over the circumstances under which he might be tempted to do so that he rendered his own assurances absurd. People covered their mouths to hide their laughter. The Braeling shook his head but accepted the king's words at face value, and the matter was considered closed.

✦ ✦ ✦

I was trying to savor what I was sure were my last days, and I couldn't. I couldn't sleep. I couldn't eat. Everything tasted sour, like fear and regret. I stayed in my little closet as much as I could, and at night I huddled in my blankets in such awful apprehension—certain that at any moment Juridius would reveal my treason—that I began to wish the waiting was over and I could die.

"Something has frightened him," said the king.

"*You* frightened him," said the queen.

"I wasn't angry at *him*."

"You were angry enough to burn the whole world down and him with it."

The king sent Petrus to check on me—as much to distract the palace physician from his own health, I think, as out of concern for mine.

"Pheris, you have to eat," Petrus told me.

He had looked in my ears and down my throat, pinched the skin on my arm and examined my fingernails. He'd sent for soup and oranges and almond cookies, and I'd turned my face away from them all. He held my bent fingers in both his hands and tried gently to straighten them. He looked at me speculatively.

"Do they hurt?"

I shrugged. They did, sometimes. My leg and my back hurt more, and they hurt more often. Sometimes the little jumps and shivers in the muscles made me want to scream, but they were usually at their worst at night, and if I lay still reciting my prayers to Ula as Melisande had taught me, they would abate for a time. Petrus made me get up to walk back and forth in front of him.

"The limp is not always so severe," said Petrus thoughtfully. I'd been curled up in my bed all day and could hardly move. "If it can be at times worse," he said, "then conversely, we may be able to make it sometimes better."

The king's ploy was a success. Petrus came every day and massaged my leg and my hand, measured the flex of my joints, and made me do stretching exercises and sit with my leg on bladders filled with hot water. "I have no illusions that we could give you a good leg, but I think we can help the one you have carry you a little more comfortably," he said. In pursuit of that goal, he slathered me with poultices and concocted tonics he tried to make me drink.

"There's something wrong with him," said Dionis, watching from the doorway.

"How finely observed, Dionis. You are astute."

"I mean more than the things that are usually wrong with him. Maybe he's dying."

I wished I were dying.

"You aren't dying," Petrus said sternly. He put his hands on either side of my head and turned my face toward him and away from the wall. He'd guessed it was no physical ailment that kept me in my bed. "You are not going to die," he said.

I knew better.

It was a month, more or less, before Erondites struck. I knew my time was up even before the double doors into the king's waiting room crashed open.

"Erondites!" The king shouted loud enough for me to hear him all the way back in my closet if I'd been there, which I wasn't, because Petrus had made me get out of bed that morning and sit in the waiting room. I was already out of sight, though, as I had heard the attendants shouting as they followed the king up the hallway. "Your Majesty, Your Majesty, please!" they'd called, and I'd leapt for cover.

The supply wagons carrying grain to Perma had been ambushed and burned.

It was a calculated attack on the stability of Attolia's rule. Her people were sick of her high taxes, tired of relinquishing their crops for her stockpiles. Twice they'd seen the Medes driven from the shores of the Little Peninsula, and they wanted to believe there was no longer any need to prepare for war. Once Cenna's play had dragged it into the open, their resentment had only grown. The farmers had grudged every seed of the grain that had burned in those wagons. To force more grain from them to replace what had been lost would require harsh measures. To leave the granaries empty would suggest that Attolia's demands had been unreasonable all along. Either way, the population would be enflamed. If they rioted and were put down, it would undermine Attolia's popularity still further.

Philologos, and behind him Sotis and Xikos, had appeared in the doorway. Everyone in the waiting room had jumped to their feet. Lamion and Ion, and Hilarion, hearing the noise, had rushed from their sleeping quarters. The king, to all appearances unhinged, was shouting at the chair behind which I cowered.

"You knew the route for those wagons, and you told the baron your grandfather!"

"Your Majesty, no!" Philo protested, all the other attendants chorusing in support: I was an idiot, I could not talk, I was too stupid to read or write, my tutor had said so. The king ignored them all, reaching around the chair to drag me out.

"Erondites has destroyed the supplies for Perma, and you told him how to do it," he said.

I shook my head, not denying that I'd done as he said, desperately trying to deny my own culpability. I hadn't wanted to help my grandfather. I hadn't wanted to betray the king. Tearing myself free from his hand at my collar, I dropped into a crouch, all my old habits coming back.

"Get your hands off your ears," said the king, slapping them away from my head. "Men are dead because of you."

I hadn't meant for that to happen. I hadn't known it would. He hauled me back up.

Hilarion, all decorum thrown aside, seized the king by the arm. "Your Majesty, you'll hurt him." The king shouldered him back and this time caught me around the neck as I tried to get away, choking me in the crook of his arm.

Seeing the knife blade of his hook in front of my face, I whimpered.

"Your Majesty, please," begged Hilarion.

"You wrote to Erondites," said the king, his voice flat with rage.

I tried to shake my head.

"Shall I cut out that lying tongue so you never use it again?" the king asked me, and I felt the cold blade hit my teeth, tasted metal or blood.

"Your Majesty!" Hilarion shouted.

The king paused at last. The attendants were staring at him in horror.

He released me and I fell to the floor.

"Send him back to his grandfather," he said bitterly. "He is an Erondites after all."

In the face of Xikos's satisfied face, Hilarion's shock, Philologos's distress, the king scowled. I didn't even care that my grandfather was going to have his way at last. I only cared that the king hated me. I reached for him and he kicked me away. Philologos took my arm then and pulled me to my feet.

Hilarion took my other arm. As I struggled, they began to drag me toward the sleeping quarters.

"I want him gone," the king said flatly.

Shuffling their feet unhappily, Hilarion and Philo turned me toward the door to the passage.

I was twisting my head to look beseechingly over my shoulder when there was a burst of light so bright it bleached every color in the room to black. The king was caught, eyes wide and mouth open, staring over my shoulder. I faced around, saw the terrifying silhouette of a figure, an impenetrable darkness limned by light, between me and the doors, and I wrenched myself free. My fear greater than all the efforts of Hilarion and Philo to hold me, I threw myself at the king, buried my face in his chest, felt the trembling in him that mirrored my own. Neither of us moved.

Eyes closed, I saw the light slowly fade from the room. When the red inside my eyelids had faded, the king spoke, his voice creaking like an unoiled pulley.

"You betrayed me to Erondites."

I nodded, admitting my guilt.

"Did you write to him?"

I shook my head, rubbing my face into his shirt.

"You can speak?"

He could cut out my stupid tongue if he would only let me stay.

"Pheris, look at me," the king said, his anger still simmering. "Can you speak?"

I couldn't lie to him again. Pulling my face away from him, I touched my fingers to my lips as if to catch the words and pull them out. I didn't expect him to understand.

"You can speak to Juridius," he said wearily. "And Juridius was here for the festival of Moira."

Blinking away tears, I nodded again.

Melisande had taught both of us the silent language she had shared with her deaf brother. She and I could communicate, but it was only Juridius who truly understood me. He was my heart's companion, and I'd shared everything with him, until the day he turned against me and joined the others at the villa as they drove me away. I'd gone to Melisande and cried and cried in her lap, thinking nothing could be worse—until Emtis had come.

"He can talk?" Xikos was the first to understand.

"With his hands," confirmed the king. "Well enough to inform Erondites where those wagons would be and when."

Before my eyes, the shock in the faces of Hilarion, Sotis, Xikander, even Philologos, turned to anger. Ion, Dionis, all of the attendants who'd spoken so freely in front of me, were realizing the depths of my deceit. Xikos pushed past Philologos and reached around Hilarion to drag me away from the king—to my death, I was sure. Whether it would be Xikos who would kill me or my grandfather was the only question.

"Stop," said the king, and Xikos paused in disbelief. None of the attendants seemed to have been aware of the great presence in the room. What they made of our reactions, I don't know.

"Your Majesty," said Ion sternly. "You cannot mean to keep a traitor among us."

"Your tune has changed."

"I was mistaken, Your Majesty. Send him away."

"So his grandfather can kill him?"

"It is no more than he deserves," claimed Dionis.

"Tell Erondites to find another heir," suggested Philologos, and Hilarion agreed.

"No one in the barons' council will object," he said.

"He is a traitor," said Xikos, which was ironic coming from a man who, if not a traitor, was certainly no friend of the king.

I think it was Xikos's words that sealed the decision in the king's mind. "Keep him," he said, adding to me, "Out of my sight would be better, Pheris, but I realize how that would turn out."

It would turn out a murder, I thought. I didn't dare meet anyone's eye. All of them were thinking of their secrets and how many of them I knew. Even Hilarion and Ion. Even Philologos was embarrassed to think of the things I'd overheard.

Into the angry silence, it was Ion who spoke. "Pheris will sit in the waiting room with us, Your Majesty. Very quietly, I am sure. And at night, he will sleep with me."

I flicked a glance up at him. He looked at me with such dislike that I quickly looked down again, but he was promising the king to keep me unharmed, and I was grateful.

"Come," said Ion, when the king said nothing. A hand on my shoulder, he guided me to a corner, where I sat on a bench against the wall. My feet dangled. The king went into his bedchamber alone and closed the door. It grew increasingly uncomfortable, but I sat, as Ion had promised, very quietly.

Others in the room were not so silent.

"The king should kill him," said Xikos.

"The king isn't interested in doing favors for Erondites," Verimius said.

"All of them should be killed," said Medander.

I thought of my mother and my brother and sisters back at the villa. I considered my uncle Sejanus, still under arrest. He'd manipulated the other attendants into behavior they were now ashamed of. He worked with the men who'd tried to assassinate the king. It was a wonder to me that he hadn't been executed long since. I thought of my brother Juridius, also a traitor. I thought of Emtis and what I had done and could not deny that the Erondites were a corrupt family.

"If the king wants him, he stays," said Ion. "We all know

why you want him gone, Medander. Stop being a cheat and you won't have to worry about what secrets the little monster knows."

The king did not leave his rooms that evening. Food was sent up from the kitchens. The attendants drank and played cards in the evening, and then Ion told me to collect my bedding and bring it to his room. Ion's room was no larger than my closet, but it had a window that looked out on the world, not onto an airshaft. It had little in it besides a bed, a table, and a chair, and seemed spacious without racks of clothes. On the table was an altar housing a row of tiny gods. I wondered which they were, but Ion flicked my ear painfully and pointed to the corner by the door.

"Sleep there," he said.

Cowed, I went to make a nest of my blankets and lie down.

The king might have bowed to the will of the gods and allowed me to remain in the palace. He had not forgiven me. I trailed after Ion, going only where he chose to go, not daring to sneak away, even to my little closet, much less out of the apartments, for fear someone would pitch me down the stairs and expect the king to be happy to hear of my death. There were no more unsupervised hours in the garden. People were careful what they said when I was near, looking significantly in my direction, putting their heads close together to speak in low voices.

The king accused Erondites of being behind the burning of the grain wagons, but my grandfather roundly denied all knowledge of the ambush. He pointed out that he had not invited Juridius to the plays, and asked why the king was not accusing my grandfather who was Susa of treason. My brother, when questioned, refused to implicate either Susa or Erondites. He claimed that a stranger in the street had asked him for the information and paid him to get it. It was an obvious lie fed to him by my grandfather or perhaps my mother. He was too young to be pressed for the truth, and they both knew it. In the end, the king had to admit that there was no proof to tie Erondites to the crime, and he was forced to withdraw his accusation.

Erondites had successfully defied the king, but it was not without cost. The king exiled Juridius. Though he was just a child, he was summoned to the capital under guard and put on a ship under the direction of the captain to be taken to the Greater Peninsula. My mother's brief reconciliation with her father was over, and the inheritance of the house of Erondites was again in doubt.

Wrapped in my blankets, listening to Ion's even breathing as he slept, I imagined the soldiers arriving at the Villa Suterpe. Had Marina fought them when they came for her beloved son, as Melisande had fought for me? Had Juridius had any warning? Had he had time to say goodbye? Did he even know, when he was taken aboard the ship, that he was going to Ferria, where my uncle Dite would take him in?

I sensed, but didn't fully understand, the rising tensions around me. With the end of the war with Eddis and Sounis and her marriage to Eugenides, Attolia had been, for the first time in her rule, a popular queen. Now her popularity, and the king's, was leaching away. I knew that there were protests in the city as food prices rose. Because I sat through the meetings with Ion, I could have told you how much the improvement to the fort at Thegmis cost, but not what the spending of that money meant to people already sick of being taxed to pay for armies and weapons and fortifications. I was focused on my own woes because I was a child and because no one had ever encouraged me to do otherwise.

Diplomatic ties were straining, and not just with the Mede ambassador, who continued to pretend the emperor had no plans to invade. None of the ambassadors from the Continent would admit what everyone knew to be true, not even Fordad, at least not publicly. He was welcome in private audiences with the king and queen, where he frankly discussed the danger, but the official Brael position was that there was no cause for concern. Everyone who wasn't a fool knew the Medes were coming, and still there were those making jokes about Cenna's play and blaming the king for the queen's preparations. It was Attolia who knew how to plan for a war.

There was talk of new attendants and the retirement of the current ones. With a few exceptions, the queen changed her attendants fairly often. Officially, it was meant to spread the honor of the appointment to different families. Unofficially, it prevented any one of the attendants from becoming too influential. Phresine and Imenia, her senior attendants, were both very careful never to use their closeness to the queen to their advantage. Iolanthe and Ileia were honored for their service and sent home with expensive gifts. They were replaced with two younger women, Caeta and Silla, who both became famous later, but for reasons unrelated to this account.

When I heard the king might change attendants, I prayed that he would not turn me out. I had no home to go to; my grandfather and my mother both wanted me dead. I hoped the king might send Xikos away, and I wasn't the only one, but it was Medander who was excused, along with Verimius. I heard the queen press the king again about making his cousin Cleon an attendant, but nothing came of it. Instead, three new attendants, Polemus, Motis, and Drusis, squeezed into the space Verimius and Medander had left.

Motis and Drusis were brothers, the younger sons of a cousin of my grandfather who was Susa. They were therefore relatives of mine, though they didn't care to recognize the connection.

"Ugh," said Drusis when he first saw me. He raised a hand.

"None of that," Ion snapped at him.

"Excuse me?" asked Drusis, as if he'd misheard, as if to ask what right Ion had to tell Drusis whom he could or could not hit.

"Lay a hand on him and I'll cut it off," said Ion grimly, a threat with great weight in the Attolian court.

Drusis shrugged and backed away with a single poisonous look for us both.

I didn't understand. Ion despised me as much as the other attendants did, and he did not defend me because of the king's favor, because that was long gone. Ion tried to live by principles that no one had ever taught me. Do not lie, do not take what is not yours, do not hurt the weak. Like Philologos, he was ashamed of letting himself be cajoled by my uncle Sejanus into tormenting the king and because of that behaved better toward me than I deserved.

CHAPTER SEVEN

*I*on was attending the king, and therefore I was with the king as well as he practiced his horsemanship on a course laid out near the Fields of War. We had arrived at the open ground along the river, too boggy for building and so left open for fairs and other gatherings, in a collection of carriages and riders. The royal stable master had brought the king's warhorse on a lead.

The way the king grumbled, any observer might have assumed the queen had shamed him into the exercise. But it was the king who was determined to improve his skill, while the queen was enjoying a rare chance to sit with nothing but needlework to occupy her under an awning that had been raised to block the sun.

Though he still refused to submit to the argument that his life was too important to risk in battle, he had grudgingly accepted that royalty did not fight on foot. Despite stories to the contrary, he was not a bad rider, but he had yet to become practiced at riding with one hand. Both he and the horse had to adjust if he was going to hold a sword and fight from horseback, and the stable master, trying to train both at the same time, had no easy task.

The beautiful warhorse Sounis had chosen for the king was as indolent as he was handsome. Yorn Fordad had suggested naming him Fryst, after the Brael god of winter, and Fryst appeared determined not to live up to the fierceness of his name. Built like a marble temple on legs, he was as placid as the king was excitable and preferred going around obstacles instead of over them—or, better yet, not going at all. Given any opportunity to stand still, he did.

"Faster, Your Majesty," called the stable master. "Faster!"

Too late.

Fryst balked at the fence the king wanted him to jump. When he stopped dead, the king sailed over the fence into the dirt on the other side of it.

The queen looked up briefly before returning to her embroidery.

Lying on the ground, the king shouted, "I think I've broken something—"

"Nothing important, I'm sure," she called back.

"My pride!"

She laughed. He got very nimbly back to his feet to glare over the fence.

When he leapt back onto Fryst, the king drove him in a circle to try the jump again. This time, when the horse balked, the king flew even higher into the air. Fryst's head went down and the king went up, rotating in midair to land upright, flourishing his arms like an acrobat jumping a bull. The queen clapped, the king bowed, and Fryst flicked his ears, looking interested for the first time that day.

A messenger coming from the palace approached Motis to whisper in his ear. Motis, rather than passing the information to the queen's senior attendant, took the man directly to the queen. The king leaned his elbows on the fence Fryst had refused to jump, waiting to hear what news was too important to wait until his riding lesson was over.

The queen called to him. "Costis's ship has been sighted off the coast."

"What flag?" asked the king.

"Round!"

This was evidently the best possible answer, and there was a great sense of relief in the air. The queen stood up. Then she sat again very quickly, and the king's smile vanished.

Phresine was at the queen's side. The king leapt the fence.

After a conference in low voices, in which Attolia insisted she was fine, the queen was lifted into her carriage. The king climbed in beside her and they rushed away, leaving the attendants to pile into the other carriages or follow on their horses. As they traveled back to the palace, people who might have smiled and waved as they passed hesitated, their smiles evaporating just as the king's had, like summer rain on hot stones. Petrus was waiting for them when they arrived. A guard had raced ahead of the royal party. The queen was tenderly conveyed to her rooms.

No one cared, or even noticed, that I had been left behind.

I had taken a few steps as everyone rushed for the carriages, but it was already too late. No one even looked back to see me watching as they pulled away.

I had no idea how to navigate my way back to the palace. I knew it was uphill. I also knew that none of the streets ran straight. There were so many turns to take, and it was so far to go on foot. I was a small, unnatural person in fancy clothes; both of those things would draw a great deal of attention, none of it benevolent. As the carriages rolled away, I stood despairing.

"Left you behind, didn't they?" said the stable master, and I swung around with relief. If I had been forgotten, I had also forgotten him.

"Probably never gave you a thought. All fine looking and smelling of perfume. They were born beautiful and mistake being beautiful for being good."

I swallowed, well aware that I was neither beautiful nor

good, and certainly not as kind as the stable master, who nodded at Fryst and said, "Well?"

I didn't understand until he squatted and linked his hands together at knee height, an invitation to mount. Hesitantly I lifted my good foot, nowhere near enough, and the master straightened, reconsidering. My hopes fell. Of course, it was ridiculous to think I could ride the king's warhorse.

Instead of giving up, the stable master took me by the shoulders and positioned me better. "Don't grab my head for balance," he told me, putting his hands around my waist. "I'll put you on your stomach and you see if you can swing your leg over as you sit up. I'll be right here holding you."

When I nodded, he lifted his hands and I flew into the air. I had just enough time to remember to grab at the front edge of the saddle with my good hand. The master held my good leg while I slid the bad one across the polished leather of the saddle, and then I was sitting up, looking between the ears of the king's warhorse, which went on obliviously working at the bit in his mouth.

"That's fine, isn't it?" said the master.

It was glorious.

"Fryst is learning all kinds of new things today," he said.

Back in the palace, I made my way to the king's apartments, my heart full of conflicting feelings—a nebulous worry for the queen and the leftover bubbling delight of my ride on the king's horse. Seeing me sway in the saddle, the stable master had stepped into Fryst's stirrup and mounted behind me. With his horse trailing on a rein, we had traveled at a walking pace through town. A very sedate first ride, and I had loved every moment of it. I smiled my thanks at the stable master who had been so unexpectedly generous.

"Go on, boy," was all he said.

The king's apartments were empty. The guards at his door guarded no one. Not a single attendant was there. I went to the queen's apartments, where I found all of them in their waiting room, sitting in silence.

"Get out," said Xikander when he noticed me, throwing a handful of something at my face. "Your hideous face has cursed our queen."

If not for the kindness of the stable master, I would have backed away. No one else was going to defend me. *They mistake being beautiful for being good.* I turned to see what Xikander had thrown. Almonds. I crouched down to pick them up. When I had all of them, I stepped to where Xikander sat beside a little gold-and-green painted table with three fragile legs, its top crowded with cups and small plates. I opened my hand to let the nuts drop one by one into the bowl he had taken them from. Then I picked up his wine and threw it in his face.

As the son of the house, I'd been protected from any direct attack by the servants. Not so from the dear members of my extended family, who lived in and around the Villa Suterpe. I used my invisibility to my advantage, but my invisibility was not my only defense. I also bit—as Xikander discovered when he leapt up to strike me. Lamion grabbed his arm, impeding him just enough to let me catch Xikander's hand and sink my teeth into the fleshy part of his palm.

Xikander shouted, smacking me with his free hand while Lamion hung on to him. Hilarion jumped up to pry the two of them apart, only to have Xikos come to his brother's defense. The gold-and-green table went over with a crash, and Luria, the queen's attendant, threw open the door to the waiting room to a scatter of broken dishes and a sudden, embarrassed silence.

I took my teeth out of Xikander's hand. Everyone else stood up and straightened their clothes. White-faced, Luria pointed at me and at the ground next to her, as if summoning a dog. I went.

Directing all the force of her glare at the king's attendants, she pulled the door closed.

"Hand," she said, and took mine to tow me into the waiting room of the queen's attendants. Caeta, Silla, and Chloe were there, pretending to embroider.

Luria cupped my cheek in her hand, looking at the damage Xikander had done, which was not much. He hadn't been able to get a good blow in.

"Grown men," said Luria, shaking her head in contempt.

I thought of the wine splashing in Xikander's face and was ashamed of myself.

She dampened a cloth and held it to my face. "You don't belong in here," she said. "Not now." She thought for a little while, looking into the fire burning on the hearth as if the answer were there. "Do you even know what's happening?" she asked. I shook my head. "The queen was going to have a baby. Now she has lost the baby, and she is very ill." She looked again at the fire. "The king will not want any of them for company—that I am sure of. He won't want you, either, but he should not be alone, and you at least will be quiet."

She took me then through a hallway to a small room near the queen's bedchamber. The king was there, in a chair by the fire, with his elbow on his knee and his head in his hand. He looked up briefly and shook his head. Luria fetched a footstool for me. Putting her hand to her lips, as if that were necessary, she sat me on the stool.

"You go to Chloe if he wants anything. You understand?"

I nodded and she went away.

The sun shone in the window without lighting the dark room. The paneled walls were painted black, with decorations leaved in gold. Wreaths of laurel surrounded pictures of manly virtue, reminding me that these were a king's apartments once, before they were occupied by the queen.

Luria came back with a tray of food and wine. The king

shook his head again, but she pressed a cup on him.

"The queen?" he asked.

"We don't know," said Luria. "Petrus is . . ." She looked down and blinked a few times, hunting for a reassuring word and not finding it. "Is doing his best."

I stayed in that corner, listening with the king to the voices in the other room. We heard the queen cry out. The king would have gone to her, but Phresine was already at the door, waving him back. For all his power and the gods' goodwill, he could no more help his queen than I could jump up and fly. Phresine came out carrying bloody cloths. She shook her head at the king and hurried past. She came back with clean towels, but her hands were still stained with blood. It was not the last trip she would make.

The king paced. I don't think he was used to being help-less. Not the way I was.

When Imenia came in and the king looked hopeful, she said quickly, "It's Teleus. He would speak with you."

The king shook his head. "Not now," he said. "Tell Teleus to . . . keep them safe."

The sky grew dark as the sun set. Imenia came to light the lamps. She brought more wood for the fire and went away without a word. She returned with more food, but again the king wouldn't eat. She gave me bread and cheese wrapped in a napkin and I gnawed at it, feeling guilty for being hungry.

Petrus came to the door and talked in a low voice to the king, and they went away together.

When the king came back, his face was wet with tears. Talking to me, because I was there and because the words forced themselves out, he said, "If the bleeding does not stop, she will die."

Imenia came to the door. "Have the sacrifices been made?" the king asked her.

"Yes, Your Majesty."

"All of them? New gods and old?"

"All."

The king sat on a stool in front of the fire and bowed his head. "Ula, goddess of the hearth and healing, tell me what I can offer to save my wife," he whispered.

Imenia had slipped away again, so it was just the king and I alone in front of the small fire as it hissed and popped. It was mostly coals, their red glow only bright enough to make everything around them seem that much darker.

"Genny . . ." It was no goddess in the fire answering the king's prayer. It was the voice of a woman, one who doted on him, but he didn't seem to hear. "Genny," she called again, but he didn't lift his head, and she was already disappearing. "Earrings!" she called as she faded away. "Ula is tired of grain and bread and cakes of corn!"

Finally he looked up, but by then she was gone. "Cakes

of corn?" he asked me. "Did you hear 'grain and bread and cakes of corn'?"

I shook my head and pinched my ear. *Earrings.*

"Earrings?" he asked.

I nodded.

"Are you certain?"

I had never been more certain of anything in my life.

"Get them," the king told me. "Get the best, the finest ones, Pheris, and bring them here."

I jumped to my feet and went rocketing through the apartments. Polemus came to the door of the king's waiting room. "The queen?" he asked, but I was already past him, only slowing when I reached the guard room and found them blocking the door, unsure if I was a messenger or an escapee. Luria, coming behind me, must have signaled, because they let me pass.

The guards at the king's apartments had no reason not to admit me, and I went straight to the bedchamber and the king's writing desk, where a small plain box held his personal things. An emerald signet ring with a carving of a dolphin on its face, a few pins, and other jewelry. The royal jewels were elsewhere, but they didn't matter. The box was locked and there was no time to worry over a key. I threw it on the ground and, perilously balanced, I smashed it with all the strength of my good leg. Then I dropped to my knees to root through the pieces. Shaking the earrings free of wooden splinters and clutching them in my fist, I struggled back to my feet to find all the king's attendants standing between me and the door. I wiped my chin and waited to see what they would do.

Hilarion stepped aside and the others followed his lead. I squared my crooked shoulder as much as I was able and walked past them. When I reached the passage outside the apartments, I began to run again, back to the king, at my best speed.

Luria waited for me in the guard room. She stopped the other attendants, allowing only me to continue to the king. She did not need to tell me to go more quietly; the silence in the queen's apartments was stricture enough.

The king looked up as I stood catching my breath in the doorway, clutching my hand to my chest.

He held out his own hand and I dropped the earrings into his palm, the ones that Heiro had given him at his investiture, with the tiny amphorae and the even tinier sprays of golden flowers.

"You're sure?" he asked.

The other jewels weren't his and they didn't matter to him. These did. For Ula, who is always given corn and bread and oil, I knew they were perfect.

He dropped from the chair to his knees. Speaking words that I didn't understand, he reached his hand so far into the fireplace that I was sure his skin was scorching in the heat.

He dropped the earrings onto the coals and used his hook to cover them. Then he sat back again with his head bowed and stayed there until Petrus and Phresine came.

Petrus was cautious, he was always cautious, but his relieved smile broke through all his hedging. The crisis had passed. The queen would live.

Hilarion came after that to tell the king that Teleus was in the waiting room, and the king nodded and rubbed his eyes with his hand. Phresine had stayed after Petrus returned to the queen. "You will send for me if she wakes?" the king asked her.

"Of course," she said, "Your Majesty." I admired the way she could make the words sound so much like "You Idiot."

The king smiled just a little. He waved me out of the room, and I followed Hilarion back to the waiting room, passing Teleus on the way. To my surprise, Hilarion took me by the hand.

"It has been a long night for everyone," he said, and he walked me himself to the king's apartments and to Ion's room, where I had been sleeping on the floor.

"I think you've earned the bed tonight," said Hilarion. "Or would you rather have your own room?"

I preferred my own little closet, so he scooped up my blankets and we went there. My mattress was still leaning against the wall. He put it on the floor and dumped my blankets. Then he helped me out of my clothes and tucked me in.

"Do you have what you need, little monster?"

I nodded. All I wanted was to lay my head down.

He patted me tentatively on the shoulder. "Rest up, then. The king will no doubt call for you tomorrow."

No one called me. I slept all day and woke in the night. There was a tray beside me with watered wine and a roasted game bird. I gnawed the meat off and tossed the bones down the airshaft, remembering the first time I'd done that. Then I cautiously poked my nose out of the closet and made my way to the attendants' waiting room. Hilarion had been kind to me earlier; he had never been cruel, but he'd never been particularly kind, either. Petrus had said the queen would live, but I had been blamed all my life for soured milk, and bad grain, and other people's carelessness. Hilarion's approval might be gone as quickly as it had come.

The attendants were talking quietly. It was only Polemus, Sotis, and Cleon. There was a three-handed game going, and Sotis was complaining about the wine. They wouldn't have been playing cards if the queen were dead. I crept back to bed and slept again.

Lamion woke me in the morning, stepping over me to get a coat for the king.

"Rise and shine, Pheris," he said. I blinked sleep and

astonishment out of my eyes, as Lamion had always called me monster and had never used my name before.

The king stayed with the queen for the next few days. The palace was very quiet, as all state business had been postponed. There were the usual whispered speculations, but there was no official news and no official mourning for a baby that had left the world before it even came into it. The only dedications made were to thank the gods for our queen's continued health.

People talked more openly about the arrival of the slave Kamet from the Mede empire. The palace guard was exuberant to welcome home Costis, one of their own. The Mede ambassador demanded that the slave be returned to his master, and all of Attolia heard of how his demands were rejected. The more astute took note of Kamet's attendance at meeting after meeting, while the less so entertained each other with stories of the king's visit to the kitchens for sweetened nuts once he was sure the queen was out of danger. That was an easier subject to make jokes about, and making jokes eased people's fears.

Very few knew about the intense effort that was orchestrated by Relius, the former secretary of the archives, after Kamet's unexpectedly public arrival, to isolate the Mede ambassador and intercept any attempt to warn his emperor that Kamet had arrived in Attolia and that the secret location of the Mede navy had almost certainly been revealed. All the king's plans relied on that embargo.

"He kept them safe for you," whispered the queen from her bed.

"He did," said the king. "I only wish he'd done it with a little less flair. Galleys racing to a ship in the middle of the harbor, by all the gods."

"Safe," whispered the queen again, and he leaned over the bed to tuck the covers around her.

"Yes," he allowed, "they are safe and your captain is a champion. Do I need to send Phresine for some lethium-laced soup?"

Her lips curled with a hint of fragile amusement, and he kissed her cheek.

A most amazing and strange thing was happening to me. Wherever I went in the palace, people greeted me. People to whom I had been invisible now nodded and smiled as we crossed paths. I was free to go anywhere I liked, with no fear of being caught alone in a stairwell or an empty room. Xikos kept his insults to himself, and even my grandfather Susa smiled grimly when we met.

"Enjoy yourself," he said, "while you can." I don't know if his warning was malice or just honesty—it was hard to tell with Susa—but I took him at his word. I went directly to the stables. Not only did the master let me ride Fryst again, he said he would look for a pony to add to the royal horses.

It was many days before the king and I were alone. He was again reading reports at the writing table in his bedroom. I was laying out a triangle on the floor using pebbles from the garden, piece by piece turning it into a spiral and then slowly changing it back again.

"Pheris," he said, and my stomach turned over. I regretted more than just my lunch.

"I lost my temper," said the king. "I frightened you and I am sorry for that. You might otherwise have come to me when Juridius threatened you."

I shook my head. The blame was not his.

"Pheris, look at me. I told the baron your grandfather that he must choose an heir young enough to be raised here in the palace because I badly need an Erondites that I can trust. I assumed it was you."

My lip quivered and I bit it—accidentally too hard—and slapped my hand to my mouth. He laughed at me, smiling very briefly before he became serious again.

"I didn't ask you, no one has asked you, if you wanted to be Erondites. I'm sorry for that, too. I am asking you now, shall we make a covenant, you and I, that I will trust you and you will trust me?" He waited, giving me time to think.

I nodded, put my forefinger to my heart and to my lip,

and opened my hand to him. He seemed to understand.

He said, "You have my word as well."

Kamet and I crossed paths often, as both of us were explor-
ing the palace anew. He was a thin, dark young man, though
of course I did not see him as young at the time. Indoors, we
passed without interacting. In the gardens, where he often
walked, I spied on him from the shrubbery. I sensed in him
a fellow feeling, of an ever-present vulnerability temporarily
lifted.

To my tutor's chagrin, my lessons had begun again. He
liked me no more than he had before, nor did I like him.
Kamet was sometimes moving through the library around
us, examining its contents as my tutor sullenly went through
the motions of teaching me and I entertained myself by confounding him. I laughed when Kamet pulled a scroll from
the shelf and got a face full of dust. His expression was such
a mixture of disgust and outrage it was impossible not to.
My tutor hushed me.

After the lesson had ended and my poor tutor had left,
Kamet approached very politely to ask if he could borrow my
chalk and slate. I slid both across the table and watched with
interest as he drew a cat and a bird with a few expert strokes.
He added neat letters in a row underneath them. Then he
pointed to the bird and looked at me expectantly. "Which
letter?" he asked. When I pointed to the one that made the

sound peh instead of bah, he raised his eyebrows.

I pointed to peh again, hoping he would give up. Much safer to enjoy my private jokes . . . privately.

Kamet's hands were slim, carefully kept, the only marks on them those of ink and a callus from a pen. Very gently, he tapped one finger on the slate. "Am I like your tutor, that you lie to me?" He sounded so disappointed that I apologetically took back my chalk and made two more letters, barely legible. My spelling was as bad as my handwriting, but he studied the marks, his head cocked to one side, and conceded.

"Indeed," he said, "it is a pigeon." Then he wrote out the word with the correct spelling for me.

At my next lesson, when I pulled my stool out from under the table, I found what I thought at first was just a rude picture of myself; I had found similar things before, with hex marks drawn across them, although not recently. When I picked it up, I was surprised to see that it was an entire scroll, folded into a codex. The first picture was indeed of me, but not meant to be unkind, only to be easily identified. Inside was a wealth of words with pictures beside them. Cat and dog and pigeon, but so many more as well, an entire vocabulary at my fingertips. Until then I'd been guessing at how letters might be assembled into words. Because my tutor was still trying to get me to identify individual letters, he'd never shown me any texts I might read. I went back to study my image, guessing that the marks underneath it spelled out my name. When my tutor came to the lesson, I hastily stuffed the codex into my vest, my secret and Kamet's.

Kamet did not speak to me again, but he nodded politely when he saw me, and I nodded back.

It was some weeks after Kamet had left Attolia that I arrived for my lesson in the library to find my tutor absent. Someone else was waiting there for me. Lightly built and very handsome, with distinguished gray patches at his temples, he wore a fine tunic with the frogs at his collar embroidered in gold thread.

"Do you know who I am?" he asked.

I nodded, my heart in my mouth. He was Relius, the former secretary of the archives and disgraced master of the queen's spies.

He said, "The king has asked me to oversee your education."

CHAPTER EIGHT

I already knew a great deal about Relius, all of it unsettling. Accused of treason, he'd been arrested, tortured by the king, pardoned by the queen, and somehow, if rumors were true, become the confidant of both. He had no official position in the palace.

"Sit," he said, waving at a stool.

I didn't want to stare at his hands, mottled with purple scars, missing several fingers. I looked at his face instead to find him watching me, eyebrows raised. Hastily, I sat. I tried to play the same tricks I had used on my tutor, but Relius would have none of it. Where Kamet had been gentle and mildly reproving, Relius was frankly intimidating.

"You don't seem to have any of the intelligence Kamet described," he said. "No, don't hunch like a turtle, just answer the question. The letter that represents the sound at the beginning of the word 'king' is what? Point."

Melisande's warnings thundered in my ears. Staring at Relius's mutilated hands, I couldn't have pointed to the correct letter if my life depended on it.

"Hmm." Relius expressed his displeasure with a delicate grunt. Then he stood, pushing the stool away from the heavy table with a scraping sound that made me flinch. "Follow me," he said, and walked out of the library. I trailed after him across the palace to the cramped but light-filled room that was part office, part study, and anteroom to his private apartment. His own collection of scrolls and books filled a shelf, and a number of beautiful maps covered the walls. I later learned that he was a cartographer and had drawn them himself. These had been his rooms all the years he had served the queen as her secretary of the archives. Baron Orutus, the new secretary, had rooms that were larger and better located, but he still resented that he'd never been offered Relius's office and that Relius still resided there. Relius might have had no official position, but his unofficial position was unassailable: he was a royal favorite.

Closing the door, he said, "Now it is just the two of us. Sit," he said, and pointed to the stool sitting next to the worktable.

I stared at his hand despite myself. He demonstrated that his misshapen fingers could still snap sharply, and I hastily moved to the stool. It was as high as my waist. Relius watched and did not offer to help as I struggled onto it. He pushed papers around on the table until he found one that was mostly blank. He dipped a pen into an inkpot and wrote out a series of numbers.

"You recognize these?" he asked, and I shook my head. I knew my letters, but the only "numbers" I'd ever learned were hatch and strike marks. Relius poured out a pile of small black pellets, the playing pieces for a game. He asked me to count out four of them, then ten, then fifty. He watched while I made five groups of ten each in order to make the counting easier, but said nothing. He walked around the study for a while, staring at the ceiling as if he were reading some messages written there.

"How old are you?" he asked. Obediently, I counted out the little black stones.

"Ah," he said. "You seem much younger."

I shrugged my shoulder and he snorted. "Yes, I can see that's no accident."

He went to stare out the window for so long he might have forgotten me. The rungs on the chair were set for people taller than I was, and my feet didn't reach them. Finally he turned around. "You may go. I will speak to the king later. Come here next time, not to the library."

Getting down from the stool was more difficult than getting up. Relius watched with no comment. When I was back on my feet, he waved me to the door and returned to looking out the window as I limped away.

A week passed, and the time for my next lesson arrived. When I rose to leave the king's waiting room, Xikander said, "I heard your tutor gave up on you and is back in the tax office. Are you still going to go to the library to pretend to learn?" I lifted my chin and stalked away, but his snicker followed me down the passageway.

As it happened, Relius wasn't in his study when I arrived. I knocked on the open door, and when he didn't answer, instead of waiting politely in the hall, I slipped inside. I went to look into a bedroom at an unmade bed, more books and papers, and a bowl of shriveled grapes. Another door led to a windowless storeroom lined with shelves.

Having determined that Relius was nowhere in the apartment, I turned to an examination of everything I could see in his study. Maps, miscellaneous papers on the table, a rack of writing tools, and a set of brass compasses, highly intriguing devices I'd never seen before. On his shelves were sheets of music, two flutes, and numerous books. I was just reaching to touch one of the flutes when Relius cleared his throat behind me. I snatched my hand back and swung around, almost tripping over my own feet.

"Another time, we will look at those. Not today. You

should return to the king's apartments."

I felt his eyes boring into the middle of my back as I went.

"Oh, did you get tired of pretending?" Xikander asked when I returned. There was a table in the waiting room that always held a plate of nuts and pastries. There was an amphora of wine as well, with partly filled cups scattered around it. I lifted a wine cup, looked at Xikander contemplatively, and when he tensed, put it back down. Hearing Sotis laughing behind me, I headed off to my closet, and that is why I wasn't with the king when the news came: the allied fleet of the Greater Powers of the Continent had "unexpectedly" met the Mede navy in the narrow straits near Hemsha. In an event described by the Pent commander of the fleet in a dispatch to his government as a "regrettable accident," the allies had sunk most of the Mede ships. The emperor of the Mede blamed the king of Attolia and was withdrawing his ambassador.

Officially, the allies had sailed into the narrow straits seeking nothing more than a source of fresh water to resupply their ships, and had come across the Medes at their mooring. Seeing the allies bearing down on them, unsure if they were under attack, the Medes had run out their guns. Some unknown sailor among the Medes had fired without orders. An allied ship, finding herself fired upon, had answered, and once that had happened, there had been no hope of stopping the confrontation. The Mede ships, all sails down, unable to maneuver, had been destroyed almost to the last one.

That night, the Mede ambassador elected to dine in his rooms.

All over the city, people were celebrating, raising their glasses in toasts to the proxy victory. They knew now that Costis's adventure with Kamet had never been about anything as petty as revenge, and there would be no more talk of "two goats and an olive tree don't make an estate."

Melheret took his formal leave from the Attolian court three days later and may well have spent that entire time preparing his exit speech. It was a work of art. The king, listening to it, leaned forward, elbows on his knees, wholly attentive to the Mede's every word, taking note of the mannered and precise language, the formal words of goodwill layered over with equally stylized insults, the genial good humor that did not hide his contempt. His compliments were conveyed in tones of condescending reproach at the way he, and by extension, his nation, had been treated.

Our king, when it was his turn to respond, sounded far more sincere. "It has been an honor to have the ambassador at our court, and my queen and I are deeply sorry that some untoward misunderstanding has cost us his company. If the emperor of the Mede feels aggrieved, surely it is unjust that we must pay the price with the loss of our ambassador's fellowship, the recent disturbing news from Hemsha having nothing to do with our Little Peninsula, and the excellent relationship between ourselves and the empire falling victim to the regrettable actions of others. In proof of that, we would like to offer you a token of our goodwill as you depart."

Melheret had prepared for this customary exchange and signaled his servant to bring forward his own gift, a bottle of scent, tiny but exquisite. "It has a most delicate aroma," he told the king. "Delightful, but of course, very short-lived." He bowed.

The king thanked him by saying, "We receive it in exactly the spirit of goodwill with which it is offered, Ambassador, and in exchange—" He turned to Ion, who handed him a flat oval case no bigger than the palm of his hand. As soon as he saw it, the ambassador patted his coat pocket, surprised to find it empty. "Your Majesty," he said sharply, his anger cutting finally through all of his stiff diplomatic posturing, "that is a private possession of mine."

"The miniature of your wife. I know. You always keep it with you, and I apologize for borrowing it without asking, but I wanted to be sure our present to you would suit."

Melheret all but snatched the case from the king's hand and opened it as if checking to be sure it had not been damaged in any way before he slid it back into his pocket. The king waved Ion forward with a case of a similar size, but a little fatter. When Melheret opened it, he blinked.

"Earrings for your wife," said the king. "To match the necklace in her portrait."

"She will be so pleased to have you home," said the queen, her voice quite kind, but the implication clear. His wife was not the only one to be pleased about the end of the Mede's tenure in Attolia. "Safe travels, Ambassador."

Melheret swallowed. "Thank you, Your Majesty."

He seemed almost dazed as he withdrew.

There were sporadic celebrations for days and then, as if the city had taken a deep breath and let all its worries go, people went back to their ordinary lives for the first time in years without the imminent threat of war. Attolia refused to release the grain from the storehouses, but she did order that work restart on the aqueduct—work that put money in people's pockets and eased for many the high price of bread.

I continued my studies with my new tutor. Relius had informed me that I could expect to meet him for an hour or so each day, beginning at dawn. Most mornings, I easily slipped past whichever attendants were sleeping in the king's waiting room. The guards, never asleep, opened the doors without a sound to let me through. On the mornings the king took his sword and sparred with the guard, I had no lesson so that I could be there when he dressed. Otherwise, he started his days quite late, and my absence from my little closet drew no attention.

Relius was not a gentle teacher, but he was a thorough one. I got used to the condescending noise he made in the back of his nose as he quizzed me on the words I knew and added more to the codex Kamet had given me. He taught me to write with a pen as well as with chalk, and one day he taught me numbers—not the marks I already knew, but Sidosian numerals. I was still quite wary of him at that time, but when he wrote the numbers out, first one through nine and then ten, I actually knocked his hand away from them, making his pen spatter ink across the scrap of paper, interrupting his explanation of the value of the null symbol. I had seen it. One and null make ten. A symbol that represented nothing increased every number it sat beside by a factor of ten. Two nulls side by side increased a number a hundredfold. Hatch and strike marks grew unwieldy with larger numbers, and it would be impossible to learn a different symbol for every amount, but with a null, one could write any number, an infinity of numbers, even.

"Pheris?" said Relius, displeased.

I ignored him. I was all but unaware of my hands squeezing, as if with my crooked fingers I was grasping at this new idea. With the numbers ordered in columns, one could see new relationships between them without laying out a pattern first.

Exasperated, Relius picked up the pen again and wrote out the symbols for addition and subtraction, multiplication and division, using simple equations to make their meaning clear. Then he left me alone.

By the time I turned my head, wincing from the shooting pains in my neck and all over my body, I found he'd retired to his armchair and that Teleus, the captain of the guard, had joined him. They were sharing a bowl of olives and watching me. Teleus put down a wine cup and rose to give me a hand as I got down from the stool.

"You're already late for the king's dressing," Relius told me as I rocked back and forth. "Go visit the stable master, and be sure you return to the royal apartments by way of the gardens."

Still dazed, I did as he said. The stable master, pleased to see me, introduced me to the pony he'd found for me to ride. A beautiful little mare, mostly a light gray, with darker spots sprinkled on her haunches. If anyone in the king's apartments wondered where I'd been, they were answered by the strong smell of horse when I returned.

Relius did not understand my fascination with patterns and numbers, but he waited patiently during my next lesson as I arranged stones and counted them and worked out the use of the symbols he'd shown me. Square patterns were easy to represent with his equations, but I could not find one to fit my triangles.

"I will send a letter to a colleague for further instruction," he promised, "if you will deign to return to the rest of today's lesson."

Relius was not always so patient, and I was not always so cooperative. I had a burning desire to learn to read, but much less devotion to my handwriting, content with any mark that vaguely resembled the shape I was trying to form.

"Those numbers," said Relius, "could have been written by pigeons tracking through the ink."

I shrugged. I knew what they were meant to be.

He shook his head. "This is your voice," he said, tapping the page.

I was the only one interested in my numbers and I already knew what they were.

"Take that idiotic look off your face, or I will beat you with a stick," Relius snapped, and I flinched.

He handed me the pen. "Try again," he said. My best efforts were still bird tracks and spills and drips. In hindsight, I was no more patient than my tutor, and as my frustration grew, my hand obeyed me less until, ultimately, I knocked the inkpot over.

"Get out." Thoroughly fed up, Relius dismissed me, and I went.

Unwilling to return to the king's waiting room, blinking away tears, I walked to the gardens instead. Working my way into the secret space I had hollowed out inside a hedge, I crouched for a while, feeling unfairly treated. Only when it was time to help dress the king did I go back to the palace. It would have been unthinkable to exercise this kind of freedom earlier, but now I did it without a thought, slipping away for hours to watch the ants and their anthills, the bees in the kitchen garden coming and going from the stacks of clay pipes that housed their hives. If there were still a few unpleasant people who might wish me ill, I only needed to avoid them, and that was not hard.

Relius was conciliatory the next day. He apologized for his temper. "I will make an effort to do better," he said, "and will expect the same from you. Are we agreed? Yes? Good. Because I don't have a stick to hit you with, and I can't be bothered to find one."

He was joking, I was almost certain.

"Start with the numbers," he said. "You like those."

After that, I began to produce slightly more legible figures and letters. But I had a long, weary way to go, and I was still unconvinced it was worth the effort.

From Relius, I learned the history of Attolia, from the arrival of the Invaders to the rise of the oligarchy, and the way the great baronial families had worked together to weaken the monarchy and divide power among themselves. Relius explained how the barons' agreement had been broken when one of them had engaged his heir to marry the princess Irene; how the other families had been angry, but outmaneuvered; and how they'd been outmaneuvered again when the queen poisoned her first bridegroom and took the throne for herself. He did not go into details on his own contributions.

He did show me my own family's part. "This chart shows the queen's family, and here, the Erondites. It's a distant connection, but many of those with closer connections were killed during the civil strife that came about after she took power."

Attolia had survived that strife by ruthlessly eliminating contenders for her throne, sparing Erondites only because he was a useful ally at the time. Until Attolia married, the baron had been content with his tenuous connection to the throne, one son in the queen's guard and another who wooed her at court. Only when Attolia chose a husband had Erondites begun to plot in earnest against the queen and against the new king.

Relius taught me about the world outside the Little Peninsula, making me memorize the names of rulers and the significant people in their courts. Sliding his bent fingers across the map he had pulled down from the wall, he showed me the Continent. "The Braelings have become so wealthy, they have made a new trade empire. The Epidi are afraid their islands will be overrun, and the Gants are fighting again with each other. If Meleo of Gant succeeds in his claim to the Southern Gant lands, he will have a nation to rival both the Braelings and the Pents. If he allies with just one of them, the Brael-Pent alliance will come apart like wet paper, and none of them can afford to be embroiled with the Mede over the little Hephestian Peninsula when that happens. All this, the Mede emperor uses to his advantage."

Relius had few maps of the Mede empire and fewer books. He was frustrated by his limited understanding of any of the languages of the empire, and much of what he knew he'd only recently learned from Kamet.

For my part, any amount of painstaking work memorizing the names and histories of people I'd never meet was worth it to learn that the area of any triangle was always one-half the number of units in its base multiplied by the number of units in its height. Relius handed me the proof written out on a piece of paper and laughed at what I am sure was a rapt expression on my face.

"Don't get spit on it," he said.

I glared at the very suggestion, realizing too late what I was revealing.

"Yes," said Relius. "I have noted the . . . shall we say, 'elective' nature of certain behaviors."

One day, after he had again reiterated that my writing was my voice and I had again rolled my eyes, though I did it with my head down, he reached around behind him and pulled a slim book from the shelf—just sheets of foolscap sewn together with no wooden covers, more a pamphlet than a book.

"This was written five hundred years ago." He held it open in front of me.

The Invitation

I will send the boy to the market
to the monger at the end of the row
for sweet shrimp and three fish, the freshest,
I will say, with their eyes still clear,
tell him to go
to the wine shop, bring an amphora
of Cleoboulos's best
buy herbs of every kind
the most sweetly scented
while I idle through the day
awaiting you.

I reached out to touch the text in wonder, amazed that paper could last so long. The ink was dark and the pages still smooth and even, though a little yellowed.

Relius rolled his eyes, much harder than I ever rolled mine. "They were copied for me by a friend. The poet is long dead, but his words are still with us, because he wrote them down." He tapped the sheet of scrap paper in front of me, covered with my wriggling attempts at letters. "And it does no good to write something that only you can read!"

I looked at the poem again. Copied by a friend.

"Yes," said Relius, well aware of what I was thinking. "Someone loves me very much, even with all my faults, and don't give me that look. You'll be in love yourself someday."

I was quite certain I would not. By then, I knew why the guard Legarus stared with such anger and misery at Baron Xortix's younger son and how Relius had been arrested for treason when his lover had turned out to be a spy for the Mede emperor. One would have thought Relius would be done with love and lovers, but I'd seen a veritable parade of them. None of his affairs lasted long, and I'd already witnessed several spats when he showed someone the door. If this friend had loved Relius for years, he or she was quite the anomaly.

Relius tapped the page in front of me. "Keep practicing," he instructed.

Yawning, I arrived one morning to find him nowhere in the office or in the rest of the apartment. This was not unusual, as he often spent his nights elsewhere. What was unusual was the intricately folded parchment on his worktable. I shouldn't have touched it, but I did, curious to see how it opened. Only when I had it mostly unfolded did it occur to me that Relius might not be pleased. I hesitated and then threw caution to the winds. When it was open, I hunched over the message inside, parsing its meaning little by little until I reached the end and sighed with relief at Kamet's instructions on how to make the folds crisp again with a straightedge.

I knew the one Kamet meant and used it to carefully refold the parchment. Then I slipped down from the stool to stretch my leg and turned to find Relius sitting in his armchair by the little stove where he heated water for his coffee.

"You become too absorbed in your work," he said. "You are used to people ignoring you, but you cannot ever assume that they are. Do you understand?"

I nodded.

"As you are interested in Kamet's message, I suggest you write back to him. Can you make the same folds with a fresh piece of parchment? Good. Tell him I am traveling. He knows where. Tell him that if the message arrives unopened, he should be safe. Add anything else you like, but be sure you put that in."

What if I get the folds wrong?

"You'll do fine. Worry more about your handwriting. Take it to Teleus in his office by noon tomorrow. He will send it on its way. You will need this," he said, handing me a key, which I took and looked at, perplexed.

"I will be gone a week or two. You may continue to come here to my study at our usual time. Keep at the *History of Savoro*. I'll ask you how far you've gotten when I get back."

Then he said, "The king will be wanting you by now," and waved me out the door without any other farewell.

I did not see him again for more than a month, and his plans for me were already astray by the next morning. When I went to the study, I was surprised and dismayed to find Baron Orutus, the new secretary of the archives, going through Relius's papers. I backed out of the doorway before he caught me watching. When I returned later, I found a new hasp screwed to the door and securely locked. I had no way to write a message and nothing to write it on.

I went first to the library in search of writing material. Though there was paper and parchment in plenty, there was nothing I could use. I tried to find a map of the empire, curious about Kamet's journey to Attolia, but when I went to a map case, I was chased away by one of the scholars, who knew I had no business there.

Frustrated and angry, I retreated almost as far as the garden before I remembered that Relius had been very clear that the message had to go to Teleus before noon. I knew there were pens and paper in the king's writing desk, but I could not fetch them without someone seeing me, and I knew better than to draw attention.

My erstwhile tutor had returned to the offices of the queen's indentured, a whole wing of the palace dedicated to the bureaucracy of the state, business, taxes, record keeping, all of it on paper. I hurried there to make a pest of myself, wandering through the offices until I found my old tutor, who tried to ignore me as I stood stubbornly looking over his shoulder. He was writing out a letter describing the crown's commitment of funds for the repair of a royal road somewhere in the west. I knew that once he was truly annoyed, he would throw down his pen in frustration and run his hands through his hair. When he did, I picked up the pen, and his inkpot as well.

"Oh, no," he protested. "No, no, no." But I was already walking away.

"Oh, let him go," I heard someone say. "It's worth an inkpot to get rid of him." I felt a smile spread across my face that disappeared when I remembered parchment. I turned back.

"Take it, take it," one of the indentured said, offering a sheaf of papers, which I let him slide under my arm. "What?" he said. "What else?" I looked from him to his desk and back. "Parchment?" he asked, astonished. "Do you know what it costs?" But he gave me a sheet of that too, as he pushed me, fairly gently, on my way.

Pleased with myself, I took the supplies out to the garden, where I could work without anyone looking over my shoulder. Hiding in the shrubbery, the paper in the dirt, I practiced a message to Kamet, complaining that I was locked out of Relius's office while he was away and telling him that if the message arrived with its intricate folds intact, he was safe. I copied it onto parchment, folded it as carefully as I could, and took it to Teleus's office. He accepted it without comment, and he too waved me on my way.

With no clear idea how far away Kamet was, I expected a reply every day. I returned again and again to check Relius's door, but it remained locked. One morning I slipped into the library before dawn to sit in the dark, waiting for enough light to see the maps. I spread them out over the tables as I looked for one that showed the Mede empire. The sun cleared the horizon, and I was able to make out the fine print before a librarian arrived to chase me out.

In the end, Relius was back before a package arrived from Kamet. One of the palace errand boys delivered it. He made a face at me, and I stuck out my tongue at him. Relius let these gestures of mutual respect pass without comment. A year earlier, the boy would have made a sign to stave off bad luck, and I would have made one as if to curse him. When Relius had gotten the package open, he handed me a squashed flower of tightly folded vellum. Unfolded, it turned out to be Kamet's map.

I'd seen the maps in the library. I'd watched Relius carefully adding information to a map of his own.

"But this one is yours," said Relius.

To keep? I wondered.

Relius nodded and tapped the key hidden under my shirt. "Out it in the garden," he suggested. So, he knew about the box I'd found while he was gone. I had hollowed out a space at the back of a hedge to call my own. In it I'd built a little shelter out of stones—stolen from the edges of the gravel paths—to keep my new pens and paper dry. One day, the shelter was gone, the stones all restored to their borders, and a brass-bound wooden box sat in its place. It had a lock and a key on a string long enough to wear around my neck.

No one but the king could have provided the box, but the king was rarely alone for more than a few moments a day and never, to my knowledge, alone with Relius. Relius was watching me in amusement.

I'd overheard many secrets in my short life, but this was the first time anyone had chosen to share a confidence with me. Being trusted was a heady feeling.

"Before you put the map away, I'd like to compare it to mine," said Relius, very seriously. "With your permission, of course."

He smoothed it as flat as possible on his worktable, and the two of us studied both maps, pointing out differences as we saw them. Twice, Relius dipped his pen in ink and made a notation on his own map.

The next day, there was another surprise. The magus of Sounis had sent a packet of information to Relius, and included in it was a folded piece of parchment for me. Opening it, I found an entire page of writing I recognized from the proof

Relius had shown me of the formula to determine the area of a triangle. It was a hastily copied excerpt from another scroll, and at the top was my favorite pattern, the bee spiral: one, one, two, three, five, eight, thirteen. It was the order of the cells in the honeycomb, and it was the pattern in the triangles I made that turned so perfectly into a spiral and then back. The scroll said the pattern was in the seeds in a pine cone and the curve of a snail shell as well. It said they all shared the same numerical form. I stared beseechingly at Relius. He expected me to read the *History of Savoro*.

He shook his head, raising his eyes to the gods. "By all means, spend the morning reading about patterns you can make with orange slices. Why would I think the history of a family that's held power on the Greater Peninsula for five hundred years would be more important?"

I had a better understanding of his humor by this time and knew he was pleased—that he'd asked the magus for the information and was happy with the results. He had another cause to be happy—the magus's handwriting was in some places unreadable. Later, I brought the parchment back to Relius to ask him to decipher several words. He laughed at me. "You see the importance of handwriting now."

He made me recopy the entire excerpt, and I still have it.

With the destruction of the Mede fleet, some tensions in Attolia had eased. The appointment of Drusis, Motis, and

Polemus gave all the attendants a chance to begin anew with the king. If Xikos and Xikander and Sotis weren't supporters, their dislike faded to resignation, and emotions, running hot for so long in the Attolian court, began to settle.

In Eddis, in contrast, sentiment was only growing against the high king. The Eddisians had not liked their queen's hasty marriage. Though they approved of Sounis, they disagreed with her decision to give up her sovereignty. Even in Sounis's own country, there were rumblings that the Medes were no longer a threat and that the need for a union of the three countries on the Little Peninsula was over.

My grandfather who was Erondites came to court. He looked me over with disgust and was much astonished when I glared back. He tossed off a laugh as he paraded past. Relius warned me that Erondites hadn't given up any more than the Mede had.

THE
BOOK
OF
PHERIS
VOLUME II

CHAPTER ONE

Costis was near enough to the capital that his name and his seal ring had been sufficient to convince the innkeeper to offer his best mount. It was lucky, because most of his emergency funds were spent. He'd ridden the horse hard, and he could feel her beginning to weaken. The sun on the horizon had spilled all but the last of its golden light, and the cloudless sky above had deepened to the hue of a silver bowl tipped upside down over the world. There was no reason to push her further. He dismounted and walked awhile to give the mare a rest. He wouldn't reach another inn before it was fully dark, so he decided to look for a farm where he could stable her for the night and get a little rest himself. Just the thought of sleep made his eyes smart.

As he walked, night fell. In the moonlight, he remounted and urged the mare on, looking for a glimmer of light on either side of the road that might offer him welcome. All was quiet in the countryside. The only sounds were those of the insects singing and the frogs peeping, the occasional high-pitched whistle of a bat circling over the open fields. In the city he traveled toward, there were long hours still to pass before noises faded, before the streets emptied and the last drunk staggered home, before long-winded arguments and murmured adorations finally dissolved into sleep. When the sun rose over the city, it would be at peace and its people would rise with high expectations of the day, setting aside the usual worries, looking forward to the plays. It was the Festival of Moira. It was a happy time.

The queen paused in the doorway.

"Is that Melheret's statue of Prokip?"

The king was working at his desk, using his hook to slide around the pages of the reports he was going through. The scattershot of little holes in state documents was the surest sign that he'd read them.

"No, it's mine," the king said, not looking up.

"And was it previously owned by the former Mede ambassador?"

"Who really owns anything?"

"Is that the statuette that the former Mede ambassador mistakenly thought he owned, and is he aware that it is here on your desk?"

"I had a cast of his statue made."

The queen waited.

"This is not the cast," the king admitted, finally turning to face her.

"And how many of the ambassadors know that you've robbed the Mede of his treasure?" She did not seem amused.

"Oh, all of them, by now," said the king. "It's been months. Even Melheret might know, though he may be out of touch out on his family's farm."

"He did quite well," agreed the queen, moving to the cushioned chair beside him, wrapping her skirts around herself as she sat, "getting himself dismissed from court before something worse happened." Eyes still on the king, she said, "We'd like something to eat."

Lamion ducked his head and excused himself, leaving them alone except for me.

Attolia continued once he was gone. "You were right—he saw past the cheap setting of the earrings."

"He'd seen those stones in your ears. He knew their value." The king had gone back to his papers.

"Obviously no one else did, or he wouldn't have made it home to his wife. You liked him."

The king thought for a minute. "He wasn't an ass, which is more than one can say for every other Mede ambassador we have met. I agree with you that he might yet prove useful."

The queen nodded in agreement and added, perhaps thinking of the contrast her husband made to the Mede's elegance, "My, how barbarian you look." The king, who had overridden Ion's disapproval earlier that day, appeared a little bit self-conscious about his attire. Ion had tried to talk him out of wearing the sleeveless leather tunic with no shirt underneath.

"I was hot," he admitted. The recent days had been unseasonably warm. "I promise to put on my fancy clothes later."

"We could move the court to the villa on Thegmis. It is cooler out of the city." She relaxed into the chair, letting its high back and its arms hold her up, then reached with one delicate foot for the stool. I leaned from where I sat to move it into position for her. She smiled and I ducked shyly back into the corner between the king's desk and the wall, reassured that she knew that I was there and did not object.

"I like it here," said the king. They both knew being out on the island of Thegmis would limit his ability to roam Attolia's capital city on his own.

The queen asked, "Why don't you have tattoos?"

The king looked down at his arm, bare except for a heavy, figured silver band just above his elbow. "It's very difficult to pass yourself off as an Attolian—or a Sounisian, for that matter—while decorated with Eddisian tattoos."

"No need to pass yourself off as anything now. Except king," she said meaningfully.

If that was bait, he didn't rise to it. "If you are suggesting our contentious Eddisian guests might like me better with tattoos, you are mistaken. One gets them at specific times and for very specific reasons. The one that goes here," he said as he raked the point of his hook lightly across the skin above the armband, "is inked when a boy enters the training house with the other boys his age. As my grandfather had spirited me away the night before, I joined a few months later, without the initiation ceremony and without a tattoo."

"And the one higher on the shoulder?"

"That is to honor the first man an Eddisian kills."

"And have you not killed a man?" she asked, knowing that he had.

He conceded those deaths with a tip of his head. "The tattoo is only for the first, and I didn't get one at the time."

She raised an eyebrow in inquiry.

"My grandfather didn't have them either," he said.

The queen knew that, and also knew he was changing ground. She was well aware of the fine line walked by Eddis's Thieves. They were granted a great deal of leeway, and occasionally severely punished for taking too much of it. The absence of tattoos made them outsiders in their own communities, and that alienation was a deliberate check on their otherwise dangerous power. A Thief could threaten the throne of Eddis but never take it, could depose a king but never be one. The question of whether one could become annux—not king, but high king over the ruler of Eddis—was the one tearing the volatile, often violent, court of Eddis apart.

If she wondered whether there was another reason the king had not gotten a tattoo on his upper arm, if perhaps no one was supposed to know about the first man the Thief of Eddis had killed, Attolia let that question lie.

"I came to ask again about your attendants," she said, as the door to the bedchamber reopened and Ion returned carrying a small table, Lamion following after with a cloth for it.

"Have they misbehaved?" Eugenides looked over his shoulder at Philologos coming in with a tray. Philo, still easily flustered, went wide-eyed and only barely stopped himself from shaking his head.

"About choosing two new companions at the Festival of Moira," said the queen.

"And sending two home?" The king looked thoughtful. "Weren't we supposed to be fostering goodwill with their families?"

"I think the palace budget would allow two more."

"They'll be stacked like kindling in their apartments." They would. The attendants' quarters were uncomfortable already. I had the space where I slept to myself because no one wanted to share a closet with me. I was quite content, but it was still a closet.

"If you will not change apartments, let us consider rotation again. They need not reside all the time with you."

The king looked relieved. "Indeed, they need not. They can have some nice rooms on Thegmis."

The queen continued on as if he had not spoken. "A new attendant from Eddis and one from Sounis to calm the waters."

"Ah," said the king. "You mean Cleon."

"And Sophos has recommended Perminder of Nilos."

"Sophos's track record for picking companions is not the best," the king pointed out.

Ion, standing behind him, looked pained.

"I meant Ion Nomenus," said the king, his wounded innocence deeply insincere.

"So, we are agreed," said the queen firmly. "You will invite them at the festival tonight."

The king demurred. "It would be better to do it in private. Something to eat?" He waved at Philo's tray.

Attolia made a face, not interested in the very food she had asked the attendants to bring. "Perhaps later." She stood and straightened her skirts and kissed him lightly on the forehead before leaving.

Sounis and Eddis had come again for the Festival of Moira. The judges were more circumspect, and that year's plays mocked safer targets. One of them was Relius: the lascivious character in the most popular play was obviously modeled on the former secretary of the archives. Another target was the former ambassador of the Mede. His character needed no pseudonym. The plays were amusing, but all the talk was still about Cenna's play from the year before. Foolish Emipopolitus's fearmongering was at the forefront of every conversation, right up until the moment the king officially invited Perminder and Cleon of Eddis to join him as attendants.

"That was a misstep," said the queen of Attolia to the queen of Eddis, after the banquet was over. They had retired together to discuss Cleon's outrageous behavior.

Eddis pulled the delicate silver crown from her head and ran her fingers through her hair, picking up small gold flecks on her hands as she did so. She began wiping them off on her skirts and then stopped, seeing that this was a poor solution to the problem. One of Attolia's attendants brought a cloth, and Eddis took it with a smile.

Ruefully she said, "I was sure Cleon would be unable to resist the chance to swan about as an attendant. He longs for respect and is just smart enough to know he'll never get it in Eddis."

Perminder, when invited to join the attendants to the king of Attolia, had stood and made a very pretty speech thanking him. Cleon had not only refused the invitation;

he'd thrown it back in the king's face. "Since when does a Thief need attendants?" he had asked. "Perhaps to carry the crown you've stolen to the altar of your god?"

Eddis said, "If I take him home now, he'll have the old men thumping him on the back and praising him to the high heavens. They are as stubborn as goats," she complained.

"You could send them to colonize the moon," Attolia suggested.

Eddis laughed briefly. "It would be easier! They'd rather leap into the Sacred Mountain than accept Gen as high king. If only he would not needle them," she said plaintively. "He burns through the last vestiges of any goodwill."

"If he were more kinglike," Attolia responded, "we both know he wouldn't be king."

"But he distances himself . . . with his fancy clothes and his Attolian accent."

"He distances himself from you," said Attolia, "so that you are still queen."

"I know that."

"I know you know that."

Eddis threw up her hands, was surprised by the towel, which she'd forgotten she held. "Cleon's too stupid to come up with the things he says. Now that he has said them, though, he is the one I must get out of my court."

"There are a number of ways to accomplish that," Attolia said, not for the first time.

Not for the first time, Eddis refused. "If I silence him with too heavy a hand, there are others who will clamor even louder. He is a thorn to be drawn out very carefully, which is why I'd so hoped to foist him off on Gen." She sighed. "Gen can only put up with so much."

Attolia agreed. "He will do something outrageous if he is pushed too far," she said, and added, "I know you know that, too."

"Well, I will not beg for Cleon again," Eddis said as she handed the towel back to Chloe. "He will apologize on his knees tomorrow, and if Gen cannot stomach him, maybe I will pitch him into the Sacred Mountain myself."

When a messenger on a lathered horse comes to the city, he draws the eye of every person in the road. They see his direction. As he turns up the streets toward the palace, Rumor, who is born in a moment, is full-grown the next. She begins to move through the town, trailing ever more elaborate finery behind her.

Costis would have reached the palace sooner if he had come by way of the headland above the city. It would have been harder on the mare, though, and he hadn't been able to bring himself to force her up the steeper path. Still, he urged her to her best pace, her hooves rattling on the stones. When he reached the lower gates of the palace, he was already dismounting as she shuddered to a halt.

The guard on duty recognized him and waved him in.

"Take good—" he started to say over his shoulder.

"We will," said a stable hand, leading the mare away.

As Costis continued on foot, Rumor outpaced him. A girl in the herb garden cutting rosemary heard the stable hand talking as he brought in the exhausted horse. She stepped to the kitchens, eager to be the first to tell her friends—and the errand boys who overheard her—that something out of the ordinary was happening. In the hallways, people saw a stranger, dirty and tired, out of place in the palace, or they saw the guard who had brought the slave Kamet out from the heart of the empire. They followed to see what more they could learn, or they dropped whatever errand they were on and began another—spreading the news of Costis's return.

Relius slipped into the reception room where the high king was sitting with Attolia on one side of him and Sounis and Eddis on the other, listening to Cleon's reluctant apology. The king's absence of interest in the proceeding was apparent and vast. It was he who was the first to notice Relius, and when Orutus, the new secretary of the archives, came in next, very red in the face, the king sat up straight. Heads turned.

Behind Orutus was General Piloxides and, behind him, Casartus, admiral of the navy. By the time the door opened to let Attolia's minister of war, Pegistus, in, there were people gathering in the hallway, peering through the doors until they closed again, and Cleon, interrupted in midspeech, was swiveling his head in bewilderment. Relius politely but relentlessly shuffled him out of the way. Orutus stood back, glowering as Relius bowed and said, "Costis brings news."

Ghasnuvidas, emperor of the Mede, had lost his ships. With no means to transport his men across the Middle Sea, he'd marched them around it instead. With much of his navy destroyed in the straits of Hemsha, he'd sent his entire army north from Kodester into Zaboar. The oligarch of Zaboar had not only allowed them entry, he had closed his harbors, trapping rumormongers inside the city walls. When the Mede forces were shuttled across the Shallow Sea in flotillas of small boats, they landed up and down the coast of Kimmer, and Kimmer too had been silent.

Unopposed, the various companies had moved separately, not uniting until they reached the empty backlands of Roa. Only when commissioners were sent ahead to arrange for markets to be set up along their route did word begin to spread of their advance.

The army passed small villages and then larger ones, marching toward roads wide enough to let them move more quickly. They bought up carts and horses, as many as they were offered, and paid in coin for them. Farmers who brought their produce to the temporary markets told their friends and neighbors that the rumors were true, there was money to be made. The army of Ghasnuvidas wasn't looting its way through Roa any more than it had through Kimmer. Its passage had been arranged in advance.

Like any prophet warning of calamity, Costis, travel worn and exhausted, was met with disbelief.

"Did you see the army with your own eyes?" Piloxides demanded.

"No," Costis admitted. "When Kamet heard rumors, I rode east until I saw the farmers' supply wagons, then I turned and rode here as quickly as I could."

"Then this is just rumor," Piloxides growled.

"And we've heard nothing from Kimmer or Roa," said Pegistus.

Orutus said, "If an army had crossed at Sukir, our trade houses would have sent word."

The door opened and closed behind him, as Eddis's minister of war and Sounis's magus arrived. It had taken Relius's messengers longer to find them.

Puzzled, the magus looked to his king. "Ghasnuvidas sends his army overland," said Sounis.

"Zaboar," said the magus heavily, and Relius nodded.

"They couldn't have crossed from Zaboar," said Orutus.

"There are no troop ships there to move them—"

"The Shallow Sea is full of ships to move them."

"There's been plague! No one would march an army into a city with plague! We've heard of it for months."

"Heard from whom?" asked Attolia.

The master of spies dropped his eyes. He admitted, "Our sources may be unreliable."

"My traders?" Attolia bristled at the possibility of betrayal.

"No, Your Majesty. The trade houses have sent no reports at all." Grudgingly, Orutus turned to Relius. "Have you heard?"

Relius shook his head. "Not I. I run no spies for my queen."

"Then all we have is this rumor," said Casartus, getting back to the point.

"It is no rumor," Costis said firmly.

"How can you be sure?" asked Eddis's minister of war, not dismissing Costis's report, only checking his reasoning.

Exhausted, Costis explained again. "The Mede commissioners are buying up every cow, every pig, every goat, every sack of grain for their commissaries, and they are paying with coin, not promises. If there's not a huge army, then I don't know what they are feeding in Roa."

"Then why didn't you go on until you'd seen it yourself?" Casartus wailed in frustration.

Costis flicked a glance at Relius. "We were not sure a

message would get through if I did not bring it."

Attolia looked to Relius as well.

"My messenger is late," he said.

"You said you ran no spies," the new secretary of the archives said bitterly.

Relius delicately shrugged. "A messenger is not a spy, secretary."

"You and Kamet were in the capital city?" Orutus turned on Costis.

"No," said Costis, "we were—" He swallowed the words he had been about to say. "Nearer the coast," he finished more cautiously. Orutus was livid.

"Based on the provisions, then, just how big do you think this army is?" the magus asked, steering the conversation away from Costis's reticence.

"Kamet said to expect seventy thousand." Costis knew no one would believe him, and Casartus wasn't the only one who threw up his hands.

"Seventy thousand?" said the magus, stunned.

"That is ridiculous!" said Casartus. "All of this—is ridiculous."

"It's impossible," said Piloxides. "How could they field an army that size?"

"By having more wealth than we can possibly imagine," the king told him.

"There is no way they could march an army that size

through Roa without Roa knowing!" Piloxides argued.

"No, they couldn't," the king agreed. "Our allies have betrayed us, Piloxides."

Not since Nussam led his forces across the isthmus to conquer the Sidosian empire had the world seen an army that size. I tried to imagine seventy thousand men marching together like a city on the move. What road could it travel? The head of the army might be in one town while the tail was in an entirely different one. And how would they make camp at night? If all the soldiers lay down to sleep side by side, how much ground would they cover? If, like my father, every soldier came with servants to accompany him, were there only a fifth as many soldiers in an army of seventy thousand, or were there seventy thousand fighting men and an army of even more? Did they bring medics, advisors, cooks? How much food would they eat? How much grain would be needed every day to feed a man, a horse, an ox? Distracted by the wealth of numbers, I let most of what was said next pass over my head.

Most scholars now agree on the number fifty thousand for the fighting men of the Mede army. At one helpmeet for every three men—a cautious estimate—there would be sixteen thousand supporters. Bu-seneth, the general in charge of the army, had forbidden the use of any carts until they reached the cultivated land of Roa. That was how he had moved a city's worth of men so quickly. By the time they'd reached the king of Roa's highways, the Medes had bought up more than six thousand horses and five thousand or more mules and donkeys and oxen.

As everyone tried to imagine the scale of the disaster, Attolia looked to Relius.

He said, "I have—"

"—taken liberties," Orutus hissed.

"—told Teleus to have the ambassadors of Kimmer and Roa arrested."

"Send word to the city walls to close the gates," ordered Attolia. "Do it now. No one is to leave the palace or leave the city until further notice."

As Relius left, Attolia turned to Costis. "Do you have any idea how close this army is now?"

"The farmers told me they were expected to have their surpluses gathered in Put for sale in a month." I had no idea where Put was, so this meant little to me.

"We have at least that long, then," said Sounis.

"There is almost no farmed land between Put and the border with Attolia to supply an army. That might slow their advance," Eddis said.

"Unless they have laid caches in those places ahead of time," said Attolia.

"All the surplus in Roa cannot feed an army that size.

How, how can they possibly lay caches?" said Casartus angrily. Both he and Orutus had taken Costis's news as a personal attack, the behavior of men very afraid of the blame that might land on their shoulders.

Attolia ignored them. Leaning forward, she addressed Sounis and Eddis. "You will want to speak privately with your own council. Let us meet again this afternoon."

To Pegistus, Piloxides, and Casartus, she said, "You will consider how to address an army of seventy thousand on our northeast border." To Costis, she said, "Get a bath and a nap. It will be a long day."

I wasn't there when they met. Nor was Relius, as Orutus had his way.

"Neither your position nor mine is official," Relius said to me. "Not even a war will dislodge Orutus's sense of self-importance."

Official or unofficial, eavesdroppers or none, every word spoken in the council chamber was common knowledge in the palace before the sun set. In the king's waiting room, the attendants picked apart the day's rumors.

"Not all of the Mede ships were sunk at Hemsha. Sounis's magus thinks they might have landed supplies at harbors west of Put, maybe at Nedus and Mesithilia."

I sat in a corner, pretending to address a math problem on my slate that the magus had set for me. Once Relius had reached out to him about the number sequence I'd found so fascinating, he and the magus had begun to negotiate a very prickly sort of friendship as they colluded in my education. It didn't surprise me at all that the magus would be so familiar with the harbors of Roa.

No one could guess how quickly an army so vast might move, but all agreed that if the Medes were to be stopped, the only chance was at the Leonyla Pass. The Medes would be coming down the coast from Roa. They would have to cross over the coastal mountains to reach the interior of Attolia, and the only place an army that size could do that was the Leonyla.

"Pegistus swears that if we fortify that pass, we could hold it forever," said Sotis. "He says we can starve the Medes out."

"If they can cache supplies at the ports in Roa, they can resupply from there as well," Motis said. "We don't have the ships to protect our ports and blockade theirs too."

"The Brael ambassador has said his king will give us ships," said his brother, Drusis.

"And why would the Braelings do that?" Xikos asked. "That would be war with the Medes, which is what they have been trying to avoid, and war with Roa, to boot."

"I don't think the Braelings need to worry about being at war with Roa," Motis pointed out, making Xikos scowl.

Drusis said what everyone was thinking. "No one needs

fifty thousand men to conquer the Little Peninsula. The Braelings have to know that the Continent will be next."

"I heard the Gants have promised troops as well," said Motis. "Ferria leads the League of Seven this year, and her ambassador says they'll send men and artillery. They all want the Medes stopped before they are sitting on Melenze's doorstep."

Xikos asked, "If we can hold the Leonyla forever, then why are the Medes attacking there?"

"That's why they are moving so fast," said Ion, who'd been sitting quietly with his feet propped on a bench, looking out the window at the darkening sky.

"They mean to get to the pass before we have time to assemble a defense," Drusis told Xikos.

"Given the bickering today in the council chamber, they may well do it," said Ion.

Yorn Fordad tipped the last of the stuffed grape leaves onto the Epidian ambassador's plate. "You were as surprised as I was, then?"

"Utterly."

"Melenze can't be pleased," said the Epidian.

"Ferria will be frantic."

"I talked to her ambassador," said Fordad. "Camoria says Ferria will leave her larger warships with the allied navy, but she's calling the fast ships home. She'll ask her merchants to bring their ships in as well. He's afraid the merchants will refuse, take their ships out of the Middle Sea entirely."

"Any word of the Roan ambassador?"

"None. They've arrested some of his retinue, but he and his junior man have disappeared into thin air."

"I suppose we can all be thankful we are not the ambassador of Kimmer today."

The Epidian agreed. "I cannot imagine a worse position to be in."

"Nor I," said Fordad.

The ambassador from Kimmer had been summoned to explain the passage of the Mede army through his country. He was still protected by his diplomatic position, but only just. That he seemed to have been left completely in the dark by his own government was all that kept Attolia from pitching him into her darkest dungeon.

The clouds were lighter gray against the black night sky. All the birds were asleep, and insects in the bushes were singing songs to their gods. Eddis was not surprised when the king arrived at her shoulder, and she didn't look in his direction. She'd heard his attendants approaching on the gravel paths, and she was well aware how much it distressed him to be announced wherever he went by their noise. She'd come to the garden to sit in the quiet and the moonlight, and she was relieved to hear the attendants' footsteps receding when Gen directed them back to the terrace to wait. The guards stayed. Teleus had been adamant that security be tightened.

When Eugenides sat beside her, she leaned against him.

"They have to support you," she said.

"They will," he reassured her. "They love a war."

"You don't know what they've been like."

"I do, actually," he said. If anyone knew the temper of the Eddisians, it was the Thief.

"And afterward?" she asked.

"Let's survive this, Helen, before we worry about that."

They were quiet, she worrying, he waiting.

Finally she said, "I know what you're thinking, and we cannot risk losing you, Gen."

"Helen, today should have made it abundantly clear to all of you what I realized staring into a fireplace full of coals praying for my wife. I cannot lose Irene. I cannot lose you and I cannot lose Sophos. Rid yourself of this notion that I alone am indispensable."

CHAPTER TWO

There was no more talk of Emipopolitus. On estates all over the Peninsula, the barons were gathering their men and equipping them for war. Every industry was directed toward the effort. Armorers were busy night and day. There were uniforms to be made, belts and boots and shoes. Carts. Saddles. Harnesses. The demands of war were endless and their fulfillment had to be recorded in exact detail, every coin spent accounted for. The queen's indentured set aside their tax records and moved into the war offices. The palace errand boys were run off their feet. Sounis and Eddis returned to the mountains, Sounis continuing on to his capital, both of them intent on rallying their people.

Perminder of Sounis remained to join the king's attendants. Eddis didn't even ask if Cleon's apology had been accepted. He returned to the mountains with her.

The ambassador from Roa was not seen again. The Attolian, Sounisian, and Eddisian ambassadors to Roa and Kimmer and Zaboar were recalled. Protests were sent to those courts and to the Greater Powers of the Continent, who were also in treaties with our treacherous allies. Attolia sent an envoy to the emperor, demanding that he withdraw his armies.

The king thought this was silly.

"The rules of the civilized world must be followed," said Fordad, mocking sincerity. He and the king were alone and he could speak freely.

The king snorted as he sipped at the liquor Fordad shared with him when the king dropped by his apartment late in the night. "If the rules of the civilized world were followed, the Mede and the Brael empires would both be the size of Attolia."

"Not true, Your Majesty," protested Fordad, still mocking. "Remember the Melian dialogues."

"Oh yes, of course," said Eugenides bitterly. "*If you have the might to do it, you have the right to do it.* The most important rule of all."

Kimmer demanded the safe return of their ambassador from Attolia, and the Attolians certainly didn't mind seeing him go. His leave-taking was not what the Mede's had been, with the king interrupting the ambassador's obsequious, exculpatory farewells to say, "I don't care what you knew or didn't know or when you didn't know it. You will be escorted to the harbor. Goodbye."

To Teleus the king added, "Be sure he's provided a closed carriage." Teleus bowed and conducted the stunned ambassador out.

I did not see Teleus return to the palace, but I heard about it that evening when he came to grouse over a bottle of wine shared with Relius. I had lately begun to review my lessons in my tutor's rooms when there were no formal dinners, and I listened to Teleus's complaints instead of reading the text Relius had set in front of me. The Kimmeran ambassador had been safe behind a carriage door when the citizens began pelting him with rotten food, but Teleus and his guards had not been so lucky. Though they had not been the intended target of the people's rage, a fair amount of diffusion in the fusillade was only to be expected. Teleus seemed to hold it as much against the king as against the ambassador.

"I don't think the king encouraged it," Relius told him, laughing. Teleus grunted. I knew he disapproved of the king, and the king disapproved of him. He was taciturn by nature, intimidating even as he relaxed over a cup of wine. The king had once called the captain of the guard stodgy to his face.

The remaining members of the diplomatic party from Roa had been arrested and were returned to their border under lock and key, a process I am sure was humiliating and uncomfortable. Still, like the Kimmeran ambassador, they were kept from any harm. One of their servants had spit at me once, and I was glad to see them gone.

It was Yorn Fordad's unhappy responsibility, as ambassador of the Braelings and also temporary representative of the Pents, to remind Attolia that the Pents had cut all diplomatic ties until there was a full and free apology from the king for attempting to murder their ambassador. The Braelings would offer the Little Peninsula their support, but the Pents would not.

"Your Majesties, I must assume that this precludes providing any ships to aid in a blockade of the Roan ports. The allied navy could be sent to your aid, but the admiral in charge of the fleet, Admiral Rullo . . ."

"Is a Pent," said the queen.

"Yes. Therefore, I cannot guarantee the allied navy's timely arrival. Not without an apology."

"Which is not going to happen," said the king sullenly, crossing his arms, slumping down in his chair.

Having grown comfortable at last in the palace, I found I was again on perilous ground when the king held out his hand to me and said, "What is that?" He was dressed and just about to leave the apartments. Lamion, Dionis, and I were to follow him that morning to his appointments.

Puzzled, I offered him the slate Relius had given me.

Before he left for Sounis, the magus of Sounis had set several problems for me. I had one of them on the slate: a circle, quartered, with the endpoints of two of the radii connected to make a triangle. I thought the king was interested in the math—the magus had told me to find an equation to describe the triangle, and I'd brought the slate with chalk to make my notes during what I knew would be interminable meetings.

The king took my slate, tipped it back and forth to look at both sides, showing no interest in the figures. He handed it to Lamion. "Get rid of that," he said, and left the apartments without another word. Then he ignored me for the rest of the day—so pointedly that I was sick that night in the necessaries. I had not been sick in months: I was eating my fill instead of living on table scraps with Melisande; I had been sleeping better, as Petrus's tonics and hot baths and his exercises, much as I mocked them, had made me more comfortable. And I had not been afraid.

The next morning, I went to Relius, unsure what I would tell him if he asked where the slate was and why I didn't have it. He didn't ask, and the slate, or one just like it, was sitting on the worktable when I arrived. Instead of standing behind me as he usually did, giving me directions and watching my work, he dragged over the other stool and sat beside me.

"Pheris," he said, speaking very gently for him, "it is hardly a secret to anyone with eyes that you come here to my study every day."

I had grown so much at ease in my new life, I did not understand what he was hinting at. I was proud to be his student.

"The slate seems small," he said. "But there are new people in the palace, and people seeing things with new eyes. When a country goes to war, it looks for enemies everywhere, and carrying this"—he tapped the slate with one misshapen finger—"you may as well be wearing a signboard on your chest like a man in a marketplace that reminds everyone who sees you that you are an Erondites . . . and that you are listening."

I looked down as if a chasm had opened in front of me, waiting only for me to fall in. I had stopped listening to the voice of Melisande in my head and had walked myself right to the edge of it. Seeing his point made, Relius patted me awkwardly on the shoulder.

"They have forgotten the burned wagons at Perma and your part in Erondites's attempts to turn the people against the king and queen. You cannot remind them. They treat you like a good-fortune amulet since the queen's illness, but an amulet is not a person, Pheris; it's a thing. An amulet does not listen and read . . . and write." He paused, seeing my distress. "You are just a boy," he said. "You should not be at play in the world of men, yet you are. We cannot change that. I know that to be regarded as a thing and not a person is painful; still, the king would see that protection last for you as long as possible. Do you understand?"

I nodded.

"Someday we will not have the Mede attacking on one hand and your grasping grandfather on the other," Relius promised. "And you will do more than carry a slate. For now, let us practice doing without one. Show me, please, how you indicate time and how much of it has passed."

No sooner was the specter of my grandfather who was Erondites raised than the man himself appeared. He was the head of the house, and he had come to the capital to offer his resources to the state. I stayed scrupulously at the side of my king, not traveling the hallways on my own even to reach Relius for my lessons. Within the week, the council of the Greater Patronoi sent a delegation to the palace, carefully choosing a time when the queen had left it to make a sacrifice at Ula's altar in the city.

Hilarion had been told that the meeting was a formality, an introduction to the sons of several barons being promoted to command in Attolia's army. When we arrived, we found not just those barons and their sons, but all the Greater Patronoi, the heads of the most powerful houses in Attolia, waiting. They filled the large council chamber, the very one where the king had chased off the Pent. The chairs at the long table had been moved to the walls, except one pointedly left for the king. When he sat, he might have

looked imperious, keeping all the men around him standing; instead, he looked like a boy about to be lectured by his
tutors.

Hilarion leaned to speak in the king's ear, but the king
shook him off. Philologos would have gone to alert the queen
until he realized, as I already had, that the brawniest of the
barons' sons were between us and the doors. To get past
them would have required an all-out brawl, and the guards
standing by would be no help; they were there to defend the
king's life, not to intervene in fights between the patronoi.
Some of them were okloi, others patronoi, and it wasn't at
all clear whose side they would come in on. Hilarion was
looking daggers at his own cousin, the head of his house.
Philologos turned beseeching eyes on his father. They were
no more use than the guards.

Erondites was there, of course, though he left it to my
grandfather who was Susa to present the patronoi's demands.
Susa began by laying out the rules of diplomacy, the importance of allies, the respect due to ambassadors and the inviolable nature of their position. The king made little hurry-up
motions, which had no effect. When the king tilted his head
back to stare at the ceiling, Susa paused in his lecture.

"Are you done?" the king lowered his head to ask.

"Only waiting for your attention, Your Majesty," said Susa.
He went on to catalog the king's transgressions: the many
examples of rudeness, the theft of the Mede ambassador's

statue, the assault on the Pent, every complaint a thread with which, loop on loop, he meant to bind the king. Susa even blamed him for the shooting of the Mede ambassador by Sounis.

Far from being humbled by this browbeating, the king progressed rapidly from impatient to resentful. One or two barons shifted anxiously and were glared at by their peers. Any weakness among their ranks put them all at risk. Erondites had convinced them that they could go back to the days when Attolia's father was a figurehead of a king and the Greater Patronoi were an oligarchy that divided the power of the state among themselves. All they needed to do was force the king's hand, press him in this moment to make a hasty decision from which he could not retreat.

"You have embarrassed our state as well as attacked a man who had every reason to believe he was safe from violence," said Susa.

"I did miss," said the king.

"That is immaterial," Susa responded pompously.

"I could have killed him."

"Your Majesty—"

"Could have winged him anyway," said the king with a shrug.

"Your Majesty should not have thrown the knife. Your Majesty should not have drawn it."

"His Majesty shouldn't have had it if he was going to

draw it," someone muttered, loudly enough to be heard across the room.

Susa waved for silence, having arrived at his conclusion at last. "We are the Greater Patronoi of Attolia, and we say the king shall apologize to the Pents."

The king was unimpressed. "Say anything you like," he said, showing his teeth.

"May I remind Your Majesty that a majority vote from the full council of barons overrules even the king?"

"If I say no, you may not remind me, then what, Susa? Will you suck the words back into your mouth?"

It was Susa's turn to shrug. "It is the law of the land, Your Majesty. In these perilous times, we must remain united. You cannot oppose your Greater Patronoi."

That was the point of Erondites's sword sliding in. With the Attolians facing their greatest enemy, the king was vulnerable, so the barons put to him this choice: submit to the barons' authority and weaken his ruling power, or risk a division that would weaken the whole state. Behind Susa, the barons nodded their heads like woodcocks, some encouraging, some stern, some smug, all of them expecting the king to bow to their demands, because Attolia needed the Pent support and because Erondites had said he would. He'd said that Susa would persuade him.

Susa was not trying to persuade him. Susa, in the guise of an elder statesman, was goading him. "Come now, Your

Majesty. You have behaved badly, and you know it. Admit your error like a man and apologize."

If the king did not submit to the Greater Patronoi, then his barons, having foolishly squared themselves up against him, would have to back down themselves, or revolt. Whether they wanted to defy the king or not, Erondites had guaranteed that a few would—and with the Mede bearing down, a few was enough. Compromises would have to be made, barons bought off. To reunite his patronoi, the king would be forced to make concessions that would weaken the throne even further.

The rest of the barons could not see Susa's malicious smile, only the king and his attendants. When the king stood to say in Susa's face, "I am not going to apologize to that mealy-mouthed, self-dealing, bootlicking Pent," Susa, with his thinning white hair and his stooped shoulders, looked the part of a wounded mentor, and the king looked ever more ridiculous.

"If the barons are unanimous—" Susa began again, ready to repeat his entire lecture, daring the king to stop him.

The king looked from baron to baron. A more experienced ruler, presented with two disastrous options, might have delayed, might have worked to divide his opponents in careful negotiations. The king was not that cautious ruler. Attolia had been prescient when she warned Eddis that he could be pushed only so far.

"The Medes advance, and all of you are still more

concerned about guarding the wine in your own wine cups!"
he said. Some of the barons had the grace to look ashamed.
"Susa has laid out the problem. I have a solution! If you truly
think the king may not oppose his united barons"—he paused
while he lifted his hand to his mouth and used his teeth to pull
the seal ring off his finger—"find yourselves another king."

He slammed the ring down on the table and stormed
out of the room, sailing right past the dithering young men
between him and the door.

He left too quickly to be called back, left the barons too
stunned to speak, even Susa, all of them staring at the ring
on the table, even Erondites taken by surprise. They should
have known better. They knew the king was impetuous, knew
how much he chafed under the demands of the throne. They
had meant to push him into doing something ill-considered,
and he had. Desperate to know what the stammering barons
would say next, I hesitated as the retinue of the king was
vanishing out the door. Knowing that if I fell too far behind,
I would never catch up, I cursed and started after Philologos,
chasing him all the way to the king's apartments.

At the door to his bedchamber, the king turned on us,
his attendants and his guard. "Why are you still following
me?" he asked.

"Where should we go, Your Majesty?" asked Hilarion as
we stood shifting from foot to foot.

"Don't call me that."

"But, Your Majes—"

He shook his head. "Merely a Thief, far from home," he corrected Hilarion. "Or I suppose prince, but no one has ever called me that. Consort?" He appeared to be thinking aloud. "Attolia has never had Continental titles, but Sounis has them. Maybe Irene will make me a duke. At any rate, I have no authority, no responsibilities, and no longer any need for attendants."

"Your Majesty, no."

"No 'Your Majesty' and 'Yes.' You can all go away, go hunting, go to town for a drink, do anything you want."

"What will you do, Your Majesty?"

"I don't know," said Eugenides, and seemed to mean it. He looked back over his shoulder. "Pack?" he said.

"You will not leave!" Philologos cried.

Eugenides's vicious humor dimmed a little. He had not considered what might come after so strenuous an abdication, that the council might take it at face value, that he might have to leave Attolia. "Philo, the council may be voting to exile me as we speak."

"What of the queen?" Philologos said in a choked voice.

Eugenides stared into the future. "I don't know. It's not up to me anymore."

He stepped into his room and closed the door in our faces.

✦ ✦ ✦

"What in the name of all the gods happened?" asked Ion, and Hilarion explained. When he was finished, Ion said, "Someone has to tell the queen."

"She probably knows already."

"Even so, we have to send a messenger."

Hilarion ran his hands through his hair, clearly not relishing this. "You and I will go. The rest of you stay here. Make sure he doesn't leave."

The other attendants, all of them having arrived in the waiting room, stared at each other and back at Hilarion. How could they stop him from leaving?

"Send to the stables. Warn them not to give him a horse. Tell the guards they aren't to let him out of the palace."

"Are you out of your mind, Hilarion?" asked Lamion. "What guard is going to tell the king of Attolia he can't leave his palace? And don't tell me it's not his palace if he is not king, because this is nonsense."

Hilarion just looked at him helplessly.

"We'll talk to the queen," said Ion, trying for calm. "Tell the stables to delay if they can, that the queen does not want the king to leave the palace."

That was a good thought.

"You can't give orders in the queen's name," Xikos pointed out.

"Go to the queen," Dionis said firmly. "Stop talking and go now."

Hilarion and Ion hurried away and the rest of us sat, the other attendants fearing for their country, while I wondered: if Eugenides truly left Attolia, what would become of me, the unwanted, unwelcome heir of Erondites?

It was an hour or more before Hilarion and Ion were able to convey their message, before the queen rose from her devotion at the altar of Ula, heard their recounting of events, and returned to the palace. Imenia came to the door of the king's apartments, bowed her head to Philologos, the highest-ranking attendant present, and said, "Her Majesty observes that it is late in the day to start a journey and suggests that His Highness rest for the afternoon and await the council's direction."

Philologos swallowed.

"Will you convey Her Majesty's message?" she prompted.

Philo nodded. "Yes," he said hoarsely, and Imenia went away again.

After rubbing his shoulders like a man who's chilled to the bone, Philologos went and knocked on the king's door.

Eugenides opened it right away. When Philo gave him the queen's message, he tilted his head to one side while he considered it. "Her Majesty is quite right, as usual. If she asks for me, please tell her I'll be reading on one of the porches." He stepped to his desk and scooped up the book of poetry that the king of Sounis had given him for his birthday. With it tucked under his arm, he headed for the passageway. Over his shoulder, he said, "You all can stay here," before his eye fell on me. "Oh, Pheris, don't be so woebegone. You can come with me if you like."

So I tagged along as he told the guards standing outside his door that they could return to their barracks. They didn't. They just anxiously trailed along as the king went looking for a quiet place to read. When people we passed stopped and bowed, Eugenides only waved at them, waggling his fingers as he passed, saying, "Never mind all that." Straightening uncertainly, they stared after him.

We ended up on one of the porches near the Comemnus tower. The day was still hot, but the porch was in the shade. There was a couch with a backrest and several stools scattered around. The king lay down and adjusted himself, then opened his book.

"Wish I'd thought to get some wine from the palace kitchens," he said.

"I'll get that for you, Your Majesty," said Hilarion from the doorway.

I hadn't realized he too had been following, but Eugenides didn't seem to be surprised.

"No, thank you, Hilarion, there's no reason you should go to the trouble."

Hilarion went anyway.

✦ ✦ ✦

Eugenides read and sipped his wine. Sometime after that, Susa appeared in the doorway of the porch, announcing himself, humming like a wasp with outrage. "Your Majesty," he said deliberately.

"No, no, Susa," said the king, without looking up. "Not Majesty. Highness, maybe. 'Eugenides' is always appropriate."

"Enough of this, you lying, irresponsible whelp."

"Whelp. That's new. People usually say viper. Or bastard. My cousins liked to throw that at me."

"You took an oath before the gods, new and old," Susa reminded him. "Your gods, and you play at abandoning it?"

"I assure you, I am in earnest, Susa," said Eugenides.

"And what of the people your games endanger?"

"You still have a queen. I am confident that she will manage," said Eugenides.

"Attolia says she leaves with you."

Eugenides's face went from a studied carelessness to utterly blank, as a slate is wiped clean. Watching from my stool, I thought to myself he had been bluffing. But Susa's moment of satisfaction was short-lived.

"She will leave with me?" Eugenides repeated.

Susa had made a mistake, perhaps a fatal one, in thinking to shame the king. Eugenides looked at him in wonder. "You ran to the queen for comfort, didn't you? You expected her to put everything right, yet again, and she refused. Tell me, did you try to order her to apologize to the Pents?"

The barons' nerves had failed long before anyone could suggest that out loud. They'd gone to the queen assuming she would somehow rein in her runaway husband. To the barons' horror, she had risen to her feet and, much like her husband, swept from the room, leaving her own ring of office teetering on the arm of her ornately carved chair.

If the barons had been surprised by the king's reaction, they were panicked by the queen's. Attolia did not threaten where she did not mean to act.

Susa was shaking with rage. "You see how you have corrupted her," he said. "It is not enough that you threaten our treaty with Eddis and Sounis, you deprive us of our queen."

"I have certainly tried to do so," Eugenides admitted calmly, laying his book on his chest and looking out over the railings at the view. "I asked her to leave with me on our wedding night."

"What?" my grandfather said, his composure further weakened. He too had believed this was all a childish bluff and suddenly felt the ground shifting under his feet.

"Oh, yes. We could have been in the Epidi Islands by now, or Mur. I would have taken her anywhere she wanted," Eugenides assured him. "She wouldn't abandon her people—she knew how Erondites would rule if she did." He shrugged. "Now, I suppose the acid from your tongue has finally eaten away at the ties that bound her here."

"And you?" asked Susa contemptuously. "Where is your loyalty to your people? The ones who made you king of Attolia?"

With a gravity I'd never seen before, Eugenides eyed Susa. "You talk about loyalty and call me to task for my oaths. What about yours, Susa? Have I not heard you swear yourself my man, my needs your needs, my honor your honor, my law your law? I was sure I did."

There was a hiccup in the baron's righteousness, just a flicker, a hand twitching in protest.

Eugenides returned to his poetry, saying dismissively, "You let Erondites push you into this, Susa. If you want him to be your king, have him."

"I do not want him to be my king, Your Majesty."

"One would never guess," said Eugenides, still looking at the page in front of him.

"We all have constraints that govern us. None of us is free to act as we choose," said Susa, battling on.

"Except me," said Eugenides. "I can do anything I want." He showed his teeth again. "Susa and Erondites, the Laimonides, all the greater barons have always flipped from side to side with every shift in power, always putting their own interests first. Now the Medes are marching, Susa, and you are all still serving yourselves. Well, I cannot rein you in. Nor, it seems, can my queen. We cannot fight the Medes and you at the same time, so we may as well go. Let Erondites be your king."

"Erondites will be the death of us all," said Susa. "The Medes—"

"Will sweep over you like the tide," Eugenides said. "In a generation," he added prophetically, "nothing will be left of Attolia but a name on an out-of-date map."

"You will not leave us to that," said Susa.

"I am not king of the Bructs," said Eugenides. "Look to Sophos for that kind of sacrifice." He cursed mildly. "I've lost my place." Holding the book open with his hand, he tried to slip the hook between the pages. Afraid he would tear them, I came from my stool to turn the pages myself, deliberately stopping at Perse's poem imploring her faithless lover to return.

Hilarion was still standing in the doorway, agony in his face.

Susa saw a ray of hope. "There are those who are loyal to you, Eugenides. Will you abandon them?"

"I cannot save them."

"You could."

Eugenides shook his head. "It is not in my power," he said. With a reproving glance at me, he said to Susa, "I told you, we cannot fight the Medes and disloyal barons too."

"Let me bring you loyal ones, then, Your Majesty," said Susa. "You know there are many who would willingly abandon Erondites."

"You, Susa? You will lead people away from Erondites?
How, when he holds your leash so tight?"

"I will let the Susa land above the Pomea go," my
grandfather said. "All of it. If you will stop this nonsense
now."

He meant my home. The Villa Suterpe was on the Susa
land above the Pomea. Though it had long been in Susa's
possession, Erondites had a better claim to it and had held
that over Susa's head for years. In offering to give up that
land and all the wealth it brought him, Susa was doing more
than rejecting Erondites's influence. He was offering to
break publicly with him.

"And you think others will follow suit? You and I both
know how Erondites keeps them cowed. How many loyal
barons, truly free of him, can you promise? Tell me honestly.
I will know if you lie."

Susa bowed his head. "One," he said.

"That's the sweet taste of truth on your tongue, probably
for the first time. One isn't enough."

"It's a beginning," argued Susa.

Eugenides shook his head.

"It's the one that matters in this farce of yours."

The king flicked a glance at him from the corner of his
eye. "One," he said, "but a lion?"

Hilarion was holding his breath. So was I. Susa dropped
to his knees.

"I am an old man, Your Majesty, but I am your man in every particular," he swore.

Eugenides snorted. "So, so, so," he said dismissively. "That's a vow for a fireside story, Susa. Was the taste of truth on your tongue too sweet?"

Susa had to agree. He said, "In Hephestia's name I swear, and may lightning strike me if I lie: I am your man, Your Majesty, in every particular, so long as you are high king and the Medes threaten us."

He held out his hand, the king's ring on his palm. "Please," he said.

Eugenides laid his book back on his chest and looked at it.

"I will settle for one, for now," he said. "But one is not enough, Susa." He took the ring. Not taking his eyes off Susa, he held it toward me, and using my good hand, I pushed it over his knuckle, back into place.

"I will bring you more supporters, Your Majesty," promised Susa. "No one wants Erondites for their king."

The barons, rattled by the outcome of their attempt to intimidate the king, greeted Susa's announcement that he had returned the ring to His Majesty with relief. Most blamed Susa for mishandling the whole business, claiming they'd only ever wanted what was best for Attolia. Those actually motivated by Attolia's desperate need for the Pents' support raged in private. The Baron Casartus threw his lover out of his apartments for merely suggesting that everything would probably work out all right in the end.

"Thank you." Eugenides bent to kiss the back of his wife's neck.

"You lost your temper," she said.

"I did," he conceded, settling on the bench beside her.

"You know how upset they get at the least hint that you are ill, that we might lose you."

"I do."

Attolia's barons needed a king, but they wanted one they could manipulate, each to their own ends, so that one house might have the upper hand and sometimes another, in a gen-teel, underhanded, secretive sort of oligarchy.

"They wanted power," said Eugenides with a shrug. "I gave it to them."

"You didn't give it to them, you threw it in their faces. You opened a contest for the throne that would have left them all fighting each other like weasels in a hole."

"I couldn't think of anything else to do," he admitted.

"I thought of any number of other—much more sensible—things to do," said Attolia.

"And?"

"Threw caution to the winds," she told him, and kissed him on the lips.

"Atté, Atté," a little later he murmured in her ear, the battle cry of the Attolians.

"You have created a monster," Erondites said, leaning forward in his chair to reach for the bottle of wine on the table. He poured himself a cup full to brimming. "There is no one now to rein him in. We know how that has gone in the past."

"We'll just have to hope this time it will be different," said Susa.

"Why would it be different? When the power of the throne increases, we see our own rights and privileges trampled."

"It's not just our privileges that are about to be trampled, Pheris," said Susa.

"What does it benefit us to be subdued by our king instead of by the Medes?"

"We might think of others besides ourselves. Occasionally."

Erondites snorted. "You might be satisfied," he said. "Don't expect me to be."

He left the court the next day, ostensibly to muster the men he would send to support the king's army. He would not travel with the army, only send his men under the command of one of his least favorite nephews.

Costis left as well. Orutus had initially refused to let him return to Roa and had even gone so far as to order Costis confined to his barracks. He should have known better.

Instead of returning to his quarters, Costis had gone directly to the king, where he had accused Orutus of abandoning Kamet to die. Orutus, following on Costis's heels into the audience room, had in turn appealed to the queen.

"If Costis is followed back to Roa, what then?"

To his surprise, Relius had supported him. "The risk is too great that both will be killed, Your Majesty."

The king would have spoken, but the queen laid a hand on his arm. "Kamet has served his purpose," she said and even Orutus winced at her pragmatism. Costis blinked as he stared straight ahead and the muscles in his jaw jumped. But the queen wasn't finished. "To risk Costis as well as Kamet is poor tactics, I agree. However, we must consider that if we order him to remain with the guard, his heart is unlikely to be in his work." She looked at him, standing so upright before them. "And how embarrassing for us all if he were to take a lesson from a poor role model and abandon his responsibilities altogether."

We all looked at the king, who looked at his toes.

The queen said to Costis, "I cannot in good conscience risk the men to ensure your safety. If you go alone, you may lead to Kamet the very thing you fear. Do you wish to take that chance?"

"I do," said Costis.

"Then go," said the queen. "And be blessed in your endeavors."

✦ ✦ ✦

The next day, Relius too departed. I arrived in the doorway
to his apartments just as he and Teleus were saying their farewells. Relius laughed at my expression, and Teleus turned to
frown at me.

"He does not approve of adult goings-on," said Relius.

"I think it's your goings-on he does not approve of," said
Teleus.

He was correct.

"That's two of you, then," said Relius airily. He didn't
like being criticized, and I think Teleus had been lecturing.
Teleus was a great believer in lectures.

Sternly, he said to Relius, "You be careful."

"I am not the one going to war," Relius pointed out.

"No," said Teleus, "you are the one poking your nose
into other people's business."

Relius rolled his eyes at the rebuke, but when Teleus continued to browbeat him, he gave that quick lift of his chin
that was as much of a concession as Teleus was likely to get.
Evidently it was enough, for Teleus kissed him again and
left.

"You," said Relius to me, "keep your opinions to yourself.
Someday you will be in love, and all your mocking of poor
Philologos will come back to haunt you."

I had been his student for too long, and I just rolled my
eyes as he had rolled his at Teleus.

He laughed and waved at the table. "Come see what I have for you."

It was a set of four leather-covered notebooks, plain but perfectly made.

"I want to know what you see while I am gone and what you think it means. I know, I know, your handwriting is still terrible. Make notes. Then go back and write more neatly when you can. Write enough that you will remember later what happened, and I will ask you questions when I return."

What if people see me writing?

"Erondites has played his hand and lost again. He cannot even crow about the return of Susa's land, as the rents are going to Marina. Erondites will not see a single copper coin while Juridius is in exile. Once the army is on the march, people will have more important things on their minds than what you are scribbling in a book."

Those were my first journals and the beginning of my histories of the life of the great king.

CHAPTER THREE

The day was bright and the sun's warmth appreciated. The riders making their way in a narrow stream up the pass from Sounis into Eddis were already high in the mountains, and whenever they moved into the shade, it sent a chill down their necks that made them shiver as if whole armies were marching over their graves.

The king of Sounis rode with his magus near the front of his forces. There'd been some disagreement about his safety there. But once before, when the woman he meant to marry had waited for him in Eddis, he'd won an argument about whether he should ride more slowly and allow half his army to march ahead of him. Now the woman was his queen, and he was even less inclined to make her wait while he inched up the winding route above the Seperchia River. The magus had to tell him quite sternly not to advance ahead of all his men.

"We are at war," the magus reminded him.

Sophos looked at the cliff on their right and the steep drop to the river on their left. "Where do you imagine the party of Mede assassins is going to leap from, Magus?"

The magus frowned and savaged him, as only the magus could, for his self-indulgence. "If the Medes are in Eddis and have murdered the queen"—he saw the king flinch and went inexorably on—"no warning would have had time to reach us. If she is lying this moment in her throne room . . . with her throat cut . . . in a pool of blood . . . we would not know it until the Mede assassins rode down the trail toward us to—"

"—be spitted by a small army of Sounisians," interrupted Sophos, angry at what he knew was a reprimand he deserved.

"—to spit the idiot king who keeps riding ahead of his men in the van," said the magus.

Sophos glowered, but he reined in his horse.

"Why must armies move so slowly?" he complained.

"You know why," said the magus, more gently.

Eddis and her party waited by the bridge across the narrow chasm of the Seperchia River. The lower part of the bridge was stone, three levels of arches that reached all the way down to the water below. The uppermost level of the bridge was made of wood. The mountain wind blowing all around, never from the same direction for very long, made every loose thing flap and jingle, tossed the horses' manes, and narrowed everyone's eyes to slits. They appeared a grim company until the Sounisians arrived and Eddis kicked her sturdy mountain pony into motion. Sounis's advance guard politely drew aside to let their king ahead of them to greet his queen. Their horses' hooves thudding on the boards, the king and queen met in the middle of the bridge. Sophos dismounted first and stepped to catch Helen as she swung from the saddle. She hung an arm around his neck and kissed him as she dropped. He had to bend to keep his lips on hers until she reached the ground. Arm in arm, they led their horses toward Eddis's company.

The men from Sounis were a day behind schedule, and Sophos apologized. "Everything took longer than expected. We started late and I could not march the men in the dark."

"The pass always slows people down," Helen reassured him. "Irene and I have taken it into account."

The bulk of Eddis's army had marched from the Aracthus Pass. Only Eddis's minister of war and her personal guard and her hardier attendants were with her. Sounis greeted those he knew by name and the rest introduced themselves, comfortable addressing him as "Your Majesty." If it still made him feel awkward to have hardened warriors bow their heads to him, he didn't let it show.

Armies, even small ones, move slowly enough that Helen and Sophos could walk together, talking quietly and bringing each other up-to-date. Their horses followed behind them, occasionally nuzzling the backs of their heads or pulling sharply on the reins to snatch at whatever they thought might be edible and within reach.

"How many trips does your father think it will take to move your men to Attolia?" Helen asked.

"Too many," said Sophos. "He doesn't think he can get them there before they need to march north." Thinking of the men who had so graciously accepted him as their king, he asked if tensions had eased in Helen's court. She shook her head.

"Gen and Attolia both asked why I didn't take Cleon out and shoot him. I think Gen was joking."

"Not Attolia," hazarded Sophos. He'd recognized Cleon among Eddis's men.

"I wasn't sure what trouble Cleon might get into, so I am keeping him with me. I wanted him well away from Therespides, as I'm sure it's Therespides encouraging him, and frankly . . ." She hesitated.

"Oh, do be frank," said Sounis, earning the smile that still made his heart seize.

Away from listening ears, with the wind blowing their words to pieces, she did not worry about being overheard. "Frankly, Cleon is too stupid to have stuck to this business so long. Frankly, it is Therespides I would like to shoot, and frankly, it would not solve the problem. There are just too many who think a Thief should not be high king over Eddis." She waved a hand at the men walking ahead of them, the honor guard behind, and lifted it in a gesture of defeat. "I cannot shoot them all."

"They were happy to have him be king of Attolia."

"He'd brought me the Gift. He'd ended the war. Most important of all, he'd be in Attolia," she emphasized.

Sounis kicked a rock down the road and had to pause to reassure his horse, who'd shied at the sound. When he caught up to Eddis, he asked hesitantly, "Gen does know the details of the marriage proposal, doesn't he?"

"That your uncle threatened to give Hamiathes's Gift to Gen, making him king, if I didn't accept Sounis's offer? Gen didn't know at the time—he must by now." Eddis glanced back at the magus riding and chatting with Gen's father a little ways behind them. Sounis did too. They both knew the mastermind of his uncle's plan.

"Gen would just have passed it on to you."

"The council would not believe it."

"They underestimated his loyalty."

"So did the magus. A rare error on his part, but—"

"Catastrophic," finished Eddis just as Sounis said, "Fortuitous," and both blushed.

"Gen has always supported you," Sounis pointed out. "And me."

Eddis hesitated. Sophos recognized her reservations and

dismissed them. "Yes, I might have won over my barons in Sounis without him, but it was Gen who gave me the courage to end a civil war with almost no bloodshed, and because of him, we entered our treaty on an equal footing with Attolia. Can Cleon truly not understand that?"

Eddis shrugged. "Cleon has never been what you would call astute. The people listening to Cleon, they think Gen has always been much too close to the throne for anyone's comfort. You cannot imagine the outrage when his father, the son of the king, married the daughter of the Thief. And if it's old news that my mother preferred my uncle but married my father to become queen, Cleon has raked it all back up again—all of the rumors about my mother's infidelity and Gen's mother's revenge. Seducing other people's lovers is a wintertime sport in Eddis. My father who was Eddis and Gen's father paid a fortune to the temple priests that year to ensure their sons' naming ceremonies were uncontested." She did not say, did not need to say, that years later those same people saw her brothers dying one by one of fever and did not think a woman could rule Eddis. "His grandfather insisted on naming Gen for his god, and people who'd thought the Thieves of Eddis were just a remnant of ancient history suddenly assumed the worst."

"Gen brought you the Gift. He made you queen," insisted Sounis.

"And I destroyed it," said Eddis. "Which made me what?"

"Queen," said Sounis firmly.

Eddis smiled at him again, but it was a sadder smile. "Even those who were grateful to Gen were worried by his popularity. When he lost his hand, they hoped the Thief in him was gone for good, and when it wasn't, sending him somewhere else to be king seemed like an excellent idea."

"Until he became high king."

"Until that," said Eddis. "They had already assumed you and I would marry. They thought that Eddis and Sounis together would be a counter to Attolia. They did not expect him to be annux."

Sophos kicked another rock, a smaller one, and this time the horse only flapped his ears in annoyance.

"You insisted we marry immediately, giving them no time to object. Do you regret that?"

"Never."

"I mean politically," he said. "Spare me my blushes."

"Never," she repeated, watching the worry lines on his forehead ease before adding, "I love your blushes too much."

Watching the two of them, Eddis's minister of war said something to the magus that made him laugh. Neither Eddis nor Sounis noticed.

In Attolia, no one was laughing. As ships disgorged Sounis's soldiers, the tent city on the Fields of War grew larger and larger. Even in the face of the Mede invasion, Attolians were unsettled by the arrival of the army of a country with which they had so recently been at war. They looked with suspicion at the Sounisian soldiers. Efforts to integrate the two armies were mixed, as Sounisian barons were uncomfortable taking orders from okloi in Attolia's standing army and the career military men of Attolia called the barons "Sometime Soldiers."

"My queen." Casartus was actually wringing his hands. "If we take the ships from Cimorene to blockade Roa, we risk losing Cimorene, and if the Mede take Cimorene, we will never drive them off." He was a good strategist and probably right. "The allied navy dawdles under the Pents' direction, and at the current rate we will not have all the forces from Sounis here to begin the march north. We must have more ships."

"Can the Neutral Islands provide us with no ships?" Attolia asked.

"We have asked, Your Majesty. They hold their ships close, worried for their own defense."

"And if Eddis were to ask?" she inquired with a trace of bitterness.

Casartus said, "I—we—do not think it will make a difference in this case, Your Majesty."

When Sounis had faced an unexpected invasion of Mede soldiers and was in desperate straits, Eugenides had had the men to send to his aid, but not the means. He'd needed a flotilla of shallow-draft vessels and he'd summoned Ornon, ambassador of Eddis, to ask the Neutral Islands to supply them.

"Since when do the Neutral Islands answer to Eddis?" Attolia had asked, sharing a grim look with her admiralty, all of whom were also taken by surprise.

"They do not," said Ornon. "We can ask, as a favor."

"A favor you assume they will grant is not neutrality," said Attolia.

Delicately, the king had explained that because Eddis was too poor to support her population, in every generation some had to leave to search for better fortune elsewhere. "Not all of them can be mercenaries," said the king.

"Helen sent her people to corrupt the Neutral Islands?"

"It was her grandfather who first encouraged Eddisians to settle on specific islands with the idea that those islands, over time, might incline in Eddis's favor."

"I see," the queen had said, indeed seeing several events in her history more clearly. The wars between Sounis, Eddis, and Attolia were over, hopefully forever, but it was still a sore point.

"Very well. Let us go to the Braelings again for advice," said Attolia.

The Braelings, however, had little to offer. When Fordad was summoned to an audience in the megaron with the king and queen, he brought his secretary and his junior ambassador. The Brael ambassador, who might have spoken more informally in other circumstances, was very precise in his speech.

"Your Majesties have our support," he assured the Attolians. "What ships we are free to commit will carry our troops and the Gants' troops, but those ships are in Manse, only loading now. We expect them to arrive in time to convey their men to Stinos before the summer windstorms arrive. They will not reach Attolia in time to move Sounis's forces, though they could continue to Roa after Stinos."

"Allowing the Medes to leisurely unload a mountain of supplies and be long gone by the time the Braels arrive," Casartus muttered.

Everyone was so carefully trying to avoid looking at the king that he had to clear his throat to get Fordad's attention. He said, "There are three large Pent ships in the harbor now, that brought grain and other supplies we have purchased. The Pents are happy enough to make money from our war."

"Indeed, Your Majesty. The Pents want you to know they have much to offer as allies if you are willing to apologize for the treatment of their ambassador, and as their special envoy, I have been empowered to accept that apology." Knowing the king all too well, Fordad warned, "My government would withdraw all support if you were to deprive the Pents, in any way, of their ships, or the use of their ships, without compensation—"

"Compensation!" interrupted the king. "Do you mean to tell me that if we seize those ships, the Pents expect me to pay for them?"

"Yes, Your Majesty," Fordad said, and named a staggering sum. The Pents were well aware of the Attolians' desperation and her empty coffers. They had sent three exquisite ships, newly constructed, with unmarked decks and creamy white sails. They meant to have their apology.

The king appeared stunned. "So, I beg the Pents' forgiveness or I come up with a king's ransom? Those are my choices, Fordad?"

"Those are your choices, Your Majesty," Fordad said regretfully. "The Pents are our allies, and the Brael will stand by our treaty with them. If you seize the property of the Pents without paying compensation, you will lose the support of my government."

"Very well," said the king, with a small sigh.

"You will apologize?" said Fordad, relieved.

"Oh, no," said the king. "I'm seizing the boats. We'll pay the compensation."

Fordad didn't think he was serious. He was trying to appear amused right up until Lamion came forward with a small carved box and opened it for the ambassador's inspection. "Foest deost Fryst!" the Brael swore, shocked into his native language.

Three matching cabochon rubies nestled in the folds of

gold velvet, each the size of his thumb, each the red of fresh blood.

Attolia, better at concealing her feelings, sounded only mildly curious as she leaned toward the king to ask, "Are those the rubies from the Attolian crown?"

"They are," said the king proudly.

"Did you spend the night picking them out?"

"I did not, though one of my ancestors did—many, many years ago. The ones in the crown are glass. They've been glass for so long that I didn't think you'd mind if we spent the real ones." He smiled at her.

"And that?" Attolia pointed as Xikos stepped forward with another small case.

"That is the diamond and sapphire collection colloquially known as the Attolian Skies."

"Which was lost during the Amanix uprising."

"Which was stolen by my great-great-grandfather during the Amanix uprising, yes."

Attolia, while continuing to stare at the king, addressed the Braeling. "I believe we have met your price, ambassador."

Fordad, his eyebrows almost at his hairline, bowed deeply, allowed that if the jewels were authenticated, the ships were theirs—and then, wary of the tension between the king and queen, he hastily excused himself and his staff with him. As he marched back to his office in the wing he shared with the remaining ambassadors, he chewed his mustache, thinking of the letters he needed to write to his government and to the Pents.

His junior ambassador asked under his breath, "Is it going to be a problem that we have just sold the Pents' ships to the Attolians?"

"I had my instructions," said Fordad.

"But no one knew he had the Attolian Skies."

"They can't blame me for that."

"Maybe the Pents will be happy with the gems," the junior ambassador suggested, trying to look on the bright side. "They are magnificent, and Attolia wasn't pleased to see her baubles spent on boats."

"Don't be stupid," snapped Fordad. "She's not concerned about what she'll wear to the next court function."

"Then what was she so angry about?" the less-experienced diplomat wondered.

"I'm not sure," said Fordad, worried. "But I wouldn't change places with the king of Attolia right now if you offered *me* the Attolian Skies."

The queen canceled the rest of their appointments. She and the king returned to her apartments in silence. The king's attendants bowed themselves to a halt in their waiting room with poorly hidden relief, and the queen's attendants continued on only a little farther before they too were grateful to excuse themselves. From several rooms away and through closed doors, we could hear the crashing noise once the queen and the king reached the queen's bedchamber.

"Oh," murmured Phresine, closer and able to identify the sound. "I think that was the Ailmené coffeepot."

Luria sighed. The queen always gave her attendants gifts from her personal possessions on special occasions, and Luria had been hoping to receive that pot when she married.

"I said I was sorry," Eugenides protested.

"Your apologies are boring," shouted Attolia.

"Oh, I know," Eugenides conceded.

"The rubies. The Attolian Skies," said Attolia. "You took them from the treasury of your god." It was not a question.

"Yes," Eugenides admitted.

"You robbed your god."

He equivocated.

"You robbed your god," she repeated.

"It's not—" He stopped, reconsidering the wisdom of what he'd been about to say. "My god allows these liberties at times."

"What times?" she asked.

He winced. One could never know for certain what might provoke the anger of a god.

"And if the Thief is mistaken when he takes liberties with the god's treasury? Then what?" She didn't wait for an answer she could guess. "You took this decision upon yourself." It was a strong, if quietly voiced, objection.

"I had to," he said helplessly, and she knew why. To protect her from the god's anger if he'd guessed wrong.

The attendants in the distant anteroom flinched as one.

"The dressing table," whispered Chloe in awe, and the others hushed her.

The jewels were authenticated. The Pent ships were handed over to the Attolians, who renamed them the *The Queen's Ruby*, *The Royal Sapphire*, and *The Attolian Diamond*, and began to ready them for cannon. Sounis and Eddis brought their small force down from the mountains, their arrival doing little to inhibit the ever-growing tensions. The Attolians, looking down their noses at the civilian soldiers of Sounis, resented being condescended to in the same way by the Eddisians. The Eddisians, most of them seasoned mercenaries, made it clear they were unimpressed by the martial skills of Sounisians and Attolians alike. The integration of the forces called for a delicate hand.

The combined military leadership of the Little Peninsula met for the first time in the large council chamber. Eugenides, the high king, sat at one end of the table, with Sounis on his right. Attolia, at the opposite end, sat with Eddis at hers. The senior advisors filled the chairs around the large table, and their staffs and junior officers stood behind them. Though Orutus would have fought tooth and nail to keep Relius himself out of the room, he made no effort to exclude me. As an attendant who couldn't stand for the entire meeting, I was permitted a small stool just behind the king. I sat with my notebook on my knees. I didn't need to lurk behind the potted lemon tree, though I might have wished myself there. It was a long and difficult meeting, with arguments over every point as men tried to assert their authority or fend off any plan of action that might diminish it. The only one who made not the least effort to impress was the annux, sitting with his usual boneless inattention. He knew as much as any Eddisian about battles and strategy, but it wasn't his area of expertise, and he saw no need to pretend it was.

Eddis had brought her minister of war and her best military advisors to Attolia. Sounis had as well. One of them was his magus, a man never gentle in his arguments, and another his father, a seasoned general, who nonetheless bridled like a proud parent at any sign of disrespect for the young king. On strategic matters, Sounis turned to his magus instead of his father, and did so while deftly managing what was clearly a prickly relationship between the two men. Again and again, Sounis's voice was a calming one in the council, soothing not only his father's ruffled feathers, but those of many others.

Where Sounis's father positively beamed with approval at his son, Eddis's minister of war glowered. The high king, slumped in his seat, catching his father's glare, slumped further.

Attolia had chosen Pegistus as her minister of war. He was younger than Eddis's minister and, unlike him, not a general of the army. His gift was for logistics, crucially important to any successful campaign, but often underappreciated. Pegistus sometimes struggled for the respect he thought he deserved, and it made him pretentious. The meeting had already gone on several hours when he was explaining in excruciating detail the network of supply caches that he'd put in place, pointing out their locations on his maps.

"None on the route our armies are marching," Eddis's minister of war pointed out. Coming from the older man, what was only an observation seemed a criticism. Eddis gave her uncle a reproving look, as if to remind him that they were all there to get along.

"We will have the material to Stinos by the time the Eddisians reach there," Pegistus promised.

"Why are the caches so small?" asked Trokides, one of Sounis's senior generals and very high-handed. He'd criticized everyone and everything throughout the meeting, and his tone put Pegistus's back up.

"We cannot store what we don't have," Pegistus said sharply, which inevitably led to a round of protests as the Attolian barons detailed their contributions and the sacrifices they'd made. I thought of the wagons that had burned at Perma and wished I was under the table instead of sitting in plain sight.

Eddis's minister of war didn't need to raise his voice to cut through the bickering. "What's your advance-to-return distribution?" he asked, and a grim silence fell.

"Ten to one," said Pegistus in the quiet. He cleared his throat, glancing at Attolia before he went on. "We have chosen to put the bulk of our supplies into the advance caches to be sure our men are at fighting strength," he said. "However, on our return there may well be some crops and we could—of course, we will," he insisted, "purchase any additional food we need."

Everyone understood.

Pegistus didn't expect to buy food from the local farms. He'd put most of the supplies into the advance caches because he'd calculated that even if the Medes were repelled, in the very best possible outcome, only one in ten of the men who marched north could be expected to return. Attolia took advantage of this moment when no one was arguing to end the meeting.

She stood up, and everyone else followed suit. Unfortunately, as they did so, Casartus asked one last question.

"Your Majesty, what of the cannon from the mountain foundry?"

"Stenides is still waiting on the iron to cast the last of them," said Eddis.

A junior naval officer on her left, a younger son of an

insignificant baron, having seen her mildness and mistaken it for meekness, said condescendingly, "The Pent ships are of little use without cannon."

Boagus immediately kicked him so hard in the back of the leg that the man dropped to his knees.

As the naval officer looked up at the queen, much astonished, Eddis said, in the same pleasant voice she'd used all day, "Now you don't have to talk down to me."

The whole room played statues as he looked from Eddis to his own queen, still seated at the end of the table.

Eddisian, Attolian, and Sounisian alike remained frozen, bent over their papers or halfway out of their chairs, unwilling to so much as shift their weight until they saw what would happen next. Was Attolia, in her own palace, to demur as her men were abused? Was Eddis to be insulted by a minor naval officer? Only Sounis and the high king appeared unconcerned. One was yawning, hand over his mouth; the other was trying to brush the wrinkles out of his silk coat as Eddis and Attolia smiled at each other like wolves recognizing members of their own pack. Attolia waved her hand, a hostess offering up her junior naval officer as a canapé.

Eddis graciously offered him a hand to rise, and the young man, who'd had plenty of time to see his life as well as his career pass before his eyes, bowed and apologized to her, to his queen, to the whole room. He even apologized to Boagus.

✦ ✦ ✦

"That was not helpful," Eddis said later to Boagus as they passed through the antechamber to the apartments she and Sounis shared in Attolia's palace, where her attendants and his were waiting to dress them for dinner.

"Didn't hurt." Boagus corrected himself: "Didn't hurt anyone but that preening boatman."

"We are striving here for cooperation, you useless, uncivilized lout."

"Who's uncivilized?" Boagus said, mocking outrage.

"You are. You are an embarrassment to your country and your queen. Get out."

Boagus laughed. "I will await Your Majesty's pleasure—"

"In the hall!"

"In the hall." He bowed and left.

Sounis had already passed through the antechamber and was pulling off his boots, having successfully waved off his attendants. He agreed with Boagus. "That idiot's sheer terror did more to unify the council than anything else in that meeting. They'll follow either of you to the ends of the Earth now."

"They won't follow Gen, though," said Eddis, frustrated either with the greater situation or the fact that her attendant, Selene, was pulling her hair as she removed its pins. She tried to pull one out herself, and the older woman impatiently brushed her hand away. "Helen? What is it?" Sounis asked.

"Cleon," she said with a sigh. "I should have shot him. I should have shot Therespides too, while I had the chance. He's not only called for a trial again, he's telling people that if we follow an untried king into battle, we will lose." Eddis stood and began to pace, rubbing her arms as if chilled and eluding Selene, who followed her back and forth, still trying to remove her earrings and unbind her hair. "And that has put the fear of the gods into them. Crodes, of all people, has asked if orders will come through me for fear that we'll be cursed if they accidentally take any direction from Gen."

Sounis considered the chaos of a battlefield. "That would be . . . unwieldy."

"It would be catastrophic."

"But they're following you. And you're following him . . . surely?"

"This isn't a problem good sense can solve," Eddis told him. "A good thumping would, but it would have to be by one of Gen's brothers. Unfortunately, I sent Temenus to march with Xenophon, and Stenides is overseeing the foundry."

Sounis put his arms around his wife, halting her, giving Selene her opportunity. The attendant started to work in earnest on the queen's hairpins. "I'm sure Gen has a plan," Sounis said as he held Eddis in place.

"If that doesn't frighten you, it should," said Eddis, glowering.

CHAPTER FOUR

The next morning the king appeared to be deep in thought as he sat with his feet hooked around a stool and his head tipped forward to let Ion clip his hair. His attendants were no longer willing to let him go even to the practice field without a nicer pair of pants, an embroidered shirt, an earring in his ear. They would have powdered his hair with gold every day if he had let them. The magus watched with amusement, having come to the bedchamber to see the king prepared for the day.

Ion stepped back to study his work. "I still say it would be handsome if you let it grow long, Your Majesty."

Ion's careless remark caught the king's wayward attention. His head came up. He snapped, "Teach me how to braid it with one hand, Ion, and I will grow it to my knees."

Ion flushed and apologized.

Waving the apology and his attendants away, the king stood to leave. As he went, the magus, immune to protocol, walked along beside him. Once they were in the passageway, he said, "Still wishing for your lost hand back, Gen?"

The king, having taken Ion's comment so badly, was unoffended by the magus's disapproval. He shrugged. "I miss it. I'm sure everyone has something about themselves they'd like to change—to dance better, sing better, be stronger or taller."

Xikos snickered. The king's occasional touchiness about his height was well-known.

The king must have heard, because he said, "In Xikos's case, be smarter than a burnt stick." Everyone else snickered. As he started down the stairs, the king continued, saying, "But if I hadn't lost the hand, I'd be another person entirely by now. Wishing for the hand back would be like wishing the man I already am to be replaced by some stranger. It would be wishing my own self out of existence, and who would want that?"

"Nicely reasoned," said the magus critically. "Now tell me why you're still snapping at your attendants." He halted, midstep. "Oh, Gen," he said ruthlessly. "It's *vanity*."

The king had also stopped. He hung his head. The magus laughed and laughed.

"How unfair to blame poor Ion," he pointed out.

To everyone's amazement, the king conceded. He said to

Ion, standing above him, "Ion, I'm sorry. I was an ass and I apologize."

Startling both the magus and the king, Ion practically leapt down the stairs. He put his arms out to blockade the way.

"Your Majesty, are you ill?" he demanded.

The king stared.

"You have been quiet this morning, and now you are being amenable."

"And I am never quiet or amenable unless at death's door?" said the king. "Thank you for that indictment of my character, Ion. No, I am not ill."

Ion looked doubtful.

"By my god, I swear I am as healthy as a horse," said the king, holding up his hand. He was smiling. Ion still didn't move.

"It's going to be a difficult day, Ion," the king said more seriously. "That's all."

Ion was suspicious but had to let him pass.

The training court where the king practiced in the mornings was empty of Attolians when we arrived. There were only Eddisians waiting for the king.

"You asked earlier who would wish you out of existence . . . ," the magus mused.

"Trust me, magus," muttered the king. "They wouldn't

like a two-handed Eugenides any better."

Hilarion was looking around in alarm. Teleus was not there, nor were any of the men the king usually sparred with. "Your Majesty? Where is the guard? What is going on?"

"My cousins have come for a sparring match," said the king. "Nothing more than that."

"On the contrary," said Cleon, stepping forward and throwing back his shoulders. He announced, "I, Cleon of Eddis, call Eugenides to trial." He sounded like a bad actor in a bad play.

The Eddisians looked embarrassed. The king murmured, "Oh heavens, what a surprise."

"It has been decided!" orated Cleon. "We cannot follow an untried king into battle!"

"I am not your king."

"Nor a high king, Gen," said Aulus, the very large man standing beside Cleon. He didn't sound particularly happy about it, but he was siding with Cleon.

Hilarion knew a disaster when he saw one looming right in front of him. "Your Majesty, no. I don't understand, but no, no." He signaled to Sotis, and Sotis started back toward the archway we'd just come through.

"Sotis, come back," said the king, and Sotis had to return. "Hilarion," said the king, putting his hand on Hilarion's shoulder. "Calm down. It's a few matches. You've seen it before."

Cleon said vehemently, "It is not just a few matches! This is a sacred matter!"

Aulus said, "Cleon, shut up."

The king said, "So, so, so. It's a few sacred matches, Hilarion, don't wet yourself."

It was not just a few matches, sacred or otherwise. The king was being disingenuous. Trying the king was an Eddisian tradition that had grown up in the years when Hamiathes's Gift had been lost. It was an intense and lengthy ritual. There hadn't been a royal trial in Hilarion's lifetime, as Eddis, when she became queen, had not had one, and when Eugenides gave her Hamiathes's Gift, he'd made her queen beyond any mortal right.

Hilarion should have put two and two together. The king had been worrying all morning, and the royal guard was nowhere to be seen. Still, the king had in the past taken on, in a very public display of skill, an entire squad of the Attolian royal guard, and that had ended well—he'd won both the matches and the guards' loyalty, even Teleus's. Remembering that, and deliberately misled, Hilarion stepped back.

An older man came forward. The zigzagging line in blue at the corner of his left eye marked him as one of Hephestia's warrior priests, and for him the king temporarily set aside his bitter humor. "Thalas," he said, greeting him with a respectful bow.

"That she may show us her approval, you come before the

Great Goddess and your subjects to be tried as king," said Thalas. Unlike Cleon, he carried his authority easily.

"As annux," the king said, and the priest nodded.

"As annux, then," said Thalas. "Will you give all you have to be judged by Eddis and by the gods?"

"I will."

"Swear in the name of the Great Goddess."

"In her name and in the name of my god, I swear."

"Do not offend the gods," the priest said to the king. Then he turned to the rest of the Eddisians and asked of them, "Do all of you swear, in the name of the Great Goddess, that you will give all you have to this, that it be a true trial?"

"In Hephestia's name," they all swore together.

"Do not offend the gods," Thalas warned again.

The first match was short and surprisingly fierce. The king won, and Hilarion relaxed a little. The second match was longer. Dionis pulled on Hilarion's sleeve and pointed. Sotis, once the king was engaged, had left the courtyard and was being escorted back in by two Eddisians. Hilarion, realizing he'd been outmaneuvered, shrugged helplessly.

The third match was when it became apparent that the Eddisians weren't following commonly accepted rules of sparring. They were playing their own game, one focused on demonstrating how hard they could hit someone with a weighted wooden stick, and there seemed to be no rules at all. The king lost the third match and hopped around on one leg swearing nonstop while he rubbed the spot where he'd been struck, just above the ankle.

Ion came forward to object to the violent play. "Your Majesty, this is not appropriate," he protested.

"He's right," growled one of the Eddisians. "Show some gods-damned respect, Gen."

"If I offend the gods, Crodes, you can leave them to tell me," the king said, straightening up. He waved Ion away, and another Eddisian stepped forward.

The fifth match was against Cleon, and the king won. "Did you not think I would give as good as I got?" he asked as Cleon, blinking at the stars in his eyes, reeled back to his place in the circle of observers.

Some of the king's opponents were almost genial. The king lost the next match to an opponent who grinned apologetically but still hit him hard enough to make him stagger. He lost the next one to another man less interested in smashing the king with a stick and more interested in testing his science. That match lasted some time. After winning it, the Eddisian bowed to the king with reluctant respect and the king, breathing hard, bowed graciously back.

One man, even larger than Aulus, with a leer of matching proportions, lunged forward after the salute so quickly that the king, even if he had deflected the sword strike, would have been flattened. Instead of sidestepping, the king dropped to all fours, tripping the giant, who stumbled over him. When the Eddisian whirled, sword raised to strike, the king sat with his knees pulled up, a mocking expression on his face. He'd clipped the giant in the knee as he passed. The match was over.

The Attolians gave a thin cheer. The giant said something in an incomprehensible accent. The king answered back with something insulting and equally incomprehensible. The giant lunged forward again, this time stopped by the priest.

"You had your chance," said Thalas.

The giant retreated to the back of the crowd, glowering, but none of his countrymen seemed to sympathize.

"Try something new every once in a while," I heard one of them say.

The king fought twelve matches against young men, those who had a right to test the man they would follow for the rest of their lives. Some now say he won all the matches. That's an exaggeration for the poets, and the kind of thing that he particularly disliked. He earned the approval, however grudging, of his peers.

The king's attendants and his guards, who had been standing around anxiously, hands hovering over their weapons, breathed a sigh of relief, all but Dionis. He'd been talking to one of the Eddisians and was moving through the crowd toward Hilarion. As Dionis passed Thalas, the priest reached out and took his arm, saying nothing, just holding him lightly at the elbow. Too respectful to throw him off, Dionis was stopped in his tracks.

There was a final match—against a seasoned warrior who represented the best of the old men, those with the years of experience to judge a new king. When the circle of Eddisians opened to admit Eddis's minister of war, the king, sweating and tired, with bruises rising all over his body, said, "I thought it would be Ornon."

"You would make short work of Ornon," said his father.

"Yes, that's what I thought, too."

Ornon, who was standing right there in the crowd, glared.

Eugenides stepped back into a fighting stance as his father raised his sword. "There won't be accusations of favoritism, will there?" he asked.

"No," promised his father.

It was an unfair match from the beginning. It was meant to be, with the king already weary and the minister fresh. The wooden swords knocked against each other, making a noise like a house being built, or one being knocked down. The sound redoubled suddenly and the king, tired as he was, scored a hit and stepped back. It was a hard hit, and the minister grunted and tapped his chest in respect.

Hilarion thought the match was over. Looking around in relief, he realized that the Eddisians had slowly been shifting position. They were not just in a circle around the match;

they were in a circle around the Attolians.

Then the king and his father crossed swords again, and Hilarion's attention returned to the match. The next hit went against the king and he retreated, circling to gain time to recover. The minister continued to press him and landed two more blows, though glancing ones, on the king's upper arm and his knee. The second blow made the king hop, but he shook off the limp and attacked again. Unlike the contests with the younger men, this was not a trial to win. It was a trial to endure.

Hilarion had had enough. As he took a step forward, the Eddisians struck. Even the guards, with their hands on their swords, had no chance. As the king and his father battled on, there was a brief all-out brawl. The Attolians went down, but they went down fighting, with two or even three Eddisians on top of them. Even I, as I rushed for my king, ready to do my feeble best for him, was scooped up by a man I hadn't realized was behind me. Aulus, holding me with my feet kicking in the air, rumbled in my ear, "Not a contest for you, little one."

I bit him so hard I tasted his blood in my mouth. With a shout, he let go of me. Afraid of falling to the ground, I could not let go of him. I held on to the cloth of his tunic with my good hand and bit down harder. Aulus bellowed like the bull he was. By then my feet had found the ground, and I stumbled away. The Eddisians nearby were laughing, and I hated them as I'd hated no one since Emtis.

Aulus could have knocked me down with ease, could have ignored me, as I was no threat to anyone. Instead, he held up both his hands, blood on his hairy forearm, and said, "Peace. Peace, warrior."

As he approached, I blew spit at him, and he stepped back again.

"My word as prince that I will lay no war on you, if you give yours to be still until this contest is done."

"Aulus, he can't give his word."

"Shut up, Boagus," said Aulus. "Do I have your word of peace?" he asked me.

The other Attolians and Perminder, the lone Sounisian, who had also given his all and had a cut above his eye and blood streaming down his face to show for it, were one by one giving their words and climbing back to their feet. The Eddisians were wiping away their own blood and rubbing their bruises. Only the guards were still pinned to the ground—the Eddisians not adding insult to injury by asking for their surrender. Reluctantly I nodded, and Aulus, very warily, reached out to shake my hand.

The king's face was swelling and one eye was almost closed. His nose and mouth were bleeding. He was staggering backward when he suddenly dropped to one knee. The minister stepped in with a blow, but the king, who'd been faking, twisted away. He stabbed the minister in the knee and swept the other leg out from under him before he could retreat. His father fell heavily and the king lashed out, kicking him so hard in the head that he lay blinking at the sky for a moment while the king staggered away.

He had won, I thought, surely. Aulus, towering over me, slowly shook his head.

"You know your limits only when you reach them," he said.

The minister got up and then they went on fighting. The king fought until he couldn't stand. When he fell, he still fought, and the minister went on beating him until the king couldn't move. Each time the minister stepped away, the king raised his sword, strokes so feeble they were harmless, but blows nonetheless. Finally the minister stepped onto the king's hand and bore down on it with all his weight. When he lifted his foot, the sword dropped from the king's hand. Eyes closed, the king still reached for it.

"Enough, Gen," his father said, bending over him.

The king swung his other arm, the one with the hook, and almost caught the minister in the face.

Sighing, the minister walked around to the other side of him and kicked him hard in the bicep.

"Enough," he said again.

The king shook his head, but that must have been the last of his strength. He tried to get up, but only made it onto his side. He pushed with his hand, but couldn't lift himself. His feet scrabbled against the ground. He couldn't get any purchase. Sobbing, I took a step forward, and Aulus gently wrapped me in his arms, pulling me back against his chest.

The minister of war trudged away, across the court to a bench against the wall, where he painfully took a seat.

The king lay very still.

I threw up.

Aulus said, "Oh for crying out loud," but didn't let go.

Teleus arrived.

Sotis hadn't made it beyond the archway that led out of the training ground. Eddisians at its entrance had turned away anyone too interested in what was going on that morning. That didn't mean that news wasn't getting out. Some of the terraces of the palace overlooked the guards' barracks below, and any soldier knows the sound of a brawl from a mile away. Word had finally reached Teleus, who'd come with men armed to the teeth and not with wooden swords.

He was restrained by the magus of Sounis, who'd been awaiting the captain's inevitable arrival. Whatever the magus said, it kept Teleus standing with his hands balled into fists while we all watched the king, the sound of the hawkers at the morning market floating over the palace wall, the sparrows and pigeons who had been driven away one by one returning to peck at the dirt.

The king moved; he reached out, feeling for his sword. Then he lay still again, blinking up at the sky. A little later, he rolled onto his side and levered himself up on one arm.

The arm still wouldn't hold him, and he lay back down.

The minister of war nodded to Crodes, who stepped soberly out to the king and squatted down to ask him if he wanted help.

We couldn't hear the king reply, but Crodes raised both hands and backed away as if from a hot fire. Returning to the minister, Crodes shrugged. "He said, 'No, thank you.'" Only the Eddisians laughed.

After what felt like a very long time, the king managed to get to his knees and then, using his wooden sword as a crutch, made it to his feet. The sword trailed on the ground behind him as he crossed the court one wobbling step at a time. His face was all blood and dirt caked together, and he could hardly see. The Eddisians lightly touched his shoulder and aimed him toward the minister of war.

I don't know what I expected, but it was not that the king would sink onto the bench and his father would enfold him in his arms, that the king would lay his head on his father's shoulder with a sigh and his father would rub his back as if he were a tiny baby.

The surly Eddisians around us all smiled like fond parents. I thought Teleus, who'd come into the ground with half the royal guard behind him, was going to tear someone's head off. No one spoke, not even Teleus. He just stared, veins showing in his forehead.

"Ready?" the minister asked the king.

"Not yet," he said, his voice muffled by his father's shoulder. "I'm trying to get through this asinine business without being sick."

Everyone looked at Aulus, and at me, and then back at the king.

At last the minister stood and lifted the king easily in his arms. He carried him back up to the palace, the Eddisians and the Attolians following, with Teleus and his guard coming behind. He met the queen on the stairs up to the higher terraces. She said nothing as he passed carrying her all-but-unconscious husband, but the look she gave the Eddisian minister of war would have melted brass, let alone lead.

In the king's antechamber, the attendants pressed forward, suddenly aggressive, like dogs on their own ground. The minister of war continued to ignore them, carrying the king all the way to his bed, where he finally laid him down.

"Your wife," he said to the king.

"Terrifying, isn't she?" the king said with his eyes closed.

The minister grunted.

"You should have left it to Ornon," the king murmured.

"You should have quit sooner," his father grumbled.

With obvious effort, the king rolled his head toward his father and blinked through one swollen eye. "Tell Thalas that," he suggested.

"How will you fight like this?" his father asked.

"I'm not allowed to fight," the king said, sounding very smug for a man with lips almost too swollen to move.

The minister grunted again. "Be sure to tell me how Thalas's approval feels when you climb on that fancy horse."

There was a silence.

"O Great Goddess, aid me," the king whispered. "I forgot about the horse."

"You're a damn fool," said his father, indulgently.

When the Eddisian queen arrived an hour or two later, Hilarion stepped over as if to block the doorway. She only smiled in amusement and went around him. "Excuse us, Hilarion," she said, dismissing him.

Hilarion tried to drag me out with him as he left, but I dug in my heels. He glanced at the king lying on the bed, recovering from the ministrations of Galen and Petrus, and threw me a murderous look, but released me. In his defense, he was not a weak-willed man, merely out of his depth.

Eddis sat on the side of the bed, and the king opened his eyes.

"Attolia is fit to be tied," she said, "or I'd leave you to your rest. She has accused us of distracting her guard from their duty."

"I did that," said the king. "I told Teleus to escort Sophos and everyone else I could think of out to the Thegmis to tour the fortifications there. He had to take half the guard."

"I assured her of that," said Eddis dryly. "Somehow she is unconvinced by my word alone." Looking down, she interlaced her fingers and unwove them again, twisting them together and pulling them apart. Abruptly, she said, "You were the one paying Therespides."

The king weighed the likely success of a lie and said, "I sent the money through Relius."

Eddis lifted her hands to cover her face. The king and I both averted our eyes, neither of us able to offer her the privacy she deserved.

When she lowered her hands, she had regained her composure, mostly. Her voice was only slightly ragged. "Have you considered, Gen, even once, that you might achieve your goals with the minimum damage to yourself and without the maximum amount of distress to those around you?" She said, "You were afraid too many of them might prefer a king, even you, to a queen who was Eddis."

"My father could stop any rebellion, but not the gradual diminishment of your authority. They'd start by those calling you Eddia and then Sounia, and if the Medes didn't come they would 'forget' you ever were Eddis. Cleon's agitating rallied them to support you as their sovereign."

"So I could rule Eddis as Irene rules Attolia and Sophos rules Sounis. But we knew the Medes would come, Gen," she said angrily. "And after you had stoked their resentment and their superstitions, the only way to bring the Eddisians around was a trial, and you told no one. You sent your guard away while it happened."

"It was better than having an Attolian-against-Eddisian riot in that courtyard," said the king, sounding just as fed up. "The magus had enough trouble stopping Teleus from starting an all-out war once the trial was over."

"You didn't warn the magus, either."

"He did fine."

"And you did not warn your queen."

"She would have led the riot."

Eddis conceded that this was probably true. She looked over his bandages and the lumps of cloth-wrapped ice packed against his bruises. "Galen?" she guessed.

"He has emptied the ice cellar. He says there is nothing that can't be fixed with enough ice."

Eddis was reluctantly amused. "What happens now between your father and your queen?"

"Well, he already hates her because she cut off my hand. Now the feeling is mutual."

"So, so, you intend to separate them for the entirety of your reign?"

The king shifted uncomfortably, looking for a softer spot on his mattress, before he confessed. "I've arranged for them to both be in the garden at the same time, entirely alone. We'll see which one leaves alive."

"You are joking."

"Only about one of them leaving alive. They might kill each other."

"Gen . . ."

"Helen, you know how it will go. They will agree, like people always do, that it's all my fault." He shifted painfully again. Not finding a better spot, he gave up with a sigh. "They are adults. They know what is at stake. They will sit next to each other on a bench without speaking until the palace bells ring the hour, and when they get up the whole matter will be finished. They will embark on a long relationship of mutual respect and admiration and lecturing me."

Eddis considered.

"I am right. I am always right. It's a curse," said the king.

Eddis nodded. This time she didn't lift her hands to cover her fractured composure, and she didn't wipe away her tears. The king reached for her, rolling painfully up on his side to take her hand.

"I'm sorry," he said softly. "If there was another way than this, I couldn't find it."

She brushed off the apology. "I've always known I was the last Eddis," she said.

She left soon after, and the king rolled back down to lie staring at the canopy over his head.

CHAPTER FIVE

To avoid waking the king if he still slept, Ion opened the
door to the bedchamber without knocking. There was no
sign of movement from the bed, so he signaled to Lamion
and Dionis to very quietly bring in the king's breakfast.
Dionis opened the cross-legged stand. As Lamion bent to
set the tray on top of it, the dish holding honeycomb slid
forward just enough to knock the wooden bowl next to it.

Deep beneath the covers, the king's eyes opened. He'd
been dreaming and now he was awake. Something was
wrong, but he couldn't place it at first. He heard the attendants, heard the sound of the tray carrying his breakfast
settling onto its stand, heard Ion, just as always, shush-
ing Lamion. None of this was unusual, and yet something
was out of the ordinary. He didn't know what it was. He
stretched his arms and legs very cautiously. He felt fine.

He felt fine.

The attendants heard the muffled sound of the king's command. "Out!"

Ion was backing away from the bed. Dionis and Lamion abandoned the breakfast tray as the king's voice got louder and louder. "Out! Out! OUT!" he shouted.

Ion slammed the door behind him and the king sat bolt upright in bed.

There I stood, on the wrong side of the door, staring. I could feel my scalp prickling and thought my hair might have been on end as well. Every cut, every bruise, every stitch that Petrus and Galen had fought to sew into the king's face the day before was gone.

"I am going to be sick," he announced. He threw off the bed linen and stumbled over to the closed stool. When he was done, he put the velvet-covered lid down and sat on it.

"I said 'Out,' didn't I?" he asked me when he'd gotten his breath back.

I shrugged helplessly.

"I know, I know. Ion would have crushed you with the door." He looked around the room. "Well," he asked me at last, "what do you think we should do now?"

I had no idea.

Still sitting on the closed stool, he ran his fingers over the stump on his right arm, and then hesitantly touched the scar on his face as if to confirm it was still there. He looked around the room as if there were an explanation hidden in a corner or behind his writing desk.

In the end, he wrote out several messages and sent me to deliver them. I slipped through the door and he locked it behind me.

Eddis and Sounis stood and stared. Attolia gently touched his face and kissed him.

"Ask the Oracle," said Eddis. "Let her guide you."

So they sent Philologos up to the temple with a message, and the high priestess came down from the heights in her chair carried by its ceremonial bearers. Arriving in the waiting room, the Oracle rolled past the disconcerted attendants and guards without taking any notice of them and stood in front of the king, not in the least overawed by his transformation. "An inconvenient miracle, Your Majesty?" There was a warning in her words, not to take the gifts of the Great Goddess lightly.

Careful not to offend, the king asked, "Will people think the trial was a sham?"

The high priestess laughed. She was a big woman, and her laugh was a rumbling, infectious sound. "You should know, my king, when the gods work miracles, no one doubts them."

It was true. Those who saw the king in the next few days stared in amazement, never in disbelief. When the high priestess of Hephestia announced that the king had been healed by the Great Goddess, a day's holiday was declared to celebrate the miracle. Extra wine was distributed among the armies. Attolia ordered vast casks sent out on carts to be shared by the people in the city. These days, it may be commonly accepted that the trial was a necessary artifice, but no one doubted this sign of the Goddess's approval at the time.

Relius had again left me the key to his study, and the king had warned Orutus not to add another lock to the door. Although my grandfather who was Erondites had failed in his latest grab at power, I preferred to be in the privacy of Relius's study when I wrote in my journals. I went there whenever I could. Describing the king's trial and its aftereffects, I concentrated on making each letter as perfectly as possible.

After the trial, the high king's authority was supreme. Suddenly the Eddisians could not be more respectful, and the Sounisians and even the Attolians followed suit. That the king looked no more martial than he had before, that he still did not sit up straight, that he still had no experience as a military leader made no difference. Sounis, Eddis, and Attolia watched more or less impassively as the court hung on his every word. Increasingly burdened by the adoration, he reminded me of a caryatid, holding up expectations that were piling higher and higher every day.

Carefully I wrote *The king told Casartus as he is not allowed into battle, his role is decorative only,* imagining my tutor reading over my shoulder. When Teleus laid his hand there, I nearly jumped out of my skin. With a long streak of ink across my page, I stared at him, half frightened and half angry.

"He said to remind you not to lose yourself in your thoughts," the captain told me.

Having successfully scared me out of my wits, Teleus might have left. Embarrassed at having forgotten Relius's lesson and having been caught out, I wished he would. Instead, Teleus put a jug of wine on the little side table and settled in his usual chair. He filled a cup and took a sip and watched me thoughtfully over the rim of it.

"You love the king," he said.

Warily, I agreed. I knew he did not.

"You love your brother."

Startled, I wondered why he asked, and considered the question carefully before I answered. I realized I would not have been so grieved by Juridius's betrayal if I had not still loved him in spite of the pain he'd already caused. Again, I nodded.

"I'm sure your mother loves her brothers as well," the captain said. "Someday you may not only love, but be in love. The object of your affections may be worthy of your love or not. May return your love . . . or not. Remember it does not make you a traitor if you love one. Nor does loving a fool mean you must be one. We do not all have to be Legarus."

I missed Relius even more than I had thought I would; without him, I could share my mind with no one. I wondered to whom Teleus could speak freely, reminded of the many hours he and Relius spent together. Glimpsing something in the adult world that I would not fully understand for many years, I slipped down off the stool and limped over to the bookshelf. Teleus watched me as I pointed at the empty space between two books, the only clean spot on the shelf, where the dust had not yet had time to settle.

"He took the poems with him?" Teleus asked. I nodded. He snorted. "Idiot."

I nodded and the captain laughed. He finished the wine in his cup, then he thumped me relatively gently on the back and left without another word.

Phresine stepped around the room lighting the lamps. Selene, who was the seniormost of the attendants who'd come down from the mountains with Eddis, was directing the setting out of the dishes. There were no more formal dinners. In the evening, the kings and queens met in Attolia's apartments for a small meal and private discussion. During the day, food came in when it was ready and was eaten wherever it was most convenient. Those in the kitchens were run off their feet, feeding the palace in shifts at bare tables on wooden dishes. The guards' mess hall had been taken over by the officers in the three armies. The guards ate outside or, if they had money, went into the town to spend it at taverns.

Earlier in the evening, Fordad had asked the king's permission to accompany the army on its march north and join in the fight against the Medes. When the king accepted, the Braeling had dropped to one knee in respect and made a flowery speech about the replacement of the three crowned heads with the one, the divinely appointed high king. The king had been visibly embarrassed. Attolia, Eddis, and Sounis had been stone-faced. None of them wished to dispute the high king's sovereignty, but the Braeling's speech made all of them uncomfortable, and if not for their very high regard for each other, it might have stirred ill will.

In the small dining room, the four of them picked at their food, almost too tired to eat. The king tried to look at the bright side. "I could use my newfound authority to insist on going into battle," he suggested.

Three heads turned, three sets of eyes locked on him, three frowns with varying indications of warning, exasperation, and irritation.

"Marvelous," said Attolia waspishly. "You run the campaign and I'll stay home."

Sounis reproved him more gently. "Gen, you know it serves no purpose for you to risk yourself on the battlefield."

Trying to ease the tensions in the room, he teased, "Are you worried you'll be taken for a wineglass warrior. Is that it?"

"That is it, Sophos; you have hit on my greatest fear," said the king. "Someone who named himself Bunny is going to outshine me on the battlefield."

"If I get too popular," Sounis assured him, "you can always poison me later." No sooner had the words come out of his mouth than he winced at his thoughtlessness. He turned to Attolia, an apology on his lips.

Already regretting her own harsh words, Attolia leaned toward the king and said in a carrying whisper, "I can show you how."

After a moment's hesitation, the others burst out laughing. Attolia bit back a smile.

It was Cleon the Eddisian who brought up the issue of the king's tattoos. Having achieved his dream, he tried to persuade the king that he should have the appropriate tattoos to commemorate the trial.

"It will please the Eddisians, Your Majesty," Cleon insisted.

"Cleon, if I have to survive anything else to please the Eddisians, I am going to throw the entire population into the sacred fire."

Cleon, never one to give up on a bad idea, approached the queen of Eddis privately.

"He has passed his trial," he insisted. "Those who fear that he has become too Attolian will see how he respects our traditions. Is it wrong to reassure them that they have an Eddisian king?"

"Cleon, he is not king of Eddis. I am Eddis." She said it even as she doubted it was still true. "Do you imagine that there is another man born in Eddis whom I would accept as high king?"

She named a few cousins and the king's brothers, both of whom were older than he was. "Should I accept Temenus or Stenides as king?" Even Cleon could see her point. She spoke slowly, trying to make him understand. "No tattooed member of my court over whom I have ruled could ever be high king over me. No Attolian could be high king over Irene, no Sounisian over Sophos."

"Still, now that he has actually earned his tattoos—"

"Earned his tattoos, Cleon?" Eddis had lost all patience. "He killed his man before he left the boys' house!"

Cleon opened his mouth and then stopped to think, possibly for the first time in his life. He wasn't sure he wanted to know who Gen had killed. "Lader?" he asked, suddenly hesitant.

"Lader," Eddis confirmed.

"He went hunting and never came back. We thought a lion got him, or a jealous husband," said Cleon.

Eddis had always known what precipitated the horrendous

shouting match between Gen and his father when the minister of war had tried to force his enrollment as a soldier. She knew why he hated the business of killing so much.

"But Lader was twice his age," Cleon pointed out. "Gen wasn't even the Thief then."

"He was sacred to his god and we all knew it, Cleon. Bumps and bruises were one thing. Lader deliberately breaking bones was another."

Cleon remembered his own part in that ugly episode and had the grace to be ashamed. "Why am I not dead, too?"

"Because I got down on my knees to the old Thief and begged for your life. You should stop making me regret it."

Cleon sat, taking it in. "It was an accident," he said hoarsely. "He wouldn't let go of the earrings. I didn't mean to hurt him so badly."

"I know," said Eddis, more gently. "I have always known that."

"You didn't beg for Lader."

"No," said Eddis sadly. "If I'd known the old man would make Gen do the killing himself, I would have begged to spare him that. But no, Cleon, I did not beg for Lader."

"So, so, so," said Cleon at last. "No tattoos."

Eddis snorted. "No, no tattoos."

Trokides, general of Sounis's armies, was posturing at the council meeting when he said, "We cannot wait any longer for the guns from Eddis. Even if they arrived today, we cannot afford to move at the slower speed of artillery."

Trenches were already being dug and the defensive walls reinforced in the narrowest part of the Leonyla Pass, but the longer the Peninsular army had to settle in, the better its chances of holding the Medes until the allied ships arrived at Stinos with the Gant and the Brael reinforcements. The longer they waited, the higher the risk that the Medes would beat them to the pass.

Trokides's arguments were sound, but he had just criticized what he called inefficiency in the Attolian army's "rolling bureaucracy," and the Attolians were loath to agree with him.

Piloxides, general of Attolia's armies, asserted, "We can certainly march the guns at any speed the Sounisians set."

One of the junior officers pointed out that the Eddisians marching from their mountains would reach the Leonyla first. "Can they not hold until we arrive?"

"The Eddisians are not fodder to be fed to the Medes so the lowlanders may show up at their leisure," one of the Eddisians said bitterly.

"Your Majesties," said Pegistus, speaking up before another argument could start. "We can march at speed, we've shown it to be true, even with the artillery." He began to lay out the pages with his calculations on the table and walked us through them.

Pegistus knew there was a measurable decrease in speed

with each additional man on the march and each additional gun. He knew the ground it covered affected the army's speed as well. He had a measure for the elevation and quality of the roads. An abundance, a wealth of numbers. He calculated the speed of men and wagons and multiplied it out in his equations, all of his solutions reinforcing his argument.

My head spun. I felt ill.

Attolia said, "You're using the speed of a grain wagon for the guns, Pegistus. The guns will not move as easily through the fords as a wagon would."

"I do not think the variance will be significant, Your Majesty."

Someone must have turned the question, as they turned every question now, back to the king. I saw him shrug and heard him say, "I've only worked with wooden ones." He was waiting for someone else to speak up, but no one did. Sick of Trokides's arrogance, they wanted to believe whatever Pegistus promised.

Under the table, the king poked Sounis in the thigh with his hook. Sounis moved his leg away, and the king dug the point of the hook in harder.

Sounis passed the problem on. "What do you think?" he asked the magus.

The magus did not reward his faith. "I would agree that artillery would be more difficult to transport. . . ." He was guessing like a student caught out by his tutor.

The king turned to his father. "Could you move an army of this size that quickly?" he asked bluntly.

The minister of war would not be baited into nationalistic boasting. He said he was quite certain how long it would take to move a smaller group of soldiers but admitted he was out of his depth when it came to moving this many men with artillery. "I must defer to Pegistus to know his own army's best speed," he said.

As the others around the table began to nod their heads, Eugenides finally, reluctantly, said, "Pegistus, your equations are beautiful, but your calculations, as I'm sure my brother Sounis is too polite to point out, are wrong."

I sighed with relief.

"Multiply them out again and you'll see the Medes would be in Stinos, never mind the Leonyla, by the time we arrived."

Once the king had pointed it out, the error was obvious. The magus in particular looked very embarrassed. Pegistus hemmed and hawed and apologized. "I must check my notes, Your Majesty."

"By all means," said the king. "But this meeting is over. We march on Trokides's direction."

As the meeting adjourned, the king asked Orutus to remain.

The queen of Attolia raised an eyebrow.

"I just wanted to ask the secretary of the archives if he

thought Pegistus's mistake was an understandable error or a deliberate attempt to slow our army."

"I will look into it, Your Majesty," Orutus promised.

Attolia and the king sat quietly together after he had excused himself.

"I miss Relius," said Attolia.

"As do I," said the king with a sigh.

While they were eating dinner that evening Sophos teased the king. "You made that pretty speech at the beginning of the meeting," he said, "telling the council to look to wiser heads than yours for decisions."

"What was I supposed to do?" wailed the king. "Let him go on thinking that you can multiply a number by eight and get a number smaller than the one you started with? You were no help."

"Well, we can't all have the insight . . . nay, the wisdom, of the high k—"

The king pitched a grape at him, and Sounis batted it away.

It was Xikos, of all people, who gave the king an opportunity to shrug off a little of the weight of his responsibilities. The king and his attendants were trudging toward his apartments. Trokides had set the date of departure for the next day, and the final attempts to organize the march had run late into the night. Everyone was exhausted and also keyed tight as harp strings.

"Your Majesty," said Xikos as we walked back through the dark where the lamps were few and far between.

"What is it, Xikos?" asked the king.

"Is it true that your cousins used to chase you through the palace of Eddis?"

The king slowed, eyeing Xikos warily.

"That they were never able to catch you?"

"We caught him sometimes," one of the larger Eddisians protested. Aulus, the one I'd thrown up on. "Unlike the Attolians, who never did."

None of the Attolians dared to say that the Attolians had indeed caught him.

"Without cheating," Aulus finished.

"Where are you going with this, Xikos?" the king asked outright.

"Two cities says we could catch you," said Xikos. He showed the gold coins resting in his palm. The other attendants stared in confusion. Ignoring them, Xikos said to the Eddisians, "If each of you will put up that much, each of us will."

"What?" cried the rest of the attendants immediately, no part of this plan.

"Deal!" the Eddisians shouted as fast.

None of them were as quick as the king, who had already slammed Xikos against the wall, pinning him in place.

"Xikos." His soft voice curled around Xikos like the hook around the attendant's neck. "Since when do you have two cities to rub together?"

Xikos, eyes white all the way around, stared over the king's shoulder.

"Aulus?" prompted the king, not taking his eyes off Xikos's face.

Aulus blew out his breath in disappointment. "Boagus and I gave him the money," he admitted.

Xikos sagged against the wall in relief.

"Why, Aulus?" the king asked.

Aulus looked at his slightly smaller partner and then back at the king.

"Come on, Gen," Boagus said. "Be a sport."

"We march tomorrow and you want to fleece my poor naive Attolians?" said the king.

While Aulus and Boagus insisted it was an entirely straightforward bet, the Attolians bridled at being labeled naive, though, in retrospect, it was clear they only partially understood the role of betting in the Eddisian court and the nature of their games.

"They don't have to bet," Aulus pointed out.

The king considered his people's traditions. The temptation was evidently too much.

"They do now," he said, "and the best is for ten barrels of the best aposta—for the guards whose competence has been mocked." To his attendants he said, "If you catch me, my fine cousins will pay for the liquor. If you do not, then you will pay for it. Is that clear? Good. Xikos, give Aulus back his money and we'll set some ground rules."

Hilarion and Ion were still protesting, Xikos was reluctantly passing over the two cities, and suddenly the king was gone. He went so fast the Attolians were left flat-footed and the Eddisians all laughing. "There are no rules!" they shouted at the Attolians. "Go! Go!"

The attendants and all the guards raced after the king, the attendants shouting for him to stop, the guards in a panic that the man they were supposed to protect was getting farther and farther away with every step. By then the king had reached the nearby light well and leapt onto its stone railing. He jumped into the open space, landing on the chandelier in its center. The wheel of iron tilted under his weight, and candles dropped down from their sockets into the rainwater cache below.

The king checked to be sure he was pursued, then used his hook to slice a rope. As one side of the chandelier dropped, he swung by his hand, building the momentum to carry him to the side of the light well, where he dropped to the balcony on the floor below. The Attolians pounding after him had to go around the edges of the well to the staircase, and by the time they started down it, the king was already going up a different one.

He kept always just ahead of his pursuers, leading them on, letting them think that with only a little bit more effort they might catch him. The guards had no choice but to stay as close as they could. The attendants, even Hilarion and Ion, had been drawn in by the thrill of the chase. The Eddisians, mostly just looking on, shouted advice. People who'd been quietly preparing to sleep got back into their clothes and left their apartments to see what the noise was about.

Not everyone was running after the king; the rest of us moved more slowly in his wake. At one point, the tail of his pursuers grew so long that he came up on it from behind, tapped the last person in the line on the shoulder, and then sped away. After that, it was less a line of pursuers and more of a mob as the Attolians moved in every direction, hoping to intercept the king.

A group of attendants saw their prey coming down a passage toward them and rushed forward. The Eddisians behind them shouted a warning as the king aimed toward a side table. Remembering how the king had pursued the Pent ambassador, the Attolians blocked the space above the table—only to grab at empty air while he slid by underneath it.

The king came up on the far side and was away again, so confident of his lead he turned and danced a few steps backward. Not content with fooling them once, he did it again. The second time, as they reached under the table, he slid on his belly across the top of it. The third time down that particular hallway, he avoided the pack of attendants blocking his path by dodging into the open door of Baron Laimonides's apartment and running through the baron's bedchamber and out the other side.

The guards watched in distress as he jumped onto a marble banister and, standing upright, slid down it. Ejected at the bottom of the slide, he tucked and rolled and came up again. Arms out, he bowed at the waist and ran away while his followers staggered to a halt, puffing and blowing.

"He'll kill himself," said Lamion.

"And the queen will kill us," said a guard.

"Don't worry," said Boagus, who wasn't chasing the king, just staying close enough behind him to enjoy the show. "He was knee-high the first time he did that on the ceremonial stairs in Eddis, in front of the whole court gathered for dinner."

"The minister beat him with a belt," chortled Cleon. "Told him to practice sword skills instead of circus tricks."

Boagus said, "The next night he slid down holding a three-foot sword he got from the armory."

"And his father beat him for that, too."

"My god," said Philologos.

"No," said Boagus. "*His* god."

"Boagus!" We heard the king from far ahead.

"What?"

"Catch me or you pay half!"

The Eddisians shouted with approval and joined in the chase. One of them declared that he would show the Attolians how it was done and reached for his knife, shouting, "First you wing him!"

Aulus knocked his hand away. "You don't wing the king, you idiot." The man cackled with embarrassment, as if only then remembering it was not the Thief he was chasing.

The halls were filling with people, helping or hindering or just watching. The king invited Sounis into the chase, but he declined on the grounds that he was much too slow. He did say he'd reward any Sounisian who caught the king with his own barrel of aposta and shouted encouragement at Perminder, running past with the king's other attendants.

Eddis and Attolia had both left their apartments and were watching from a balcony of one of the interior courts, where they could get the best sense of the state of the chase.

"They will not actually kill him," Eddis told her as several of her cousins rushed past.

"Not on purpose," said Attolia dryly.

"It will be over soon," said Eddis. "Now that he has woken the entire palace."

On the floor above them, the shouts of the pursuers were growing louder. The king erupted into the air over their heads, arms and legs windmilling as he reached for the outermost ring of the chandelier. It was a longer jump than the previous one, across an open court much larger than a light well, and he didn't make it. Instead of landing on the chandelier, he barely caught the edge, swinging below it, his legs kicking, lighted candles raining down on all sides.

The king held on a moment more. Then, like the candles, he fell.

Eddis seized Attolia by the hand.

There was the sound of a tremendous splash. The Eddisians, the Attolians, the Sounisians crowded to the railings to look down at the king in the cistern below. It held all the water drained from the roofs of that wing of the palace and was so deep the king had to paddle to keep his head above water.

He flicked the hair from his eyes, the drops of water glinting like gold in the light of the remaining candles. He made his way to the side of the tank, where there were stairs leading out of the cistern. He rose from the water like Atimonia leaving her bath, and after a formal salute to the queens, he slipped into a dark passageway and was gone.

As quiet slowly returned to the palace, Attolia found the king in her bedroom peeling off his wet clothes.

"Unkingly," she said.

"My god, I hope so," said the king.

CHAPTER SIX

Only a few hours later, the soldiers began mustering on the Fields of War. The kings and queens of Eddis, Sounis, and Attolia would ride out of the palace, past the cheering crowds, to lead the largest army seen in their lifetimes. In his royal bedchamber, the king of Attolia, annux of Attolia, Sounis, and Eddis, stood staring at his clothes. With no time to devote to fashion, he'd left the creation of his parade suit to his attendants. They were long past the days of spoiling his coats with ink stains and bringing him mismatched stockings.

"Thank you, Ion," said the king. "It's a credit to your work and the tailor's."

Ion was fussing over the jacket, straightening the wedges of ribbons that were to drape from each shoulder.

The king was only just dressed when the queen arrived. She saw the full glory of the parade suit and waved the attendants still working on his buttons out of the room. After she'd gently closed the door behind them, she drew herself to her full height and swept down in a rare full courtesy to her king.

"Stop," the king moaned quietly.

Attolia rose, saying, "So elegant, so colorful, so—"

"Don't—"

"Kingly."

I knew, because I'd been there when Hilarion and Ion had worked with the tailor, that they had been determined to make a suit that would be admired by all who saw it as the king rode out of the city. I thought it was splendid.

"I look like a pitneen," said the king.

He did. The colors of the suit were exactly those of the little birds that flocked in the winterberry bushes in the early spring, gorging on the fruit as it fermented. At the Villa Suterpe, I'd found them blinking and incapacitated on the paths. I should have seen the similarity earlier.

"A very regal pitneen," said Attolia. Her smile fading, she asked, "Was this deliberate?" I caught my breath. I liked Hilarion and Ion both.

"Worse," said the king. "It is an unsolicited gesture of the deepest, sincerest support, and it's far too late to make any changes."

The queen's expression didn't alter, but her shoulders quivered.

"For gods' sakes, throw a cup of wine on me," begged the king.

Attolia shook her head. "They are right," she assured him. "It is just the thing that will impress the city as you ride out."

"They want a pitneen for a king?"

"They want a spectacle. And you are . . ." Her voice trailed off. She was pointing to the cloth in the king's hand, hanging like an empty sack. "What is that?"

"It's the hat," said the king in despair.

"Ohhh," she breathed as she pulled it from his hand. It was a long, shapeless velvet sack, lightly padded around the opening to stiffen it above his brow. She put it on his head, then carefully draped it down his back, giving him exactly the profile of a bird. She had to sit down.

The king swept the headgear off. "Once we are on the road, I expect you to do your duty with the wine cup," he said before he yanked the door open and stalked out. The queen composed herself and followed.

Eddis stared openmouthed.

"Not a word," warned the king.

Her eyes sparkled. She might have been a banker seeing every loan repaid at once, and she too lowered herself in a courtesy to the king. Perhaps glimpsing the sudden uncertainty in Hilarion's face, as she rose she assured the king that not even her attendants could have done better. Hilarion relaxed.

Eddis wore a perfectly ordinary Eddisian uniform, the only concession to her status a plain silver circlet on her head. Sounis, also in uniform, was standing by with his lips so tightly pressed together they were invisible.

Everyone was very subdued as they listened to the directions, repeated three times by the anxious palace official in charge, how the royal party would exit from the palace and parade through the city. Attolia and the king were to lead the way from the room. Sounis and Eddis would follow. The attendants of all four of them lined up in order of precedence, and in the rigor and the silence of the ceremonial moment was the song of the little bird that announces itself even as it hides, calling "look-at-me, look-at-me, look-at-me" from the bushes.

The high king didn't turn a hair. The queen of Eddis poked her husband. Sounis looked back with wounded innocence. It was the last lighthearted moment for a long time.

When we reached the courtyard where the horses were waiting, my pony was among them. She was named Pepper, after the sprinkling of black dots on her white flanks, but I called her Snap because the stable master had taught me to snap my fingers, and taught her to come to me when I did. He'd also commissioned a special saddle for me, and every free moment I'd had I'd gone to him for riding lessons.

While careful not to draw attention to myself, I had obsessively checked to be sure my name was included on every list of the king's attendants. I was determined not to be left behind, and if anyone considered the matter even for a moment, I knew I would be.

As I'd hoped, everyone around me was much too preoccupied to notice the stable master boosting me into the saddle. I rode behind the king through the city, surrounded by the shouting crowds, and my heart lifted. We moved at a snail's pace while mothers held up their children to see the kings and queens as they passed. Even those who were older and wiser and knew what lay in our future waved and shouted, buoying our spirits against privations to come. If only wars could be won on the strength of the cheering when they begin, instead of the blood and the pain and the horror that feed the gods of discord.

By noon, we had not made it more than a mile from the city and I was already paying for the heady feelings of participation with an ever-increasing discomfort in my hip and my back. I had never ridden for more than an hour or two at a time. I'd had no way of knowing what it might be like to ride all day.

Snap carried me as carefully as an egg in a cup, and we fell farther and farther behind the king. Marchers and carts passed us by. Panic fluttered just under my breastbone when

I saw the magus waiting at the side of the road. I was sure he was going to send me back to the city. Instead, he turned his horse as I approached and rode beside me.

He claimed to have seen a crested sinerine fly past. "They are quite rare on this side of the Middle Sea. Shall we take a look for the nest?"

Warily, I went along as he led the way off the road. He helped me to dismount and we tied our horses. The magus followed a narrow path into the trees, going slowly so that I could limp after him, the stiffness slowly easing as I moved. Much to the surprise of us both, we did find the colony of birds. Their nests were remarkable, like a hundred knitted socks all hanging in the branches of a tree. Though the magus was very obviously delighted, the sinerines were an excuse for me to stretch my leg, and we both knew it.

When he helped me back onto my pony, he asked if I was feeling better, and I nodded.

"Are you lying?" he asked me frankly.

Defeated, I nodded again. There was no way to deny that even with the special saddle, my whole body hurt. Every individual sinew seemed to be drawing itself as tight as the strings on a lute. I'd focused so narrowly on getting far enough that I couldn't be sent back, I hadn't considered what an impossible position I would be in if I couldn't keep up.

"The first day is the hardest," the magus reassured me.

Then he flagged down a wagon. He loaded me into it, and to my surprise climbed in after me, tying his horse beside Snap at the tailboard. For the rest of the afternoon he chatted amiably with the blacksmiths squeezed onto the benches with their anvils and their tools. It was a very different side of the acid-tongued man I'd heard flaying opponents in arguments over the council table.

As the sun settled toward the horizon, Sotis came back with dinner in a basket and several bottles of wine. As darkness fell, we pulled into a makeshift camp beside the road. The magus stepped from the wagon to the back of his horse and held out a hand to me to help me onto Snap. I didn't take it, afraid of falling if he unbalanced me. When he saw how much trouble I had standing, one of the blacksmiths lifted me as easily as another man might lift a lamb and handed me into the magus's arms.

The magus rode nearly an hour more in the dark, Snap dutifully following behind, passing campfires and tents pitched on either side, finally reaching the spot where the tents of the royal party were pitched beside the even larger council tent. The magus handed me down to Petrus, who was waiting with hot water and his tinctures ready.

Because he was busy with me, it was not Petrus, but Galen who discovered the king was feverish. The king insisted he was not ill, merely overheated by his elaborate clothing. Petrus felt that Galen encroached on his prerogative as the

Attolian royal physician. Galen was jealous of his privileges as the healer who had cared for the king since his youth. In the morning, when there was no sign of the fever, Petrus said the king was well enough to travel and Galen disagreed.

The king would have overridden Galen's concern, but Sounis, to everyone's surprise, dug in his heels and absolutely refused to ride on until both Galen and Petrus said the king was well enough to continue. As a result, I had that extra day to rest as soldiers marched past the royal pavilions, lowering their voices and casting worried looks at one another.

The next day the king and I were both ready to ride. Galen and Petrus watched the king like a hawk while the magus supervised me no less strictly. I rode for the first few hours, a little more comfortably without the stopping and starting of the first day's march. When Snap and I had fallen back as far as the blacksmiths, they welcomed us into their wagon, out of the goodness of their hearts, or in expectation of the baskets one of the king's attendants would deliver later in the day. The magus often joined us, quizzing me with math problems and watching as I tried to mark answers on my slate while the cart bumped over the ruts in the road. Every few miles, he made me do Petrus's stretching exercises, and he insisted I get down to walk whenever the wagon was stopped. Each day, I rode a little longer, and eventually, I was able to step from the tail of the wagon onto Snap's back and ride to where the royal tents were being pitched. If it seems unlikely that I could make up my lost distance at the end of the day, one must consider the universal truth of armies. The larger they are, the more slowly they move.

An army moves like a caterpillar thinning itself out over the day, with the guns pulled by teams of twenty and forty horses dropping farther and farther behind, and as the army passes it leaves the road in worse condition for men and wagons that follow. Every ford stops progress for hours. Every cart that gets stuck slows every one behind it. The head must always halt while there is still time in the day to allow the long body to slowly contract again. Sometimes actual caterpillars move faster.

We were already falling behind Pegistus's best predictions.

Every day after the day's march, trailed by his attendants and his guards, the king walked through the camp, so that the sight of him might reassure those worried about his health.

"What is it, Gen?" Eddis asked, breaking the silence between them. She and the king had walked more than a mile back along the course of their march, and they'd have to turn back soon.

"I am useless," said the king, throwing up his hand. "Worse than useless. I could be in the capital, drinking wine and eating cheese. I could do it there as well as here, and

I wouldn't have slowed everything down even further by sweating in that hideous padded jacket."

Eddis hid her smile. So much changed, and so much remained exactly the same. She tipped her head at the men all around who were watching their king as he passed. "They believe in you. They need to see you."

"We've had this conversation before," said the king. "Last time, I was just getting over being sick in the shrubbery outside the hospital."

"And I think I told you pull yourself together then, too."

"I hate being a symbol."

"I thought you wanted to be a figurehead?"

"That's entirely different," he said haughtily, and Eddis dug an elbow into his side.

"It is," said the king. "I was not raised to be sovereign. You and Irene and even Sophos were. I would have made a fool of myself if I'd tried to seize the reins from Irene. Still would."

"You're not an utter failure," Eddis said, deliberately condescending, and he smiled at the backhanded compliment.

"I cannot prosecute a war, Helen," he said, his smile quickly gone. "But I can fight in one. It's because I can that I think I should. If I'm not willing to fight in this war, how is that just?"

"I have lived through too many winters in the mountains, seen too many men willing to fight to the death over a spilled cup of wine, to think dying for a cause makes that cause just," answered Eddis. "You went again to Hephestia's temple and the high priestess gave you an answer you didn't want to hear. Xanthe told me."

The king grumbled. "I should have asked the goddess privately."

"You could have been in the hypocausts, Gen, and everyone would have known all about it. You should be used to that by now."

Seeking a clearer answer to his question, the king had gone back to the temple. Again, he had steered me through the curtains, though this time as I pushed through them, his hand had fallen away. I'd arrived in the treasury alone to find the high priestess waiting. The king did not appear for a long time, and when he did, he seemed deeply shaken. The Oracle had looked him over in smug satisfaction. In that sonorous, resounding voice that sent chills down my back, she'd said something in the archaic language I didn't understand. In plain language she added, "*Do not overreach.* That is your answer, Eugenides."

The king had returned very subdued to the palace.

"The gods' messages are known for their opacity," he complained to Eddis. "Except, of course, in hindsight, when it's too late."

"Stop whining," said Eddis. "Go to bed. Do not overreach. That seems clear."

"The Oracle is Attolian. The only archaic she knows is from temple ceremonies. *Peris upus s'tatix.* It doesn't mean 'Don't overreach.'"

Eddis reluctantly agreed. "It's . . . danger in . . . excess?" she translated hesitantly.

"You're almost as bad. Did you pay no attention to your tutors?"

"Not if I could help it," she said, unembarrassed. "I was outside chasing your brothers with a stick."

"Well, rest assured that the gods are not interested in how many pieces of cake I eat. You missed the reflexive. It's a warning against self-indulgence."

"I think you're quibbling."

"Helen," he said, exasperated. "I don't want to go into battle. I am afraid of what I might become. What if I've let you and Irene and Sophos tell me I shouldn't fight because that's what I wanted to hear?"

She had to think about that for a while. "You have to trust yourself," she said finally.

"I don't know if I can."

"Then you'll have to trust us."

Eddis returned to the council tent.

"Is it his pride?" Attolia asked without looking up from the counters she was sliding across a map.

"No," said Eddis. Standing beside her to lean over the

map, she pointed to an area of high ground. Attolia moved a marker.

"It is only that he doubts himself, as we all do. As we should," said Eddis.

"I thought he might measure himself against his brothers or his cousins."

"He has never done that."

"Do you?" Attolia asked, genuinely curious.

"I did once. I outgrew it, and I understood my cousins better when I did."

"But you can fight."

"We both can, Irene. We both will, if we have to." She laid an arm around Attolia's shoulder. "But the call of life is as powerful as the call of death, and it is no weakness to answer to it," she said quietly.

It was another week or more when one of the queen's attendants gave the secret away. It was nothing, only a second cushion for the seat she brought for the queen, but the king noticed and Eddis noticed him noticing. As the discussion of the army's route for the next day went on uninterrupted, Eddis dropped her eyes. She'd suspected earlier, but had said nothing. Sounis was looking from Eddis to Eugenides to Attolia, and he too guessed.

By the end of the meeting, everyone present was desperate to excuse themselves. Most of those in the council, including his father, thought the king's temper was rising because of frustration with our slow progress. The queen's attendants knew better. There were apologetic glances cast at the queen and worried ones cast elsewhere. Attolia remained impassive.

After excusing themselves so hastily, the royal councilors lingered outside the tent. The king of Sounis and the queen of Eddis made no bones about the fact that they were eavesdropping.

The king of Attolia was at his most childish.

"Why didn't you say something before we marched?"

Unusually, Attolia was no more reasonable. "What difference do you think it would have made if I had?" she said snappishly.

"I can't go into battle, but you can march to war? The king may not risk his life, but the queen can?"

"It isn't easy for anyone to stand helplessly by while someone invades their country. It is not easier for me because I am a woman. It is not a special burden you alone bear that you cannot fight in this war."

"You will go back to the capital."

"I will not," said Attolia.

"You will. You just said—you cannot fight the Medes."

"And you, who would not know what to do with a company of pikemen if you found them in a basket—you would lead this army? With your generals who do not know a wain from a wheelbarrow? I should leave you here surrounded by idiots who cannot understand that you must feed your army if you want it to fight? Is that in any way satisfying?" she asked.

We all heard the sounds of inkpots or perhaps map weights or troop counters hitting the canvas walls of the tent. Something larger smacked into the fabric— making an imprint for a moment before it was gone. "No, it is NOT satisfying!" shouted the king.

It was probably a wine bottle. It didn't break when it landed on the overlapping carpets that covered the ground. The knife that came next protruded six inches—harmlessly, because the tent walls sloped, and no one would be leaning with an ear to just that spot on the canvas. One hoped.

"That was inappropriate," said Attolia.

"Inappropriate?" shouted the king. "You in your state on your way to war is inappropriate!"

"I did not become inappropriate all by myself!" she shouted back.

"Do you imagine I don't know that?"

Sounis looked at Eddis, pained.

"His mother and father used to shout at each other," Eddis said, trying to sound reassuring.

There was a crashing noise. Sounis said, "I don't understand."

Eddis said, hesitating as she put her thoughts into words, "I think they have to show their worst selves sometimes in order to be sure that even at their worst they are loved. Irene knows how frightened he is."

The king didn't sound frightened.

"Any minute," said Eddis, "he will realize—" As if her words were magic, silence fell in the tent and Eddis finished in a whisper. "How frightened she is."

With a gesture and an authority that Sounis could only envy, Eddis waved off those lingering nearby and moved the perimeter of the guards away from the tent, giving the two inside space that might afford the privacy that canvas walls could not.

CHAPTER SEVEN

The Medes had made it to the Leonyla Pass and were camped on the inland side of it. No one was surprised when messengers brought the news. It had taken almost twice as long to make the march as Pegistus's estimates had predicted. Carts had broken down, gun carriages had mired in streambeds, progress through bottlenecks had been slowed by disorganization. Still, a little flame of hope had burned in every heart that if the Peninsula's armies had moved so slowly, the Mede army, which was so much larger, must be moving even more slowly. Indeed, the camp forming below the pass held only the forward part of the Mede's forces.

"It grows every day," said Trokides. "By the time we reach the Leonyla, we may well face the whole of the Mede army on open ground." He only said what everyone was thinking, but it was hard to have our hope snuffed out.

The ships that the king had seized from the Pents had arrived in Stinos and were offloading the troops they'd ferried from the capital. Yorn Fordad was on one of them and, riding south from Stinos, he brought better news: the Pents had given in. Recognizing the threat the Medes posed, they had ended their delaying tactics and were sailing to secure Cimorene and the Straits of Thegmis. More support, ships, arms, and soldiers were being sent by all the powers of the Continent.

It was a great relief to know that we would not fight alone against the Medes. The aid, though, would not come without cost. The countries of the Lesser Peninsula would pay for it in treaties and trade concessions and loss of their independence. They would be occupied by the troops from foreign nations and might not see them gone again for a lifetime.

In grim meetings, Attolia and Eddis remade their strategy yet again. They knew the Medes would march on Stinos first. They could not move south and leave a fort behind them in enemy hands.

"We must slow the Medes' approach to Stinos, delaying them, if we can, until the Continent's forces arrive to relieve us," said Attolia. "Failing that, we garrison Stinos and retreat with the bulk of our forces. If the Braelings and Gants arrive in time to lift the siege, the Medes will be caught between our army to the south and the incoming forces of the Continent."

And if the Braelings' ships did not arrive before the tiny garrison was overcome, the Continental ships would reach Stinos only to find it held by the Medes. Stinos was the lone port north of the mountains that ran down Attolia's eastern coast and south of the Leonyla. With it in Mede hands, the Continent would be unable to land their troops and would be forced to withdraw. Without the Continent's assistance, the Peninsular armies would be ground to pieces as the Medes moved south.

There was an alternative left undiscussed, its existence hinted at by averted eyes and pursed lips: Eddis and Sounis could abandon Attolia, turn, and ride for the mountains. In Eddis, they could hold out for years, leaving the lowlands to fall to the Medes. The allies from the Continent would eventually drive the Medes back again, and a puppet government would be installed in Attolia, but Eddis and perhaps even Sounis might remain free. Attolia would be lost either way, and her generals knew it. They looked at their Eddisian and Sounisian counterparts with weary resignation.

"Sounis will not run," said her king.

"Nor Eddis," said her queen.

"Then we address ourselves to moving faster," said Attolia crisply. "To meet the Medes as soon as possible and slow their advance."

They abandoned the artillery and most of the baggage train, leaving them to catch up when possible. I might have been left behind too, but by then I'd grown accustomed to riding for hours at a time, so I was there when we camped on the ridge above the Leonyla Valley. I saw with my own eyes the Medes waiting for us.

Confident of their ability to advance whenever they chose, the Medes had made no effort to extend their base camp. They were leisurely waiting for all their forces to come through the narrow pass behind them. When we attacked, it was only against their vanguard, and we fought for the next three days. Each day a hundred years long.

Lamion was killed the second day. He had asked permission to fight with his father and his brothers and cousins. The king had released him. Drusis had petitioned to be released as well, leaving his brother, Motis, to attend the king. It was a difficult decision all the attendants had to make. So long as the king did not go into battle, neither did they. They would have to desert his service or risk their reputations by appearing to be hiding behind his skirts. When Philologos's father came to talk privately with the king, Philologos had stormed into the council tent saying he would not abandon his responsibilities to the king, not even for the glory of war. Even Xikos said that must have taken its own kind of courage, and no one so much as hinted that his father might have come to ask the king not to release Philologos—to keep his only son and heir safe.

✦ ✦ ✦

A hospital was set up in Lartius, a small town well south of the battleground and inland. Most of Attolia's attendants and Eddis's were there. Attolia had selected Chloe to stay with her, and Eddis had chosen Selene. The king had attempted to order Attolia back to Lartius as well, without success.

The waters of the Pinosh River are a mesh of meandering streams that finally join together just before they drop into the narrow chasm that cuts through the hills to the coast. The valley above the pass was broad enough for a battleground, but not so wide that the Mede army could encircle us. When we met the enemy, we had the rising ground behind us. As we retreated farther and farther, we would cross the ridge that was the watershed between the Leonyla and the long, sloping plain down to Stinos. The Medes would have a wider and wider front on which to attack.

On the morning of the fourth day, as dawn was breaking, a messenger from the Medes rode out across the open ground, inviting our high king and Sounis to a parley. It was unclear whether the insult to the queens was calculated or accidental.

It was the kind of day with brilliant blue skies and scudding black-bottomed clouds filled with rain. The sun as it rose higher turned the bright greens of the marshy ground to gleaming gold, picking out all the colors in the tents of the gathered armies. As the parley party gathered, the royal pennants blew and snapped in the wind.

Attolia would accompany the king, but both Sounis and Eddis would stay back out of an abundance of caution. They were all together as they waited for the Mede party to move first from its encampment. When it finally did, their horses shifted, stamping their feet and throwing up their heads, revealing their riders' tightening grip on the reins.

"Gods defend us," one of the generals said under his breath. Everyone heard it.

"What is it?" asked Xenophon the Eddisian. His eyes were not the best.

"Elephants," the king answered grimly. "They are coming out on their elephants."

The elephants had been brought through the pass only the day before, dragging the Mede artillery. This was the first time they'd appeared on the battlefield, their ponderous steps eating up the ground between the camps.

No one would look directly at the king. Even Fryst, with the personality of a plow horse, would go wild when confronted by an animal ten times his size, and the king was no rider to handle a badly spooked horse.

As if unaware of this looming humiliation, the king suddenly said, "I really want one of those."

"One of what?" asked Attolia, distracted.

"An elephant," said the king, and repeated it a little louder. "I want an elephant."

"An elephant," said Attolia. She briefly lifted her fingers to her temple and after a deep breath she asked, "Where do you imagine you would keep an elephant?"

The king squinted speculatively at the enormous animals. "That's a good point. They are much too big to go in the stables. Philo," he said, "run and get me the melons from the breakfast table." Philologos ran as if he were being chased by wild dogs and was back with three small melons before the king and queen began their stately ride down the slope out toward the Medes. As they went, the king was stuffing the melons, each the size of his fist, into the front of his tunic, and everyone could hear him still talking.

"We could keep it in the guard's bathhouse! There's plenty of room."

"And the guards will bathe . . . ?"

"In the palace reservoir."

"Our drinking water," the queen objected.

The king's plans grew more grandiose as his voice grew fainter. "We'll build your aqueduct. We'll make another reservoir."

"It would be cheaper to build a larger stable," Attolia said as they were almost out of earshot. The king swept off his ridiculous hat and bowed from the saddle as if this was just the conclusion he'd been leading her toward.

"So, so, so! We'll build a new house for our elephant."

"Your elephant," said Attolia.

I noticed that he didn't put the hat back on.

Instead of riding all the way to the Mede parley, the king and queen and their councilors dismounted and walked. The king was assiduous in assisting the queen over the mud churned by the days of fighting, making the Medes wait. When he'd reached firmer ground, the king took out a melon and split it with his hook as they walked. It was the Medes who had problems with unruly mounts. One strained its trunk forward, reaching for the king.

Hilarion, who by order of precedence had the long-seeing scope, described what he saw to the rest of us.

"He's fed it to the elephant. Gods all around us, he's patting it on the nose and the other elephants are crowded in! He'll be trampled."

But he was not. Those in charge of the elephants forced them back. The Medes climbed down, and the rest of the parley was carried out on even ground.

The general sent by the emperor to conquer the Little Peninsula was a stocky, grizzled veteran. If he was disappointed not to be speaking from the back of the elephant, it didn't show. He introduced himself as Bu-seneth and without other preamble asked for the high king's surrender.

The king didn't answer. Instead he leaned to look around Bu-seneth.

"Nahuseresh?" he said. "Why are you there with the junior officers? Come up and say hello." The king waved him forward.

Nahuseresh stared without speaking.

Noting the muscles tightening in the Mede general's jaw, the king murmured, "I'm sure he's a great help to you."

Addressing Attolia, Bu-seneth said, "Carry a message to Sophos, king of Sounis and Eddis. Tell him we will accept his surrender. We are not here to make war on peaceful people."

"Then go home again," Attolia suggested.

Bu-seneth scowled and the parley was over. The Medes had not expected a surrender; their goal had been to intimidate. If the king had blunted the awe-inspiring effect of the elephants, we soon learned the damage they could do.

At the end of the day, the council tent had been moved and reassembled, its distance from the battlefield not just a sign of the day's retreat, but of new caution.

Out on the coast, the damp sea air turned to mist and rolled inland like a tide, squeezing through the narrow pass to spread over the dead and muffle the cries of the wounded. This was the first time we saw it, the fog they called the Leonyla's tongue. It licked the back of the neck and made a man shiver from head to toe. It left everyone damp and chilled through.

Eddis asked the king to move through the camp, to speak to the soldiers and encourage them.

"You cannot mean that," the king said bitterly. "Send someone they can respect."

"Sophos will go as well. It's a big army, Gen," said Eddis.

"At least act like a king," said Attolia, acid in her voice.

It had been a long, miserable day. The king might have been angry. Instead, he smiled and kissed her gently. "I will go pretend to be the best high king there ever was," he promised.

In the growing dark, as other activities stopped and men turned to handwork, mending, and sharpening the tools of war, the king and Hilarion, Dionis, Ion, and I wandered from campfire to fire through the dripping fog, chatting for a few moments and moving on. As the night air grew cooler, one of the king's guards offered the king his cloak and, after protesting, the king reluctantly accepted. No one wanted him to be ill again.

At one campfire the soldiers offered up a cup of wine, and he sat to drink with them. He tested the waters carefully. All were veterans, all of them old enough to be his father. They'd lost battles before and they were ready to set aside the ills of the day to savor the warmth of the fire and the life that still flowed through their veins.

"Without war, there would be no heroes," said one man.

"Would that be a bad thing?" asked the king.

"That's a woman's question," one man responded dismissively.

"Perhaps my wife can tell me the answer, then," said the king with a dangerous smile.

"Take my advice," said another man, one with a scar that puckered his skin from his forehead, across his cheek, and down to his chin. "Never let your wife tell you anything."

His friends all laughed. Hilarion opened his mouth to call them to account, but the king reached out to cover his mouth. Hilarion was so surprised, as he looked down at the king's hand, that his eyes crossed, and the men around the fire slapped their knees and rocked back and forth. Hilarion realized what the king had already seen: these soldiers had meant no insult to the queen. With his right arm and his hook covered by the borrowed cloak, the men had no idea who the king was. They'd offered a drink to a couple of passing strangers, oblivious to the guards waiting beyond the light of their fire.

"When you return home from war," a skinny whip of a man said thoughtfully when the merriment had subsided, "you see your wife and your children and you know you have protected them. They are safe and well and you are safe and well. There's nothing like that feeling. Nothing else in your whole life will ever compare to it."

"And you swear you'll never go to war again, but you

do," said the man with the scar, shaking his head at his own decisions.

"What man will stay in his bed when the Medes are coming?" the whip-thin man asked. "Who wants to say ten years from now, 'I had a good nap that day!'" He spoke in a querulous old man's voice. "No one will remember their nap. They'll remember this."

"Tomorrow we will fight for our homes and our wives and our children."

The king shrugged then, and a little of his bitterness was back. "Not I."

They still did not know him. Looking him over, they assumed him to be one of the many indispensable servants of war.

"Well, we wouldn't be able to fight without your help, son."

"Blacksmith?" the thin man asked.

"Nah," pointed out the man with the scar, "no pox. He's no blacksmith and no farrier. Cooper?"

The king shook his head.

"Cook, are you?"

Again, Hilarion would have said something, but seeing the king's frown, he bit his tongue. The men saw it too, and misread his intent. "Don't you tease him," they said. They did not doubt Hilarion was a fighting man. "None of us can get along without the cooks."

"But I want to fight!" insisted the king. He slumped dramatically and added, "My wife won't let me."

They roared. The man with the scar slapped his leg. "Didn't I say never listen to your wife?" And they all laughed even louder.

"She doesn't want you to lose your good looks, end up like Lefkis with his face split."

"Spindly kid like you," said Lefkis, pinching the king's right arm above the elbow, not noticing the straps under the heavy cloth. "Stay in the cook tent," he said.

The king pretended to be insulted. He muscled up his other arm and said he would destroy the Medes single-handed if she would only let him go.

"You'll have your chance in time," the men assured him as they sobered again. They knew that every man would fight, coopers, cooks, and all.

"I'll tell you what," said Lefkis, pulling a glove out of his belt and handing it to the king. "If you ever make it into battle and out again, you bring this to me so I'll know you, and we'll make sure you get a double ration of wine that day."

Taking the glove, the king stood and bowed and thanked them for the wine and said he must go. His wife would be expecting him. Far more cheerful than they'd been earlier, they waved him on his way.

✦ ✦ ✦

There had never been any expectation that we would stop the Mede advance, only slow it. Three of the next five days, we fought and retreated. On the sixth, the Medes requested another parley. After very little debate, the queens agreed to send Attolia and the king again, for no other reason than it meant a morning of rest for our soldiers. The Medes came out on horses this time, no need for petty intimidation. Again, Bu-seneth asked for complete surrender, and again Attolia refused him. As the two parties turned away from each other, Nahuseresh delivered an unscripted announcement from behind the Mede general. "I have found Kamet!"

Attolia laid a hand on the king's arm to caution him, as he swung around angrily.

Bu-seneth had turned on Nahuseresh and was pushing him back. Attolia's former ambassador, who foolishly thought she had fallen for his seductive offers of support from the Mede emperor and from him, had been humiliated and had returned to the empire in disgrace. His hatred of Attolia and her husband was a personal affair, and the king's hatred of Nahuseresh was the same. It was at Nahuseresh's instigation that Attolia had cut off the king's hand, and the king blamed him for it. Why the king felt such animosity for Nahuseresh and not for Attolia, I do not know. People are no less mysterious than the gods. If an author's account of any man is tidy, you must believe it has been made so in contrast with the truth, which is rarely clear and never simple.

Nahuseresh shouted past Bu-seneth's ear. "I found him in Roa! My men took their time cutting him to pieces. Oh, I see your queen restrains you! Come out and fight like a king, Eugenides, instead of a sneak thief hiding behind your wife's skirts!"

Bu-seneth pushed Nahuseresh one way and Attolia dragged the king the other, ending the parley.

That day we watched in horror as a wing of the Mede's horse broke through our lines and cut off a group of Eddisians. Mede infantry drove in after the horsemen. Attolia looked for a rider to carry her orders to the Attolian reserves. "I'll take the message," said the king, fed up with sitting still, and he was off before anyone could stop him. His attendants galloped after him, but I stayed, as Snap would not have been able to keep up. We turned our attention back to the battle.

"What is it, Pheris?" said Attolia a little later, as I reached to tug her sleeve. "I have no time for games."

I pointed at the white horse leading the reinforcements.

The Eddisians, hard pressed, could see him coming, Fryst glorious with mane and tail flying, the king with his sword held high. Behind the Mede line, Nahuseresh reared his horse into the air and stabbed at the sky with his own sword, exultant at having drawn the king out at last.

Faster and faster Fryst came, not slowing even as they approached the men locked in battle. Where another horse might have leapt into the fray, Fryst, predictably, dug his front hooves into the muddy ground. Head down and heels up, he sent the king flying in his pitneen-colored coat.

I had the observation glass. Philologos had handed it to me before riding out after the king. I watched the king rotate in the air, straight as a pike, arms thrust out to either side. He spun as the weight of his sword arm dragged him off-balance. Still spinning, he landed in front of Nahuseresh, swinging the sword along the ground like a scythe, slicing into the hock of Nahuseresh's horse and bringing it down, screaming.

I saw all that before Trokides snatched the scope away. Even then I could make out Nahuseresh as he dragged himself free of his horse. He ran away—feet flying and arms pumping, head tipped back like an athlete racing for a finish line, with the king, like a reckless fool, chasing after him. The king followed Nahuseresh farther and farther onto enemy ground as Nahuseresh outpaced him on feet winged with fear, every step carrying the king away from his own men.

From the council tent, we heard the roar of the Eddisians. "Annux! Annux!" they cried as they surged forward to save him. I was terrified and exhilarated. The queens were livid. The Medes were driven back.

It was not the miracle described in Pollimius's history. The tiny Peninsular army did not push back the entirety of the Mede forces. The Medes outmatched us by such numbers that they sent only a partial force to every battle. Their confidence was so high that they were unprepared for a setback. They did not have their reserves in order, and what might have been a hesitation in their advance became a full-scale retreat. Legend makers will exaggerate, but the truth is extraordinary enough and needs no embellishments: the Medes withdrew in chaos; Nahuseresh seized another man's horse and fled from the king.

As the rest of the army secured the ground they had painfully won, the king returned to camp. His father had taken him up on his horse and the two rode together, surrounded by smiling Eddisians. When they reached the royal tents, the king slipped down, but he didn't approach Attolia or Eddis, who were waiting for him. He followed after his father, who was marching grim-faced for the tent Eddis's senior advisors shared.

The attendants hesitantly went after the king but stopped when the minister of war slipped the cords and snapped the tent flap down in their faces. Again, tents by their nature are poor at providing privacy. There was a clearly audible sound of flesh contacting flesh and we all heard the minister of war say, after a moment, "Get up."

"Why would I do that?" the king asked, bleary voiced. He must have done so, as there was another meaty smack. Hilarion and Ion stood looking uncertain, not knowing if they should rush to defend their king or spare him any witnesses to his humiliation. Before they could make up their minds, the tent flap was flipped aside and the minister stumped out.

The king lay on his back on the carpet. One side of his face was red and white with the imprint of the minister's fingers all in a row. As we watched, the white was fading to red to match the rest of that side of his face.

"Get Petrus," said Hilarion to Medander, but the king flapped his hand.

"Leave Petrus to those who need him more," he said as he struggled to sit up. He had plenty of help to get to his feet. "Please tell the queens and Sounis and the rest in the council tent that I will join them," he mumbled, "soon." Sinking onto a campstool, he tipped his head into his palm.

When he was ready to stand again, the attendants led him to his tent, washed him, and put him in clean clothes, oddly quiet for people who had just seen their overmatched army win an unanticipated victory. They trailed behind the king

like schoolboys to the council tent, where he stood with his
face swollen and purple on one side and apologized to the
queens and to Sounis and to his councilors for his aston-
ishingly selfish behavior. Sounis sat next to his own father,
looking sympathetic. His magus stood behind him, looking
very grave. There was a pained silence until Sounis hesitantly
pointed out that the prophecy hadn't actually said clearly
that the king couldn't fight.

"I think we all know I wasn't thinking of the prophecy,
Sophos," said the king. "Though I thank you for the excuse."

There were a couple of small smiles.

"You were thinking of Kamet," said Eddis sympathetically.

"You weren't thinking at all," snapped Attolia, less forgiving. "Did you hear Nahuseresh say a single word of Costis?"

"No?" the king said uncertainly.

"Nahuseresh said his men had killed Kamet. You can be
sure they had to kill Costis first. Yet Nahuseresh never mentioned him. Tell me how you see Kamet captured and dead
and Costis nowhere in his story?"

Feeling foolish, the king said humbly, "I . . . can't actually
see a way."

"Indeed," chided Attolia. "He taunted you with guess-
work. Costis would not sit like a pigeon waiting for his neck
to be wrung. We will wait for a message from Roa before we
hold any funerals."

She looked around at the other silent councilors. "We

have enough to grieve over already, but not a defeat—not today. We have retaken the ground lost and established our front camps closer to the Leonyla. I believe the question before us, my king, is—do you fight tomorrow?"

The king looked at his father. Looked at his queen. "That is not my decision," he said.

The queen nodded impassively and turned the question over to the councilors. They were interrupted in their deliberations by the sound of cheering.

"What is all that noise?" Trokides asked.

Hilarion, pleased with himself, said, "I think a man got his glove back."

In a city of tents filled with exhausted men under the quiet stars, Eugenides lay in bed, listening to the muffled sounds of others who were still awake. He watched the shadows of torches that burned all night play across the canvas walls around him. It was late and his face hurt, but that was not why he couldn't sleep.

"It is like being a sheepdog who suddenly turns on the sheep," he said. "It feels utterly right in the moment, never afterward. That's why I wouldn't let someone else send me into battle. I never wanted to fight until I believed it was necessary. I do," he said, as if he was trying to convince himself. "I do believe it is necessary." He still sounded unsure.

"Your father will regret that slap to the head," Attolia murmured into her pillow.

"Oh, that was just the final round of an old argument. It was so important to him that I not be the Thief, that I be a soldier instead, and now that I'm finally doing what he always wanted, he has to tell me to stop."

"Maddening," agreed Attolia in the voice of experience.

Eugenides sighed. "People should be more careful what they ask me for."

CHAPTER EIGHT

The Peninsular armies had won the day because the men were rallying to their high king, all of them, Eddisians and Sounisians and Attolians alike. The royal councilors were in rare agreement: it would be foolish to undermine this new sense of unification. The king even prevailed in his desire to fight on foot, beside his Eddisians, and for the next three days our armies did not retreat. The Medes continued to send out only a portion of their forces, and the Peninsular armies fought bloody battles to hold their ground.

Philologos was wounded. It was only a slash to his shoulder, but enough to keep him out of the fighting for a while. Cleon the Eddisian died fighting at the king's side, one of three of the king's cousins who died in a single day. The king's oldest brother, Temenus, came that evening and sat with the king alone before the two of them went off to observe the private rites sacred to the Eddisians.

It was his cousin who was Eddis who came slowly one evening, head down, to the Attolians' tent with word of the explosion in the foundry that had killed Stenides, the king's favorite brother. The body was far away in Eddis. There would be no rites to observe until they returned to the mountains, if they ever returned to the mountains.

"He should have been making watches," said the king, holding the delicate green-and-gold timepiece Stenides had made him, opening the case and squeezing it closed again with a tight, precise snap, shrugging up one shoulder to wipe away his tears. Then he left to find his father and Temenus, his remaining brother, to bring them the news.

Perminder of Sounis distinguished himself, helping the king of Sounis off the field when he was thrown from his horse. We called Perminder the black sheep because of the tight curls in his hair, and that evening Eddis joked about the Lion being carried by the Lamb. She was not the only one to make jokes that sounded forced. Any levity was harder and harder to find. Sense was hard to find. A man was shot through the head by a bolt and lived to tell about it. My cousin, who'd been sent by my grandfather to command the men of Erondites, lost a single finger to a sword cut and died a few days later of an infection in the wound.

✦　✦　✦

The Medes, like houseguests who don't want to be impolite, rarely fought into the evening. When they withdrew from the field, the Peninsular armies did the same. As the sun set, the king and queen of Attolia would walk through the camp, between the long rows of tents, past regularly spaced cook fires and work sites. The ground that had been pasture a few weeks earlier was hard-packed dirt except where it was mixed with wastewater to a slippery, stinking mud. All around them, blacksmiths and barrel makers, fletchers, armorers, gunsmiths, and leatherworkers were engaged in making and remaking what was needed for an army of ten thousand men.

The king offered the queen his hand as she picked her way around a puddle. Because the Medes had not mustered to war that morning, the soldiers, at least, were having a day of rest. They slept through all the noise, most of them laid out in their tents, but some stretched out by the cold ashes of the fires they'd lain down by the night before.

When they reached the edge of the encampment, Attolia led the king into the open space beyond it. She did not intend to go out to the farthest pickets, just far enough that they could speak quietly without being overheard. There was a low stone wall. It had once served to divide one family's land from another's. Those property rights moot at the moment, it made an adequate bench.

He wanted to ask if she was tired, but didn't. She knew it and was grateful.

"You're quiet," she said.

"You're busy," he said. He hadn't wanted to interrupt her as she assessed her forces.

"I've seen what I needed to see. Eddis and I will talk later. What woke you last night?"

"The dead," he said, and Attolia nodded. They woke her as well. The king toed the trampled and torn grass and said, "I thought it was wrong to sit back on a hillside watching men die and now . . . I am not sure. From above, I can see men on both sides trapped in a war over which they have no control. On the field, I care about nothing but striking down anyone who strikes at me."

She took his hand. "Your morality up on the hillside is an illusion, no more real than the freedom you imagine you have from it in battle." She had seen enough to know. "All wars make men monsters, all wars and all men."

"And women?" he asked.

"Women, too," Attolia confirmed.

Every day the priests and priestess with the army prayed for the arrival of the Brael ships at Stinos.

Some of the tactics used to delay the Medes worked well, some did not. "They seem so familiar with the terrain," said Pegistus. "They must have sent scouts well ahead of their army."

Sounis pointed to the campaign map. "We diked here to support the field guns."

"We moved them back three days ago."

"I know, but the dike diverts this streamlet, so it now runs into the flat here." He pointed. Attolia and Eddis leaned over, along with Pegistus.

"Whoever has informed the Medes so well of the terrain might not know about this," said Sounis. "If we lure their cavalry here, they will founder."

Attolia and Eddis nodded and moved their markers, wrote out their orders, and the Medes lost an entire troop of their men and their horses.

The king had sent Fordad to the harbor at Stinos, but instead of troops he returned with the worst possible news. The Etisians, the late summer windstorms, had come early. The winds from the north would drive the Brael ships back, delaying their arrival.

Fordad's words were a body blow. I saw men stagger, clutching their heads. The Medes, committing only part of their forces every day, were as strong as they'd been when they first passed through the Leonyla. Our army was exhausted. We might have lost ground all the way back to Stinos in the next few days but for the encouragement of those who went again from fireside to fireside—the kings and queens, the officers of the army, the barons who went to their sons and their cousins and stirred them to give everything they had. Instead of losing ground, step by bitter step, we advanced.

"Bu-seneth has an army of conscripts," said the magus cynically, warning the council against false hope. "He uses us to train his soldiers for war."

Whatever the cause, overconfidence or poor training, the Medes left an opening in their lines and Attolia, in spite of fears that it was a trap, ordered her forces forward. We had a day of glory. Moving our encampments, we took over the fortifications the Medes themselves had constructed and were still outside the range of the barrel guns.

After that, Bu-seneth did not take the field for several days. Perhaps he was licking his wounds, or perhaps reinforcing the motivation of his unwilling soldiers.

Only the king failed to appreciate the reprieve. After a morning of his fruitless pacing, Yorn Fordad suggested his energy might be better spent on horseback in the afternoon. "The men in your outposts would be cheered to see you," he pointed out.

The Peninsular armies had been pushed all the way back to the fields east of Lartia and then had advanced again to the top of the ridge that separated the valley of the Pinosh River above the Leonyla from the watershed to the east, running down toward Stinos. The ridge was long and open, and small companies of men had been posted far out from the main camp to warn us if the Medes made an attempt to encircle our forces. Those soldiers had not had the benefit of royal encouragement, and so it was agreed that the king would ride out in the afternoon to visit them.

We followed a road that was really no more than a wagon track through the thin trees. The king was laughing at something Philologos had said as we neared a cairn of stones, a kind of grave marker not uncommon this far north. I saw a man standing near it and my heart leapt into my mouth. I was certain he meant the king no good. The king must have seen him too. He pulled up, making Fryst throw his head. When I looked again, the man at the cairn had disappeared.

"Your Majesty?" Philologos asked.

"I thought I saw a dead man. . . ."

The king eased up on the reins, Fryst took a step, there was a flash of light and a sound so loud that I didn't hear it with my ears but felt it crash through my chest.

Then I was on my back, blue sky overhead, and my heart pounding. The air was full of smoke and muffled sounds. I heard, "To the king!" as if from far away and I rolled over, dragging my arms underneath me, too weak to push myself up from the ground. I lay like a baby, my feet scrabbling in the dirt.

Just ahead was the king—I knew him by the coat Hilarion had made him wear—lying partly under Fryst, the horse just as still as he was. There were men on horseback coming through the smoke in the air. They dismounted and walked through the bodies, looking right and left, killing as they came. When they reached Fryst, they tried to pull the king free, but had to lift the horse off him first. I saw Hilarion stagger up, his face covered in blood, shouting something—I couldn't hear what. I saw a Mede drive a sword through his chest. Then they tied the body of the king over a horse and led it away.

By the time I made it to my feet, there were others up, and they too were holding their heads, stumbling in pain and confusion. Many of the horses had run away, but not Snap. I called her with my fingers, but I couldn't hear any sound and obviously neither could she. She looked as puzzle-headed as I felt. I reeled toward her and she shied a little. Unlike the other horses, who were dodging their stagger-ing, injured riders, Snap was used to my awkward gait and swinging arms. If I was even more unsteady than usual, she didn't back away, and I was able to catch her reins in my good hand. With that contact, we both were steadier. Snap's eyes rolled, but she let me pull her to the body of the king's horse. I climbed on top of poor Fryst and from there onto Snap's back.

I hadn't checked her for any injuries, but she gamely started off. I could feel some unevenness in her gait at first. Her hooves made no sound, or rather I heard none, only a roaring of wind in my ears. I couldn't guide her; I could only cling with my good hand to the saddle, hunched over with all my weight in one stirrup. I hung on, tears streaming down my face, wailing, I'm sure, like a shade escaped from the underworld. The Medes looked back over their shoulders and mocked me.

The explosion had been heard for miles, and the Medes were racing away ahead of any pursuers. Snap couldn't keep up, but she hammered on as best she could. Her gait got steadier as she recovered from the shock of the explosion, and I was able to pull myself better into my saddle and tighten the strap across my leg. I had no illusions that I would be of any use to the king. I only knew that I must reach his side if I could.

The Mede encampment, a city of tents ten times the size of our own, was well prepared to repel any attempt at a rescue. The men at the barricades saw me. They could have shot at me, they could have taken poor Snap's feet out from under her; they did neither. They snatched at Snap's reins, but she was having none of that. She galloped through the pickets, dodging and weaving as I clung to the saddle. It was no more than a game to the Mede soldiers, and once we were past, they returned to their positions.

Snap took me to the center of the camp, where I slid off her back and frantically made my way between the stamping horses to where the king lay on the ground. I dropped over him as if I could somehow protect him, only to be dragged up and tossed aside.

✦ ✦ ✦

The king lived, it seemed, for they patted his cheeks and tipped a pitcher of water on his face. He didn't move as a man bent over him, tugging at his hook. The man fell back, clutching his hand and swearing. Someone else brought a broad leather strap, and they buckled the king's arms to his chest. I heard him groan as they rolled him over. When they lifted him to his feet, one of his legs couldn't bear weight. As they walked him forward, his head hanging down, it buckled under him.

I tried to follow, meaning to stay with him no matter what, to be his support to the bitterest end, but just as we reached the open doorway of a tent, someone pushed me hard from behind and I fell heavily. The muffled uproar in my ears had faded, and as I lay on the ground struggling for breath, I heard it quite clearly when my grandfather who was Erondites said, "Welcome, Eugenides," from inside the tent.

There was a stack of campaign trunks just inside the doorway of the tent. While there were still men standing between me and my grandfather, I scrambled toward them, fleeing like a mouse into the space between the trunks and the curving side of the tent. I hid myself there. I abandoned my king.

"You must be surprised to see me." My grandfather sounded smug.

"What?" said the king, evidently still deaf.

My grandfather repeated himself, louder.

"No," said the king. "You are no surprise, Erondites. You," he said to someone else, "are Ion Nomenus?"

"Yes," someone said softly.

"Yes?"

"Yes!"

"You are a surprise," admitted the king.

Nahuseresh, impatient at being ignored, said, "Enough introductions, Thief."

"King."

"Bastard," said Nahuseresh. "A sneaking Thief who has stolen a throne."

"It was never yours," said the king mildly.

"Why does he still have this?" Nahuseresh said, his voice as sharp as the blade on the inside edge of the king's hook.

"Don't!" one of the guards shouted from outside the open doorway. I heard Nahuseresh hiss.

The king mocked him. "The last man who tried that is missing a finger," he said.

I hoped Nahuseresh's fingers were gone, but he probably would not have remained in the tent if he'd been seriously injured.

Bu-seneth said, "You'll sign a surrender and take an oath of loyalty to our emperor. You will accept Nahuseresh as your prime minister, and when your people have disbanded their armies, you will be returned to them."

"What?"

Bu-seneth had to repeat himself.

"I will not," said the king.

I cannot bring myself to describe what happened next. Crouching, head pounding, I listened to treason, torture, and betrayal. I would have fled then, giving myself away as I tried to escape the sound and the choking, sickening smell of irons heated in the fire. I would have left my king all alone. I know it and I have never forgiven myself.

All that saved me was the unexpected kindness of the traitor Ion Nomenus. I crept out from behind the trunk and locked eyes with him—a slim, serious-looking man standing on the far side of the tent. He had been waiting for me to appear, and with a glance at the men bent over the king, he gave a tiny shake of his head. With the slightest motion of his fingers, he waved me back.

So I stayed. I listened to Bu-seneth's frustration growing as they could get nothing from the king, not even a sound. Peering out from my hiding place, I saw Nahuseresh bear down with all his weight on the king's injured knee.

"Tell me again that you are king," he said, lording over him.

The king broke his silence to oblige, saying in a conversational tone, "Annux, if you prefer."

"Annux?" Nahuseresh said contemptuously. "You are

a puppet, dancing for the queen. She will know her place when I rule over her."

"When I am dead," the king said, his voice breathy, "you will still have to fight my armies. And the Braels. And the Gants."

At his words, Bu-seneth and my grandfather and Nahuseresh all straightened to share a smile with each other.

"Oh, Eugenides," Nahuseresh mocked him. "The Continental Powers? Do you really think they are coming to save you?"

"I do, actually," said the king.

"They sent you to your death," said my grandfather.

"You lie," said the king.

"I do not," Erondites answered. "You think the Continental Powers are your allies. You are wrong. They do not fear the Medes. *You* are the danger. You took Attolia, subdued Eddis and Sounis. You summon ships—the Neutral Islands deliver them up. You control the passes and the sea roads. You threaten their trade routes, Eugenides. The Medes, the Continent, they cannot allow another power to grow on the shores of the Middle Sea."

"You fool," said Nahuseresh. "Who do you think put the bomb in the cairn?"

Bu-seneth said something contemptuous that I did not understand. To the king, he said, very seriously, "That you survived was our good fortune. The gods delivered you to us."

Nahuseresh pressed down again on the king's knee, making him gasp in pain.

"The Continent musters its armies in Melenze," said Bu-seneth. "They promised you aid to ensure that you would march north—to spend your armies against ours. When the Little Peninsula has given its all, only then will they step up to fight. Your cause is lost, Eugenides. You waste the lives of your men by persevering."

"So you say," the king spat.

"Let your soldiers go home," said the general. "The emperor bears them no ill will. Disband your armies now and I promise you, on my honor, that you will still be king while you live and your throne will pass to the emperor only after your death."

"No!" protested Nahuseresh, outraged. "I am to rule Attolia!"

Bu-seneth knew that a change in tone, a surprising moment of compassion, can break down the most resistant prisoner. He repeated the offer. "You have no heir—you've seen that your wife cannot bear you one. Be king under our emperor, defy the Continental Powers that have betrayed you. Sign the surrender, Eugenides, and I will send Nahuseresh home rolled in a rug."

"You would not dare," said Nahuseresh.

Bu-seneth had been sitting on a stool by the brazier. Slowly he rose to his feet. I'd been drawn out from my hiding space and any of them could have seen me, but I could not look away from this contest, nor could anyone else. I might have risen to my feet and danced without drawing their attention.

"Do you think anyone cares about your ambitions?" Bu-seneth asked Nahuseresh. "Do you think your brother cares? He does not. You are not the next ruler of Attolia; you were never meant to be. You are a laughingstock sent here so that you would be out of their way instead of whining uselessly underfoot."

The king must have had all his wits still about him, because he was shaking with laughter as well as with pain. "Useless," he choked. "And you called me a fool! How could you not see that it is Erondites who is meant to pull my strings?"

My grandfather's smirk was all the proof Nahuseresh needed.

"Sign the surrender," Nahuseresh snarled, kicking the king until Bu-seneth pushed him back. Nahuseresh went on shouting, "The Braels are not coming! The Gants are not coming! You will die and your silly truce will break, your armies will scatter, and we will beat them one by one, burn your fields and destroy every city, every town, burn it all to the ground."

"No," said the king, his voice shaking.

"There is no one coming to save you, Eugenides!"

"I don't believe you," he said.

He did. I could hear it in his voice and so could Bu-seneth. The general ordered Nahuseresh back like a man directing a dog. Then he returned to persuasion. "I have honed my soldiers on yours, and our battles have served their purpose. My men are ready, and tomorrow we will begin in earnest to destroy your armies. Sign or die, Eugenides; either way, you have lost. Sign and you save their lives. That is all you can accomplish here."

Nahuseresh yanked the irons out of the fire, sending sparks flying dangerously into the air to fall and singe the carpets. This time, the king did not bear the pain in silence. He screamed. Then he wept. In terrible pain, he did not surrender to save himself; he gave in to save his people. With a shaking hand, he signed at the bottom of the vellum sheet that Erondites held in front of him. He accepted Erondites as prime minister and left his kingdom at his death to the emperor of the Mede.

Bu-seneth, having gotten what he wanted, stepped back uninterested as Nahuseresh vented his humiliation and his rage. Kicking at Eugenides, Nahuseresh shouted, "You will be a puppet and my brother will pull your strings. All you will ever be is a thief. Admit it." He tried to stamp on the king's fingers but missed. "Show us what you can steal now!" he snarled as the guards lifted the king onto a stretcher.

Ion Nomenus had taken the signed surrender away to sand the ink. Done with the task, he moved as if without purpose to stand by the doorway, blocking me from view. As they lifted the king, he flicked his hand behind his back and I rolled under the canvas onto the wet grass outside.

It had grown dark and a light rain was falling. I could hear the king sobbing as they carried him past, crying out that he was the king, he was Attolis, he was annux still. Tears streaking my own face, I got to my feet and limped after him. The men holding him saw me and shrugged at one another. I followed them as they took him to a small tent with a cot in it and nothing else. They chained him and left. They did not try to confine me and were right not to bother.

After a while, the sound of the king's gasping and crying lessened and he fell silent. I lifted my face and saw through the tears in my own eyes that there were none in his. He was looking back at me with a face like an open grave. Then he smiled, and a chill like the ones I felt in Hephestia's temple shuddered down my back.

He slid his hand free of the manacle around his wrist and probed in the embroidered cuff of the opposite sleeve. He eased out a knife with a triangular blade no longer than his finger and used it to slice through the leather strap around his chest. He put the knife away and worked his way along a row of tiny invisible pockets until he found the key he wanted. He unlocked the chain around his waist and sat up, using his sleeve to wipe his face clear of the last signs of his suffering, silently mocking my amazement.

He made the sign of needle and thread with his fingers, pointed to the gaudy colors on the front of his coat, and tapped the pocket at his wrist. Then he lifted his hand to make the sign for excellent.

That tailor has terrible taste, but he knows where I like my pockets.

He tipped his head at my astonishment and used the sign for my tutor. *Relius.*

I had guessed that Relius had shown him my signs; that wasn't what surprised me. Relius was clumsy and slow. Eugenides wasn't signing like him or even like Melisande. He was communicating as Juridius and I did. Not only was everything he said clear, he knew the sign for my tutor, and I had never taught that to Relius. Why would I have needed to?

Eugenides unlocked the chains around his ankle and poked a finger with distaste through the burned holes in his clothes. He splayed his first two fingers and held them to his chin—making a forked beard. I knew who he meant.

Nahuseresh tells me I am not king. We'll see if he really prefers the Thief.

Another sign whose meaning was easy to guess.

But you're hurt.

Not as badly as Nahuseresh thinks.

Your leg—

He shook his head, almost pitying me. His face crumpled and he wiped back and forth under his nose, mimicking his earlier suffering.

My cousins know better than to trust my tears. You should, too.

He raised an eyebrow when I didn't laugh. Every moment the air seemed tighter, the ringing in my ears seemed higher. I could feel myself shaking as if it were cold. He ruffled my hair, a reassuring gesture that had no effect.

He glanced up. *I need a heavier rain.* There was a rumble in the sky, then a patter on the canvas above us that gradually increased to a drumming sound.

He indicated I should help him out of his coat. He winced and scowled as I pulled it off him, then he wrapped me in it and put me into his place on the cot. Rolling me to face away from the doorway of the tent and covering me with the blanket the guards had left, he artfully arranged the folds to make me look larger. He patted my shoulder. *Wait for me.* Then he rolled under the fabric edge of the tent, just as I had rolled out from Bu-seneth's.

I listened to the sound of the rain and shivered.

There was sticky blood all over me. My face was pocked with tiny wounds. As I touched my cheek, I found a bit of rock embedded in the skin below my eye and picked it out. There was drying blood from my nose and mouth, and my head ached, the pain pressing against my skull from the inside out as if my head were an overfull wineskin ready to burst.

It seemed like a very long time to me before Eugenides returned. When he did, we took the coat and my own blue tunic and arranged them under the blanket, their bright colors peeping out to catch the light of a lantern if the guards looked in on us.

It will do. He nodded with eerie certainty. *Don't be afraid.* He might have meant that I should not be afraid of the Medes, but I think he meant that I should not fear him, either. I did, though. He was terrifying, even more than he had been when he confronted the Pent. I was more frightened than I had been when he learned the grain wagons had been burned. I still followed him out from under the side of the tent into the dark.

In the pouring rain, even two figures as strange as the king and I were anonymous as men hurried past with their heads down. Eugenides confidently led the way across the camp. There were two guards at the entryway to Bu-seneth's tent, and we circled around to the back. The stakes that held the walls down were meant to keep out the wind, not trespassers. When Eugenides lifted the fabric, I pushed underneath it, afraid to meet the general on the far side, but more afraid to disobey. I came face-to-face not with the general, but with the man who'd saved me. He lay on his back only a foot or two away, his eyes closed and his chest soaked in blood. I scrambled away from him as quickly as I could as Eugenides rolled in after me.

"Ion Nomenus," he said, speaking aloud, though quietly enough not to reach the ears of the guards outside. "He should have stayed in his pigpen."

Sickened, I turned away. The whole tent reeked.

Eugenides said, "If there is a hue and cry, hide yourself behind the chests again. No one will expect to find you here, and I will come for you when my work is done." Then he was gone.

I settled tentatively on the cot where I think Ion Nomenus had probably slept. It was behind a partition made by the campaign trunks and Bu-seneth's traveling desk. There was a stool near the head of the cot holding a miniature set of household gods and three small plain figures, two men and a woman, mementos of his family, probably. I swallowed, wondering who would miss him.

There was a sound, something wet and intermittent I had not heard at first over the drumming of the rain. Ion Nomenus's eyes were partly open. He blinked.

"Water?" he whispered.

I fetched him a cup of watered wine from a carafe on the desk, dipping the end of my sleeve in the cup and dribbling the wine on his lips. The wound in his chest sucked and bubbled. He blinked again, his eyelids growing heavier.

I wanted to tell him he would be all right, but we both knew he would not. All that was left was for him to make some sound loud enough for the men standing by outside to hear, and I and the king too would be prisoners again. I hated to think of covering his mouth.

He tucked his chin, trying to see the wound in his chest.

I shook my head at him. *Don't look.*

His head fell back. The wound sucked.

He could have called out—I think he had enough strength. I don't know if the guards would have heard him. I know he didn't try.

He whispered, "I always looked out . . . for myself." He drew another painful, burbling breath. "No more of that now."

He was staring at me through the narrow opening of his eyelids that was all he could manage. "So . . . just once I can . . . choose a side for better reasons." He coughed and squeezed his eyes shut, knowing he must swallow the blood or let it out. It ran down over his chin.

"Tell my king . . ." he whispered, then changed his mind. "No, don't tell him," he said. ". . . no more of that now."

It was the last thing he said.

When Eugenides returned, he found me still crouching there next to Ion Nomenus.

Come, Pheris. He lifted the edge of the tent for me. Miserably, I crawled around Ion Nomenus to join him.

There was a distant sound of shouting. The king nudged me in the opposite direction as men hurried by, their eyes passing over us. I don't know if they didn't see us or if they didn't care. We walked, unnoticed by anyone through the city of tents. It seemed to go on forever, and when we finally reached the edge of it, my heart sank even lower. Terrified of being caught, I had not even considered how far we had to go.

"Courage," said the king in my ear.

We passed the Mede pickets, again without being noticed. Perhaps the king guided us away from the sentries; I never saw them. We stumbled out to the empty land between the two enemy camps, through the scrub and the churned-up mud, sinking into the marshy ground and wading across the shallow streams. The king paused several times to look back, but he seemed expectant, not fearful.

The rain had stopped and some of the clouds had cleared. I fixed my eyes on the distant light of campfires. The king was limping more heavily, and I worried with every step that my leg might give way entirely. The king began to utter the most outrageous vulgarities. Traveling with soldiers for weeks, I had not heard such language.

At last we approached a copse of trees, difficult to make out in the dark, and the king fell silent. Leaning more heavily on me, he bent to find a stick and knocked it against a tree trunk, alerting the sentry that we were almost on top of him. We heard him scramble to his feet, and the sing of steel as he drew his weapon.

"Halt," he said in the dark ahead of us.

"We did," said the king.

"Password," said the unseen soldier, very officious, no doubt embarrassed that we'd come so close without him noticing.

The king asked me if I knew it.

I shook my head. It had been "sword of Clemon" the day before, but it would already have been changed.

"Get your officer," said Eugenides to the soldier.

"The password," insisted the soldier.

"GET YOUR OFFICER!" the king roared. There was a crashing in the bushes all around us as soldiers drew weapons and raced in our direction. The man on picket directly in front of us finally unshuttered his lantern. His officer, stumbling into the lighted area, shouted, "Who's there?"

"Attolis Eugenides Eugenideides," said the king. "By the will of the Great Goddess, annux over Hephestia's Peninsula, king of Attolia, king over Sounis, and Eddis, king from the Macheddic Mountains to the sea, king from the Melenzetti Pass to the River Lusimina, and by my oath to my god, now and for my life, Thief of Eddis."

✦ ✦ ✦

They took him away from me. They brought him a horse and helped him mount, and he rode off. Soaking wet, aching all over, I watched him go. When someone behind me dropped a blanket over my shoulders, I flailed in panic.

"Sorry, sorry," the man said, steadying me. He came around to where I could see him, as he gently tugged the blanket tighter. He put his hands on my arms and waited for my nod before lifting me into the arms of someone on a horse who bent down to take me. We followed the king back into the camp.

The soldiers lined our path and cheered, some firing guns into the air, spending precious ammunition to celebrate. When we reached the council tent, it was aglow in the darkness, all its lamps still burning. In front of it, Attolia, Eddis, and Sounis waited quietly, surrounded by the royal councilors who had been debating through the night. As Eugenides carefully dismounted, Attolia stepped forward. She might have taken him in her arms, but she hesitated, and that opportunity passed. "Welcome back, my king," she said very formally.

"We have much to discuss," said Eugenides, and passed by her to enter the council tent.

CHAPTER NINE

*H*e lowered himself into his seat and leaned back by inches. He closed his eyes, but his expression remained hard as stone. Eddis, Attolia, and Sounis did not take their seats beside him. They stood by as the tent filled with silent men. The king had returned from the enemy, but no one here was cheering. Uneasily, they waited.

When Eugenides opened his eyes, he announced into the silence, "The powers of the Continent have led us here with moon promises. There are no reinforcements coming to Stinos."

As the men in the tent looked at one another in horror, I followed the king's line of sight. He was watching the Brael. By the time I turned my eyes back to the king, he had seen all he needed. Until that moment, I don't think he'd truly believed the Braels had betrayed us.

I don't know if Fordad would have admitted the truth or denied it. Eugenides slowly shook his head, and the ambassador remained silent.

In the tightly packed tent, a space opened between Fordad and the doorway. He bowed and left, looking neither to the left or the right, passing Petrus at the doorway as he entered with his carrying case of remedies. As Petrus headed for the king, the space made for Fordad began to close, and Petrus was brought to a halt.

Eugenides was searching the men standing around his council table, noting who was there and who was not.

He said, "Hilarion. Who else?"

Petrus answered for the dead. "Xikos. Perminder. Sotis will not live long." He paused, hating to say it, but knowing the king was waiting. "Philologos."

Poor Philo, who everyone had tried to protect, had been riding beside the king. The bomb hidden in the cairn of stones had killed him instantly.

"The guard?" Eugenides was emotionless.

Teleus, captain of the guard said, "Clovis is dead, and all of his squad. Treagus and most of his squad as well. Legarus and Trulo from Aristogiton's."

Eugenides nodded. "We will avenge them. Marshal the men to attack at dawn. They must be ready as soon as there is light to see."

Barons, generals, the other royal councilors anxiously

turned to Attolia, to Eddis, to Sounis, their trusted military leaders, only to find Eugenides's adamantine conviction reflected in all three faces.

"Your Majesty." It was my grandfather Susa, a braver man in that moment than ever before. "We all want vengeance, but if it is true that the Continent has abandoned us, we cannot be foolish." Almost begging, he said, "We must retreat, Your Majesty, not attack."

Eugenides didn't answer. He appeared to be waiting. "Brother," he murmured, "a single spark will do."

Through the open front of the tent, light flared in the black night, larger than campfires, larger than bonfires. There was a sound like a thunderclap, loud but distant, rolling through the air. More explosions followed the first; flames as high as the trees shot into the air, thunder boomed again. The king didn't even turn his head.

"The Medes' powder stores," he said.

We could hear a sound like men screaming, though men's voices could not have carried so far.

"The elephants," said the king. He rested his head wearily in his hand. "They are stampeding through the camp."

"That will wake Bu-seneth," Trokides said bitterly.

"No," said the king. "Bu-seneth woke earlier. Nothing will ever wake him again."

I was not the only one who shuddered, though I was

the only one who had seen the Mede general on his back with his throat cut, his tent reeking of blood and ashes, the small triangular knife from the king's pocket sunk in his chest, pinning a singed scrap of vellum in place. All that was left of the surrender was the deceptively docile signature of Eugenides.

"The Mede keep an orderly camp. It was easy to find their officers. I am sorry I could not find Nahuseresh or Erondites. Nahuseresh says I am a bastard, not a king." I saw Attolia follow his gaze, this time to Eddis, as the king continued. "A Thief and not a king. He wanted to know what I can steal now, and I look forward to showing him."

To Susa, he said, "We will have no better chance than this."

Susa bowed deeply. "We will marshal the men, Your Majesty."

In silence, everyone else bowed, first in the direction of the king, then to Attolia, Sounis, and Eddis, before they headed to their tasks. Then those three took their leave as well. Sounis bent to say something to Eddis and then followed his father away to rouse the Sounisians. No one spoke a word until Petrus screwed up his courage and stepped forward.

The king said, "Not now."

Petrus girded his loins. "There may be no time later for the proper care of the wounds," he said. He meant that the king would put him off right up until the dawn when he rode into battle.

The king shook his head again, and mild-mannered Petrus gave in. He withdrew, and I knew why. Even I did not want to be near the king. I followed Attolia and Eddis as they withdrew from Attolia's tent. The maps and markers, the campaign tools were all in the council tent with the king, but there was a campaign desk with paper and pens to lay out their battle plans. Attolia ignored it. She turned to face Eddis.

"Once, when I said he had saved me, you said I had saved him. From what?"

Eddis didn't need to answer. Saved him from becoming the Thief, the murderous figure sitting alone with his dead.

Attolia said, "Gen's father didn't want him to be the Thief. But it was his father who gave him the gold to go after Hamiathes's Gift." Each step led to the next. "His father didn't care about a mythical rock; he just wanted his son out of Eddis."

"Yes," said Eddis.

"Because your council had just voted to kill him."

"Yes," said Eddis again.

"They have always been afraid of him."

"Afraid of what he would become."

"And you? Have you been afraid?"

Eddis was amused. "No." She shook her head.

Attolia didn't believe her. "But you've always known he could take your throne."

"No." Eddis's amusement gone, she said fiercely, "What I have always known is that I am the last Eddis, that my country will not outlast my lifetime. That it will be destroyed in the fires of the Sacred Mountain or overrun by invaders, or it *might* become part of a new country, under a new king, with a new name. Which would you hope for if you were me?"

"I don't understand why you don't hate him," said Attolia.

"The same reason you don't and Sophos doesn't, because of who he is," Eddis said softly.

"And who is he now?" Attolia cried, and Eddis took the stricken queen in her arms, pulling her close to comfort her.

"He is still our Gen, Irene. He can bear his god a little while without losing himself." A movement outside the tent caught her eye, and she said with forced lightness, "And look there, Emipopolitus's enemies have united against him."

Attolia opened her eyes to see that mild-mannered Petrus had not given up; he'd gone to his rival and recruited his aid. By the light of a single lantern, he and Galen were approaching the council tent together.

"Galen will not be turned away," said Eddis. "Gen is not the first Thief Galen has cared for."

Neither Galen nor Petrus came out again for a while, and when they did, they both had that satisfied look of men who have met a challenge and overcome it. By then, the soldiers already awakened by the return of the king and the explosions in the Mede camp were well on their way to being ready for battle. Their officers were meeting in Attolia's tent to discuss the plan for the day.

In the gray light of false dawn, the Medes were readying as well, but their war elephants were gone, their camp in disarray and many of their officers dead. They sent a messenger asking for a parley, stalling for time.

The king, in fresh clothes, his hair still wet from washing, climbed into the saddle of the horse they'd brought him. He pulled the reins experimentally, and the horse obediently turned in place. When Yorn Fordad approached, lifting his hand as if to lay it on the king's knee in friendship, the horse danced aside, leaving the hand hovering in the air before the Brael gave up and let it drop.

Fordad said apologetically, "Please understand, Your Majesty, that I acted in obedience to my king."

Eugenides laughed. "When I lie, Fordad, I don't beg people to forgive me for it."

Fordad bowed stiffly and said, "I will pray for your victory on the field, Your Majesty."

"Pray that I triumph today, Fordad, or that I die," said Eugenides, bending from the back of the horse to look the Braeling in the eye. "If I live through this day and I am not king, then all that remains will be the Thief, and every sovereign of the Continent who betrayed me will wake choking on their own blood, I swear it. Your king in his innermost chamber, with his rune stones laid out on the table and his ship lamps by his bed and his curtains trimmed in beads of carved jet, he will not be the first one to die, but the last. I say it three times, Fordad. It will be so. It will be so. It will be so."

As Fordad staggered back, the king jerked at the reins of his horse and rode to the parley. In the confusion that followed, the Braeling took a horse and rode for Stinos and was not seen in Attolia again.

For the first time, Eddis and Sounis as well as Attolia and Eugenides rode down to the parley with the remaining Mede generals and Nahuseresh, who had taken charge of them. Uneasily, the Mede officers stood behind their self-proclaimed leader. They knew the cost of failing their emperor, and none of them had wanted to be in command, afraid their careers and perhaps their lives might already be over.

Arriving in front of them, the king smiled. "But where is Erondites?" he asked.

"I am in command here," Nahuseresh announced.

Eugenides ignored him. "We can hardly negotiate without the man in charge." He raised his voice. "Erondites!" he called toward the scattered tents in the distance. Standing in the stirrups, he called again, roaring at the top of his lungs, "Erondites!" And a bolt of lightning cracked the sky. It struck a tent in the Mede camp. Canvas blossomed into black smoke and red flame. As the tent burned, Eugenides said to the stunned Mede, "That is all the parley that happens today."

In eerie silence, unbroken by any sound from either army, the king rode back across the empty battlefield. When he pulled up outside the council tent, his father dismounted and approached, laying a hand on the king's leg. Feeling the tremor in it, he opened his arms to catch the king as he fell.

INTERREGNUM

*E*ugenides was standing in the dark, alone.

He blinked, held his hand before his face, saw nothing. He rubbed his eyes and swung around, careful to keep his balance, but there was no light anywhere. The ground was hard under his feet, but not a floor. Small stones stuck beneath his boots made a scraping noise. Soft at first, there was a sound of voices in the distance, but their words and the direction from which they came were unclear.

He stretched one foot forward, accustomed to moving in darkness, and paused. There was a light as he waited, growing from a pinprick to the size of a candle flame. It was a candle flame, held in the hand of a man he recognized.

Lader, said Eugenides.

Indeed, said Lader. Exactly as you made me.

I did not make you, said Eugenides.

You made me dead. Stopped all change at this moment, made me this man forever.

You made yourself. I did not make that man that you were when you died.

Lader dismissed the objection with a shrug. It doesn't change your responsibility for killing all the men that I might have become.

I am not a judge to know if you would be a better man if you had lived. You broke the laws and offended the gods. I kept the laws and killed you.

Did you? asked Lader. Did you strike because I had offended the gods, or because you hated me?

Because you offended the gods.

Speak truth, Eugenides, Lader compelled him.

Because I hated you.

Lader stepped forward, holding the candle higher, its flame casting brighter light and deeper shadows. The candle burned, but Eugenides could feel no heat from it. He did not take his eyes off Lader's face.

Here is a message from the gods, Thief. Beware the house of Erondites. What an Erondites knows will destroy you. Beware, Eugenides. Your greatest danger will come from the tongueless one, if you allow it. You know I speak the truth. No one lies here.

The candle flame guttered and went out. Eugenides was alone again.

CHAPTER TEN

The tent walls were glowing in the light of the afternoon sun when the king rolled over on his bed and opened his eyes. Attolia was on a chair beside him, her lap desk balanced across her knees, only functional because she'd had a supporting leg added to the underside. Reaching out, the king touched her very gently, as if she might be a dream. "Are you well?" he asked.

"Of course I am well," she said. "Are you?"

"I am. I was someplace—dark—I can't remember. The Medes?" he asked, waking more fully.

"Routed after the death of Erondites," Attolia reassured him. "For three days we've driven them back."

"Erondites is dead, then?"

"Yes. It was his tent that burned, and they have identified his body."

"Three days?" he said, taking note of the unusual quiet all around the tent.

"We are some distance behind the battle line. Nahuseresh has failed to rally his army and Eddis has pushed the Medes deep into the narrow part of the Pinosh Valley. We have captured a great many prisoners, including . . ." She paused, savoring the moment.

"Tell me," said the king, impatient.

"Three elephants," she said with the barest hint of smugness, "and two of their handlers."

"My queen," said the king, raising himself on his elbows. "My excellent queen."

"The handlers' uniforms were distinctive," said Attolia. "We saw them at the first parley. I offered a bounty for any prisoners in those uniforms brought to me alive, and they, in turn, helped capture their animals. If you are feeling well enough, I will send Pheris with a message to break our camp here. What is it?" I heard her ask.

Sitting on stools outside the door of the tent, Chloe and I were the only attendants waiting on Attolia and the king. I was hanging on every word; Chloe, very prim, was trying to look as if she wasn't.

We both heard the king say, very slowly, as if trying to remember, "My dream. I was in the dark and Lader came with a prophecy for me." He spoke slowly, but with growing certainty. "He said to beware the house of Erondites. What an Erondites knows will destroy me, and my greatest danger will come from the tongueless one."

Chloe, sitting across from me, narrowed her eyes. It dawned on me only then that with my grandfather's death, I had become Erondites, not just a member of my family, the head of it. Instead of any feeling of triumph at how the tables had turned, I felt sick. I shook my head violently at Chloe. Her expression didn't change.

"Lader?" I heard the queen ask.

"Lader," the king confirmed. "Not someone who wishes me well. Pheris," he said, and I knew that he knew I'd heard every word. Shaking, I rose from the stool and went into the tent. He lay in the rumpled bedclothes, his hair going in all directions as it always did in the morning, his face creased with sleep. He smiled, and it was the smile I knew.

My fears eased, though Attolia's expression remained speculative.

"You know the story of the potter and the prophet?" the king asked me.

Indeed I did.

"This prophecy—it was not Moira bringing me a message from the Great Goddess. This was a truth delivered by a man who hates me. I will not go breaking all my pots on his say-so. Do you understand? Now find me Teleus, please, and send him here. After that, carry Her Majesty's message to the camp master."

✦ ✦ ✦

I did as I was told, and as I returned to the king I met Teleus, just leaving the royal tent. With a stern expression and a hand on my shoulder, he steered me away from the entrance. I tried to resist. The dire words I'd heard in the king's tent were like carrion crows. I had felt their truth in my bones and I was frightened. Teleus pushed me firmly toward a fire ring some distance away. These burned patches, with their rustic seating and a barren expanse of trampled ground, were all that remained of the tent city that had been there a few days before.

Taking a seat on an upturned log, Teleus folded his hands. "The Braelings and the other Powers have betrayed us," he said at last, as if I didn't know that better than anyone. "The king has just informed me that before he left the capital, Relius shared his travel plans with Fordad."

Every thought of Lader's prophecy flew out of my head.

"We have not heard anything from Relius since he left the capital," Teleus said.

I started to shake my head, but managed to draw it only a little to one side, as if I were trying to move the weight of the world with my chin. Hilarion was dead, Lamion, Sotis, even Xikos, a death I wouldn't have guessed I would mourn and yet did. I would not accept another. The day Relius had left, Teleus had told him to be careful and Relius had mocked him. It was Teleus who was going to war, Teleus who would be in danger, not Relius.

"We had hoped that he was just unable to get a message through to us." Teleus was looking down at his hands, trying to get the words out. "He isn't coming back, Pheris."

I miss Relius. The queen had said it to the king when Pegistus's calculations for the march had been so badly off. They'd been afraid already that something had gone wrong.

Grief strikes in strange ways. I would never have expected that I would weep someday for Xikos, or that I would see Xortix's younger son sobbing his heart out when he learned that the lover he'd betrayed had died, or that, losing Relius, I would think of all the words I'd written with such care in the journals he'd given me, words that he would never read if he was dead—and that my first tears for him would be tears of rage. We sat and cried together, Teleus and I, by the ashes of the dead fire, as the men broke up the few remaining tents in the camp. Then Teleus wiped my face with his sleeve and sent me back to the king.

I was in the royal tent, rolling the bed linens to go into a trunk, when a messenger arrived, bringing word from Sounis that a new prisoner had been taken.

"Is it Nahuseresh?" asked the king hopefully. No other prisoner came to mind that was worth sending a messenger on a hard ride when the king would already be on his way to the main camp very soon.

"It's Sejanus, Your Majesty."

The king paused in the act of stuffing one foot into his trousers. He let me help him attach the straps of his hook and cuff, but all the ceremony of dressing and undressing him had long since been surrendered to the demands of war. "I suppose I should have wondered before now what he might be up to," the king said thoughtfully. "Pheris, leave the packing for someone else and fetch Teleus. I want to go as soon as possible, and I want you with me."

We rode into the main camp as the sun was dropping toward the horizon. The tents were all aglow in the slanting light, and there was a breeze to blow the stink away. It looked like a scene from a storybook, but the king's mood was as foul as the sewage in the mud between the brightly colored tents.

The sides of the council tent had been rolled up. The table in the center had been moved away to leave space in front of the four folding chairs draped with cloth and cushioned with furs. The king sat with Attolia on his left and Eddis and Sounis to his right as Sejanus was brought to them in chains.

"I came to warn you," he protested on his knees.

"No," said the king. "You escaped your arrest and came to join your father. Finding him dead, you are pretending you came to warn me."

"I didn't know he was dead," insisted Sejanus.

"My condolences," said the king.

I'm not sure I would have known my uncle if we'd met on the road. Thin and filthy, his long hair in tangles, he looked nothing like the urbane visitor at the Villa Suterpe. He knew me, though. He looked in every direction except mine.

"Tell me, Sejanus," said the king. "Isolated as you were, how did you discover this plot against me?"

"My father arranged my escape, I admit that. As soon as I was free, though, I came here to warn you."

"Directly," the king said in utter disbelief.

"Directly!"

The king appeared to consider, then shook his head again. "No. It doesn't seem more plausible no matter how many times you repeat it."

"Your Majesty, please—"

"You know what would make it easier to believe, Sejanus? If you told me the names of the others who conspired with your father."

"I don't know who they are," said my uncle, too quickly.

"You don't?" asked the king. "Are you sure? You couldn't point out one or two?" He gestured at the assembled barons, hidden among them those who had conspired with Erondites. My grandfather could not have acted alone. Sejanus might have given away a conspirator with a single glance, but he didn't. He was studying the dirt in front of him with all his attention.

"You have escaped the custody imposed by your king. The penalty for that is death," said the king.

"I am not afraid to die, Your Majesty," Sejanus said proudly.

The king shifted, sitting forward with his elbows on his knees to ask, "What *are* you afraid of, Sejanus?"

"Your Majesty, even if you torture me, I cannot give you names I do not know." Brave words.

Remembering the brazier in Bu-seneth's tent and the rack of hot irons, the sound and the smell of them, I felt my gorge rise. There was a sense of momentum, as if the king was somehow hurtling forward like a runaway cart as he said, "You do know them and you will give them to me."

None of the people in that tent would have protested if the king had ordered Sejanus carved into pieces. None of those standing in ranks around the tent, either. All of them would have said it was because he was their king and they were his loyal subjects. The truth is, they were frightened. Even Susa. They'd all seen the king when he returned from the Mede camp, and not one of them would cross him. Some of those standing in the tent were already making plans to flee.

I knew it was wrong—that the king who had so recently suffered at the Medes' hands would use those tools on another man, and my secret, most monstrous self whispered, "Better him than me. Better that Erondites than this one."

"Secure him for the night," said the king. "We will deal with him in the morning."

The guard put Sejanus in a goat pen. The gate of the pen was tied closed with rawhide, its security not so much in its fencing as in the men posted to keep an eye on the prisoner at all times. With its sides made of staves lashed loosely together, everyone could see his humiliation. As a light rain fell, soaking Sejanus and the blanket they had given him, people came to stare. No one jeered, though; no one said anything at all, unsettled and unsure why.

Eddis went to speak to the king, and Ion, on the king's orders, had to turn her away. She went to Attolia with her concerns, and Attolia told her about Lader's warning.

"Lader was always poisonous," said Eddis.

"His words are still prophecy. The gods themselves say that what Sejanus knows will destroy the king," said Attolia. "He must give up the names of those who have committed treason. It is an ugly business. I see your concerns, but the law is clear."

Eddis said, "Sejanus used every weaseling trick he knew to torment Gen. Even if Gen had his own reasons for allowing it, he came to hate Sejanus and those wounds still bleed. I am afraid emotion clouds his reason."

"Then it is good that he has the law to guide him."

Eddis frowned. "The law may not be enough."

"Pheris," Sejanus called to me in a carrying whisper. I had walked past the pen three times already, making excuse after excuse to pass that way. I was trying to see the man I remembered in the abject prisoner huddled under a damp blanket. I knew he was an enemy of my king. I also knew that when I had been the monster in the Villa Suterpe, he had been kind to me.

"Pheris," he begged. "Please. Come closer."

Reluctantly I approached and crouched by the pen.

He held his hand out between the stakes. "This is my last ring," he said. "Take it."

I wasn't stupid enough to go so near.

"Take it." He shook it in his hand. "I have promised it to a man who will lead you to safety. Can you understand me?" He narrowed his eyes, searching my face for some sign of comprehension. "Alestis was a stable boy on our estate when your mother and I were your age. Alestis, can you remember that name? We were friends and he will take you to your grandmother. You will give him my ring as payment. Do you understand?"

He tossed the ring. I didn't catch it and it dropped into the grass by my feet.

"Hey," said the guard, noticing us, and Sejanus pulled back his hand. "Move along there," said the guard.

"Take the ring," whispered Sejanus. "Take it and give it to Alestis."

I scooped it up and left without looking at him again. I admit that I was intrigued that Sejanus had given to me the last thing he had of any value, but the idea of him helping me seemed as implausible as the claims he'd made to the king. I took the ring back to the tent I shared with the other attendants. The space inside had at the outset been quite crowded, with a cot and a trunk for each of us. The trunks were still there, but half the cots were gone. I pulled out of my trunk the box I'd brought from my hiding place in the palace garden what felt like eons ago, where I kept my pens and ink bottles and small pieces of paper, my counters, my collection of odds and ends.

I laid out all my small treasures on my cot, adding the ring to my various patterns and finding none that pleased me. I moved the pieces, the rocks and the feathers, the buttons and coins, the gold cufflink I'd slipped from the sleeve of Xikos's coat. He'd assumed he'd lost it. He didn't take good care of his things and with one gone, he'd had to pay for a new set. He was so angry and never guessed it was me. The memory had been a little spot of glee before, but now it ached like a bruise.

The ring didn't fit, the cufflink was a bruise, my regrets

were a road my thoughts traveled down until they came inevitably to Emtis. Emtis was the reason I feared that I was, as my family called me, a monster. He'd hurt me and I'd thought I was justified in hurting him. Perhaps I would have been if I'd acted from fear alone. Instead, I'd taken revenge and only afterward asked what my hate had made of me.

I thought of the king, haunted by Lader. I thought of how much he hated Sejanus and I thought about the prophecy. Sejanus had mocked and humiliated the king. So had many others, but it was Sejanus who had come so close to killing him. The king had seen him directing the assassins in the garden without recognizing the danger. He'd survived that attack by inches. Fear and hatred twine together. Looking at the stones and the delicate feather of a wren, Xikos's cufflink and Sejanus's ring, I saw a pattern. I saw the relationship between all the pieces, hate, fear, revenge, remorse. I saw it as if it were one of the magus's equations and I could calculate the outcome. Whatever it was that Sejanus knew, learning it would destroy the king.

I picked up the ring—one single piece removed from the pattern, and all of it was altered. I packed up my treasures and put Sejanus's ring back in my pocket. On a page pulled from my journals, using penmanship that would have made Relius proud, I wrote out a message requesting a horse and signed it with Baron Orutus's name. No one would question it if the secretary of the archives sent for a horse, and no one would doubt that it was the secretary's order when it was delivered by the king's most easily identifiable attendant.

This masterstroke of deception turned out to be entirely unnecessary. After hunting through the camp for the man Alestis and seeing in an instant I would get no help from him, I went to the spot on the horse lines where the royal horses were picketed, to find the stable master expecting me.

"Shall I have her saddled?"

He took my blank stare for concern.

"She has a few more pepper spots, and I've put cream on them. Otherwise she's as sound as a drum."

Snap. In the chaos after the powder exploded in the Mede camp, she too had made her escape. She'd been found the next day wandering the Attolian picket lines, looking for her friends. The master sent a groom to fetch her, and once I had petted her all over and kissed her clever nose, he helped me to mount, assuming that I was taking her for a ride to celebrate.

As the camp settled for the night and Ion and Medander waited on the king, I wandered among the tents. Back in the capital, when the armies had been mustering, the soldiers had been out at all hours drinking in the taverns or swaggering through the streets. In the camp, the men who had fought through one day and knew they might have to do so the next were more inclined to get a good night's sleep.

Those who stayed at the fires, sharing their wine and talking together, kept their voices low.

Passing Sejanus's pen, I mooned theatrically over a honey cake I had slipped from the royal table, and his guards, as I thought they would, lunged at me as if to snatch it away. I might be instantly recognizable, might have the king's favor, but I was still a small person with a treat, and I made a tempting victim. Perhaps they were only teasing, but I cowered as if afraid and offered them the wineskin I was also carrying instead. They took it, thanking me for the "gift," and I hurried off.

I circled back to see them sharing the wine and waited out of sight until they had fallen asleep with Petrus's lethium inside them. With a blanket over my shoulder and a large melon under my arm, I went to untie the knots that closed the pen.

"What are you doing?" Sejanus hissed at me.

As I pulled the sagging gate open, I put a crooked finger to my lips. The guards were not deeply asleep and silence was crucial.

"Pheris, I must stay here or they will catch us both," Sejanus whispered.

I waited.

"Did Alestis send you?"

I nodded.

"Can he get us both free?" Hope gave his voice a desperate edge.

I nodded again. Lying is just letting people believe what they want to be true.

When I'd found Alestis, with the other Erondites soldiers, he'd seen me watching, and his look of contempt had been all I had needed to know that Sejanus had been mistaken in his friendship.

Carrying my blanket into the muddy pen, I arranged Sejanus's blanket over it, putting the melon underneath to give the semblance of a head under the cloth. Then I handed Sejanus Sotis's clothes. Ion's would have been a better fit, but Ion would have noticed them missing. Dressed in fine clothes, with his messy hair tied back, Sejanus was able to stroll past the picket lines like a man avoiding the stinking latrines, headed out into the woods to do his business.

I'd gone ahead, as if doing the same, and waited to lead him to where I'd tied my pony. I looked in the wrong thicket at first—they are all the same in the dark—lending too much verisimilitude to my show of idiocy for Sejanus. For a moment, I thought Snap had pulled free and we were doomed.

"Where is Alestis?" he asked me, repeating the question several times. Finally, blinking, I produced a rolled paper and handed it to him. He unrolled it in the dark and shrugged helplessly. "I have no light. Did the stupid bastard think I can read this in the dark?"

I handed him a waxed folder of matches. He squatted

down beside me to take them. "I'm sorry," he said, apologizing for his angry words. "I am sorry and I did not mean to frighten you." He patted me gently. "Thank you for the matches."

When he'd read the instructions, which I had written out in a scrawl no better than Alestis's might be, we mounted the pony. Sejanus's long legs hung past the stirrups and Snap grunted with the effort of carrying us both. Sejanus patted her, too.

We headed toward the ridge to the north and west side of the camp, splashing through shallow streams and weaving between the spindly trees. As the ground rose, the forest thickened and it was harder to stay on course. Sejanus climbed down to lead the pony while searching for a trace of a path to follow. Finally he found one that took us to the edge of the valley. It continued with the rocky cliffs on one side and the woods on the other, until we reached the stone marker we were seeking. I looped Snap's reins around the stele loosely so she could pull herself free, but I hoped she wouldn't do so too soon. Then we began to climb.

I'd grown much stronger in the time I'd been an attendant. I had been with the king for the three days he slept and I was quite rested. Even so, I had to move very slowly on the steep slope or risk a bone-breaking fall. I could feel Sejanus's impatience, yet he didn't rush me and he held my hand in the steeper parts, to be sure I didn't lose my balance. When I checked again and again to see how high we had climbed, he encouraged me.

"Don't look, you'll be all right."

When we reached a place where the trail flattened out on a narrow ledge, I hesitated, trying to screw up my courage. He saw it and he urged me to take a rest.

"We just have to be over the ridge by daylight," he said. "They cannot waste time chasing us if they don't know which way we've gone."

Cursing my weakness, I sat down beside him. Saving the king from himself was a harder business than I'd expected.

When Sejanus began to talk, I think it was to himself as much as to me. "I had a brother like you once. His name was Pheris too." Seeing me startle, he said, "No, not you, another Pheris, my brother Pheris. He was older than me, older than Dite. They gave him my father's, and *his* father's name, before they knew he was . . . that he was like you."

So I'd had an uncle I had never heard of as well as Dite, whom I'd completely forgotten about.

"Our father wanted to get rid of the baby. When they are born like that they are usually id—" He looked sideways at me and bit the word back. "Everyone thought the baby would die, but our nurse loved him and she kept him alive. She was always bringing him out and showing everyone how clever he was—because he *was* clever, but it didn't matter.

She got my father to play chess with him once, and when Pheris won, my father threw the board at him. We all knew who lost that game, but Melisande never learned."

She had, I thought.

Sejanus got back to his feet. Instead of rambling to the sky, he bent to speak directly to me. "I'm going to take you to my mother. The king will seize all the Erondites land, but she has a small unwedded estate he can't touch. She loved my brother. She will be happy to see you, and if Melisande still lives, she will send for her, too." He took my hand, reassuring me. "No one is going to hurt you. The king will not have you for a fool to mock in his court." In the dim light, he searched my face for comprehension and I nodded, reassuring him in turn.

Instead of seizing the opportunity I had right in front of me, I trailed after him like the idiot he thought I was, keeping one eye on the path and one on the ground below us, as he told me about his mother and incidentally about himself, and how he had ended up at the villa where he'd been a prisoner. "I was comfortable; no one was unkind," he said. "It took me a long time to realize that nothing I did would ever matter again. I'd been someone important and I'd thrown that away. For something so stupid, too. Here, take my hand, it's slippery."

He was helping me at every turn, though he was more tired than I was, and we soon had to rest again.

"My father wanted a puppet; I wanted Eugenides dead. Once he was gone, I was sure the queen would marry Dite. Dite loved her so much." Bone weary, he struggled back to his feet and, spreading his legs to brace himself, he offered me a hand. "I had a lot of time to think in that villa," he said. "I had been wrong about everything—Dite, the queen, the king. I hated my father and I ended up just like him."

He must have guessed what I would have asked, if I could have. Why had he let my grandfather help him escape?

He laughed at himself. "I wanted to be someone who mattered again," he admitted. "I'd never had the courage to stand up to my father the way Marina and Dite did. When the Medes offered me money to kill the king, I thought it was a stroke of luck—Dite would marry the queen and I would be out from under my father forever."

We were so high that on any steep spot on the trail I could have taken us both to our deaths, and Sejanus continued to hold my hand. I was still listening to him, and we'd nearly reached the end of our climb.

"He didn't ask me if I wanted to escape; he just arranged it. I hated him so much. I meant to go straight to the king. Reveal all my father's plans. I thought I might redeem myself."

But he hadn't told the king his father's plans.

"My father was dead and his conspiracy with him. All those men who were trapped in his web were free. Most of them didn't know he was treating with the Medes; some have done nothing more than give Erondites gold when he demanded it. All of them, if they aren't executed, will see their estates confiscated, their families ruined."

He was making excuses for them and for himself. "No one could stand up to my father. That's why Marina ran off. Only Dite ever defied him to his face—Dite the poet, Dite who played the flute and cried when he shot his first dove. My father despised Dite. The king thought he was striking such a blow against Erondites, but I'm sure he was delighted when his disobedient son was exiled, and the whole court would have known it. That's why no one dared to cross him—he always got his way in the end."

He tugged on my hand. I'd slowed, waiting to see what he said next. Did he realize that what he said about his father was what the other attendants said about Sejanus? That he always got his way?

He sensed my reluctance. "Pheris, if the king learns who conspired against him, if he destroys their houses, he will never be able to trust anyone again. He will be another Attolia, starting a new rebellion with each one he puts down, and my father will have his way even from beyond the grave. I can stop that. You don't believe me? No, you are making that face because you have no idea what I'm talking about. I am just nattering away, trying to convince myself. Maybe I am running away because I'm afraid. I don't know. I *am* afraid, that's the truth."

I slipped my hand free. Resting it on his arm, I watched his face closely in the moonlight, thinking about lies and how we want to believe them. I wanted to believe that he cared about the barons, his country, his countrymen.

His laugh was bleak.

"Poor imbecile. It's all right. Everything will be all right. Let's get moving."

We had nearly reached the spine of the ridge and I had run out of time. I began to back away.

"Pheris?" He looked down at me. There was just enough light that I could see his shoulders sag with exhaustion. "I'm sorry I called you an imbecile. Please don't be angry."

Maybe I was the one who was just afraid—afraid of dying, afraid of making another mistake as I had with Emtis. I don't know.

I'm not going with you.

"What do you mean?" he said, stunned. "You have to— you have to come with me."

As I had guessed, Juridius and I were not the first babies that Melisande had taught our secret, silent language.

I dug into the purse at my waist and pulled out his ring. I tossed it to him, high in the air so that it would be easy to catch. He still nearly missed it, leaving it until it was almost too late to put out his hands. He cupped the ring to his chest, continuing to stare down at me.

You can sell it to someone and get what you need with the coin.

He took a single step toward me and I was already turning to run down the trail, knowing I would fall.

"I'm sorry, I'm sorry," he called, holding out his hands, stepping deliberately back. "I will not chase you, I promise. But Pheris, you must come with me."

What happened to your brother?

He looked at me so sadly and said nothing.

Your father killed him.

It took him a long time to speak. "The morning after my grandfather died, when Melisande went to wake him, Pheris was dead."

I understood. It's hard to call your father a murderer, easier to say he was a traitor to his country than to say that he had suffocated his own son in his bed. I'd known all my life that my mother, but for spite, might have done the same to me. It is only now, as a grown man, that I can write it out in so many words.

"Come with me, Pheris. Alestis has arranged—"

Alestis arranged nothing.

"What?"

My pony. My directions.

"I don't understand," Sejanus said. "Marina told me you were not like our brother."

She doesn't know me.

Melisande had seen how cleverness failed to protect my uncle and had changed her tactics. Knowing my mother would otherwise have paraded me like a trophy prisoner in front of her father, knowing that when he lost patience with it, my life would be over, Melisande had insisted I play the fool.

"Pheris, come with me," begged Sejanus. "We will fetch Melisande to my mother's villa. She can have a ripe old age with us and you will be safe."

Safe? Because I don't matter?

"You cannot go back to the king."

I will serve him.

"You are Erondites. He will kill you."

I shook my head, not believing it. The men who took my wine would blame themselves for falling asleep. They would be punished, I knew, but I was stupid with my own cleverness and I told myself they'd brought it on themselves.

"You will lie to your king?" my uncle asked.

As you lied to him. We are liars, all the Erondites.

Sejanus thought back over the trail we had climbed, the narrow places, the ledges and the steep drops. He was realizing how close to death he had been, how close both of us had been.

I play chess, too.

He nodded, remembering his clever brother. "He would have sacrificed a pawn to eliminate a knight. Pheris, my mother loved him. She would take you in and be glad," he said. "Someday, we could approach the king . . ."

I shook my head and he gave up.

"Can you get back down on your own?" he asked, worried for me.

I nodded. I didn't know anything of the kind, but I let him believe what he wanted to believe.

"Then thank you, and thank you for this." He held up the ring.

Gods' blessings on your road.

"And on yours," said Sejanus. "Will you write to your grandmother?"

I will.

"Pheris." I had already started down, but I paused to look over my shoulder. "My brother was the best of the Erondites. He would be honored that you share his name."

Sejanus climbed on and I began the dangerous descent, hoping my pony was still waiting for me.

I got back to the camp just as the sun was rising. The descent had turned out to be safer than the climb, though hard on my clothes, as I slithered down most of it on my side. Snap had not pulled herself free, and I rode her close enough to camp to be sure she would find the picket lines again on her own. I slipped her bridle off and hung it over her withers, hoping the groom who found her in the morning would be puzzled, but not alarmed, by the empty saddle. I pushed her in the direction of the other horses and made my own way back, coming to the sentry and waiting to be recognized.

"Did you fall in your own hole?" he asked sarcastically, and I looked away. "Do you need a hand?" he asked more kindly, and I shook my head as if embarrassed. My bad leg ached fiercely and I limped at a snail's pace past Sejanus's pen and looked through the fencing. The wet blanket was still huddled in the center. The guards had been changed and no one was any the wiser. With the very last of my strength, I made it back to the attendants' tent and crawled into my cot.

CHAPTER ELEVEN

The camp was in an uproar when I woke. Groggy, I fumbled my way back into my clothes, my body so stiff that I fell twice and finally sat on the ground to put my feet into the legs of my trousers. Only when I had them on did I realize how filthy they were. It was no wonder the sentry had asked if I was all right. I had to undress and find another pair in my trunk. I left off my tunic, which was almost as dirty, and went in my shirt to the council tent. When I reached the tent, it was already full, and when I tried to slip in among the other attendants, Ion eyed me with a wrinkled brow and then stepped between me and the king.

The pickets had been alerted, the camp had been searched, but there was no sign of my uncle or his means of escape. The king was enraged, not the cold fury we'd seen before, but the heat of a temper burning out of control. He shouted at Teleus and at Baron Anacritus, who had charge of the camp. Neither could shout back, but Teleus was sorely tempted. Anacritus was afraid. The king promised death to anyone who had aided my uncle. Too late, I was afraid for the men I'd tricked into drinking lethium-laced wine.

No one was certain which guards to blame or I would have lived with the guilt for their deaths on my conscience. Before the king could condemn them all, as he might have done at that moment, word arrived that Nahuseresh had rallied his army. The Medes were marshaling to attack, and the king was ready to fly to pieces with frustration.

Over the three days that he had slept, Attolia and Eddis had driven the Peninsular armies relentlessly. They had succeeded in pushing the enemy all the way to the pass. Part of the Mede forces were already in the narrow gorge of the Pinosh River and hemmed in, as we were, by the steep sides of the Leonyla Valley. Their superior numbers were no longer the advantage they had been. To force the Medes to retreat any farther, though, would be to push a stopper into an already full bottle. The task would only grow more difficult as the battle lines narrowed and our men grew more exhausted.

"I want Sejanus," the king insisted.

"Gen," said Sounis, very sharply for him.

War is never just about men killing with swords and guns. Time is a weapon, and so is hunger. The Medes had abandoned most of their baggage train when they were routed after the death of Bu-seneth. If the Peninsular armies held their ground—only a few days, perhaps just one day more—the Medes would have to withdraw or starve. No one could be spared to hunt Sejanus. All of the Little Peninsula's resources needed to be committed to battle.

Grinding his teeth, the king gave in.

"Afterward, then," he said to Attolia.

"Afterward," she agreed. They both knew that Sejanus, with days to make good on his escape, would be impossible to find.

The queens issued their orders. Much had changed since the first contentious council meetings of the combined armies, and there was little need for discussion or even elaboration of their instructions. Sounis and one company of reserves would swing to one side of the valley; the king would take the other. All the rest of their forces would be committed to pushing the Medes back into the Leonyla Pass.

Neither Sounis nor the king would be risked in battle unless the main forces failed. If the Medes broke out, the two companies of reserves would fall on them in a pincer movement, their only hope to delay the enemy and give the queens time to escape. Teleus and a small company selected from the royal guard would see them safely to the mountains of Eddis.

Propelled by my words to my uncle the night before, in a desire to have a life that mattered, I followed the king out of the tent. Ion tried to pull me back. Pushing him away, I caught the king's eye.

"Stop it, Ion," said the king. "He is not the Erondites I'm worried about. What is it, Pheris?" His eyebrows shot up. He said, "No."

Stubbornly, I stood my ground.

"You will stay with the queens."

I had grown stronger over the previous year, strong enough to ride hard after the king and return with him from the Mede camp, strong enough to climb the steep sides of the Leonyla Valley and only be stiff and sore the next day. But the fundamentals had not changed. I could not ride hard, day after day, without rest. If our forces were defeated, as the queens fled, they would have to slow their pace or leave me behind. I would never make it to the mountains of Eddis.

"Get him his pony," said the king.

While everyone else was making their preparations, I was hastily cleaning as much of the dirt off my tunic as I could. I had no breastplate to strap on, no sword to wear. As we assembled around him, the king gave me a long knife, kneeling to buckle it around my waist himself.

"In a lifetime of stupid things, this may be the stupidest

thing I have ever done," he said to me. "But if I am told to watch Erondites, by the gods, I will. You stay close, do you understand?" He knew he could not keep me safe, and he was afraid for me. He looked me in the eye and said, "To hell with Lader if he thinks I will not trust you."

We rode into position, and I did stay close to the king. Ion was on one side of him and I on the other.

We could see across the valley to Sounis and his reserves, mostly Sounisians. His father was with him as well as his magus. On our side, except for the attendants, the soldiers were Eddisians. Eddis's minister of war was there, and many of the men were the king's close cousins.

We milled in place, some standing in their stirrups to get a better view of the battlefield through the thin trees downhill from us. The Medes were slow to enter the fight, the sounds of battle dim in the distance. The morning sun had burned off the mist that had come through the Leonyla the night before, and the sky overhead was cloudless. The grass was green, fed by the many streamlets of the Pinosh. A brown-and-white spotwing butterfly bobbled from the tiny yellow flowers of the chipweed to the larger blossoms of the trumpet grass.

There was a whistle in the air, like a hawk screeching over and over again, and someone must have finally turned to look for it.

It wasn't a hawk. To my horror, Ion pointed at a figure waving from high up on the ridge.

"Does anyone have a glass?" asked the king. I didn't need one. My back was bent, but my eyes were excellent.

"I think it's Sejanus," said Motis.

"Crossbow!" Ion shouted, and he leapt at the king, sweeping him off his horse. They both fell heavily to the ground while the rest of us, paralyzed, watched the slow arc of a crossbow quarrel against the sky. It landed some distance away. Cursing, the king shoved Ion away and got to his feet, holding his ribs.

"Damnation, Ion. Even if he'd hit me, which is next to impossible at that distance, the bolt would bounce off a linen shirt, never mind a breastplate. Someone go catch my horse." Unlike poor Fryst, the horse had not dropped back to a walk and was some distance away.

Several men had pistols and raised them to fire at Sejanus.

"Don't waste the shot," said the minister of war. "What does he think he's doing?"

Sejanus appeared to be waving the crossbow over his head and then pointing at us emphatically. I turned my pony toward where I'd seen the quarrel fall.

"Pheris?" I heard the king behind me.

I struggled to hold my reins and communicate at the same time.

"Find what?" asked the king.

Quarrel. Impatiently I made a long arc with my hand.

"The shot from the crossbow," the king said. "Find it." Men jumped down from their horses to look through the grass. Sejanus waited above us.

The bolt was almost completely buried in the ground, only the message wrapped around it visible. Motis brought it to the king, who passed it to his father to untie and unroll. The minister pulled the paper free, creased it so that it would stay flat, and handed it back.

My heart leapt into my throat. It was my note, my words scrawled on the scrap of paper torn from my journals. The king glanced briefly at what I'd written, then flipped the page over to read the words added clumsily in charcoal on the back.

"Mede. Naupent," the king read out loud.

As one, we all turned to look up at Sejanus. He was waving his arms over his head, crossed at the wrist and then wide open, the universal signal of distress, of warning.

"Naupent?" asked the king's father.

"It's a tiny pass," the king answered thoughtfully. "Just a footpath, but it's way over the hills from the coast."

"Is there a watch on it?"

"I don't know, I assume so." Attolia, who would have known, was too far away to ask.

"How would the Medes know about it?" Ion asked.

"Erondites," said the king. We all looked up at Sejanus.

"And this is Erondites's son," said his father. "Do you trust him?"

"No," said the king. He was still staring at the note and then up at Sejanus. If the king took his men to the pass, there would be only Sounis and his company to slow the Medes if the Peninsular army was overwhelmed. He shook his head. He squinted at the minister of war. "Should I?" he asked.

The minister of war considered. He'd heard the sounds of the fighting. He had seen enough of it through the trees to say, "For an army with no supplies and overwhelming numbers, they aren't pressing their advantage. They mustered late in the day, which might have been disorganization or might not. They might be waiting."

The king was quiet, still thinking. "'Naupent' means tongueless. The pass is so high the mist from the sea doesn't come through it." He was staring at me. I was still frozen by the sight of my words written on the paper in his hand. "It was never about you," said the king, as if a weight had been lifted. With my treacherous uncle on the hillside above, I was less certain. I prayed to the Great Goddess that the king was right. "Send a message to the council tent," the king ordered Ion. "We'll go to the pass."

"Not you," said the minister of war.

The king looked around at the open field. "Were you going to leave me here alone? Or do you mean to leave my guard and go by yourself?"

The minister frowned.

"Do you know where the pass lies?" the king asked. "Do any of you?" They did not.

"I will ride with you," said the king to his father. Before the minister could protest, he added reasonably, "I can go to ground when we get close."

There was no way to take horses up to the Naupent except to ride first out of the narrow part of the valley. Sounis and his reserves, Attolia and Eddis in front of the council tent, seeing the men wheeling on their horses and racing away, must have been dumbfounded. The king's messenger, once he reached the council tent, was sent on to Sounis with the news and with orders to divide the reserves and send half to take up the king's place.

We rode hard until we came to a path that climbed into the hills above the Pinosh, Snap doing her best to keep up. In time, I was clinging to her back as she trotted along the very ridge that Sejanus and I had climbed toward the night before. Sejanus was waiting there for us.

"The Medes are marching up to the Naupent. They mean to attack from the rear and capture the queens."

The king jerked his head toward the back of our little troop, and Sejanus went looking for someone to lift him onto a horse. No one would meet his eyes. Their horses stamped and threw up their heads.

It was Ion who finally held out a hand to Sejanus, and then we were on our way again, pushing our horses as fast as they could go up the hillsides and along their ridges until we reached the next hillside to climb. Snap's short legs were no longer a disadvantage, and she was a nimble climber. I, however, was having more and more trouble staying in the saddle as she swayed and lurched. I was exhausted before the ride began and was beginning to shake. At a wide spot in the trail, one of the soldiers pulled up beside me and held out his hands. I unbuckled the straps across my thighs and leaned toward him. He pulled me off my pony and settled me on his lap, which was no doubt safer but even more terrifying, as my legs dangled over every abyss we passed and my life hung on a man's forearm. I didn't even know his name and I do not believe he survived the battle at Naupent, as I did not see him again.

The king stopped his horse beside an outcropping like a rocky shoulder sticking out of the hillside. The trail disappeared around it and then reappeared on a slope some distance away, switchbacking upward to a notch in the knife edge of the mountain above us.

"We are close enough now," said the king. "You can see the way from here. Pheris and I will wait for reinforcements from the queens."

The minister of war nodded stern approval. He leaned to embrace his son, then he bowed his head to his high king and led the way forward. Ion hesitated, but the king waved him on. Dionis and Motis followed. My bearer deposited me back on Snap, and the man who had been leading her handed me back the reins. I sat on my pony, feeling weak and cheated as everyone else rode to glory, not really understanding that most of them were riding to their deaths. The last man had passed around a curve in the trail and the sound of horse hooves on rock was fading when I looked at the king, wondering how he could have given up his chance and mine to fight against the Medes.

He said, "This is no time to argue with my father." Then he pointed over my shoulder to the much fainter track behind me.

We turned our horses and began to climb. The ascent was much steeper at first than the route the minister of war had taken, and the horses had to scramble to get up it. Once they had, we could see that, like the other route, our path climbed all the way to the skyline. We watched as the minister of war reached it and passed through. Then we rode up after him.

Up close, the Naupent was a passage between sheer rock walls, so narrow I could have reached from Snap's back and touched them on either side. On the other side of it, we discovered the remains of the Attolian guard. Their bodies were scattered among those of the Mede advance party that the minister of war had killed in turn.

The open ground below the Naupent on the seaward side was cupped like a shallow bowl, tilted as if to spill its contents down the hill. There was even a trickle of a stream that pooled just before the lip of it, like a libation waiting to be poured out. Beyond that, the ground dropped too steeply to be seen from where we sat. Farther away, though, we could make out the route down to the Gulf and coming up it, their weapons shining in the sun, the Mede.

The Minister of War had ordered his men into formation on either side of the narrow streamlet. He looked over his shoulder as the king rode down to join them.

"I lied," said the king.

"I know," said his father. He pointed to the space he'd left open and the king moved into position.

CHAPTER TWELVE

The sun was rising as the queen of Attolia rode into the narrow passage of the Naupent, the hoofbeats of horses echoing behind her like ragged heartbeats. The mist ahead of her, held at the very threshold of the pass by the warm dry air inland, might have been a solid wall of gray stone. Crossing into it, Attolia found herself alone in a ghostly pale world as the ground underfoot went from gravel to grass and the hoofbeats behind her slowly faded.

She was listening with all her heart, but the only thing she could make out was the squeak of leather tack from the riders she'd brought with her. She sensed their presence on either side but could no longer see them.

"Your Majesty," someone on her left called quietly. It was Teleus, and she knew he'd found the first of the dead. She turned her horse in his direction.

Some of the bodies were laid in an orderly row; the others were scattered as if, by the time they had fallen, there had been no one to help them off the field. There was still silence as all ears listened for the slightest sound, a call for help, even a moan. The mist, catching the sun, was dissolving, revealing more and more bodies as it faded away, Attolian, Eddisian, and Mede.

Attolia and Eddis had been successful beyond all expectation. They had beaten back the Medes, forcing their enemy to retreat into the narrow gorge of the Leonyla, pushing them beyond the defensive walls built centuries earlier to narrow the already narrow passage. The Peninsula held those walls now, the gates of the Leonyla, and they could hold them indefinitely so long as they did not falter. The Peninsula had the advantage, and the advantage must not be wasted in grieving. Even for the death of the king.

Attolia had guessed what she would find and had made Eddis stay behind. They knew the pass had been held, because the Medes had not come through it. They also knew it had been held at terrible cost, because none of those who had gone to defend it had returned. No messenger even to tell the fate of the defenders, most of them Eddis's uncles and cousins, her high king, her Thief.

Attolia, her voice firmly under control, said, "Gather in our dead. Leave the enemy where they lie."

"There is no fuel for a pyre," said Teleus beside her.

"We will carry the dead through the Naupent and down to the fields of the Leonyla. They will have their due—their rites and their pyres—with our other fallen." A pyre that burns seven days for a high king, she thought.

The mist was receding faster, as if the horses coming through the pass had opened the way for the warm air, and it was flowing into the valley in a rush. So many bodies, lying tangled together, piled one on top of another, covering the ground. And still not a sound from anywhere around them.

"Only sleeping," Attolia said aloud.

"My queen?" Teleus thought he had misheard.

She swung down from her horse, landing heavily, catching the captain for balance. "They are sleeping, Teleus. We must wake them."

"My queen," Teleus said again, afraid for her as she moved from man to man, crouching over them, shaking them, saying, "Wake up, wake up."

He went after her. He hesitated, then he placed his hands on her shoulders. "My queen." He had no other words, and only the warmth of his touch in the chill morning air to offer. His voice penetrated my darkness, and slowly I opened my eyes to find myself lying in the wet grass where I had collapsed.

The day before, the minister of war had watched in amusement as the king tried to send me away from the battle line and I'd stubbornly refused to go. When the king turned to him for help, though, the minister had accomplished easily what the king could not. "There will be a pool under the laurels," he'd said, pointing to where the twisted mountain trees grew along the stream bed. "Collect every bottle and sack the men have and fill them there. Be ready when we call for water." When I still hesitated, the look he gave me was so stern, Snap was carrying me away before I knew I'd given in.

"Thank you," I heard the king say behind me.

"He should live to tell the tale," said his father. "Gods willing he will not fill it with nonsense for our great-grandchildren to read."

So I had helped the wounded back from the fighting, offering those who wanted water a sip and doing what I could to ease their passing. Then, as the Medes continued to flow into the shallow cup of the battlefield, over the lip of it like a libation running in reverse, rising against us in an endless tide, I had used my little knife, staggered and stabbed, striking at knees and thighs, certain I was going to die, only I had not.

As the sun had dropped and the shadow of the ridge reached out over us, the flow of the enemy had slowed then begun to recede. Their cause lost, the Medes had withdrawn, taking the path back down to the sea, descending into the mist as it rose to greet them, leaving those of us still alive to sink to the ground, too exhausted even to call out to one another as the mist covered us as well, not with cold and damp, but with darkness.

Now I rolled over and the horse nearest me danced away in surprise.

I was still blinking when Attolia stepped to my side and sank to the ground, too ungainly to bend down. She took my face quite gently in her hands and brushed my hair back from my face. "The king, Pheris. Does he live?"

I'd seen him toward the end of the battle, but he had stumbled away from me, into the mist.

Attolia turned to Teleus. "Look for the living," she said. "Gather in the dead. I will look for the king."

Pulling her robes a little higher, she picked her way across the slope of the battlefield, and I staggered after her. It was a miracle I could move at all. At first I concentrated on putting one foot in front of the other, but as I woke a little more, I stared into the faces of the dead as I passed. They were transformed, their skin as pale and hard as stone, their blood black, and the dew gathered on their hair and their eyelashes anointed them like sacred oil. They were easy to distinguish even in death by their uniforms or by the cloth bands on their arms. I looked at the foreign army and thought they too must be men of many different places, but I could not read the language of their faces and uniforms. In death, they were anonymous.

When we found the king, he lay unmoving, his face in the

curve of his arm. He'd been alive, I was certain, at the end of the day, but he was as still as the dead when the queen dropped beside him, calling his name.

On the ground next to the king lay the minister of war, each drop of condensation on his lifeless face glinting like a diamond in the strengthening light of the day. As I watched, the king woke and saw his father and remembered that his father was dead.

As he sat up, Attolia circled the king with her arms. He laid his head on her shoulder and drew his hand very gently around her. Wordless, the queen stared at the bodies scattered over the grass as if wondering where to begin grieving. When her eyes narrowed, I knew she'd seen Nahuseresh's body. It was not far away.

"Did your father kill him?" Attolia asked, catching at one small detail in the maelstrom of grief.

"The poets can say so," said the king, his voice hoarse from shouting and from weeping. "My father fell early in the day, and Nahuseresh was alive much later than that. I have no idea who killed him." His voice roughened further as the tears still to be shed began to rise. "I saw my father fall. I was too far away."

Leaving them to their grief, I picked my way back uphill.

Men moved from body to body, checking each for signs of life. The wounded who had slept through the night, dreaming dreams they would remember for the rest of their lives, slowly blinked awake when they were shaken. Each as he was found was brought up and laid with the other wounded to be cared for as best as we could manage. Our men had brought mules packed with blankets and bandaging. Once they had found all the living, they began to bring up the dead and laid them in their orderly rows as well. Few had survived, but all those who'd made it through the day had lived through the night.

In time, the king and queen made their way back up the slope. I was just sitting, growing stiffer by the minute, not even trying to make myself useful. Though I was not physically injured, I was much damaged in spirit. The swelling pain of my abused back and my leg seemed somehow a proper balance to the pain in my heart. I had found Ion, and he lived. Motis was dead. Dionis badly wounded. He held out his hand to me when he saw me, and I knelt beside him to take it. He was deathly pale but assured me he would live. I did not believe him.

I overheard the king talking and caught the name of my uncle. I had not seen Sejanus, living or dead, that morning, and I pricked up my ears. The king said he wanted him found if he still lived. I staggered to my feet, stretched my aching leg, and went to look for him.

I looked first among the wounded, as it was faster than looking through the dead, and if he was dead, then he was beyond aid or worry. I found him carrying water. I bent near him where he crouched over a soldier, holding his flask and letting the water drop a bit at a time into the man's mouth.

I tapped his shoulder. *The king is asking for you.*

"What does he say?" he asked, keeping his voice low.

I don't know, only that he asks if you live still.

Rising to his feet, Sejanus handed me the waterskin. Then he headed up through the last strands of mist, toward the pass, without waiting to discover if the king saw him as a savior or a traitor.

I took his flask and continued from one injured man to the next, offering each a drink. I was there, the flask dangling from my hand, when they brought Sejanus back down from the pass, holding him tight by the arms.

As the pyres for our dead burned, the Mede retreated farther. Those among them who most feared their emperor's displeasure had paid the ultimate price for their failure, and the rest were going home.

I had failed my king. Sejanus was under arrest again and the king, wild with grief, was determined to learn what would destroy him. Nothing I'd done had made a difference, and nothing I had done could have. If Sejanus had escaped entirely, if I had pushed my uncle to his death, if he'd died at the Naupent, the king would still have been determined to learn, at any cost, who had participated in Erondites's conspiracy, who among his subjects had worked to slow our advance to the Leonyla.

Eddis tried to talk him out of his obsession. "You can't do this."

"I can do anything I want!" he snapped.

"Gen!" she said, very close to losing her own temper, as she too was overwhelmed with grief. She continued more quietly. "You forget that you are not the only one your grandfather taught that lesson. Unlike all the other people who hear you"—she waved expansively at the camp full of people around them—"I know the rest of what he said: if you are queen, you can do anything you want—but never *everything* you want. He said to choose wisely. Gen, this single-minded pursuit of yours, I cannot tell you what catastrophe might come of it; I can only tell you it is unwise. You are king—"

"Am I?" the king interrupted airily. "I do not seem to be. If I were king, my orders would be obeyed."

With the Medes retreating, he had insisted that Attolia, heavily pregnant, should return to the safety of the capital. She'd refused to do so. He had commanded and she still had refused. He had stopped short of ordering Teleus to take the queen against her will. That Teleus wouldn't have obeyed the order perhaps was all that stopped the king from giving it.

Eddis had had enough. She bowed her head. "You are king of kings," she said, "and king of fools if you think you can give orders to your wife and expect her to obey."

The pyre for the king's father burned for three days. As its ashes cooled, the king summoned Sejanus. The walls around the council tent again were lifted and the tents on all sides had been struck to allow room for the crowd to gather. Again the fur-draped chairs were lined up, and again Sejanus was brought in chains before the rulers of the Lesser Peninsula. The high king had not slept for days, and his face was hollowed out with exhaustion, his eyes rimmed in red.

"I came to warn you," my uncle protested.

"You knew the Medes were there because you conspired with your father. Again, Sejanus, you change sides to save yourself."

"I—"

"You escaped and could have gone anywhere, yet you went to the Naupent. Why?"

"I didn't go to the Naupent," Sejanus insisted. He was hell-bent on telling the truth, though he knew he would not be believed. "I went in the opposite direction, but there was a woman in the woods. She said that if I turned around, I would meet a man with a message for me, so I did. I found one of the sentries from the pass, badly wounded. He had taken the wrong path down from the pass. When he asked me to carry the warning to you, I said I would."

"You met a woman in the woods?" said the king in disbelief. "Who was this mystery woman?"

"She appeared to be my childhood nurse, Melisande." Sejanus shrugged. The king hesitated, almost as if he did believe then, but he shook it off.

"And this sentry, where is he?" he asked.

Pegistus answered him. "Several of the sentries posted to the Naupent are still missing."

"I warned you. Isn't that the important part? I fought for you," Sejanus said hopelessly.

"The Erondites have always been excellent at joining the winning side once they know which side that is. It doesn't make them any less traitorous."

"You are my king," said Sejanus, and repeated it when the people around the tent recoiled at his audacity. "You are my king, I swear to you. I have been loyal to you since I left the villa where I was under arrest."

"If that is so, Sejanus, tell me: who conspired with your father?"

Sejanus considered one last time. "It is not my place to decide what my king should know and not know. If you ask again, I will tell you." He lifted his chained hands in supplication and said, "I am not begging for myself, I am begging for them. Please, don't ask."

I was not the only one who saw the king on the brink.

Eddis and Sounis watched helplessly. But Attolia drew him back. Lightly, she laid her hand on his. "My king," she said, "the old Erondites was dead already when someone helped Sejanus escape. Whoever did so did not act in fear of his father. Ask for that name first." She was looking at me.

Sejanus, who had been so careful not to indict another with his eyes, was caught off guard. He followed the direction of her gaze, and so did the king.

"No." Sejanus lunged forward and was pulled up by his chains. As he tried to take back his error, his carefully considered words turned to babbling. "It was my fault. It was all my fault. I arranged the escape and I forced Pheris to help me. Don't blame him. In the end, he wouldn't come with me. He came back to you. Please," he said again and again. "Please have some mercy."

My uncle had told the truth when he knew no one would believe him. I would not let him lie for me. I had done what I thought was right and I would not deceive my king. I stepped before the king.

I drugged the guards. I freed my uncle. Break this pot first.

I watched for the blood to drain from his face.

Instead, after a moment of astonishment, the king laughed. His amusement laced with bitterness, he shook his head.

"My dear," he said to the queen, acknowledging a point scored. "How neatly you chain them together."

"Turnabout is fair play," murmured Attolia.

The king dropped his chin to his chest and seemed lost in thought, as a breeze blew through the quiet tent, kicking up the colorful silk streamers hanging from corner poles, making the ends of them dance and sending a shiver down the backs of our necks. "Pheris," he said when he lifted his head. "You freed Sejanus and you helped him to escape." Instead of enraged, he appeared only exhausted.

I thought he would ask me why I had betrayed him, and I was ready.

"Shall I pardon him, then?"

That was a question I was unprepared to answer. I stood blinking, utterly at a loss, as Sejanus and the king waited for my answer. I thought back over all I knew of him, and over all I knew of myself, too.

I don't know.

"We never know, Pheris," said the king. "Decide anyway. For me."

That made it easier. For him, the answer was obvious. *Yes.*

"Will he betray me again?"

The hair rose at the back of my neck.

Never.

Eddis's eyes narrowed. Sounis tilted his head as if listening for a sound in the silent tent. Attolia looked away, as if uninterested.

The king announced, "The Erondites's patrimony will be

divided. One part to you, Pheris, one to Dite, and one to you, Sejanus. None of you will inherit from the others, all will return to the crown if you have no heirs."

Sejanus was staring as if he doubted his ears.

The king looked at him with dislike. Then he stood and left the low dais without another word, stalking off to the tent he shared with the queen and pulling the fabric over the doorway with finality. The queen instructed the guards to unchain Sejanus, and they hesitantly complied. Everything felt off-kilter and uncertain.

"Pheris?" said the queen.

Sejanus had come to kneel at my feet.

"You are the head of his house," said the queen gently.

I had no idea what to do.

"Perhaps Sejanus should join your kinsmen. The guards can escort him to their tents."

I nodded, my head bobbing like a fisher bird's, and the guards led Sejanus away. When he was gone, the queen said to me, "Where the king gives his heart, he gives it completely."

The king slept all afternoon. When he woke and saw me sitting nearby, he said, "I trusted you." I thought it was an accusation at first, and then I understood. He sent me to fetch Eddis, and when she came to his tent, he asked her point-blank how to make Attolia return to the palace.

"Eugenides," she said, thoroughly exasperated. "You

never *ask* for anything. My garnet earrings. The rubies from the Attolian Crown."

"They weren't from—" He started to argue, but Eddis scowled so fiercely, he subsided.

"*Ask her,*" said Eddis.

After she left, the king washed his face and combed his hair, put on his parade suit, now repaired to its former glory, and went to meet Attolia as she was leaving the council tent. He approached and took her hand. She frowned warily, but declined to draw it back. The king dropped to his knees, and then she did try to pull back, but it was too late; he wouldn't let go.

"My queen," he said with every appearance of humility. "No man, not even a king, should think he can command his wife, so I have come to ask you, please, will you return to the capital?"

The men filtering out the door of the council tent saw the tableau and hesitated. Unwilling to intrude, they stepped aside, but they didn't go on about their business. They waited to see what would happen. Those passing the council tent paused. Anyone within sight of it began to draw near, and seeing them moving, people farther away did the same.

As the crowd grew, Attolia searched it for Eddis and found her smiling serenely next to Sounis.

"I see that we all have our hands on each other's hearts," Attolia said acidly.

"You have defeated the enemy," said the king. "Pick your generals. I will go with them to drive the last of the Medes from our shores, and you can go safely home. I am not ordering, I am merely asking."

Attolia tried to pull him up.

"You were merely asking," she pointed out.

"And will go on asking, from right here, in the mud, until you agree."

The crowd of onlookers was growing.

"You do not know a wagon from a wheelbarrow," Attolia said.

"That is so," agreed the king earnestly. "I will let your generals guide me, I swear."

"You make more promises than the moon," said Attolia.

"A man may do many strange things and not feel he has broken a promise if he keeps his faith with the one to whom he made it." Very briefly, he glanced at me.

Attolia, looking away, appeared to be listening to something only she could hear. "So, so, so," she said at last. "It is time for me to turn to woman's work. I will go, my king."

"Thank you," the king said in relief, climbing back to his feet and trying to wipe the mud off his knees. "Take Eddis with you."

Eddis made a small choking sound, and Attolia's eyebrows rose in speculation.

The king said, "Forgive me. I misspoke. What I meant to

say was, would you please take Eddis with you?"

"Helen?" Sounis asked uncertainly.

"He's slow," the king said in a stage whisper to Attolia. "He does eventually catch on."

"Yes," Eddis said, her cheeks reddening. She stepped out from the crowd to join Attolia. "Yes," she said as they stood arm in arm. "We will both go, not that you were asking," she said to the king.

Nudges were followed by smiles, and as the news was passed back through the ranks of those gathering to hear it, there were cheers. Once they'd quieted a little, the king said, "Take Sounis, too."

"What?" Sounis was not sure he'd heard properly.

"Yes," said the king. "All three of you. Go confer with your barons, your patronoi lesser and greater, your okloi, your townspeople and their mayors." He spoke to Eddis and Sounis and Attolia, but he addressed everyone around him, his joking demeanor gone. "The Medes will return, and if not the Medes, others who want to control the Lesser Peninsula, this land of Hephestia's making. The treaty between Sounis and Eddis and Attolia cannot be fixed in one person, in one life as ephemeral as the rain in summer. There must be a charter of one law for everyone, with one council drawn from all three countries so that in future they may select a new high king, as they do in Sounis. We need an unbreakable union, and only you three can make it."

To Attolia, he added hesitantly, "The right to be high king cannot be passed to our child."

The queen nodded. "To be king or queen of Attolia is enough," she said.

To Eddis, the king said, "There will be land grants in Sounis and Attolia to the veterans of this war." She nodded as well, knowing that the offer of good land would empty her mountain country. To the king of Sounis, he said, "Take the magus. He was born for this," and they all laughed.

The king did not say, did not need to say, that he must be absent. He would remain in the north as long as necessary for them to forge an agreement, though it meant he could not be with his queen.

That was how, with his knees covered in mud, Eugenides united the three countries into one.

CHAPTER THIRTEEN

*E*ven in Stinos's protected harbor, the Etisian winds blowing across the decks of the *Ruby*, the *Diamond*, and the *Sapphire* made the rigging hum. The tops of all the waves were white, and the few clouds in the sky scudded past like runaway sheep. With the wind behind them, the *Ruby* and the *Diamond* would carry Eddis and Attolia and Sounis back to the city of Attolia in days, not weeks.

The king had accompanied the travelers out to the ships. As he said his farewells, Eddis drew him close. With the wind blowing her words away, only he heard them.

"Gen," she said. "Be careful."

"Of course," he promised.

"I dreamed of the eruption again last night," she told him, and he sobered.

Eddis nodded. She too had thought that the gods would

be pleased by the unification of the three countries. "Do not offend the gods," she warned him, though neither of them could guess what that might mean.

Once the ships had left the harbor, we set out to drive the Medes north along the Attolian coast toward Roa, fighting their rear guard in skirmishes, hunting through the woods for deserters who meant to hide and turn bandit rather than go back to the empire. It was an ugly business, and Sejanus died before we reached the border. It was a gut wound that quickly turned septic. I wished for the royal physicians, either of them, but the healers in the hospital tent assured me that there was nothing even Galen or Petrus could have done.

I sat next to Sejanus, washing him in lavender water as the fever set in, promising him I would write to his mother, that I would write to his brother Dite, that I would forgive my own brother, Juridius. As his thoughts wandered back in time, he told me about his brother Pheris, about the games he would devise pitting his agile mind against his brothers' and sister's agile bodies.

"Your mother wasn't always so ruthless," he said. "It was Pheris's death that hollowed out Marina's heart. We have weak hearts, the Erondites."

No, not you. It was your stupid head that got you into trouble.

He smiled, but as the fever burned, he grew more anxious, worrying over the past. He plucked at the blanket with his hands and turned his head fretfully. I struggled to soothe him; there was little I could do. As I replaced his pillow for the hundredth time, the king came to the doorway of the hospital tent. He hooked a foot through a campstool and slid it near to Sejanus's cot. Staying there some time, he spoke quietly with Sejanus.

My uncle asked about Dite and learned for the first time that his older brother was the music master in the court of Ferria.

"He is free to come home whenever he chooses. He might not, though," the king warned gently. "He's very happy there."

"He is?" Sejanus asked, his voice thready.

He hadn't known. His only contact with the world had been messages smuggled in by his father, and his father had never mentioned his other living son, hadn't cared what had become of him.

The king said, "Juridius is with him. When he is ready, he too may come home." They talked about the Erondites estate and what part of it Sejanus would choose to be in my hands. Before he left, the king bent over my uncle, brushed his hair gently aside, and kissed him on the forehead. Sejanus, much eased, died a few hours later.

When the ashes of his pyre had cooled, I climbed onto my pony to catch up with the king. On the road I passed

companies of soldiers marching back toward Attolia. The
Medes' inclination to fight dropped with each mile they
retreated, and more and more of our soldiers were being
released to return home. I stayed the nights in whatever
camp I found convenient. I was easily recognized and welcomed, a marvel to me then, and even now. At some point,
as the king already had, I crossed the border into Roa.

Harrying the Medes, the king had not hesitated to enter
Roa uninvited. He was not at all surprised, though, when
he reached the small harbor town of Nedus, to find a party
waiting for him, sent by the king of Roa. In the strictest
terms, the spokesman warned Eugenides off from further
trespassing lest he risk creating ill will.

"Me create ill will?" said our king.

"Indeed," said the spokesman, a weedy man, with his
long hair blowing in his face, making it difficult to take him
seriously. "I remind you that there are treaties between Roa
and Attolia!"

"There were treaties between Roa and Attolia when your
king allowed the Mede army to march past him without a
peep."

"It is not for you to say how the Mede will be treated on
land that does not belong to the Attolians."

"That is certainly true," the king conceded.

"Then we shall tell our king that you are turning back,"
the spokesman said.

"You can tell His Majesty whatever you like," said our king cheerfully. Then he rode past them into the town.

The *Sapphire* had recently reached the harbor after beating its way north against the wind. Her captain was waiting at the gangplank to welcome the king on board.

"Their Majesties?" the king asked him, cutting short the ceremonial greetings.

"All have safely reached the city," the captain assured him. "Her Majesty who is Eddis has decided to remain in Attolia at the request of the royal physicians." When he saw the concern in the king's face, he added, "The physicians would like to attend both of Their Majesties."

"Getting along like a house on fire, are they?"

"Evidently," said the captain.

The king did not appear any less worried, but they moved on to discuss unloading the supplies on the ship and how best to bring the wounded on board before it sailed south again. When they had finished their arrangements, the king rode back to his army. He was unsurprised to find the Roans still milling in confusion outside the town. They felt their message had not landed as it ought to have.

They tried to deliver it again, but the king waved them away, saying. "I will pursue the Medes until they are no longer a threat. Offer them your support or don't, as you like. I think you will find you have welcomed poor guests into your home. As for broken treaties, tell your king to think very carefully before he raises that issue with me."

When the *Sapphire* had departed, the king left a garrison to secure the harbor, and we carried on along the coast of Roa.

Late one night as I was longing for the cot that was set up and waiting for me in the tent I shared with Ion, the king and Ion and I were listening to Pegistus and Trokides argue over the council table. These were the two generals that Attolia and Eddis had tasked with the campaign to rout the Medes, under the nominal supervision of the high king. Eddis had lost her senior general, Xenophon, as well as her minister of war in the battle for the Leonyla. Sounis had wanted his magus with him for the negotiations in the capital and had sent his father to the capital of Sounis to supervise matters there. While there were other candidates, Trokides was a reliable soldier and Pegistus a careful planner. If neither of them was a cunning strategist, chasing the Medes had not called for great military innovation.

Unfortunately, without cooler heads to mediate between them, they fought over everything. While they were both full of self-importance, they were not stupid—their disagreements, though fiery, usually ended in some grumbling accord, and the king did not intervene in them. He did occasionally lay his head down on the table and feign sleep or threaten them with dire forms of execution, which they ignored.

That night, we had camped on a bluff above a narrow but fast-moving river. Trokides felt we should knock together rafts and cross the river as quickly as possible. Pegistus had sent scouts to look for a ford, and he wanted to wait until they returned. The king, with his head resting on the back of his seat and a wine cup in his hand, was glancing from Trokides to Pegistus and back again with diminishing patience when a guard stepped into the doorway. Trokides and Pegistus glared equally at the interruption, but the king's expression was more hopeful.

"They're at the pickets, Your Majesty," said the guard with a broad smile. "Both of them."

It was Costis and Kamet. They were brought to the council tent a little later and greeted with embraces and kisses. I smiled shyly at Kamet, hardly recognizing the tidy scribe with the worldly air I'd seen in Attolia's palace. His hair had grown shaggy and he was dressed in what appeared to be a remanufactured blanket.

Costis had made it safely back to the temple complex to find Kamet waiting. By the time Nahuseresh's men had arrived on the hunt through small towns up and down the coast of Roa, Costis and Kamet had made their way into the hills to shelter in an abandoned shepherd's hut. Costis had found and prepared it during the months he was pretending to be a naturalist and keeping an eye on the Ellid Sea for signs of the Mede ships. Carefully scouting from their hiding place, Costis had seen the retreat of the Medes and had been watching and waiting, hoping the Attolians would be on their heels.

"You smell like sheep," the king said to Kamet.

"Your Majesty, it's been awful," Kamet responded. "I had to sleep on the floor. It's not the sheep I smell of."

"Costis," the king said reprovingly.

"He is alive," Costis said. It made me smile again to hear him sound so much like his captain, Teleus.

Trokides and Pegistus were eager to get back to their argument and happy to draw Costis and Kamet into it. They had been working from the limited information brought in by scouts, and local knowledge was what they needed.

"There are fords upstream," said Kamet. "The bluffs on either side of the Lusimina just get higher and the river narrower. The only other ford is downstream, at least two days away."

"Then we must cross here," said Trokides triumphantly.

"They are in the woods on the opposite bank. They are going to shoot anyone trying to cross in a boat," insisted Pegistus.

I'd been trying to remember where I'd heard the name of the river.

"What is it, Pheris?"

The river. The name.

"Lusimina?" the king asked, checking with Kamet to see if he'd heard correctly.

Slowly the memory I needed floated to the surface of my mind.

After the ambush, when we returned to our camp, the watchmen asked who you were.

The king blinked, as if he had trouble recalling that night.

Remember what you said. By the will of the Great Goddess, king of Attolia, king over Sounis and Eddis . . . king over all the land from . . . the mountains . . .

I didn't have a sign for Macheddic, or Melenzetti for that matter. Seeing my frustration, the king reached for the charcoal stick they'd been using to mark the map and handed it to me. He tapped a bare spot on the vellum. Slowly at first, and then with increasing confidence, I wrote out the words "king from the Macheddic Mountains to the sea, king from the Melenzetti Pass to the River Lusimina."

"Did I say that?" the king asked.

Yes.

I was Erondites. I knew what would destroy the king and would not let Lader triumph from beyond the grave. *Do not overreach.*

"Your Majesty?" Pegistus prompted impatiently.

"We will not cross the river," the king said slowly, but with certainty.

Trokides was outraged. "On the word of a child?" he said.

"Your Majesty?" Pegistus protested. "If the Medes turn and come this way again, Roa will not stop them."

"No," said the king. "We will build a fort here and garrison it."

"On Roa's land?" Pegistus was horrified.

"No, not on Roa's land," said the king. It had been in his mind all along to make the king of Roa pay for his treachery. Eugenides moved his hand across the map. "This is Attolia now."

"And if the king of Roa objects?" Trokides asked, quite reasonably.

The king shrugged. "He can send his complaints to the courts of the Greater Powers of the Continent or to his new friend Ghasnuvidas, emperor of the Mede, and see who comes to his aid. This land is Attolia, and we will march no farther."

Far away in the capital city of Attolia, Eddis woke in the dark. She'd been dreaming, as she had so many times before, of a dark night and the crisp mountain air of Eddis, the sky full of stars shining so bright on the Sacred Mountain that the snow on its slopes glowed even though there was no moon. She'd dreamed she was on the roof walks of her palace, looking over her city, and the quiet night was shattered by a crack and then a roar as the mountaintop exploded into a ball of fire and gouts of flame shot into the air, only to be hidden by an ever-expanding cloud of smoke. She had run through the palace, desperate to reach the streets to warn the people. The snow on the slopes was melting, some of it turning to steam but the rest into a burning river of mud and lava that would roll down the slopes to sweep over her city and fill the mountain valley.

"Helen?" murmured her husband beside her. Circling her with his arm, he pulled her close, shifting her bulk with an ease she envied. "Nightmare?" he asked.

"I ran through the streets and they were empty, Sophos. The windows, the doors, they were boarded over and everyone was gone. The Sacred Mountain was erupting and there was no one there."

The terrible tension was fading, and she was already falling back asleep to dream again. She wasn't in her palace or in Eddis. This time, she was looking over the rooftops of some other city, seeing them fill with people who'd felt the ground shaking under their feet, heard the rumbling of the distant explosion, and come out to watch the eruption taking place far away.

CHAPTER FOURTEEN

Over the next few weeks, the Peninsula's soldiers put down their weapons and began felling trees to make room for a sturdy fort. They dug trenches and laid the courses for stone walls while the king exchanged letters and messengers with the king of Roa. There was posturing and threats. Roa sent a new spokesman, shifty-eyed and provoking. We did not know it then, but Roa had bribed the remaining Mede officers to make a stand on the far side of the Lusimina. The Medes were indeed lying in wait, as Pegistus had feared. However, our king would not be baited into crossing the river, and every day more of the enemy's soldiers disappeared on their way home. As the deserters had nothing but their weapons and the clothes on their backs, they soon turned to looting the countryside as they went.

"Remind your king that, unlike the Medes, the Attolians

have always been good neighbors," Eugenides told Roa's ambassador. "Our losses have been steep because of his betrayal, and this small parcel of land is all we seek as compensation."

When it was clear that he would receive no support from the army of Ghasnuvidas, the king of Roa capitulated. Some historians would have you believe that Roa's land was seized outright, but I myself watched the treaties being written and know that there were agreements and payments made in exchange for what, in all honesty, was a stretch of empty forest and two small coastal towns.

The stone walls of the new fort were waist-high in places when news came that Attolia had safely delivered twins. All work stopped for three days of celebration. I think the king might have appreciated a quiet moment to reflect on this great change in his life, on what it meant to lose a father and to become one, but he was king, and the momentous birth of not one heir for Attolia, but two, was a public event and not a private one. There was more news, equally momentous. The Charter of the Three States had been drafted, and the king could return home.

Half of the forces remaining were left to garrison the new fort on the Lusimina, and the others marched with the king back along the coast toward Nedus, where the *Sapphire* was waiting to take him to the capital. On the way, the king detoured to climb up the hill to the temples at Reyatimi, the sanctuary where Costis and Kamet had been watching for the Mede invasion.

In each of the temples, the king made a dedication. At all but two of them, he offered up a gold tablet inscribed with his gratitude for the safe delivery of his children. At the altar of Ula, though, he left a set of gold earrings he'd had cast from the coins in the treasury abandoned in the Mede camp after the death of Bu-seneth. The last temple he visited was that of the Reyatimus, which is what they called the Sky God in that place. The king was met in the forecourt by a priest who eyed him warily.

"Eugenides." The priest called him by name. "It is rare a Thief comes to our doors."

"I would make an offering, if it is not unwelcome."

"Your god and ours have a tempestuous relationship," the priest demurred, his gaze resting on the object the king held.

"They have their moments of cooperation," the king reminded him. His smile fading, he indicated the helmet he held under his arm. "This was my father's. I would dedicate it with a sum sufficient to build a new altar in the temple, if you will accept it."

The priest nodded. He reached to take the helmet, saying, "No offering from a son to honor his father is unwelcome here."

We did not have the Etisians to blow us home, and the whole way the king was impatiently pacing the length of the *Sapphire* or scrambling into the rigging to kick his heels high above her decks. It gave Ion indigestion. As our ship rounded Cape Elydia, they lit the signal fires on the headland, and we saw the beacons catch fire along the coast. By the time we docked, the whole city and most of the population of the nearby countryside had filled the streets.

Standing at the *Sapphire*'s railing, the king grumbled, "Crowds of people, shouting at me. My least favorite thing."

The captain appeared surprised by the response to a hero's welcome. Trokides had spent more time with the king than the captain had. He said something too quiet to be heard above the sound of the crowd.

"What was that?" the king asked him.

"It's just that you have so many least favorite things, Your Majesty," said Trokides, in a deliberately bland voice.

Pegistus snickered.

"I can have you both ganched, you know," said the king over his shoulder as he started down the gangplank.

He walked up from the harbor at a snail's pace. Everyone wanted to touch the king, to catch his sleeve, to embrace him. With every step he was kissing someone or being kissed, while those who couldn't squeeze into the streets leaned from the windows above to shower us all with flowers. When at last he reached the steps leading up to Attolia's palace, the king gently detached the last few grasping hands before he slipped between the ranks of the royal guards. Those of us who had accompanied him that far turned aside to make our way around to a less ostentatious entry into the palace. As Ion tugged me by the hand, lest I be lost in the confusion, the king slowly, solemnly climbed the steps to where Attolia, Sounis, and Eddis awaited him.

Arriving at the top, he said to his queen, "You could have sent a carriage," and she said back to him, "You could have ridden the horse."

He had walked right past the horse waiting for him at the dock, draped in silk and velvet, saddle and bridle decorated in gems worth a king's ransom. Grinding his teeth, Teleus had reordered the guard to convey him on foot, but the crowd had been impossible to control. All of us around the king had received similar treatment, at least as many flower petals and almost as many kisses.

Attolia courtesied to her king, and the people roared with approval. He brushed petals off his shoulders and bowed in return. "My queen," he said over the noise of the crowd. "You are well?"

"I am well," she told him. He stepped to kiss her and the cheering grew even louder.

The king and Sounis exchanged bows. When he came to Eddis, the king caught her by the hand.

"Let me spare you the bow or the courtesy, cousin," he said, and kissed her on the forehead. The noise was deafening.

"Crowds of people, shouting at you!" said Eddis. He could read her lips.

"My least favorite thing!" he shouted back.

For some time they stood, waving to the crowd and listening to the cheers. Then, with one final wave, they retreated through the forecourt and into the palace. When the doors closed behind us, it was blissfully quiet, the sound from outside reduced to no more than a murmur.

"You are well?" said the king, searching Attolia's face, now that the audience around them was smaller.

"I am," she reassured him.

"And the children?"

"Come and see," she said. Leaving Eddis and Sounis to manage the ceremonial expectations of the court, Attolia led the king to the anteroom of the royal nursery.

The king stood, shifting from foot to foot, excited and anxious by turns. Phresine came first, with the prince. Like any nurse, she eyed the king suspiciously. "Lower your arms, I'm not a giant," she said sharply. "There, now. Your hand under his head, that's it," she instructed him before finally releasing the bundle wrapped in Attolian blue and gold. "Your son," she said as she stepped back, ceremony creeping in again, as if there were any ritual that could further enrich that first moment a man holds his child.

Hesitantly the king cradled the baby in his good arm. "So

serious," he said, looking into the tiny face in awe.

"They do not smile at first, Your Majesty," said Phresine.

When Attolia cleared her throat, the king dragged his eyes away from the baby. "I thought he should carry your father's name," she said.

"Not your father's?" asked the king. This was a prince of Attolia, and the queen's father's name had precedence.

Attolia said softly, "Your father's name would honor my house." The king nodded without speaking. Attolia reached to take her son as Luria was bringing out the princess. We'd heard her wailing in the nursery, and she was still fretting as Luria laid her in the king's arms. Captured by the sight of an unfamiliar face, she fell silent. The king looked into his daughter's eyes as he had looked into his son's, and his smile faded.

"Gen?" said Attolia, suddenly afraid. Phresine's arms were reaching for the princess as the king drew the baby away.

"It's nothing," he said. "It's only that I can see now what my grandfather must have seen, what every Thief before me has seen." With growing confidence, he shifted the bundle onto his other arm and used his finger to brush the baby's cheek. Smiling again, he said, "She is Eugenia, and if she falls, her god will catch her." Less solemnly, he added, "I could pitch her off the roof to show y—"

"No."

"It's what they do in Eddis. Of course, they wait until there's been a heavy snowfall, but—"

"No!"

"Do you mind?" he asked, his voice serious again, because Attolia believed in his gods, worshipped his gods in their temples, but she did not love them.

"I do not mind," said Attolia, equally serious until she added, "She cannot be more trouble than her father." She tucked the blanket a little tighter around the child in her arms. "Hector," she affirmed for her son. "And Eugenia," for her daughter.

"A king and his Thief," said Eugenides.

That evening in the megaron, as the tables were being pushed back after dinner, one of the musicians played a scatter of notes on his pipe. They were the opening notes of an Eddisian line dance and easily recognized, even as the music master was frantically hushing the player.

The king, who'd been half asleep, sat bolt upright.

"Dance with me?" he said to Attolia.

Puzzled, Attolia agreed. They always led the first dance.

"Splendid," said the king. "I was afraid I'd have to ask Eddis and she's as big as a house."

"You would have to put me in a wheelbarrow and roll me around the room," said Eddis.

"Oh, but we aren't dancing here," said the king. He

jumped to his feet and headed for the musicians.

The music master was bowing and apologizing. "I'm so very sorry, Your Majesty. It won't happen again. It was entirely inappropriate."

"No, it wasn't, and it will happen again, but not here," said the king. "Pick up your instruments, all of you, and follow me. Everyone, follow me," he said to the gathered patronoi of Eddis and Sounis and Attolia, and they did. They paraded after him up the ceremonial staircases and along the passageway that led to the narrower stairs that in turn led to the roof—even Eddis, with Sounis hovering near her like an anxious sheepdog.

The sun was just setting, the sky was blue and gold, and all the clouds were blushing pink as people poured out onto the guard walks that surround the roofs of the palace. There was plenty of room. The king pointed out a convenient space for the musicians and waved to everyone else to take their places. Holding the queen's hand, he picked his way up the tiled roof of the ceremonial hall to the peak. Attolia, accompanying, was as surefooted as the king. Once at the peak, they waited for the music master to bring his players to order, and when the musicians began to play, Eugenides and Irene danced.

Effortlessly they performed the steps of the traditional line dance, moving forward and back, along the ridge of the roof, careless of the steep slope on either side. At the end of

the dance, the king released Attolia and bowed as she courtesied. Then he descended to catch Eddis by the hand. Eddis
protested, he cajoled, and together they climbed up the roof.
Attolia, meanwhile, had taken Sounis by the hand and led
him up as well. He looked far more anxious than the other
three, but as the musicians played, the four of them danced
gracefully to the music, and then they descended, each to
select a new partner.

Everyone else was dancing on the flat guard walks—Ion
and his new wife smiling at each other, Celia and Lavia
laughing. Phresine danced with Trokides. Baron Anacritus
danced with his wife and then with his lover, while his wife
was dancing with the king. Much to my surprise, Chloe
had singled out the magus, who seemed very pleased at the
attention. Costis was dancing with his younger sister when I
saw Kamet approach Teleus, who'd propped himself against
a crenelated wall.

The captain refused to dance, his grief for Relius so
all-encompassing that even the king handled him gently.
It would be many long months before Meleo the Gant
succeeded in subduing his southern neighbors and before
the Pents, sensing the coming changes in their alliance
with the Braels, changed tack with the Lesser Peninsula.
Dropping their demands for an apology from the king, they
would release the prisoner they'd secretly held and send him
home. Teleus and I would cry happier tears together then.

That night, as we celebrated the return of the high king and the new charter that unified the Peninsula, I am not sure how many saw the handsome young men with goat feet, the celadon-skinned women with leaves and flowers in their hair moving from partner to partner. Anacritus danced with a woman covered in silvery scales. An imposing figure in a flowing blue robe bowed stiffly to the king before offering a hand to Attolia. Relinquishing her, the king turned with a smile to dance with a woman whose skirts billowed as if in a wind that touched nothing else.

When Moira descended from the rooftop to offer me her hand, I shook my head, gesturing to my bent leg.

"Pheris, how foolish," said Moira, "to think that means you cannot dance." When she held out her hand again, I took it.

After a time, the light left the sky and the darkness settled in, the musicians fell silent, and the king led us down from the rooftop. Peace stole over the palace and the long day was over. The three countries, Sounis, Eddis, and Attolia, were one, and the gods were pleased.

THE END

Alyta's Missing Earring

"*E*ugenides," said one of the fates.

"What?"

"We know you are lurking. What are you up to?"

"Nothing," said the god of Thieves. Then he shrugged. "Hiding."

"From whom this time?"

"Alyta."

All three fates lifted their heads in surprise. Alyta, though the daughter of the storm god, was one of the gentler goddesses.

"She wants a favor," said the god of thieves.

Sphea, the spinner, nodded in understanding. The gods and goddesses often came to the half-bred mortal son of the Earth, asking him to use the gifts given to him by the Great Goddess on their behalf.

"What could Alyta need stolen?" Metiri asked as she measured out a length of her sister's spinning.

Eugenides waved his hands, as if pestered by gnats. "Whatever it is, I am not stealing it. I already told her that." He drew close to Hega, looking over her shoulder at the pattern on her loom. "I thought there would be more red," he said.

Hega snorted.

While the weaver's fingers were occupied elsewhere on her loom, the god of Thieves deftly shifted several of her threads. When Hega moved her fingers back, she felt the change.

"You've made a knot," she complained.

"Just a twist," said Eugenides. "A little one."

"And look, these threads are out of order now. I will have to unweave this whole section, and Sphea's new yarn will have to wait."

"Then let it stay," Eugenides suggested. Whispering in her ear, he said, "It looks better, this. Doesn't it? Say it does."

Hega gave an irritated sigh, but she left the twist in the weave that Eugenides had made. "But no red," she grumbled. "That comes later."

Periphys moved lightly, the leaves dipping at her passing, the occasional spent blossom falling in her wake. She had a specific objective and wandered a little less than usual on her way.

"Sister," she called as she alighted on a terrace overlooking the lower slopes of the Sacred Mountain. "Stop your drizzle, please," said Periphys, unmantling her hair. "I'm all wet from coming up the valley."

Alyta had been soothed by the sound of water dripping from the branches of the conifers that surrounded her home, but she took pleasure in pleasing others; the pattering of droplets eased, and Periphys blew the clouds away. She sat beside Alyta in the weak sunlight.

"You must have heard us calling. So what keeps you home while we are missing you?"

"I did not hear," Alyta said. "I'm sorry. I was lost in my thoughts."

"Thinking what?" probed Periphys, a penetrating if not powerful wind.

"I was wondering if lovers are more trouble than they're worth," said Alyta.

"Cello is," Periphys answered promptly.

"Cello is my favorite," Alyta reminded her. "I love him best."

"Then he should be happy with that," grumbled Periphys, "and not strive so hard to keep you all for himself."

"You're jealous," said Alyta gently.

"He's greedy," said Periphys pettishly.

Alyta didn't argue that. "But a little greediness in one's lover is not a terrible thing," she said. "Not when it gives me pleasure to indulge it."

"Maybe not," said Periphys. "But I see something is the matter. So tell your sister what it is, and I will see if I can help."

Alyta had had many lovers and many children, but had settled on Cello, one of the mountains and the son of the Earth and Sky, as her husband. He had begged her to belong only to him, and she had agreed.

Cello had a friend, Ente, son of the goddess of discord. Angry at losing Cello to his new love, he was determined to ruin their marriage. With that in mind, he had stolen Alyta's earring, one of a set that Cello had given her.

"Ente will wear it," Alyta explained. "And Cello will assume I gave it to him and think I am still taking lovers in spite of my promise."

"Tell him otherwise. Before he even sees Ente."

"I'm sure I could," said Alyta thoughtfully, "but perhaps he would be hurt that I would think he could be so easily deceived."

"Then tell him after he sees Ente."

"But if he is deceived, I might be the one hurt."

"Then he doesn't deserve you," Periphys pointed out.

"But I like him too much to let him go," said Alyta, not disagreeing with her sister, just pointing out other factors to consider. "And I do not see why I or Cello should suffer for something that is Ente's fault."

"Well, if Cello finds out that Ente has lied, it's Ente who will suffer," said Periphys. "He risks all of Cello's love because he will not share any of it." Privately, she thought Ente and Cello rather deserved each other, but she'd never liked Cello. His mountainous form seemed so often to be in her way.

"Ente is too clever to lie outright," said Alyta. "If he's caught, he will only say he found the earring in the woods and meant nothing by wearing it."

"Then you will have to get the earring back," said Periphys. "And you know who will help."

In the tavern, Gen sat drumming his heels on the side of the bench seat underneath him. The dirt floor was uneven, eroded under the table by sweeping, and his feet didn't reach the ground.

His grandfather frowned at the noise and Gen stopped, his shoulders drooping. The tavern was no more than a shed tacked onto the side of a stable, with a bar that ran its length and, across a narrow aisle, a few booths lined up against the outside wall. The food and drink were no reason to visit. The bread on a plate in front of Gen was filled with grit and the wine was sour, but the tavern keeper chatted with the men at the bar, relaying news from distant places, and that was what they'd come for. Gen had knocked his feet against the wood partly in frustration, partly in defeat. More noise would make no difference. He couldn't hear.

Or rather, all he could hear was the men sitting in the booth behind him. They were telling coarse jokes and laughing about something they'd done that they thought very amusing, and they were loud enough to cover all the more important conversation at the bar.

He gathered they'd been sent by their master to steal something from a woman who had rebuffed his advances. Their master meant to wear the earring they'd stolen and pretend the woman, Alyta, had given it to him. The man would have it in his ear, and when Alyta's husband saw it, he would think the man was his wife's lover and be enraged. Drunk and cruel, the men were laughing at the harm their master intended.

Gen felt sorry for the woman. He caught his grandfather's eye and nodded at the men, but the old man shook his head. It was not their business. Their business was the news from Kathodicia. He'd taken the seat opposite Gen so that he could see the faces of the men talking to the tavern keeper and understand their words better. Gen knew he should have picked that side of the table as well and that his grandfather would tell him off for his mistake later.

Still, it was easy, as they rose to leave, to take the earring, lying temptingly close inside the coat pocket of one of the men. None of them noticed, but of course his grandfather did. Once they were outside, he seized Gen by the arm and shook him hard.

"When he sticks his hand in that pocket and finds that earring gone, who will they blame?" he asked. "The tavern keeper on the other side of the bar? The men who stood with their backs to the booths? No. They will blame the strangers sitting behind them, the ones who walked right past the coat hanging on a hook."

He was angry because the men were very likely to chase them and because they'd be remembered as thieves if they came back to that tavern anytime soon.

"And for nothing," Gen's grandfather told him. "Alyta, whoever she is, will not have her earring back, and when her husband notices, he will still think she's given it to her lover."

Gen hadn't thought of that.

"Get yourself into the woods. I will steal one of the horses and pick you up. We cannot afford to linger here."

They rode hard, and Gen's teeth rattled in his head as he held on tight to his grandfather's coat. When they finally slowed to rest the horse, Gen pulled out the earring to look at it. It was surpassingly beautiful. A tiny lapis urn hung on three golden chains from a solid gold ring. It held sprays of miniature flowers, with blossoms made of seed pearls and leaves enameled in yellow and green. The patterning on the urn was so delicate that even Gen's young eyes had difficulty making it out.

"Let me see it," said his grandfather.

Reluctantly, Gen held out his palm.

His grandfather shook his head.

"You can't keep it."

Gen was truculent.

"We steal in the service of our god and in the service of our king. To do otherwise is common theft and as wrong in you as it is in any man."

"We're keeping the horse," Gen pointed out.

"You use the Thief's skills for yourself, and you will lose the favor of our god."

"But I didn't use the skills for myself," Gen protested. He'd used them for Alyta, who'd done nothing to deserve her husband's anger.

"Are you sure?" asked his grandfather. "When you look at that very fine earring, don't you want to keep it?"

"Yes," Gen admitted. He'd never seen anything like it.

His grandfather had set aside his anger by then, and his words were more compelling for it. "Without the god's favor, you will fall," he warned. "And never know what you have lost until you hit the ground."

Gen didn't say anything; he had no interest in a smack that would make his ears ring all day. Shaking his head, the old Thief stopped the horse and shifted in the saddle so he could look his grandson in the eye. "That earring goes on an altar as soon as we reach the city. You can take it to the temple of Alyta. She will be happy to receive it on behalf of her namesake, I am sure."

Embroidered in swirls of silver thread, the fine silk of her pearl-gray shawl lay like a cloud lightly wrapping her shoulders. The deep purple of her gown was the color of the mountains at sunset, its pattern shot through with streaks of silvery blue that widened as they descended until they met together in the skirt that fell to the floor in ripples around her feet.

"Do you know who I am?" the queen asked as she spun gracefully around to show off the costume.

"A goddess," said the king, with a certainty that brought color to her cheeks. "But I don't know which one," he admitted.

It would be the first time in years, since before the war with the Medes, since before she was married, that a traditional midsummer banquet would be held in Attolia's palace, and all over the city, people were planning their costumes. When she had ruled alone, Attolia had dressed as Hephestia, sole head of the pantheon of the Eddisian gods, but with a king by her side, that costume had been put away. She had spent the morning closeted with her attendants, selecting a new one.

"Alyta," said the queen.

"Goddess of the mountain rain?" the king said, a little wary.

"Phresine suggested it—"

"And I get to play her jealous husband?" said the king, remembering days when he had been secretly afraid his world might dissolve like a sugar cone in the rain. "Remind me to have Phresine cast into outer darkness."

"—because I am a descendent of the goddess," said Attolia, ignoring him. "Or am supposed to be, on my mother's side, and you are Eugenides."

He didn't understand. "I am Eugenides," he said, puzzled. "Do I not need a costume? I might like this idea better now."

"No, you go as your god," said Attolia, as if this connection between Alyta and the Thief were clear. The king's face remained blank.

"You do not know the story of Alyta's earring? Phresine told it to me," said the queen.

"Oh, indeed," said the king, loudly enough that the queen's attendants could hear it from where they sat in the waiting room. "Phresine, source of all the edifying stories I have somehow never heard before!"

So Attolia retold it for him. How Alyta's earring was stolen by a troublemaker and how the god of Thieves stole it back for her. How, in return, Alyta had promised him his heart's desire.

"And what was that?" asked the king.

"No one knows," the queen answered. "When anyone asks, the man playing the Thief always refuses to tell."

The king nodded. Attolia reached out and took his hand. "It's a fine idea," he said, without meeting her eye. When he looked up at last, he stood to share the tenderest of kisses. "You are any man's heart's desire," he said.

So a tailor began to work through the night on a suit of soft, silvery-brown moleskin, and while he worked, the king lay awake.

The celebration of the equinox was a celebration of peace and stability, of the stars and planets in their courses, of all things right in the world. It was a time to set aside worries and hard work and revel in the confidence of good things to come, that confidence often expanding into extravagance and socially sanctioned silliness. When the queen descended the grand staircase, dressed as the goddess Alyta, with her king by her side, in a suit not brown, not gray, but somewhere in between, with no crown but thrush feathers woven into a ring on his head, the cheering could be heard by the guards in their places up on the roof walks.

Still, the court knew their mercurial king well, heard the brittleness behind his laugh, saw the distraction behind his smile, and behind their own smiles began checking ledgers for any missteps they might have made. Eugenides mostly observed while his wife ruled, but his observation was as keen as a razor's edge and sometimes as dangerous.

They were not surprised, only unsettled, when he disappeared, as he still could, from a hall filled with people. They looked to their queen, and because she hid her worries far better than her husband did, they were reassured that whatever occupied the king, it was no concern of theirs. The wine flowed, the music played, and the court danced while the king took his invisible paths out of the palace and across the city, revelers passing him in the street too busy with their own entertainment to see anything but another Eugenides, one of a thousand out that night celebrating.

In the temple of Alyta, the king did not approach the altar. He sat instead at the back of the nave, head tipped down, examining his boots as he tapped their toes together, remembering a visit to the temple made many years earlier.

His grandfather had sent him in alone. Gen had stood some time debating with himself as he shifted from foot to foot. He could have hidden the earring in his boot or under his belt; his grandfather would have been none the wiser. Cynical, even at such a young age, he suspected that the earring would make it no closer to the goddess's treasure room than the high priestess's pocket. She would sell it for its gold in the market. Even more than giving up the earring, he hated the idea of its delicate beauty being melted away to nothing but an indistinguishable lump of metal, no matter how precious.

His grandfather's warning had been very clear, and logical as well. "You jump best when you believe in yourself. You believe in yourself because you know you are the Thief. Fail to deliver up to the gods what you know they demand, and you will never be the Thief. Not here." He'd poked him in the chest. "Not here, where it matters most."

At last, with a sigh, Gen had reached up to slip the earring over the edge of the wide, shallow bowl on the altar. He was too short to see, but he heard it slide down the metal surface until it plinked ever so lightly against the other offerings inside.

When he turned to leave, he found he was not alone after all—a figure stood near the entry door, dressed in the flowing robes of Alyta's priestesses. As he approached, she stepped to meet him, stopping him with a hand on his shoulder. She was very tall—he remembered that, but everyone is tall to a child.

"Thank you," she had said. "It was a generous gift." And he had suspected, even then, that the generosity was not in the reluctant release of the earring, but in its theft.

"And in return, you will have your heart's desire, little Thief," she had promised, and bent to kiss his cheek before she'd sent him blinking into the sunlight where, when his eyes cleared, he found his grandfather waiting.

"Took you long enough," the old man said, and they went to sell the horse.

✦ ✦ ✦

He'd thought he knew his own heart's desire. He wanted to be the Thief of Eddis. When his cousins mocked him, when his father shouted at him, when his grandfather shouted at him, for different reasons, all he wanted was to be the Thief someday. But he'd had other desires since, and he could only wonder which of them had been granted by the goddess.

She'd called him "little Thief" then. He'd been so overwhelmed by the sight of her, he hadn't even noticed. He'd staggered out of the dark temple into the bright day, thinking the spots in front of his eyes had been caused by the sun.

He did not see Moira when she arrived, did not sense her presence until she settled next to him on the bench. "Asking more humble questions, Eugenides?" she teased. Then she relented. "No, I see. You haven't asked because you are so afraid of the answer. Does she really love you? Did she have any choice?" Gentler than she had ever been before, Moira leaned close and spoke quietly in his ear. "Alyta, goddess of the mountain rain, goddess who fills the streams in summer, loves all her children and all who descend from them, and she is ever gentle in their care."

When Eugenides did not respond, she went on. "Ask yourself, Eugenides: why that orange tree? Why that tamarisk bush? She had promised you your heart's desire while a child of hers was alone in the world and unhappy. See, Eugenides," Moira said, holding out a finger from each of her hands and interlinking them. "Only two threads brought together, two threads that touched," she reassured him. "Nothing more than that. And everything else left up to you."

SOME PERSONS OF SIGNIFICANCE:
A LIST OF CHARACTERS IN THE QUEEN'S THIEF NOVELS

Agape: Youngest daughter of the Eddisian baron Phoros. She is a cousin to the queen of Eddis and to Eugenides the thief. She is nicer than her sister Hegite.

Aglaia: One of Attolia's attendants.

Akretenesh: The Mede Ambassador to Sounis.

Alenia: A duchess in Eddis who was incensed when Eugenides stole her emerald earrings.

Alyta: A gentle goddess of welcome rain, rain in the distance, and rain in the mountains. She is known for having many lovers and many children, mortal and immortal.

Ambiades: The Magus's apprentice. His grandfather was executed for conspiring against the king of Sounis. Gen calls him Useless the Elder.

Anacritus: An Attolian baron with a wife and a lover. He is a strong supporter of the queen.

Anet: The sky god in the Mede pantheon.

Ansel: Free servant of Melheret, the Mede ambassador to Attolia.

Aracthus: An Eddisian god. Associated with the River Aracthus.

Aristogiton: A friend of Costis and a soldier in the Attolian guard. Costis borrows his name when he needs an alias.

Artadorus: Another baron with a wife and a lover. He's been roped into Baron Erondites schemes before. At the Baron's suggestion, he misreported the kind of grain he grows in order to pay less in taxes.

Attolia: Irene, queen of Attolia.

Aulus: An Eddisian soldier and minor prince of Eddis enlisted as an ad hoc nanny for the king of Attolia.

✦ ✦ ✦

Benno: A guard hired by Roamanj to accompany his caravan.

Boagus: An Eddisian soldier and babysitter of Eugenides.

Brinna: The head cook in Attolia's kitchens.

✦ ✦ ✦

Caeta: One of Attolia's attendants.

Casartus: Admiral of Attolia's navy.

Cassa: Owner of the honeyed hives in the Mede epic of Immakuk and Ennikar.

Cello: A mountain god. Lover of Alyta.

Chloe: A younger attendant of Attolia.

Cleon of Attolia: One of the king's attendants.

Cleon of Eddis: A dim-witted, but not evil, cousin of Eugenides. Eddis proposed him as an attendant for the high king, but Cleon spectacularly rejected the king's invitation.

Cletus: An Attolian baron, supporter of the queen.

Costis: Costis Ormentiedes, a soldier in the Attolian guard. He is unwillingly embroiled in the politics of the court by Eugenides.

Crodes: A soldier of Eddis. Cousin to the queen and to Eugenides.

✦ ✦ ✦

Death: Lord of the Underworld. Brother of the Queen of the Night.

Dionis: One of Eugenides's attendants.

Diurnes: A member of Costis's squad in the Attolian guard.

Drusis: A new attendant to the king. Motis and Drusis are brothers.

✦ ✦ ✦

Earth: The origin goddess in the Eddisian creation stories.

Eddis: Helen, queen of Eddis.

Efkis: An Attolian baron. Because of Eugenides's schemes, he was thought to have betrayed the Queen of Attolia.

Elia: One of the queen of Attolia's attendants.

Enkelis: An ambitious lieutenant in the Attolian guard, briefly promoted to captain by the queen of Attolia.

Ennikar: One of the heroes in the Mede epic of Immakuk and Ennikar.

Ephrata: An Attolian baron.

Erondites: An Attolian baron, one of Attolia's oldest enemies. Father of Erondites the Younger and Sejanus.

Erondites the Younger, called Dite: Baron Erondites's son and one of Attolia's most fervent supporters.

Eugenides: An Eddisian who served as the queen's thief of Eddis before becoming king of Attolia. Also called Gen.

Eugenides: The Eddisians' god of thieves.

✦ ✦ ✦

Galen: Eddis's palace physician.

Ghasnuvidas: Emperor of the Mede. He has been diagnosed with an incurable disease that leaves lesions on the skin, and he has passed over his own sons in order to name his nephew as his heir.

Godekker: An escaped slave living in hiding in Zaboar. He agrees to hide Kamet and Costis.

✦ ✦ ✦

Hamiathes: A mythological king of Eddis. To reward him, he was given Hamiathes's Gift, which conferred immortality and the throne of Eddis.

Hegite: Daughter of the Eddisian baron Phoros. Older sister of Agape.

Heiro: Daughter of one of the barons in the Attolian court. Eugenides dances with her but not with her older sister, Themis.

Hemke: A shepherd on the salt flats of the Mede empire.

Hephestia: The Great Goddess. Head of the Eddisian pantheon. Goddess of volcanoes. She is the daughter of Earth and Sky. They have given her the power of their lightning bolts and earthquakes.

Hespira: In the Eddisian story of Hespira and Horreon, she was lured to the underworld by the goddess Meridite, who wanted her to marry Horreon, Meridite's son.

Hilarion: The oldest of Eugenides's attendants.

Hippias: The Secretary of Attolia's archives until his unexpected death. He was replaced by Orutus.

Horreon: An Eddisian god, the son of the goddess Meridite. He was a blacksmith who made magical armor forged in the fire of the Hephestial Mountain.

✦ ✦ ✦

Ileia: One of Attolia's senior attendants.

Imenia: One of Attolia's senior attendants.

Immakuk: One of the heroes from the Mede epic of Immakuk and Ennikar.

Ion: One of Eugenides's attendants

Ion Nomenus: He was the faithless attendant to Sophos when he was held captive by the Mede ambassador Akretenesh and the Sounisian Baron Brimedius.

Iolanthe: One of Attolia's senior attendants.

✦ ✦ ✦

Jeffa: The former secretary of Nahuseresh. When he died, Kamet took his place.

✦ ✦ ✦

Kamet: An enslaved Setran, private secretary to Nahuseresh.

Kepet: A Setran slave dealer in the Mede empire.

Kununigadak the Devourer: A terrifying monster who guards the gates of the underworld in the stories of Immakuk and Ennikar.

✦ ✦ ✦

Lader: A very unpleasant cousin of Eugenides. Deceased.

Laecdomon: A disruptive member of Aristogiton's squad in the Attolian guard and an agent of Baron Erondites.

Laela: A slave in the househould of Nahuseresh. A friend of Kamet's.

Lamion: One of Eugenides's attendants.

Lavia: One of Attolia's attendants.

Legarus: One of the men in Aristogiton's squad in the guard. He is quite beautiful and uses it to what he thinks is his advantage.

Luria: One of Attolia's attendants.

Lyopidus: The mortal brother of the god Eugenides. Jealous of his brother's powers, he asked Eugenides to steal the Sky's lightning bolts and died when they set the world on fire.

✦ ✦ ✦

The magus: One of the king's most powerful advisors; a scholar.

Marin: One of Nahuseresh's dancing girls. He and Kamet were both in love with her.

Marina Erondites Susa: The only daughter of the Baron Erondites, she was disinherited when she married against her father's will.

Medander: One of the king of Attolia's attendants.

Melheret: The Mede ambassador to Attolia.

Meridite: An Eddisian goddess. Mother of armorer Horreon.

Minister of War: Eugenides's father.

Minos: An Attolian baron. Publicly a supporter of the queen.

Miras: One of the new gods of Attolia, god of light and arrows. Worshiped by soldiers.

Moira: Messenger goddess of the Eddisian pantheon and also a record keeper. Her name means *fate*.

Motis: Became an attendant when two of the king's attendants were retired. Motis and Drusis are brothers.

✦ ✦ ✦

Nahuseresh: The Mede ambassador to Attolia. Nephew of the emperor; younger brother of the heir to the emperor. He attempted to woo the queen of Attolia as a means to her throne and failed.

Neheeled: Nahuseresh's older brother, heir to the Mede Empire.

Ne Malia: Mede goddess of the moon, fertility, and rebirth.

Nine Gods: The main pantheon of the new Attolian gods. They defeated the giants.

Nuri: A Mede god of the river and the flood.

✦ ✦ ✦

Olcthemenes: In the Eddisian stories of the old gods,

Olcthemenes was the tailor who turned a blanket into a suit of clothes for the god Eugenides.

Olmia: In the Eddisian stories of the old gods, Olmia the weaver made a hat from bird feathers for the god Eugenides.

Onarkus: The head of the queen of Attolia's kitchen.

Oneis: A heroic figure from the Epic of Oneis.

The Oracle: Oracle and high priestess at the new temple being built for Hephestia above the palace in Attolia.

Ornon: A minster to the queen of Eddis. Ambassador to Attolia. Subsequently Attolia's ambassador to the Mede empire.

Orutus: Secretary of Attolia's archives, which is to say, her master of spies.

✦ ✦ ✦

Pegistus: Attolia's Minister of War.

Pelles: One of Eugenides's attendants.

Periphys: A goddess, one of the lighter winds.

Permindor of Nilos: Also called Perminder of Sounis, he was proposed by Sophos to be a new attendant to the high king.

Petrus: Attolia's personal physician for years.

Pheris Mostrus Erondites: The nephew of Dite and Sejanus, and the firstborn grandson of Marina, the only daughter of the Baron Erondites. He shares his name with his grandfather who is Erondites.

Philia: One of the goddesses of the Attolian pantheon. She is goddess of mercy.

Philologos: Youngest but highest ranking of Eugenides's attendants.

Phoros: A baron in Eddis; father of Agape, Hegite, and two other daughters.

Phresine: Oldest of Attolia's attendants.

Piloxides: A general of Attolia's armed forces.

Pol: Captain of Sophos's father's guard; a soldier.

Polemus: A new attendant to the king.

Polyfemus: One of the giants who supposedly built the old walls of Sounis's prison and the roads of Eddis.

Proas: An Eddisian god of green and growing things.

Prokep: A Mede god; a statue of him was made by the sculptor Sudesh.

✦ ✦ ✦

Queen of the Night: Sister of Death and mother of Unse-Sek.

✦ ✦ ✦

Relius: He was the secretary of the Archives, with many, many, lovers; one of whom turned out to be a spy for the Mede Emperor.

Roamanj: A caravan master who hires Costis and Kamet as guards.

✦ ✦ ✦

Sejanus: The youngest child of Baron Erondites.

Senabid: A character in skits, a slave who makes a fool of his master.

Shef: A slave dealer in the Mede Empire.

Shesmegah: In the Mede pantheon, goddess of mercy, forgiveness, and second chances.

Silla: One of the Queen of Attolia's attendants.

Sky (god): Created by Earth, he is the second god in the Eddisian pantheon.

Snap: Also called Pepper. Pheris's pony.

Sophos (Useless the Younger): Apprentice of the magus;

future duke; nephew of the king and his heir. He becomes king of Sounis.

Sotis: One of Eugenides's senior attendants.

Sounis: Sophos's uncle and king of Sounis. He had no children of his own. In exchange for his half-brother's support he has named his nephew, Sophos, as his heir.

Stadicos: One of Attolia's barons, corrupted by the Mede ambassador, Nahuseresh.

Stenides: Eugenides's brother, a watchmaker.

Susa: One of Attolia's barons. Devious, but not necessarily an enemy of the queen. He is baron over the lands where Costis's family has their farm.

✦ ✦ ✦

Teleus: The captain of the Royal Guard. He only has one lover.

Temenus: Gen's brother, a soldier.

Tenep: Usually the most gentle of the gods, she turns her anger on the world when Ennikar steals from her.

Thales: Wrote about the basic elements of the universe; Eugenides was copying his scroll before he went on his mission to Attolia.

Thalia: Costis's younger sister.

Themis: Erondites recruits Themis and hopes to make her the king's mistress, but Eugenides only dances with Themis's younger sister, Heiro.

Therespides: An Eddisian known for his philandering. Also known for selling information to anyone who will pay him.

Timos: Cousin of Eugenides and Eddis. He dies stopping Attolia's advance up the main pass into Eddis.

Titus: Gen's cousin who once broke several of Gen's ribs in a beating.

Trokides: A general of Sounis's armed forces

✦ ✦ ✦

Ula: Goddess of the hearth and healing.

Unse-Sek: A terrible monster that roamed the isthmus in the stories of Immakuk and Ennikar, child of the Queen of the Night.

✦ ✦ ✦

Verimius: One of the king's attendants. He has a wife and various lovers until he was sent home from the Attolian court.

✦ ✦ ✦

Witch of Urkell: In the Epic of Immakuk and Ennikar, she is Ennikar's lover and the daughter of Ninur.

✦ ✦ ✦

Xanthe: Eddis's most senior attendant.

Xenophon: One of Eddis's generals.

Xikander: One of the king's less pleasant attendants. Poor Gen has so many unpleasant attendants. Xikander and Xikos are brothers.

Xikos: Another one of the king's unpleasant attendants. Xikander and Xikos are brothers.

✦ ✦ ✦

Zerchus: A cook in Attolia's kitchens.

Pinosh River

Lartius